MORTA

MORTAL SUNS

Tanith Lee

THE OVERLOOK PRESS
Woodstock & New York

First published in the United States in 2003 by
The Overlook Press, Peter Mayer Publishers, Inc.
Woodstock & New York

WOODSTOCK:
One Overlook Drive
Woodstock, NY 12498
www.overlookpress.com
[for individual orders, bulk and special sales, contact our Woodstock office]

NEW YORK:
141 Wooster Street
New York, NY 10012

∞ The paper used in this book meets the requirements for paper
permanence as described in the ANSI Z39.48-1992 standard.

Library of Congress Cataloging-in-Publication Data

Lee, Tanith.
Mortal suns / Tanith Lee.
p. cm.

1. Kings and rulers—Succession—Fiction. 2. Children and disabilities—Fiction.
3. Abnormalities, Human—Fiction. 4. Princesses—Fiction. I. Title.
PR6062.E4163 M67 2003   823'.914—dc21   2003042047

Book design and type formatting by Bernard Schleifer
Printed in the United States of America
ISBN 1-58567-207-6
FIRST EDITION
1 3 5 7 9 8 6 4 2

C O N T E N T S

Akhemony & the Sun Lands

NOTE ON PRONUNCIATION

In the Sun Lands, the letter C is always pronounced as K,
Although CH is pronounced as in the word <u>charge</u>.
The letter Y is always hard, as in <u>try</u>, except at the end of a word: Ak–<u>hem</u>–<u>onee</u>.
The letters AI are pronounced as in the word <u>rain</u>.

Conversely, among the Pesh, the letters AI rhyme with the word <u>sigh</u>.

Into the Hand of the gods
I give myself. And lie still.

QERAB

The words that are spoken
before the dance begins

IN TEN YEARS, I shall be younger than I am tonight. And since I am now one hundred years of age, this prospect pleases and inspires me.

At Sin Dhul, City of the Moon, I am called the Poetess, and by some, the Seer. They say to me that, through all the Empire-Continent of Pesh Sandu, I have been given these titles. My name is Sirai. But in my youth, I had another name. Indeed, I had two names.

Today, Prince Shajhima visited me, here in my sequestered tower in the desert. He brought a great baggage of gifts, much of it food, which my few servants eyed gladly, I will not say greedily. Our diet is often simple, and visitors seldom come, but for the owls and ravens that alight on the tower top, and the nightingale which sometimes sings in the garden. Even the nightingale has been absent some time.

The Prince and I sat talking for an hour or so on the roof, under the awning. The sky was dressed in its afternoon blue, but later it was the richer blue of night, and stars appeared like the lighted windows of an upper world. I enjoy the Prince's company. Now over fifty, he reminds me of his father—the Battle-Prince, also called Shajhima—when he had reached this age. Now and then, not thinking, I search for the sword scar his father had upon the left hand and, not seeing it, I am for a moment puzzled. So old age is.

I told the Prince I had decided to write down something about my life, my early life, before his father carried me here, a captive barbarian slave, unable to walk, and chained—not with iron, but with despair.

Prince Shajhima assured me he would like to read such a book. At first I feared he would be the only one unwise enough to do so. Then my chosen scribe, Dobzah, who even now pens these words, came up and said she too was eager for the narrative.

She must put down now that all this, which will be written, shall be by my voice and her hand. I am unable to write so much. But Dobzah is younger than I, and strong. I trust her, and will trust her with my life in these pages.

To picture Sirai, you need only visualize a very old woman, unveiled, thin and pale, her grey hair still long though less abundant, piled on her head. To picture Dobzah, think of the clever, bright-eyed sparrow, whose wings, in the story, outmatch the storm.

After the Prince had left us for the City, which lies five miles away over the desert. Dobzah and I played a game with silver pieces on a fine bone board.

I told Dobzah that I would use, as a heading for the various parts of my life, a word from my own continent, the Sun Lands, the word *Stroia*. Which indicates those phrases that are spoken during the dance, to give meaning to it. For my life has been a sort of dance, and I value dancing highly, for it taught me how to walk over the world.

Because I am so old, I know soon I must die. But I have no fear, for I have learned something of the ways of God. After death I will wander, I believe, ten or so years about the earth, to expiate my sins, to learn and teach the final lessons. Then, a young girl again, I will go on to Paradise—that heaven beyond all heavens, which all men hope for and many deny. Never doubt. Heaven is there.

But perhaps already I am embarking on that purgatory wandering which precedes delight. For this book will be for me a tortuous return into the past. At my age, I find, I can look back and behold my own self, more clearly than I see others now, just as one may see oneself in dreams. That girl, that child I was, I view half remotely, but also with tenderness, as if I had given birth to her. But I bore only one child, a son, and him I never knew. My own self, I know as I know not one other. Strangely, too, it seems to me now, gazing back into the amber darkness of the past, I can see and divine events which, at the time, were hidden from me. And I can become, almost at a wish, the spectator at scenes which, while I lived adjacent to them, I had no knowledge of. Yet there are things too I may not look at, and perhaps God conceals them, lest I die before this task is done.

Tonight we listen, Dobzah and I, for the nightingale. But she does not sing. The upper pool, with the tree that is her throne, are glimmering both, mystical with night. At the lower pool, where the washing is done and the women sing, someone has left a jar, which shines dim white, a moon in a cloud.

Shall I begin my history tonight? After supper, and before moonrise. Dobzah says to me, *Yes.*

And now, for a second, I feel afraid. I, so old I have outlived, as they say here, a thousand roses. Old Sirai in her tower, fears her journey back into her golden youth. But it is to be done. It shall be done.

Come, Dobzah. Let us go and eat the beautiful foods that Prince Shajhima brought, then light the lamp and fill the silent air the nightingale disdains, with this song of words, this dance of life.

Annotation by the Hand of Dobzah

Here I set my vow. I will be faithful to the words of my mistress, Sirai, Moon-Poetess of Sin Dhul.

Sharash J'um.

1st Stroia

Birth: The House of Death

I

Darkness, which at Sunfall had come down like black lions to the shore, stood foursquare now on the night hours of earliest morning. But above, Phaidix had lit the cold stars with her arrows. And in the palace below, as always, many lights were burning bright.

From the amphitheater of the hills, the whole chamber of the night lay quiet, sounding—faintly, steadily—only with the Heart of the Land of Akhemony. In the mysterious folds of night's garment, nothing seemed to stir. Perhaps a fox was running through the winter grass. Perhaps an owl, or some even more supernatural creature, floated between earth and heaven.

Then, thin and sure as a razor, piercing everything, there flew out one high torn note: a scream of pain and fury—and terror.

Things without name or form raised their heads and stared. The stars stared down, and Phaidix's cruel moon stared as it rose out of the Lakesea.

While among the courts of the palace came a sudden fluttering of the light, like wings

The Daystar, Queen Hetsa, sat upright on the birthing couch, supported by her attendants. All were crying and shuddering in fright, all but the queen. She had spent her first panic and horror in her scream. Now, cleared of it, she pointed at the midwife with one hard, crystal forefinger.

"*What have you done?*"

"I? I, madam? Nothing—it's not—"

"Your potions. Some *witchcraft.*"

"*No*, madam. How could I possibly—"

"You shall be flayed alive, do you hear?"

The midwife shrank, and turning with thoughtless distress, slapped her assistant across the cheek. This woman staggered back, still clutching the awful burden to her breast.

But Hetsa was sinking in a faint. Her labor had lasted over ten hours, and down the couch, all down the white linen, ran scarlet evidence of the cost.

The room was full of shadows, also turning red as the lamps burned low, so that everything seemed at last awash with the blood of birth, not least the tall crimson pillars with their capitals of coiling serpents. In one corner, cool clear light flickered alone at the shrine of the Arteptan birth goddess, Bandri.

On some impulse, the assistant of the midwife scuttled there, and putting the bundle on the altar, began herself to sob.

Bandri, of big-bellied black marble, watched impassively behind her veil of offering smoke. All things may occur, she seemed to say. Even this, in the apartment of a queen.

Hetsa was reviving.

She pushed the herbal cup away, and raised herself again. She had been beautiful a month ago, her long, gilded hair and pure skin blossoming from the culmination of a healthy pregnancy. Now she was a hag, a rag. But she spoke finally very low.

"All you in this room—not a word, not a *word*. Don't touch me. Take that thing—one of you—anyone of you—and carry it where it must go. I don't want to be told. I don't want to hear a *word*. It's dead."

From the red shadow then, the old woman came out, the old nurse that they called Crow Claw.

She must have been lurking there, by the curtains. No one knew how she got in, but you could not keep her out, not if she wished otherwise.

She stood upright and thin as a stick in her black, her heavy ornaments, with her colorless cracked plate of a face flushed by the lamps.

"The child came too fast, was too eager, that's why."

Hetsa looked as if she would spit like a cat. "What do I care? Why—*why*— she's dead to me."

"I know what you mean to do," said Crow Claw. Her countenance had no expression whatsoever, and yet, when the light dipped and lifted, many visible thoughts seemed to pass up and down like birds, crows perhaps, across a wall. "I can't stop you."

"Be silent, you insolent old bitch—"

"I will say what I must."

In the fire, a log burst. One more bloody reflected flame shot to the ceiling.

"Please . . . let her speak, madam," said the midwife.

Hetsa snarled. She saw the midwife respected the witch more than a Daystar queen, but Hetsa had already known this. Her loins were leaden and cold, and perhaps she would bleed to death now, in the aftermath of this travesty. She might need a witch.

"Before you are rid of your child," said Crow Claw, "you must name her."

"*Name* her! Are you mad?"

"Madam," said the midwife. She was bolder now she had understood she had nothing to fear. Witnesses could attest to her skills. It was the queen's womb that was at fault. And there were too many well-born women in this room to kill. They would have to be bribed instead. "If you send her—*there*, she must have her name. She can't go down into that place without it. You must take pity. It would be— a blasphemy."

Hetsa buried her face in her hands, and tore her hair. The women were too unnerved to stop her. Besides, in this mood, she was very dangerous.

"Then I'll name her," said Hetsa at last. Sweat and powder had dried in lines on her face. Her mouth was red from biting. She looked hideous. "She shall be *Cemira*."

One or two exclaimed, shocked despite everything.

"Madam—that's the name of a monster—"

"And so she is!" screamed Hetsa. She reared up from the couch like a snake, shrieking, howling, until once again her body abandoned her to her emotions, and dropped senseless and silent.

Crow Claw went to the shrine of Bandri and lifted up the bundle in its robe of rich silk that had been laid ready, but certainly not for *it*.

The faces of the very old and of the utterly young sometimes resemble one another, and did so now.

"If it was a daughter, it was to have been called *Calistra*," muttered the midwife.

Crow Claw looked down at the child. It gazed back blindly, moving a little, not crying. It was alive, and if one had not seen all, perfect.

"Well. She is Cemira now. *You are named.*"

"May we be forgiven," someone whispered.

Two lamps, another and another, trembled, faded, went out.

His House had been built west in Akhemony, under Mt. Koi, many hundreds of years before, where the first black terrace of the mountain was laid by the gods. Above Koi, the Mountain of the Heart ascended. Here, of all places, the Heartbeat of the Land sounded most loudly.

It was a three-day journey, but in winter might take five, or seven days, depending on the roads.

The two soldiers rode blank-faced, in the black livery of the temple. Their swords and knives were honed, and their eyes sharp. Bandits grew more shy in the hills at wintertime, but were not unheard of, and although this mission was sanctified, now and then cutthroats and outcasts might chance the wrath of heaven. After all, there was the small casket of gold to be considered, a Daystar's gift to Thon.

The person of the child was holy, and for this reason an ugly sallow priestess accompanied them, in her black-curtained litter slung between two ponies, and attended by an outrider. She fed the child at the infrequent stipulated times, with the watered milk of a black ewe. Almost continuously, already, the child might be heard wailing from hunger, and once the milk curdled, there would be no more. Lucky for it, the cold had kept the milk four days. And, although the peaks that rose above them were chalked with white, no snow had fallen here; there were making good time and would reach the House tonight.

Late in the afternoon, the road slanted upward again, the enclosing rocks drew away, and the slopes of Koi were fully and awesomely revealed, half darkly dense, half transparently drifting on the settling mist. Behind, Heart Mountain was itself an iron ghost. Ethereal, it rested its white skull in the dome of the sky, its base quite lost.

The temple guard drew rein. They, and the outrider, bowed to their horses' necks, touching their own hearts that echoed the beating from the mountain core so exactly.

She too, the sullen and unlovely priestess, peered from the litter, touched her heart, and bowed. She did not bother to show the baby, only leaving it to wail on from hunger and cold and desolation, amid the cushions of the litter.

The great Sun was down, on their left hand now, and the lesser sun, the Daystar, was herself setting, when the party reached the Phaidix Rock. At the spot where the pale marble Phaidix rode her mountain lion, her bow raised and tarnished silver arrow poised to catch, at some point of the night, the moon on its tip, the soldiers halted, and the priestess got out, with the pain-singing child in her grip.

Up the road, straight now as a rule, stood the oblong portico of the Temple of Thon, the House of Death.

Two pairs of black pillars—four, Thon's sacred number—with carved whitish capitals of bone, and the ancient black-bronze bowl between them, the height of a man just before full growth, was sending up its never-ending stream of smoke.

Leftwards, the road tumbled gradually away. Far down there, the decayed sunset of the greater Sun still hung a cloud-caught drift of frigid, mauvish red, into which the Daystar was vanishing with only a silvery streak. Up the flanks of both mountains ran a single, deathly, colorless ribbon, Koi's the brighter.

In the House of Death, an eye was always watching.

Now, out of the impenetrable black of the doorway, two black figures came. Within their hoods, a black void was to be seen, as with the door.

Although the soldiers were Thon's, and had been so, each of them, for ten years or more, they were not immune. Their features pointed, hollowed. One was sweating in the bitter air.

It was the priestess who spoke up.

"I bring a daughter for Thon."

The two black figures stood immobile. All light drained from Koi, from the Heart. On the road, dusk gathered and swelled. The Phaidix shone strangely for a moment, like ice, and was extinguished.

"Enter then."

The voice, disembodied, did not come from the beings on the track, but out of some vast mouth-chamber of the temple itself.

Boldly, perhaps only because her ugliness had made her a fool, the priestess went quickly forward, up the road, towards the temple.

As she did this, the two faceless figures turned about, and moved ahead of her.

Soldiers and outrider followed. They knew quite well that for them there would be austere comforts in this place: mulled wine, and roasted meat, of a hare perhaps, a creature sacred to Thon; beds warm enough, if not luxurious and no one to share them. Nothing then, to fear. Even so, they hung back as they rode, on their very bones, these men, making towards that doorway of high, impenetrable black, beyond the smoking bowl that smelled of storms and wormwood.

For the child, it gave one last lost squeal, and grew as still, quite properly, as death.

My first memory.

Of the earliest memories, only one, which is composed of dozens, one image repeated and repeated, perhaps changeable, ever the same. The memory of Death.

It is the Arteptans who are black. A mysterious and scholarly race, their cities, tombs, and monuments of polished stone, tower beyond the ground, touching sky, as elsewhere, usually, only the landscape does, the architecture of gods.

Thon was not black, despite his colors—the black robes of his priesthood and soldiers, the black of his temples and his animals— hares, black foxes, the hill leopard, black sheep and goat and cow, the crow and raven. One could never for a moment confuse the warm ebony of human skin for the lifelessness of that other black. Besides, black, in this land, was not the color of mourning.

He rears out of the darkness of the inmost shrine, where the four torches find him. He did so then and, in my mind, he does so yet.

Thus: the sudden burst of light, upon that colossal, perhaps disembodied head, seen high in the black air—the face was corpse-white, the eyes dull silver ringed with red. The lips were purple, bruised but not from kissing. His teeth, yellow, pointed like stakes. And from this face, the hair strewn back as if by a gale—*standing on end*. The hair of Thon, the god of death, is blood, made of blood, the blood exploding from a wound, the blood we see in nightmares, if we have truly sinned.

Of course, the statue is only nine feet in height. But to a child, or infant, crouching on the floor of the area already scattered with so many bones, the head will seem to swim in space, since he is robed in black like his priests, and has no form, is only like a pillar, without hands or feet, without torso, legs, or arms. He has no phallus. Evidently, for Thon is not the giver but the Taker of Life.

"Do any remain?"

It was a ritual question. Tonight it was virtually rhetorical. Sometimes the pious, consigning their unwanted babies or youngest children—none over the age of one year was acceptable—to the House of Thon, left provision. And so a secret priest would come, and administer a little food, for that particular child. In this case, the gift of gold was specifically for the god, that had been made most clear. This baby was to be left, in the sanctum, without covering or nurture of any sort. Thereafter, the decreed four nights would pass, and the three or four days before and between.

Supposedly the slough of some woman of the queens' courts, this one had only had to survive three days, four nights. That had been random, fate, dependent on the hour of arrival. Even so, newborn, it could not possibly have survived. The sanctum was also deadly chill, and the baby had lain stripped naked at the footless foot of the god, among the skeletons of all the others who had perished there through the centuries.

"I will open the door, and see."

The ritual answer.

They stood, the two priestesses of Thon, black-robed, the black mask, half a black eggshell, over each face, eyes glimmering at the slits, pitiless from more than shadow.

Held high, the new torch flared.

Bones like curious treasure, all shades, from brown to sheerest snowy white. And the black stretches where they had been pushed and swept aside. Here and there in the enormous room, were a few less clean, whose owners had died more recently.

Below the edifice of the god, the baby lay, the daughter of Queen Hetsa, sixteenth Daystar of the Great Sun, the King.

"Look—it's moving."

"No. Some trick of the torch."

"We must be sure."

"Of course."

If any lived, it was now unlawful not to take them up. Seldom did any live, even those who had been fed. It was not an onerous or repetitive task, to descend to the floor of the pit. Once in a hundred times, perhaps, did they have to do it.

When they bent over the baby it rolled its head, looking up at them. Its eyes were black, as if they had drunk up, wanting anything else, the dark. It had no voice. Had it ever tried, down here, to scream for rescue, or an answer?

"What is the name?"

"I forget—some dreadful one. The mother was insane."

"Not surprising. You see?"

"It's deformed. It hasn't any feet."

"Nor it has. It's accursed. Surely, we ought to leave it here, despite the law."

"I didn't hear you, sister."

One of the priestesses of Thon bent and picked up the baby, which had come into the world so fast it had left its feet behind in the stuff of chaos. "Come along now, I'll take it."

"No, I have it. I remember the name. Cemira."

Feeling the heat of a living body, after the frozen and ungiving stone of the sanctum, the child began finally, faintly to whimper.

"Hush," said the priestess. The child stared up into the black eggshell of face, the slits of pitiless eyes. Were they pitiless? Instinctively, the woman rocked the child, and carried it off, to where they would warm for it a little milk, which anyway might kill it, now, after this interval of famine.

"The child is dead. She is dead, and your servant, Lord Thon. Accept her. Her name, Cemira, has been entered upon your list. She rests helpless on your knees. She is dead, and she is yours. *Alcos emai.*"

After six days, once the fever had departed, and the baby was found able to see, hear, move and make noises, the priests pronounced her dead. That is, alive, and a slave of the Temple of Thon, in Akhemony.

Whether cripple or whole, witless or wise, from now until her physical ending, she would serve here the blood-haired god.

Alcos emai, used at the finish of countless prayers, means in that tongue, *So it is.*

2

I can see her quite distinctly, the child. This must be the first memory of self. She is leaning on her two little canes, with their rests propped under her arms. She wears the long, black child's tunic that reaches to the floor, where her feet would be, if she had any. Under the tunic is the black, sleeved shift. Like all the children, all the priests and priestesses when unmasked in the House of Thon, she is waxy pale. She has a small pointed face like that of a small cat, cut from lunar opal, with big ringed eyes. Her mouth turns down, not from temper or displeasure, but like a dry flower that is dying. Her hair, between straight and coiled, is golden as the metal fringes on the robe of her father, the Great Sun, King Akreon, in the palace at Oceaxis—Lakesea—to the east. The father she has never, and never will ever see. Except—across the river of time.

Someone called to the children, the five of them who were in the porch, watching the snow settle on the kitchen court.

"You and you. You, you. You."

Although they were permitted to keep their given names, their only possession, the names were never spoken. Death was an eater of titles, as of flesh.

The children approached the black-faced, unfeatured priestess. She was the tall, thin one they were particularly frightened of.

"Why are you idling here? Haven't you anything to do?"

"The snow," said the littlest child, a boy of about two and a half. Until the age of four—the sacred number—male and female went unsegregated. It had been noticed long before that sometimes the tiny girls could comfort the tiny boys, and the tiny boys lend the tiny girls a sense of duty. These were the male and female role—virtues, here, servitors, succorers, which were offered to them as ideals.

Along with that, they had, from the third to the seventh year, a rudimentary schooling. To read the texts of the temple, copy letters, such things made them more useful. But, too, their work was in the laundry, in the kitchen, sweeping the long stone floors, clearing up old blood spilled by the outer altars.

At twelve, they would learn more specific arts. The boys butchering and woodwork, and other skills to maintain the temple. The girls might make candles, sew, or rear the animals of the precincts, preparing them for their ultimate destiny of sacrifice or table.

Any who were apt could rise, if there were a vacant place, to the ranks of the lowest priesthood. The god had chosen them anyway, by allowing them to survive the initial test, in the sanctum. They could expect no other life.

Of the very few who dared to run away, generally the harsh mountains killed them. If not, caught by the grown servants of Thon, their own future incarnation—now lost—they were taken at once to a lower room, a sort of natural cave existing under the temple, and locked in there in blackness, with nothing but an injunction to speak a prayer of apology. Unlike the sanctum, with its corpses and skeletons, there was no chance to outlive this punishment. The cave door was not opened again until half a year had passed. The remains were removed, and flung down the side of Koi, into a ditch that ran below.

Sometimes there had been more than two hundred children together in the House of Death. From all Akhemony they might come, or farther. Now there were only eleven.

None of the five in the courtyard had grown accustomed to snow, though they had seen it each winter of their not-yet four years of life.

The boy, bemused, for a moment was made stupid.

"It's cold to touch."

"*Is* it? Is *snow* cold? Go out then, ninny, and lie down on it, and enjoy it."

The boy began to cry. Then stopped. He gave no other protest. None of them did so.

He walked out into the court, and lay on the white covering, face down. He did not wriggle very much.

After the priestess had counted slowly aloud to the number four hundred, also sacred to Thon, she told the child he might get up.

He came back staggering, biting his lip at the scald of the snow, which had burned his cheeks.

Then all five were sent about their business.

"And you, child, you, the useless one. Go back in there. You should be peeling vegetables since you can't stand up. A curse, these misfits, these freaks. Thon should have taken you, but even he didn't want you. Perhaps he'll never let you die, you displease him so."

The freak, Cemira, went with downcast eyes. Most days she peeled vegetables and scoured pots, hour upon hour. Her hands were raw from the cold of the mountain temple, and the heat of the too-hot, greasy water, and cut by kitchen knives too large for her. And somehow these hands would twitch about as if looking for her feet. Of course, her feet would have saved her. She would not have been in the House of Thon, if she had been born with feet. She would have been a king's daughter. But she did not know that.

She moved slowly, and the watcher, the thin priestess, had an urge, not for the only time, to kick away the crutches and see this one fall. But she contented herself with another order.

"*Hurry*! Be quick, you lazy idiot-child."

The outer room of the kitchen, where routine tasks were seen to, was dark and not warm. Beyond the window, as Cemira resumed her work, the snow dizzied down. Sometimes the flakes spun in through the unshuttered opening, and sizzled out in the flame of the meager brazier below.

The, children rose at dawn, and retired at dusk. Summer meant a longer sweating day, winter a longer, icy night.

Perhaps the seasons, the nights and days—that is, heat and cold, blackness and light—were the only proper markers of Cemira's time. Was night, huddled on the narrow pallet, covered by one thin blanket, better than the monotonous and uncertain day? Yes, night was better, for with night, burning or freezing, eventually came sleep. But was summer better than winter?

During the cold months, the children might have to lean into one of the wells to crack the ice with a stone. Once one had plummeted, and so died.

The snow, miraculous and soft, was cruel. Yet silver shone in down-hanging icicles, and once, a living mountain lynx, the shade of milk, stood by the statue of Phaidix and her lion, also her beast, licking at her obdurate foot. Someone had said blood or malt must have been smeared there, but why? In the House of Thon they did not offer to any other god—not even the Sun. And Phaidix any way did not like blood. When the lynx melted away down the mountain, its flowery paw-marks stayed six days, in the closing ice.

In summer, different flowers grew about the statue, and inappropriately about the porticoes of Thon. White and honey, the priests came with brands and scorched them away. But it must be done over and over, for the flowers came back, blooming on and on.

From the courts, in summer, you might look up and see the kites and eagles, motionless, a mile high in violet air. When storms came down over the Heart Mountain, the sky hung alternately low, with enormous clouds, damson and smouldering black, and in them were the shapes of the mountains themselves upside down, or the shape of the temple, sculpted heavily in smoke.

But in summer, too, on every forty-fourth day, each child, however young, must go, to sprinkle fresh blood at the pillar-base of the god in the inner sanctum. And then it stank, that place of bones. Worse than the butchers' yard, worse than the latrines, worse than all worsenesses, that hole of death to which they had almost been added. After twelve years of age, there would be further duties in the sanctum. They had to do with the stacking up and tidying of the skeletons, and the washing of the face of Thon.

Cemira was almost four. She had asked one of the kinder priestesses, the one who had taught her, prematurely, to sew, and sometimes rubbed scented fat into her hands, when their chapped soreness cracked and bled on the linen.

"You're in your fourth year. Almost four."

How did she know? She must have consulted the record of Cemira's entry to the temple . . . Or she was that other one, who had rocked the baby in her arms.

Two years earlier, sometimes, this priestess had taken Cemira on her knees, and brushed her hair for a long time. The priestess had murmured, above the shining, rippling fleece of the child's hair, "You're my baby. You're my baby I should have had." And, once, "They told me, it had golden hair, even in the hour of its birth."

Cemira, however, did not remember this. Only at her tenth decade will Sirai recall that Cemira heard it.

Poor woman. Presumably she had lost her own child, either in reality or unstable fancy. Poor woman. She was kind, in her fashion.

By the table where Cemira sat, peeling, cutting—already she was exhausted with sitting—leaned the sticks, the canes. They hurt her, but they were all she had. They meant mobility.

She wanted to sleep. No one was there, though through the door, the kitchen moved to black forms, gushing with steam and thick with the odor of meats, for the higher priests dined well one day in four. Cemira let her head droop.

She was immediately elsewhere. Where was it? In the sky. A bird carried her, the cloth of her tunic caught in its claws. Irrationally she was not alarmed. Below she saw the temple, the smallest thing in the world. Enormous clouds, quite solid, and touched rosily with a sinking Sun, formed buildings that were all like the temple, the only edifice she had consciously seen, but far more huge, more charming in design. Most wonderful of all, she moved without needing feet, and had no pain.

A pot met the floor with a nearby crash. A lower priestess cursed the pot, and then must speak the prayer to Thon asking his forgiveness for her curse.

Cemira woke. Exquisite escape quite over, she resumed peeling the roots. Returned to earth, and her crutches.

Annotation by the Hand of Dobzah

I can confirm that my mistress, Sirai, has to this day, under her arms, the faint small marks of her first wooden walking canes. These are two silver scars formed each like a sickle moon.

3

Countless legends, dramas and songs, in a variety of lands, are concerned with the notion of justice, of the severe payment for vicious deeds, and the rewards of honor and tenderness.

Hetsa, the Daystar Queen, sixteenth wife of Akreon, had heard such stories often: they had run off her marble skin like rain.

It was a spring afternoon. Hetsa was sitting in her royal apartment, awaiting her lover.

The apartment had altered rather from the earlier scene, when it had been splashed by blood and bloody light, reeking of oils and aromatics and the act of birth. The walls were recently repainted, a token gift of the King's. He had never been discourteous. Behind the pillars, on the creamy plaster, a procession of maidens, bearing fruit, accompanied by long-tailed birds, pipers, and garlanded gazelles, went prettily around three sides to a gilt shrine of Gemli, the Ipyran goddess of joy. A proper compliment, for Hetsa was the daughter of an Ipyran king. In fact the shrine had been placed at the very spot where Bandri, the birth goddess, had waited, over four years ago. Now Bandri was nowhere to be seen.

That same night, they had informed Akreon his child, a daughter, had died, a pity, but not, demonstrably, so unlucky and ill-omened as the truth. Nor such a tragedy as it would have been thought, had the baby been male.

Nevertheless, in the month after the death-birth, Akreon took another new queen, a Daystar picked from Oceaxis itself. He had seen her at a noble's house, where they had taken care he should. She had ankle-length hair the color of young barley, a pale yellow almost green, and she was just thirteen.

As this Lesser Sun arose, Hetsa completely declined. She did not invite a lover for one whole year, but after that they arrived in generous quantities.

That was not unheard of, or rather, providing nothing was heard, it was possible. Akreon had his own pleasures, and his several duties, as uppermost priest and war-leader of the land. He liked women as a pastime. He did not, intellectually, think about them. It was his steward, primed to the work, who from time to time suggested the generosity of a necklace, or a repainted chamber.

Hetsa's women were rustling and giggling in the outer room. They had a turtle, the size of a dog and with a shell like old jade, and were playing with it by the pool. It was supposed ancient, and able to predict things. Now certainly it raised its petted head, and the outer doors were opened.

The merchant Mokpor came through, with one slave. His caravan had come back from the south this morning, and Hetsa had expected nothing less.

Hetsa's Maiden, Ermias, entered, bowed, and smiled secretively. For a second, Hetsa was irritated by this. She kept order by means of sudden malice, and presents.

"Why are you grinning like an ape?"

Ermias's smile vanished at once.

"I have toothache, madam. It draws up my mouth."

"Have the tooth pulled out then. Who has come?"

"The merchant, madam. He's waiting—" Ermias had meant to say, smiling still, *impatiently*. Instead she added, "In the outer room."

"Is he. Has he the web-silk from Bulos?"

"Oh yes, madam."

"And the riverine pearls?"

"I'm sure." Ermias wondered uneasily if she would need to have a tooth pulled in point of fact. Hetsa remembered, curious things, and might in two months' time, demand to look in her mouth. But no, Errnias would say she had sought out old Crow Claw. The witch was not so often seen about now, but one could always pretend. Crow Claw's magic would easily put right one of Ermias's perfectly sound molars.

"Send him in to me. His slave may stay outside. And shut the door. I don't want them all running to other maids, with stories of what I've bought. That happened last time. No sooner had I got my dress made up, than that cunning one, that serpent Stabia, appeared in just the same embroidered stuff. She's too old to wear it and too fat, and should have known better."

"Yes, madam." Ermias thought that Hetsa should also recollect leaning at her mirror of burnished silver, and sighing, while Ermias dressed her hair, over the little poem Mokpor had sent her. "His eyes are like stars," Hetsa had exclaimed. Perhaps they were, they needed to be, when his poetry was so bad.

Ermias went to the middle door and waved Mokpor peremptorily forward. As he modestly obeyed, she saw him give her a look, her slender form and darkly curling tresses, probably her gold earrings too. Not an utter fool, Mokpor. When the queen was done with him, Ermias might be available. He smiled. Ermias tossed her head, letting him admire her supple neck that was three years younger than Hetsa's.

"Radiant Sun!"

Mokpor knelt gracefully on one knee, as the middle door closed at his back. Kneeling was the manner of Oriali, the Eastern Towns, from which he had come. It also displayed his fine legs, in pale leather boots and firm leggings. Deliberately, he always misnamed the queens, not as Daystars, but as Suns, an honorific allowed only princes, and the Sun-Consort.

"Well, you're late."

"I was delayed."

"You dawdled."

"How could I, my glamorous and gleaming one? How *would* I, when I was to come here?" His starry eyes flashed. His fair hair sparkled with attention, thickly curled, like the narrow Eastern beard around his jaw. She had said, she liked his trace of accent.

He was exceedingly well-dressed. Hetsa's patronage had decidedly helped him. That first evening, when he had come with an example of the new liquid flame-red dye from Artepta, he had seen at once, his luck was in.

Now Hetsa signalled languidly to his box. Oh. She was in a mood.

"What have you got to show me?"

Mokpor took another chance. He rose, strode to her, and lifted her to her feet as easily as if she were a doll, squeezing her close. "My blazing need for you, my queen. Can you feel it?"

Hetsa turned her face. Mokpor chased her mouth with his own, and caught it. After a moment she responded to his kiss.

He knew better than to question her. She was often out of temper. But then, she was a woman. She had lost a child years ago, they said, and it had spoilt her looks. But she was still toothsome enough, and when he had pinned her as she liked, and was racing within her, bending now and then to beard-tickle and suck her breasts, Mokpor was not unhappy.

Outside, at the command of Ermias—that minx—some musicians were playing loudly with gourd-harps, drums, and bells. A good thing. Mokpor was aware not everyone could get noises like that out of a queen.

She would buy the spangled cloth, too. He would tell her it was the color of her eyes.

Beyond the wide window, open to the passage of spring day . . .

Hetsa contemplated, at first dreamily, the constant sounds of the palace. A noise of trotting horses, a rift of distant laughter. Birds singing in the gardens that ran down to the lip of the shore. The soft lap and whisper of the Lakesea, nearly calm today as water in a cup.

From the outer room, Ermias had taken the other girls, and the green turtle, probably, away. But the guardsman would stand at the outer doors, and some ready, serviceable slave would be there in a corner, waiting stoically.

All was peace, smooth as if combed. Why then, this sense of a problem, stealing near?

She need do nothing. There, on that rail, her excuse if any were required, hung the lovely, half-transparent, honeyish web-silk, with its threads and stipples of brightness. And Mokpor had left her, as a tribute a flagon of Bulote perfume, the kind that had esoteric ingredients and was mixed in the temples of the love goddess. This had flattered Hetsa. That he should gift her, so for a moment she had become his beloved mistress, rather than his queen. The cloth, of course, was expensive, but then, she did not often overspend—unlike others.

Her body was warm, sated. He had told her he had gone mad almost, during his month away from her. And he had possessed her vigorously twice, and a third time done things to her with tongue and fingers and a wicked little wand, until her shriek set the vessels on her mirror-table ringing.

And yet, now, this. What was it? *What?*

She raised herself on one elbow and glanced about the room. The day was stilly mellow there, the shadows under furniture, drifting in curtains, tiles, lucent and lengthening only somewhat.

Two hours surely, before the sunset of the great Sun, and then another until the smaller sun, the Daystar, had followed him into the mountains behind Oceaxis.

Yet this—was a night-foreboding, was it not? She had heard it spoken of. The little fear that came with the breeze of evening, something old women felt. The promise of death.

It was . . . it was that sound. That sound of a drum she could hear, not music, not the hoofs of horses—a drum out of time with the other Drum, the Heart of the Land.

Any music played in Akhemony might only be partnered to that tempo, the rhythm of the Heart on Heart Mountain. That was easy to do, for one no longer *heard* the Heart Drum, without conscious effort. Men's hearts simply beat with it, in their breasts, so they said. She had not found it quite like that, when first she came here.

And now this—this did not keep time at all.

Knock knock-knock. Tap-tap. Tap.

Hetsa gave a cry. Her face was rigid and hard with fright.

It was not a sound. It was—a pummeling, like something jumping, *twitching*—in her belly.

She started to her feet and her gown, undone, half on, slid off her body.

She stared down at her stomach, that, four years ago, with massage and diet, had regained, mostly, its firmness. Even the pale feathers on its surface, where the skin had been stretched, were hardly visible.

Drum-skin stretched—

Drum-skin. Knock. Tap, tap.

Kick. Kick-kick.

Something inside her, something inside her womb. *Kicking.*

Hetsa snatched a garment. Like a terrified child she ran to the outer doors.

The guard turned in astonishment.

"Fetch my women! Fetch Ermias!"

The stoical slave rose up, and ran.

He had an instant's unease, when the pompous official stopped him. In his golden collars, with the attendant walking behind, the man's summons to the Hall might have meant trouble. Just out of Hetsa's apartment, however, Mokpor learned he was only to attend the Sunset Offering, a notable honor. Apparently, the Sun-Consort herself wished to see his wares.

Mokpor made time to visit the public rooms of the palace and bathe the scent of Queen Hetsa from his body. One never knew. If the King were closely to pass him, Akreon might catch that heady smell, and, who knew, maybe remember it belonged solely to him.

Never before had this merchant had the priviledge of entering the Great Hall at Oceaxis.

He had been told it was the length of twenty-six tall men, lying head to foot, and more than half that across. In construction it was an oblong; but within the oblong, the gigantic pillars, which were apparently each one, plated with gold one inch thick, formed an oval. At the sea end, which faced east, the Sun and the Daystar would be visible at their rising, and here, on the East Terrace, the priests made an offering with every dawn. In his youth, a king would normally participate in this. Akreon, at fifty-six years, did so no longer.

West, which faced towards the mountains, where, on clearer days Koi might be made out, and behind Koi, on the clearest, the Heart, another terrace extended. And here, the priests, and still, Akreon, saluted the fall of both Suns into the mountains inland, and so into the Sea of Sleep that lay under the world.

The way into the Hall was up a steep precipice of steps—one hundred and seventy, or one hundred and seventy-three, or -four of them, depending on who told you, or your own mathematics. The Hall was the highest point of Oceaxis, and from far off, the gold glint of the roof of it might be picked out, so one might say, offhand, to a caravan, *See that? The palace.*

There were three landings on the stairs which led to the East

Terrace. On each landing were small gold statues, on plinths of gilded bronze, images of the god, the Sun, in his various nonhuman guises— the horse with chariot, ram and bull, the eagle, the boar. Death liked the ram, too, Mokpor remembered. While in Oriali the ram meant benign fortune, so he would bow to it. Being the second landing, he was slightly winded, any way, and glad of a reason to pause.

The terrace that looked east to the Lakesea was, beyond the house shadow, glowing and windblown, for a stiff breeze was coming off the water in the westering light. Its waves, too, were frisky now, and gilded, like the plinths, and the mosaic underfoot. The gods thought of everything.

Over the big altar, flawless snowy marble, stood the image of the true Great Sun, the solar deity as a young man, prince and hunter, with bow and knife. He was naked, his member sheathed in a Sunburst, and there was gold in his marble hair.

The altar was clean as a diligent wife's kitchen.

Various people were straying or standing on the Terrace. Mokpor beheld their jewelry with artistic esteem. Their wind-shaken clothes were estimable in other ways.

He avoided their eyes, in the correct underling mode. And once, when some noble turned on him a relentless flaring glare, Mokpor dipped his knee and bowed his curly head. No, not a fool.

Beyond the east doors, with their inlay of enamel, bronze, and copper, the gargantuan Hall.

"Stay close," he said to his slave.

He had noticed before, a slave did not always have a sensible dismay and awe at the great works of the civilized world. Obviously, a slave could attempt so very little, possibly there was to him—since no chance of gain—no logic in reverence.

If the gold on the pillars was an inch thick, one could not be sure. But the pillars were massive, dark yellow, and the gold ringed them, around and around, until the eyes slipped off in a swoon. The ceiling was flat and very high, resting on pillar-tops of black and gold. Painted figures showed a battle on the walls. And, near the roof, was the giant skull of a lion, large as a man's torso, they said killed by King Okos in his boyhood.

There were carved benches about the room and tables, chairs, and the high seats reached by steps, these set with colored stones. But more urgent than anything was the central Hearth.

One had heard of the Hearth, too.

It was the Sun, in his two aspects of a king, the young man and the old. They kneeled back to back. They were of solid brass, much blackened from many hundred years, and worn and softened also, the features and muscles rubbed too silken, and the raging manes of hair, the old man's pouring beard, planed down by time from standing fires to the plaiting contours of sheepswool.

They were fearsome though. And had in their heads optical diamonds. Refracting now, the diamond eyes of the old king, turned to the West Terrace.

These two aspects of the god held on their knees the fire pits. And the Hearth fires burned there, low, the flames the bounty of the Sun, which must never, even in the midnight of death, be let go out.

Instinctively almost, Mokpor glanced up.

Around the smoke hole in the roof, were the two corresponding icons of the Daystar, girl and hag. Each arched over, holding out her hands to receive above the semen-smoke of the fires from the loins of the Sun. The buttery electrum of these figures had become almost entirely black. If they had ever had eyes, they were no longer to be seen.

Such was the fate of women. Subservient, smirched, blinded. Mokpor, irresistibly, recollected his mother, a woman of seventeen, who had disappeared in his ninth year.

Akreon, the Great Sun on earth, had spent the fine day hunting in the hilly forests just northwest of Oceaxis.

Returning, possibly he had looked out from the higher ground, it was an inevitable view. The pristine thriving town, wreathed by its wintered orchards and olive groves, its farms, spearcast east its port, fixed solidly into the inland sea called a lake. Birds and smokes rose from the shining roofs, and on the good, common road below, perhaps a score of carts passed, with the early produce of the land, and cattle maybe were driven in for the market tomorrow.

Or else, he paid no particular heed. He had seen these sights often, for he had spent many winters at Oceaxis, and summers too. It was a choice spot.

Besides, how could he assess this treasury of his possessions here, this king who ruled, as his father and grandfather had ruled, from Ipyra and distant Uaria in the north and west, through all Akhemony, to the remotest isles beyond Artepta and Charchis. To feel this kingship over in his hands or mind, he would do what men generally do, with such personal enormity of ownership. It must be reduced to the workable and everyday, the subject of inspections and reports. And, too, it must be magnified far, far beyond the everyday, into the unearthly power of a god: the subject of prayer.

For Akreon knew himself divine—he was the Great Sun. In his veins ran the fires of eternity, the light of heaven. And he had grasped this, from his first awareness, over half a century before.

Probably then, he did not give the region of Oceaxis a glance. He had had splendid exercise, and wanted the bath, some wine, and then, after the Sunset Offering, his dinner. He had brought down two bucks in the wood. King-killed meat was highly prized, not least by the King.

It was a complacent god perhaps, then, whom Mokpor the merchant saw emerge on to the West Terrace, as the sun reached the edge of the day. A god in the form of a strong, muscular man, carrying only a modicum of extra flesh, and without any iron in the rays of his darkly golden hair. A high color intensified light grey eyes. His handsomeness was blurred only a little, less than the god of the fireplace.

Women had been crazy for Akreon in his youth, one heard, and a few men also. But he was not incontinent, and only after his forty-fifth year did he turn fully from his consort, whom they said he loved, to other women, and to child-girls.

He wore a crimson tunic appropriate to the occasion, floured with powdered gold, and with borders of gold bullion so heavy they dragged the material.

All the higher court had migrated now, out on to the West Terrace. Over beyond the phantom slope of Koi, the sky was coagulating into a rich amethystine rose.

Mokpor took in everything, carefully. One was questioned by the envious, and if one got things wrong in the telling, disbelieved.

A mile away, in the town, the temple gongs were sounding. As they stopped, silence came sacredly down.

Even the wind dropped.

In stasis: the guardsmen in their bronze, glittering, the court in their silks and furs. The glow, carmine now, tinting the white crests of helmets, the pillars at the doorway, the cheeks of women like peaches, sparks in the drops of gems.

In his metallic unbroken voice, the boy priest at the altar sang out through the bell of the air.

> *Splendor of leaving,*
> *Beauty of going away,*
> *We stand powerless at the Gate of Night.*
> *Do not forget us, O Greatest God.*
> *Do not forget.*

An elder priest gave the cup of incense into the hand of the King. Akreon poured the gum forth in a glaucous stream. Smoke rose black on the carmine of the sinking Sun. And framed, adrift in fire, the Daystar, hovering like a silver boat. She must always wait her hour alone above the world, offering her lantern of reassurance, before she might follow the God.

This was mystic, holy.

Mokpor's throat closed with emotion. The ethic of these minutes was more valid than any description of appearances or jewels, of who stood where, any mortal glory.

When the noise came, he jumped violently.

A clang—the cup had dropped from Akreon's ringed hand. It rolled along the terrace. Startled, a few small cries had answered it.

Akreon pointed at the Sun. "Look! By the God's Knife, two of them!"

"My lord—" the priest, at Akreon's side, not quite so tall as the King.

"Do you see, priest? *Two* Suns."

A murmur rising now on the West Terrace, as the wind rose, coming back over the house from the Lakesea.

Garments ruffled, fluttering of things.

"Two Suns!"

Akreon's face was inflamed not by blood and sunfall, but with excitement. He shook the priest roughly. Akreon was known for his courtesy, his piety.

"My lord—do you mean, the great Sun and the Daystar?"

"No. In God's Name—Are you blind?"

Akreon stared about him. He seemed puzzled now.

"My lord —"

"The Sun is there twice over. Two Suns. Going down now over Koi and the Heart."

Akreon turned back to watch to the last this portent, which only he could make out.

The single Sun—though he had struggled, Mokpor could only find one—sank suddenly. Was gone.

Akreon shrugged. He turned again, nodded to the priest, who was very pale. Akreon spoke reasonably. "Forgive me, sir. I'd thought it would be visible to all."

The priest said, into the utter silence, into the rising of the twilight as the shadow ascended, "We must seek the response of the god, my lord. What you have seen—was granted only to you."

True luck. Mokpor grinned inwardly, in glee, pushing away the religious and superstitious terror he still kept clamped upon his diplomatic face.

Of all the times he could have been invited to the ceremony, the gods had allowed him this one. The sunset when the King had seen a vision.

Ushered into the apartment of the Sun-Consort, Udrombis, in the hour before dinner, he found her as he had expected, cool and quiet. Nothing at all might have happened anywhere.

She talked to him a few moments of his travels. She was known for her tact and her ability to put at ease the nervous . . . to make nervous too, those too much at ease. She had been lovely in her youth, at twelve, when the King had wed her. She was forty-eight now. Tall, heavy, faultlessly elegant. Her Arteptan blood showed in her ropes of jet-black hair, worn long despite their grayer strands, and the polished agates of her eyes.

In another chair sat the other, lesser queen, the Daystar Stabia, the Consort's close friend. They had been amiable companions for years and, if ever rivals, were so no more.

Mokpor had noted, down a long lamplit room beyond this one, where two sleek dogs lay on the tiles, two male golden children, eleven and nine years old, playing a board game couthly, just out of earshot— one assumed, Udrombis's youngest son, and Stabia's only son. Friends also, apparently.

He began to realize quite quickly, as she looked at his dextrous display of the cloth, that he was not really here to sell her anything. At least, not web-silk.

"Such delicate fabrics. Yes. I will take those, and those. And Stabia, let me have this, for you."

Stabia inclined her head, "Thank you, madam. You're very kind."

They were formal before him. And Stabia, the younger, was like a bolster. She would look more like one, in the selected silk.

"Please sit, sir. Try those sweets, they're quite tasty. I mustn't keep you too long from your meal."

It was Stabia who rose, and gestured to the group of Maidens behind the chairs, that they might go. As they did so, moving on into the second room, they drew across a long heavy curtain. The two sons of the Sun were hidden.

Stabia said, "The Sun-Consort wishes to confide in you, Mokpor. Don't be agitated at what she says."

At once the scented hair rose on Mokpor's head, and his belly griped. What was coming?

"Queen Hetsa," said Udrombis, in her mild, eloquent voice, "has taken you as her lover."

The chamber whirled. Mokpor watched all the decorations hurry past. He shut his eyes and tried not to wet himself. "High Lady—I have enemies—someone has—"

"Lied? No. Of course not. You must understand, sir, my task, in this last third of my life, is to care for the household of the King. To this end, I have those who are able to tell me things. Your habit with the Daystar, Hetsa, is but one of many I've learned of."

Mokpor threw himself flat on the floor.

To his horror, as he did so, he heard fat Stabia stifle a laugh.

Udrombis said, levelly, "My desire isn't to distress you. The King, I know, will never lie with Hetsa again. He was warned from it, after the stillbirth. He loves best his last queen, the little girl from the town. She's only seventeen, even now. And she's born him a pair of healthy children. If the King were to wish to see Hetsa again, he would inform me. I would then advise him that she was not quite well. That's all. She does no harm, therefore, and nor do you. One must be sensible in these matters. There have been other cases."

Mokpor began to weep. It was Stabia who leaned over him and, of all things, wiped his eyes and nose briskly with a corner of her over-mantle. She, a queen, gave him his cup of wine. He drank it down.

Sitting on the floor then, like one of their sons—he *had* been nine once, and his mother seventeen—he listened to what Udrombis wanted.

"But—"

"One has heard things. Strange things. I would like to know who or what had incurred such supernatural activity in the apartment of Queen Hetsa."

"Her women—Ermias—couldn't you send for *her*?"

"Ermias is a Maiden. Loyal to her mistress, I hope. *You*, sir, are this Daystar's intimate."

Mokpor hung his head. One day, when he was elderly, this would make a story worth recounting. He would need to be elderly, to have got over the shock.

Crow Claw had been located.

Perhaps it was not so strange that Ermias had found her at last after dark, in the garden of Phaidix, under the wall.

Crow Claw had been making an offering of milk at the small stone altar. The statue was crude, very old. It smelled nastily of milk poured there. The moon goddess who had charge of the stars, did not care for blood, since when she hunted animals, or murdered men, their death was delightful and they did not bleed.

"Crow, you have to come and see to Queen Hetsa."

"I'm too old."

Ermias raised her brows. She put, without delay, the silver ornament, a girl dancing, into the witch's hand.

"Take this. And come."

"Why?"

"She's sick and making a fuss. Screaming—"

"Why?"

Ermias bent near. "She says—feet are running about in her *womb*."

Crow Claw gazed up at the night sky. Phaidix's moon was rising on the sea, the bow, strung with its invisible cord.

"I have seen those feet. They scurry about her room."

Ermias made a sign over her heart, a protective, unbroken circle. "*Don't* speak of that."

"Her girls saw it. Three of them have seen it."

"*No*."

"And the turtle, the ancient one. She sees. Her eyes *follow* them."

Ermias had come to Hetsa in the year after the business of the baby in Hetsa's apartment. Ermias had replaced the chief of Hestsa's women, who had fled back to her kindred in the hills. This girl had had dreams, of disembodied silver feet that *ran* and *jumped*—and *skipped* across the floors.

Hetsa had heard nothing of any of this. The rumors had only eventually reached Udrombis.

They climbed up a level of the palace, Ermias supporting the crone, now and then thinking of a grandmother in her father's house, who had had no teeth. Crow Claw had teeth. She could bite with them, had left one tooth in a man's hand, years ago.

Ermias noticed it was the second time today there had been notions of teeth—some omen?

In Hetsa's rooms, the shadows are another color now. The raw greys and browns of mourning.

The lamps tend to go out, as if the oil were bad.

Hetsa lies wide-eyed. Her hands grip her belly. She feels them, kicking her, *kicking* her. The feet of the dead child left behind.

The physician has examined her, and told her nothing at all is amiss. She is nervous; woman's trouble, hysteria. That is the cause of this.

But the physician's medicine has not helped, and Hetsa knows.

Beholding the witch, like the very last shadow bending near, Hetsa says nothing.

Crow Claw peered down.

"I see them," the witch said presently. "They are there."

"What shall I do?" Hetsa sounded like a ghost. She expected soon to die.

"Confess," said Crow Claw. "That is all that must be done. Be open with your foulness, the deformed baby—what you did with it. The name you gave it. Tonight is a night among nights."

The women mumbled.

Crow Claw folded her robes about her. In four years, she had aged not one iota.

From the Great Hall, up in the sky, a cheerful loud noise blossomed with the dinner. The men were singing, maybe even the King. The queens would be chattering, laughing. And from the Hearthfire of the double Sun god, the semen-smoke would lift to the doubled hands of the Daystar. All was well. The Suns invoked, must rise tomorrow. The vision of the King could bode only good.

"Confess," said Crow Claw. "Or die."

Below in the garden, a black fox, got in at a hole in the wall, was drinking the milk of Phaidix under the moon.

4

As predicted, the Sun rose. The Daystar rose. In the way of days, this one passed.

Night came again, over the lands of the Sun, creeping through dark Artepta, enfolding watery Bulos in a cloak of shade, clambering now on the backs of Oriali, clasping Ipyra of the burning caves, pushing across the Lakesea, moonless in cloud, smothering Oceaxis, and gushing on to put out the colors and contours of the continent's central basin, Akhemony, the "King's Own Land." At the mountains, the tide expanded, climbed the Heart and Koi and Airis; spilled, poured down into the waste of waves and islands that was Uaria, and so swept on into the mouth of the Unknown, the seas beyond the world.

It was a three-day journey, but that was for those who would pause to rest. For these riders, posted with horses along the route, much of a day and a night sufficed.

Coming as they must to the smoking House of Thon, in the darkness, they drew rein on the track, where, in their torchlight, the Phaidix rode her lion.

And here, unsheathing their swords, they saluted her, the armed men. The metal of the, swords, pherom-steel, had been made in the earliest times from her fallen stars.

That which watched in the House presently sent out four black figures on the road.

No word exchanged. Nothing. The horses sidling a little, hard held. A faint luminescence in the valleys below that might indicate that morning was appearing in a dream. No other thing, save, somewhere, hundreds of feet above, the trickle of one tiny pebble.

The watchers on the track watched from their ovoid faces. The men sat their horses, meeting hidden eyes.

Then the riders wheeled about, and raced on over the passes of Koi, their torches breaking wreaths of gold.

They must reach the crown of the land, the Mountain of the Heart, before the Sun returned.

An ultimate noise roused the five youngest children in their dormitory. The night had been cold, and four of them had doubled together two by two, for warmth. Only the freak, Cemira, had been left alone.

With their heads ringing from the clashing squall of the gong, they dropped from their pallets and stood up, to meet this new disaster. For the gong was only sounded in a time of calamity. They had been told that long ago.

As four poised on the icy floor, Cemira swung herself upright by use of her canes. Like all of them, she was naked. She hung there, the slender white verticals of her legs ending where the ankle bones should have begun, like stalks from which, the flowers had been cleanly, tidily, severed.

"*The most terrible has occurred.*"

The priestess spoke to them in a voice of coldest iron. It must be, as once or twice had been threatened, the end of the world.

Two began to sob.

The priestess shouted, once. They were dumb.

"Dress yourselves. Come to the Death Altar. Be very quick. If you are late, you'll be beaten. To mark you for life."

Life? *She* would have no fear of world's end, even when the mountains collapsed and the sky broke on the roof in fragments.

They ran about when she was gone, pulling on their clothes, moaning, and presently rushing out. Cemira was the last only because it was more awkward for her.

As her sticks swung her hurtfully through the passages, she was passed by priests and priestesses who also ran, speechlessly.

Yes, the world was to end.

Was she sorry? She did not question herself, this little girl. She had only miseries to lose. The one who taught her to sew, any way, soothing her chapped hands, had sometimes told her of another aspect of Thon. Then he was the Veiled One, who shut the eyes of the sufferer with his gentle breath, and brought the Sleep of Night, which might be full of beautiful dreams.

The Death Altar lay in the forepart of the temple. It was the sole public hall of the house, to which, very rarely, suppliants might come, wishing to show honor to some deceased relative or lover. But usually such people would take themselves to temples of the towns, not here. For Thon's house in the hills of Akhemony was not kept for remembrance.

When the child reached the hall, it was packed full, and full too of the smells of unwashed morning bodies and mouths, and the rope-thick smoke that gusted from the Altar. Nearby, a black cow stood tethered, tossing her head in fear, for she scented old blood around the drain, which could never quite be washed away.

There was no chanting. No words were being said. There was no true sound.

The child listened. She heard her heart beating. No, it was the Heartbeat from the mountain, the Heart of the Land of Akhemony. This was what she heard.

All her life, her four into five years, she had heard it, and mostly here, so loud, so omnipotent in this place. Heard it so long, she no longer heard it at all, although every hymn of the temple took its tempo from that beat.

The smoke roiled into the roof, up to the wide black beams. There was no statue. Thon showed himself only in the sanctum. They said, he was too terrible for others to look on until, presumably, they must.

She was sorry for the cow. She had fed it yesterday. They had told her in the kitchen it need not be killed for another month, and that was for food, which would have been better, because the butcher's yard was kept quite clean, and there it might not have noticed the odor of blood—

Nearby, another child, adrift in the adult crowd, threw up from terror on the floor.

A priestess turned, quickly, and slapped it.

Yes, yes, let the world end now.

I see myself as if from above. I see myself standing there, as I had then to stand, on my canes. Almost mindless I was with lack of life and knowledge. I weep for her, that little child I was.

Annotation by the Hand of Dobzah

I wish to say that, at this point of her narrative, tears ran from the eyes of Sirai. But only for a moment. I have never seen her weep before except for another, but it is always very swift. I tried to catch one tear once in a bottle. When she saw what I did, she burst out laughing at me. And her tears stopped.

Up on the peak of the Heart, it was possible to see, across the earth, the initial trace of light that must be a messenger of the Sun.

The riders had reached the lower platform. They might go no further. Perhaps, they could not have done, for here the Drumbeat juddered them, made them dizzy and half faint. The land—seemed to dance. One man staggered down from his horse. His torch fell. He lay full-length on the ground, clutching at the rocks.

All about, the gathered height, still, in disturbed darkness, spring-dashed with the most silver, or the most dirty snow. But above, the pinnacle-peak, its round, dim disk of cave, was garbed gleaming in clandestine virgin white. And where the stream darted over and down, not long unfrozen, catching torchlight, the magical greenish flowers grew.

The priest who had ridden with them, the Sun priest from Oceaxis, had come to the boulder where the horn hung on its chain.

The chain was rusty. He must scrape and scrabble to reach the instrument. Having it, he did not wipe the filthy lip, that would be sacrilege. Since boyhood, one of four, he had been trained to sound such a horn, against this hour. He lifted the horn to his mouth, drew breath into his mighty lungs, that a diver for pearls in the Bulote rivers might have envied. He kissed the horn lip. Tang of age and bitterness—

Even over the rampage of the Drum, that thundered and blasted down at them, turning the mountain in a cauldron of sound, the horn was audible. A lost and appalling lowing had come from it, and went on, like the cry of the world herself.

Then the priest, breath exhausted, let go the note, which hung a moment more above the thunder of the Drum, swilled between cliffs of stone and air, paled like dye in water, vanished.

Shivering, the priest got up again. His life had been, partly, for this. It was unthinkable he would ever have to do it again.

He, and the soldiers of the King, stood, agonized and one-dimensional, between land and heaven.

Then—

Then.

The Drum, the Heart—

Stopped.

One of the soldiers screamed. He clapped his hands to his head. A fellow caught him and threw him down before he plunged to his death over the ledge of the mountain.

And now, only this . . .

The wind whined, curled over, and came back, whining. They heard the tinselly crinkle of the waterfall.

The horses shook their heads, the bridles jingling.

The priest spoke softly, not to bruise the Heart-stopped air: "The Great Sun is dead."

In his youth he had known this, once, at the death of Akreon's father. He had not been on the mountain then, he had been younger, then. He buried his face in his hands, and stood motionless, as the soldiers swayed or reeled, or crawled around him.

The temple was built of shrieking. In the midst of it, as they ran against her, as they fell and tumbled on the floor, Cemira hung on her canes, and saw the throat of the cow slashed by a howling priest, her outcry tangled in all the rest.

After that the world spun over and Cemira sprawled, just as the thin priestess had wished to see.

Cemira lay on the floor, kicked and stumbled on by others with feet.

Her head tolled an abysm of emptiness. It was as if she had gone deaf. Or, had died.

The blackness covered her, and yet, still conscious, she bobbed on the sea of it. This *must* be death. And death was as horrible as living.

But someone now snatched her up. She was borne, whirling, through the whirling world, away and away. She clung with all her might. Did she wish after all to survive, then? This curtailed body, did it have the temerity to long for life?

"Ssh. It's the worst moment. In a second—it will be over. Hush. My baby. I know, I know. Hold me. Yes. Oh, let the gods make it end!"

Unknown to Cemira, known to the priestess who held her, the kind priestess who had sought her in the maelstrom, up in the peak of Heart Mountain the drummer was already taking up again his Drumsticks. To him, maybe worse than to any other, this abysmal hesitation in the rhythm of his days. He craned into the gloom of the sanctified cave, his flaming madman's eyes straining upon the reefs of time, seeking the new moment in which—to *resume*.

It came.

The sticks flared high, struck down.

From his body of bronze, the Drum of brass and bullshide, the savage crescendo bellowed, and the earth tilted and crashed back upon its axis.

Cemira raised her head. Her hair was soaked with her tears and those of the priestess, whose mask was also wet, and askew. For the flick of an eye, Cemira saw the old white face, a stranger's, gathered in seams, the sad visible eye, quite human. But the priestess adjusted her mask.

"There now. All over."

"What was—what was—" Cemira had been deprived temporarily of the power of language.

"The Great King has died. Probably at Oceaxis. The Heart must stop, to show the heart of the King has stopped. Do you see?" Cemira shook her head, and was giddy. "Well, it's over now. And there's a new King. So the Drum beats on."

In fact, in Akhemony, the new King had only just learned his status. The messengers had not reached his estates quite in time. So he had been out before sunup, looking at the vine-stocks, making offerings for their spring growth, when the lesion of the Drum smashed down through the land.

He, too, fell on his knees, trembling, most of his balance gone. This happened to many, or worse. You often heard it, so and so died when the King died. One's heart could not beat in time to the Drum from birth, and stay unmoved at its hiatus. The two slaves were facedown.

Yet when the Drum recommenced, knowing it was now beating for him, Akreon's heir, born thirty-four years in the past to the Sun-Consort, Udrombis, lurched to his feet, and held himself frowning in his own arms. He had always known it would come, but, as with the cow in Thon's temple, Glardor had thought it would not come so soon.

Because of the turmoil that persisted in the House of Thon, the priestess was able to take Cemira away with her, to her cell. She should not have done this. Later she would have to make a confession of her error, though it would be forgiven her, seeing what happened next. In the cramped stony space, the priestess lit her brazier, and took the child on her lap. She fed her cold porridge and honey, a treat she had been saving for herself.

Cemira could only eat a little.

"Will it happen again?"

"The Sun keep us from it. No. No, not for years. Not until you're a grown woman. Perhaps not until you're old."

Cemira knew she would be old here, in Thon's House. She could not imagine this, but neither could she imagine anything else. Except, to fly with eagles in the sky.

A long time after, there were footsteps outside. A man's voice called, "Are you here?"

There was no choice in the matter of replying. "Yes."

The priest came in around the black leather curtain. He stood looking at the priestess and the little girl, dark and pale, from his flat-faced mask.

"Is this the child from Oceaxis?"

"Yes, she is."

"Can she walk?"

"No. She hasn't any feet."

"Good," said the priest. This ironic comment indicated only that he had found the one he sought. "Are those her canes? Bring her."

They went up through the temple to a bleak room behind the Death Altar, the room where supplicants came, if they ever did, to pay the priesthood and have their details entered on a tablet.

Here the soldier stood, upright and steady as he had not been, five hours earlier, on the shaking, soundless platform under the peak of the Heart.

To Cemira, he was of a frightening magnificent hardness. His insectile carapace of bronze, his helm with its snow-plume. The gems in the pommel of his sword. His cloak was the scarlet of the god's blood-hair, and he wore over it the insignia of Queen Udrombis, a lion, stitched out in gold.

"Does she speak?"

" . . .Yes."

"Child—is your given name Cemira?"

Cemira stared. Personal names were not to be spoken, only one, the name of Death.

"You said she could talk." He was impatient, but more with himself than with the child. He had been ashamed, nearly fainting when the Drum stopped. He was an athlete, an accomplished charioteer, a champion. He had fought the battles of the King and, at twenty years of age, had killed more than fifty men, and sired more than ten. After his shame, her deformity meant little.

To the child, the gorgeousness of his *seen*, unmasked face, in its frame of metal and metallic hair, his tall male body, so clean and strong, so blameless of anything but slaughter and sex, were beautiful, and nearly sorcerous. She had quite forgotten the priestess.

Perhaps he saw the fear melt from her eyes to fearful admiration. He had a little daughter too, in the hills below Mt. Airis. He crouched down and lightly put his firm young finger on the tip of her nose. "Can you give me a smile? It's good news. Queen Udrombis has sent me to bring you home."

5

The queens were in mourning, as was all Akhemony. And so, the Daystar Hetsa walked barefoot over the reflective floors of the palace, in a dull brown robe, without a jewel, to attend the summons of the Sun-Consort.

Only once before had Udrombis spoken to Hetsa. That had been on the festal evening Hetsa, then only sixteen, had gone up to the bed-chamber of the King. Udrombis was then quite amiable. She did not seem jealous, but stern only in her words. She had made sure Hetsa, the daughter of a barbaric Karrad-king in Ipyra, knew the facts of congress, and inspected her clothes, and asked what perfumes had been used. Hetsa had been told she must be worthy of the honor of her role. She was to serve the mighty Sun. In this her own, Hetsa's, honor lay. Hetsa had thought privately the Great Queen made a great to-do about it. Akreon had already had Hetsa, in her father's house. What had honor to do with lust? It was riches that Hetsa wanted, standing, to be at Oceaxis. But she was outwardly timid and respectful. You did not cross the Consort. One had heard this and that, even in the wilds of Ipyra.

The huge room was exquisite, yet quite sparsely furnished. Udrombis did not care for clutter. On vast basalt paws, the two lions lay, holding up the writing table. She had scrolls, books, curiosities from many lands. She was as excellent, they said, as a temple scribe, and despite her age, her eyes were keen. Too keen, perhaps.

"Lady!" Hetsa bowed very low, and remained bent over.

She had been told to leave her attendant at the door. There was no one to help her. Hetsa, unlike that first time, was shaking with anxiety.

Udrombis sat in her chair of carved cedar, looking at her, or not, making no sound. A minute passed, and Hetsa gave a gasp.

"Please, be comfortable, Daystar," said the Sun-Consort, gently. "That chair should be quite pleasant. You haven't been well."

Hetsa straightened, found the seat, and sat.

She had attempted, before coming here, to make some plan, but obviously there was little she could do or say, now. The witch had forced her to write out the truth, the thing she had done previously, so long ago—the dreadful baby, undoubtedly long dead . . . How could it have been important? And yet, the beating in her womb had ceased, once the document, signed with Hetsa's illiterate wiggle, had been carried off for the Consort's attention.

Crow Claw sat watching her then, in the spent glare of the lamps. Old mischief-maker, old horror. It was her fault.

The following noon, waking from a dazed drugged sleep, Hetsa had learned other more vital things had occurred. Her petty crime was flung to second place.

"Madam," said Hetsa now, in a breathless, crumbling voice, "our loss of the King—is terrible for everyone, and for all the lands. But for you—your anguish—my most humble condolences—"

"You are very tender, Daystar, to remember me, in your own misfortune."

Hetsa shuddered. She broke out, "Oh, madam—I—was so young—I was frightened and foolish and wrongly advised. I thought only of the King's honor—a deformed child—I—I—"

"You should then, as now," said Udrombis, "have consulted with me." She folded her white hands one over another. The gesture was implacable, like her smooth face. She had few lines. They said she was massaged daily—not for vanity, but to be worthy of her office. Even now, she would need to be worthy. No longer a King's consort, even so, she remained a King's mother.

As they talked together—if so you could call it—Glardor would be riding from his estates. The funeral of Akreon could not take place until the heir arrived.

Hetsa thought, oddly, in the depths of her unease, of Akreon's firm, fierce, summer body, embalmed now, packed with spices, stiff and *dead*.

The Sun declines, said the verse, *Kings go down also to their rest*.

He had foreseen it, had he not, standing on the terrace in the sun-fall, two suns descending together, the god, and the god-King, as one.

Did Udrombis mind it? Her keen eyes were dry. And yet, the black irises seemed veiled a little. She would continue with her duties, of which Hetsa's sin was one. But within her heart, who could know?

Hetsa hated Udrombis in that instant. Hated her, priggish, stupid, dangerous, tyranical bitch.

"I can't say to you, Hetsa," said Queen Udrombis slowly, measuring out her doleful words, "that your act can be overlooked." Hetsa gave a shrill cry. Udrombis ignored it. "You must come with me into the next room. There the priests have prepared the altar before Ia, who as you will know is our judge in Akhemony. In deference to you, I've added an icon of the Ipyran deity."

Hetsa, insensible apparently to this kindness, got up, threw herself on her knees—Mokpor again?—and wailed. "Oh, madam—madam—don't—"

Udrombis, too, rose up.

When she did this, she seemed to tower four miles over Hetsa on the floor.

The Great Queen's mourning robes were of the palest grey, shot almost invisibly with silver. Her hair had been covered with a grey, soft gauze held by a circlet of milky amber. Her feet were bare.

"You must come with me now and confess to your indiscretion aloud, at the altar. There together we shall seek to secure for you a cleansed soul."

"Madam—don't—don't—"

Udrombis said flatly, "What is it?"

"I don't want to die!"

Udrombis sighed. "You needn't fear death, Hetsa. Don't be afraid. But I insist upon this."

Hetsa floundered to her feet. She wrung her hands and tried to kiss the fingers of the Queen. Udrombis removed her person, slightly, and left Hetsa flailing at the air.

"Thank you—thank you—"

Beyond the curtain, in the tiled room where, on a side table of inlaid ivory, ivory figures stood against figures of bloody cinnabar, in some deserted game, the proposed altar had been set up behind a screen.

Here, at the Queen's instigation, before the statue of Ia, a creature with the head of a man and the body of a bird, perhaps an owl, Hetsa flooded forth her deeds.

When everything had been said, Udrombis, a priestess too by right of her station, cast down the costly incense for the god. And some even for the small Ipyran god, who was only a bird. The vapors lifted.

"It's done. You are free of it."

"Oh, madam."

Hetsa did not think to ask Udrombis if the deformed baby had lived. Of course, it had not. Probably pious Udrombis, so sharp for the honor of the King's house, was glad enough that it had died in the sanctum of Thon.

Udrombis then, with her own hand, an ultimate mark of notice that Hetsa did not miss, poured out for Hetsa a goblet of wine. Hetsa was happy to receive it, her mouth had been so parched. She reasoned that the Queen must wish some service from her, and to this end had terrified her, and let her go. Hetsa was somewhat concerned as to what Udrombis would demand. But anything was better than dying, at twenty-two years of age, in this apartment.

When the cup, of fine greenish glass, dropped on the tiles and smashed, Udrombis, having engineered the omen, was still not indifferent to it.

She had not wanted, anyway, to retain the cup through which she had, swiftly and painlessly, poisoned the Daystar Hetsa. And in something of the same vein, she had dispatched Hetsa herself. Udrombis took no interest in causing hurt or horror for their own sake. She desired all souls forgiven, to have their chance in death. But like any good wife, any good widow, now, she kept the floors of her husband's house swept clean.

6

My father Akreon, the Great Sun of All the Lands, was found in his bed one hour after sunrise.

He lay on his back, most of his body under the furs and silken sheet. His face was serene and slightly smiling. Both his arms had been raised high, the big hands spread open, as if to welcome the Sun that was climbing up the window, at the couch's foot.

At first, his body-slave thought him alive. Then in terror learned that, though he held out his arms, they were hard as iron. As was indeed the whole of his frame, even his toes. Even his phallus, which was erect.

He was also lushly tanned. A day's hunting in the spring forest could not have given him such luster. He was the shade of an athlete who has raced under the hottest summer sun.

The awe which accrued to this particular death was not, then, amazing.

Akreon's father, my grandfather, King Okos, had died at the age of ninety, frail, and olive-colored as a cricket.

I came back to Oceaxis as the heir did, my half brother Glardor, who was almost thirty years my senior. He came with pomp, in some style. I, on the front of the soldier's horse, my beautiful bronzen soldier that I loved, and whose name I have forgotten, as I forget little else—I wonder why that is? Is it I was not yet used to names? Or perhaps love itself, the purest love of childhood, has smoothed that name from the tablet, to keep for him his privacy.

Udrombis, a clever woman, had not wanted me much to be seen, until she had got a look at me herself. She did not know what she would find. Typically, in the way of her justice, I, being royal, must live. But I might be all Hetsa had thought me. I might not be much use.

I entered the palace again by night, and perhaps I had been drugged just a touch.

Huge ceilings float over me, and the torches swim and flash. Horses' hooves echo along my brain. Then, a soft bed, the first soft bed I have ever known, and this, like sleep itself, enfolds me, and I sink down, to fly among the eagles in heaven.

A massive storm raged over Akhemony. The sky was black and the clouds curdled with lightning. The water of the inland sea was churning, serpent green. Hailstones, that some claimed burned, fell in the streets of Oceaxis.

I myself have read the records and histories, which showed that, with every Kingly death, such extremities of weather displayed themselves.

At the death of an earlier Sun King, a solar eclipse occurred, bringing such fear that many killed themselves on the spot. But that had been long ago.

In any case, before noon the wind dropped. The almost tideless sea, and every fire in Oceaxis, stood still, and was flattened, as if by great invisible hands.

The Sun Temple had been laid, stones brought, they said, by eagles, on a natural height above the town. Pines and cedars clothed the hill, the sacred trees of the Sun god's shade. And near the hill's head, the oak trees, and red marroi, from whose bark was distilled the occult drink of priestly visions. All these had bent and rushed to the wind, and now were stones. It was dark as twilight, or so I recall, as we climbed the hill, in hundreds, everyone on foot. Everyone, of course, save I.

The temple was built upon three terraces. It was white, but the columns painted ochre, rose, scarlet, and gilded with burnished bronze and hammered gold. The roof lifted too, into a column, a white chimney flecked, as it seemed, with specks of diamond and emerald, blinking eyes of green and silver fire. This chimney was itself the height of a tall tree.

No one had said anything to me. No one had prepared me. I had been got up, washed, and given—to me amazing—food. They had dressed me plainly. Now a muscular slave carried me in his arms. He did not like me. I was used to that. But at his side walked such a pretty, pretty woman. She entranced me. Her curling black hair, with glints in it; her earrings. She, too, wore the plainest weave, and I could tell she was angry, or unnerved. She disliked me also. I did not know yet, properly, her name was Ermias, and we were all in disguise. Udrombis had decreed I had some rights, covertly, to behold my father's funeral.

First the drums began to rumble. They were the lesser drums of the temple, but matching themselves to that other eternal Heart Drum which I, in my lifetime, have heard broken not once but thrice.

Above our immediate crowd, the merchants and traders, the minor officials, and captains' wives with their servants, up there, the highest persons. And in their ranks, unlike our own, the strictest segregation. To one side were the courtiers, the lords, and to the other, the noble women of the King's court.

But one's eye went higher yet. To the upper terrace. Oh yes, surely they too must be gods.

Grey and brown were the colors of mourning in our lands. Yet, aloft, such browns, such greys, fawnskin, lion-pelt, the most dappled silks, the pearls of the deepest rivers.

The princes stood to the male side, the right, near where the fire-basket blazed up on its stand against the thick sky, top bowed and spread like the very shape of the cedars.

Foremost were the sons of Udrombis. Her youngest, Amdysos, golden, handsome, eleven years old, clad in a grey that was white. And his elder brother, Pherox, a youth named for the metal of swords, and who had a silver tooth, his black hair like the lion's mane. And, before them, the oldest son, the heir, the King, Glardor the rising Sun.

No one would know now, gazing up to him, that he had been, even one moment, unready.

He was so like the King, the King who had died. He had got, from nature, the tan the King uncannily had had, the kiss of the god. For Glardor was a man for hunting too, and for husbandry in open fields. Around his brow ran the band of lead that betokened his loss. His garments were of sober grey, with one stripe of bullion the width of an arm.

Behind these three sons of the Consort, ranged the other sons, the men and boys got on Daystar queens. All were comely, all seemed honed by the promise of perfection. The fruit of the princesses of north and west, of east and south, the province-kingdoms of the Sun. But near Amdysos, stood his friend, the son of Stabia, who was friend to the Queen.

For nine, this boy was very tall, very beautiful. They said he had a chariot already, nor quite a toy one, and he and Amdysos raced in miniature the sacred Race of the Sun that was held at Airis in the summer, by grown men, for the amusement of the gods. But they invented its obstacles, since no man who had faced them must reveal them.

On the other side, farthest from the fire, were the royal women. The dead King's queens, seventeen in number, and their daughters—countless, these—drooping in their dove and rain shades. But there, the last and youngest queen, sheltered at the side of the Consort, the little girl from Oceaxis, weeping openly in her veil. Her sons were babies. They had been left behind.

The harps were conjuring the musics of lament. A boy priest raised his arms, almost in an imitation of the gesture of the corpse, whose arms, for dignity, had been broken to fit the bier.

How are we to live?
There is no sorrow unknown to men.
Birth sends us to a house of shadows,
And at the end, to Night.

They were bearing forward the body of the King.

The chariot approaches, a chariot of steel, painted with closed eyes, drawn by white geldings—Death does not procreate. Drapes like cobwebs trail the road.

Out comes the bier, open. Only Akreon has been gloriously dressed for this day. He wears crimson and gold. From his cadaver waft the sweetest, most appetizing odors. He smells like confectionery from a kitchen I have never yet known. And the bath of a rapturous and celebrated courtesan.

I saw him ascend the stair. Up the terraces, borne high. I think I glimpsed his face, but it was painted, and flowers had been put into his hair, a wreath of white narcissus, the best the spring could give, since the green blossoms at the Heart must not be plucked.

In the hall of the temple was enormous space. The roof, about the tapering O of the chimney, had stars set into a ceiling stained violet like the sky. Phaidix kept her altar on the female side, but the watch flame was out. The giant altar of the Sun lay under the chimney, empty but for its two fires.

The chanting was now like the sound of bees in a cavern, or the noise one hears in the head when one is sick. How do I know? I was a child in the crowd below the terraces, yet, I have seen it, the going up of my father.

Four of his soldiers lifted Akreon to the altar, where he stretched, magnificent, between the two dishes of fire, an offering to the god.

Udrombis, the Consort, stepped forward. She tore her garment, a religious gesture, its passion foreign to her, yet executed with such control, such forethought, it had great power. Beneath the robe of sand and silver, another of white and silver. With her right hand she scattered upon her lord the funeral wine meant to represent her heart's blood, as—outward show apart—perhaps it did.

At this moment, the sky above the temple portentously cleared.

A rift appeared in the cloud, and the Sun, at its apex, seared through the aperture of the chimney. To those within, the intimates of the dead, his children and women, the wonder was vouchsafed.

A shaft, burning like molten gold, split suddenly down through the funnel of the chimney, where every facet of a gem scorched out in reply.

The Queen stepped back.

Directly upon the breast of the King, the shaft was fired, striking the jewels of his collar, so that a splash of fire shot back into the air. For some moments, he lay suspended, seeming to levitate in a blaze of light, and then, unconscionable, undeniable, the thin smokes began to issue from his body.

Those in the temple held their breath, perhaps. Or waited, with instructed silence, still, like the trees, as stones.

The smoke unfurled, massing, permeating the temple with the scent of rare spices and perfumes.

As the King's body erupted into brilliant flame, the priests' voices, the boys' clear altos and the sonorous bass, sprang like the fire to uprushing life.

Akreon's body was burning, there on the altar of the god. For the god had sent his fire to bring this chosen son into the upper air. The god received Akreon, and the priests sang loudly, as if in joy, and triumph.

From the terraces below, the smoke was visible now, pouring up towards the golden wheel of Sun, and breaking sky. The air was heavy with a delicious and cloying odor.

The slave who held the child murmured very low, "He is going up. My eyes witness the ascension of Akreon, the Great Sun." All the crowd was murmuring this.

The child stared in vain, striving to see the body of the King, sailing to heaven in the grip of an eagle, but seeing only . . . smoke.

Is it possible I wondered even then, on the nature of what God might be?

I cannot say that I did, for I had understood nothing of the ritual of a King's cremation in Akhemony, and no one had explained—the demonstration, its reality. Who indeed, of those who knew, would tell a child, a crippled girl child at that, the substance of the miracle of the sunfire?

That, in the innermost circle of the temple roof, the chimney, were concealed various craftily angled mirrors of burnished pherom and silver. That these, put ready to receive it, would focus down the light of the noonday Sun, on to the altar below. At this spot, normally, a vessel of syrup or wine was left standing for the god. But at the time of a King's obsequies, it was a King who lay there. And it was the jewelry on his breast which took the shaft of the Sun.

Soldiers on campaign know well enough this trick. The focusing of the Sun off a shield or blade, to start a cook-fire.

And that—was all it was. The ray of heaven, the fire from the god. Science, applied.

And yet, evidently, there had been a miracle. I learned in my later years how, if the sky were overcast, a concealed panel might be opened in the chimney side, that gave down on the inner room of the fane. Light could then be shone upward another way to the mirrors, and so in turn the ray would leap out and, if more reluctantly, the pyre be started, apparently still through supernatural means.

But, it had not been needed, this final ploy of the priests. The clouds had cleared for Akreon. The Sun had come to claim him after all.

Ermias oversaw the child's bath. A slave washed the little girl carefully, without undue roughness or sensitivity. She even sponged, rinsed, and dried the stumps of the white ankles. They were like marble, delicately veined with the shadows of bones ending within. The skin was scarcely thickened there, but neither very feeling.

After the bath, another slave brought a supper, some milk and bread and candies.

The child was carried to and put into her small bed, that had such astonishing softness. She had been rather worried that she was not allowed her canes at all.

She lay awake, now the door was closed and all the servants had gone, listening to the noises in the outer room.

It was growing dark.

Before a small altar, that had a statue of cheerful Gemli, as the child would discover, burned a low, reddish lamp. It cast one rose upon the ceiling. All else turned impenetrable.

But outside, Ermias had received the merchant Mokpor. They were drinking, and eating savouries together.

Ermias had been annoyed. She had vented none of that on the child, but then, she did not like the child, was somewhat repulsed by the child, so had no favors to take away.

The disguise of a wife of Oceaxis had irritated Ermias, who was wellborn; how else had she been the Maiden of a Daystar queen. Now, Ermias was also promoted. Dressed again in silk, she had upon her hand the gold ring set with a yellowish fragment, that denoted her the guardian of a royal infant. She had been right to draw an omen from the talk of teeth. This in the ring was a sliver of tooth from a stallion of the Sun god.

The child could not sleep.

She heard Ermias laughing, and the laugh was husky, sexual, and low. It sounded to her like the laugh of a witch, for in the dormitory of Thon's House, sometimes awful old tales of the backlands had been rehearsed.

Afraid in the dark, only the small charm of the bed, the red rose of the lamp to comfort her, uncomforted now, the child began to cry. But stifling her tears, naturally, as she had learned to do.

Something came gliding up out of nothingness.

Dark on darkness, blotting out the rose, it leaned towards her. It smelled of herbs, of frosty spring night, of mothy, musty dryness.

The child caught her breath.

"What is it now? Are you frightened, little girl?" The voice was ancient as a shard, but very gentle. A hand, moistureless as an antique parchment, settled on the child's forehead. It reminded her of the priestess that she had already, callous with innocence, abandoned.

Outside, again, sluggish, bubbling, Ermias laughed.

"Is she a witch?" whispered the child.

The crone laughed now. Old woman's laugh, past such deceits, cindery and warm.

"She? Ah, no. What you hear is what a woman does with a man when she likes him. She may make another noise soon. You may think he's hurt her. Don't trouble. It means that she is happy."

Soothed by voice and hand, the child accepted these words, uncomprehendingly. The real witch was at her side, but she did not know it. In the dark, the black eyes of Crow Claw were luminous and profound as those of some animal of night.

"What's your name?" said the witch.

The child said, solemn, "Cemira."

"Yes, I thought it was. But now you have another name."

"She told me," said the child, guilty and uneasy, "but—I forget." Not yet was she accustomed to names.

"Shall *I* tell?" The child waited. "Yes, I will. They call you here *Calistra*." The witch took her hand from the child's flesh and used it instead to tuck in the covers. The priestess had once or twice done this very thing, in the child's babyhood. Now it seemed right, a fundamental. "But there's the other name."

"She said—*it was a monster*."

"She in the other room? That one?" As if in answer, Ermias gave a loud groan. "Hark at her," said Crow Claw. "Do you think she knows anything, except how to make noises?"

"Cemira," said the child, almost boldly.

"Cemira. It is a monster, in its way. One of the Secret Beasts of the moon goddess. It walks on its hands and has a silvery tail. Sometimes it asks questions, and if it can't be answered, it *laughs*. Not the way *that* one does, out there with her man. It is a beast of Phaidix's, a beast of fire that's white. Which name do you want?"

"Both!" said the child. She was greedy for names at last.

"That's good. Then you have two. It's agreed. But the other name is the name of a King's daughter, and you must use it."

"Ca—listra."

"Calistra."

Ermias gave a squeal, like a hare in a trap.

Had I been still alone, I would have been petrified. I had only heard such sounds given off in pain. But I knew now. This was some silly thing she did. Ermias was silly, even if she had power over me. There was yet the Great Queen, however, whom I must meet in forty days, when the time of the first of the Four Stages of Mourning was over.

But if I had meant to speak of this to my new friend in the darkness, she silenced me. "Sleep now," she said.

And she began to sing to me, in her eldritch, cracked, and cindery voice. At once I seemed on a river, floating to a sea. All fear, even the awakened buds of hope, if such I had in me, left me. I was at peace. I was no one, but part of all things, which therefore were not my enemies. On her raft of song I flowed into the ocean of sleep, and as sleepers and the dying do, left the world behind.

2ND STROIA

THE SNAKE, THE EAGLE

I

FROM THE LOWER SLOPES of Mt. Airis, you could see over into Ipyra.

Steep gorges dropped to green forest, a green river sparkled, white with rapids. Beyond were cliffs and ravines, and in the midst, mountains which sometimes cracked and burst out with fire. In caves of sulfur, ancient women dreamed and sent strange messages to the world. Somewhere in the maze of the crags was said to be an entry to Thon's kingdom underground, where Tithaxeli, the River of Death, inexorably moved, without seeming motion, towards the land of death.

Another way, one could look south and east towards the Lakesea. It was like a piece of sky that had fallen out of place.

"No chance of it, then."

"Well, they said she was foraging towards Ipyra and might go over. We did our best."

Amdysos, fourteen years of age, a Sun Prince, son of a dead Sun, was philosophical enough. One must do one's utmost, try everything. That seen to, it was with the gods. He said so, quietly.

"The gods could have given her to us," said Klyton. At twelve, he was more impatient, or perhaps it had nothing to do with his years. "I offered to the Sun. And to Phaidix, too, because the pig's her animal sometimes, isn't it?"

"I think so. Well. Well, maybe she's in their protection."

"A pig."

"Perhaps she's in farrow, Klyton. We may have to wait until all that's done with."

"What, and let her spawn ten or so monstrosities just like herself, to rampage over the farms and villages?"

The she-pig they spoke of was said to be of unusual size, twice or three times that of a normal animal. Now and then, it had happened, beasts that were too large, or even too small, appeared, especially in Akhemony and Ipyra. Klyton and Amdysos had seen, throughout their lives, the trophies on various walls, and at the rustic palace under Airis, for example, the skin of a boar that had been the height of a horse, and the deer skull, miniature as that of a rabbit, with perfect jutting horns.

They had wanted this pig, and gone out to get her, telling no one the plan. The farms round about had a name for her: Thon's Daughter. It was that bad. She had killed seven times, the last a girl on the day after her wedding. Hearing of the family's grief, Klyton's eyes, which were the color of the distant green river, had filled with raging tears. However, it was never wise, however irritated one was, to be sharp with the gods.

"Of course, the people may have exaggerated," said Amdysos now.

"Don't you believe the stories?"

"Do you?"

Klyton considered. He said, "The lion skull at Oceaxis, in the Great Hall. That's real, isn't it?"

"I always thought so. But—it could be a clever artifact. King Okos took the lion when he was fifteen. He speared it and cut the neck vein. But it's enormous. Could he have?"

"Perhaps he had some help."

"Oh, yes, there's always that. And the spear could have been tinctured with a drug. Even so."

"My mother," said Klyton, "told me once she had a pet deer as a girl, that was only knee-high. It never grew."

"That's a small animal though. Giant size is another matter."

They sat, looking down at Ipyra. The country had been quiet for some eight years. In the last argument with Akhemony, a rebellious force had ridden as far as the river below, painted and tattooed tribesmen, feral as wolves, and the conniving chiefs who owed the Great Sun fealty and wanted to forget. But Akreon had squashed the uprising with his sword, his army beating the rebels back, filling the water with corpses, passing on up into the crags. He had brought two wives back from that campaign in Ipyra, one of whom had now been, like Akreon, three years dead.

There were always some conflicts. Kings might even encourage them, you sometimes suspected, to keep the army trim. The talk was of trouble brewing southwards now, with Sirma. If so, it would be their first chance, the Sun Princes seated on Mt. Airis, to distinguish themselves in battle, since they were thought too young before.

The dogs were running about the forested upper slope, playing and barking, with no need to hold silent, their long hair streaming against summer green. Above, Airis had touched the sky and formed one solitary, foamy cloud.

Below through the trees, Klyton could make out the Akhemonian side curving through stages of fields and vineyards to the little town, with the summer palace perched on its rock. It had been a fortress once, until replaced by the Sword House, two miles along the mountain road. Udrombis brought her own court here in the hottest months, which meant Stabia had also come. Young men did not mind it. It meant less schooling, and this was wonderful hunting country. Soon, too, there would be the Sun Race. You could not quite see the stadium this far over.

Only the elusive quality of the demon pig had spoilt the day.

Klyton polished his knife carefully, though it had done nothing. This was a pherom blade, and had a pommel of deep red stone, incised with an eagle, his chosen blazon. Good weapons and gear should always be treated with respect. At twelve, he too was well-made, well-cared for, his skin like fine bronze overlaid with pure gold. He was long in the leg, his shoulders already wide for his age; he had clever musician's hands, properly calloused. His profile could have come from one of the archaic coins—his looks went back some way. Plaited for safety, hair more gold than all the rest, hung to his waist.

Dark-eyed Amdysos, only a little less beautiful, stared down into Ipyra, but he was dreaming of valor and old wars. It was Klyton who was thinking.

The Heartbeat came faint but steady on this air as the drone of the bees, in the clover fields below. At Airis it was, of course, not so loud as in Oceaxis. They said, going away to a war, leaving the land behind, the *sound* behind, you heard noises in the head, and the stars turned over all night in your dreams. Leaving it gradually, on march, there was a sense of loss. Returning, in victory, it was worth any trial, better than the homecoming to family, wife or lover, to hear the sound again, beating, beating for ever.

Klyton was not thinking of the Heart. He smiled.

He said, "Did you see the girl in the temple, Amdysos? I mean the little one."

"Which? Who?"

"The baby. She had topaz hair down to her lap. She outshone all the queens—not Udrombis, the rest. She'll be something by the time she's ready."

Amdysos glanced at him, curious. He had already started with girls, and had been at pains to make little of it, in case Klyton should feel left behind. Klyton was only twelve, though one tended to forget. What was this, now?

"A child? Do you mean marriageable, or what?"

"Sun's Light, no. Only a brat. Our half sister presumably, anyway. But pretty as pain."

Amdysos offhandedly made the circle. This expression, meant to placate skittish gods of toothache and minor injury, had never appealed to him.

"Whose was she?"

"How do I know? Do you think I pounded about asking? I just noticed her. She was worth a glance. Of course, sometimes when they have it so young, they lose their looks at ten."

"Oh. Indeed."

"But it was odd. In the responses, she didn't get up. They had to lift her by her elbows. And put her back. She was carried in a chair."

"She's crippled then," said Amdysos. He scowled. "Such children used to be given to Thon."

"That's the old ways. What they do in the back hills. That's if they don't just leave them on the ground for lynxes and wolves."

"It might be better. Would you want to live disadvantaged like that? It would be like going to battle with your hands tied together."

Klyton said, slowly, "I'd rather have the chance at life."

The dogs barked madly, and fell dumb.

Both boys looked up, and in their turn, changed to granite.

Up on the slope, a huge whitish shape had come out of the trees.

Through the year after Akreon's death, there had been many portents. The moon was seen to be red, or steel. Stars rained into the Lakesea. And a spotless scarlet bull was born in the pens at Artepta, with a white sun-flash on its brow, a tuft from whose tail was sent to Akhemony, to gift the new King.

Maybe the pig was a remnant of these things.

She was not as mighty as they had said, but still, she was extraordinarily big, and though clearly female, her tusks extended the length of a man's forearm.

She swung her head, looking at the two dogs, which had flattened themselves down now as though in homage. She did not seem angry.

Klyton's hand twitched over the boar spears. His eyes glowed at her. If she was not enraged, he was. Half the day searching, and now this.

"No—wait—" Amdysos caught his wrist. "*Look*."

Behind the pig trotted two little ones, the shade of pinkish amber, young as a morning, scarcely on their feet.

"She is a murderess," said Klyton, very low.

"And a mother. She's not going to run at us. The gods would curse us if we took her unprovoked, seeing the litter."

"She's sloughed out of season," said Klyton.

"Yes, but she's not a normal pig."

The creature bent her head, snuffing at something. The leveling sun picked out in gold the lethal dainty bristles of her snout. Her tusks were white as snow, as if she had never done more with them than gore a tree.

She looked peaceful, grazing like a ewe.

Klyton rose, and rising, raised the spear. The action was fluid. A streak like one of the meteors tore down his arm, the spear stem—and then Amdysos shouted out.

The pig started. She jerked aside, as the spear, its cast interrupted, dropped well short. Rather than brace herself for a charge now, she shook herself, and swinging abruptly around, nudged the little pink pig-children away, over the rocks, and back into the green shadows of the wood. She might only have found the bare mountain too warm.

"By the *Knife*! *Why* did you—"

"I'd said. A mother."

"Damn it, Amdysos. You'd give a cripple child to Thon. What does a bloody pig matter?"

"I'm sorry. It wasn't right."

Klyton flamed. In his fury he might himself have fallen straight from heaven. Amdysos, who was fearless in everything, turned his head, as if from a blow.

A wind rustled down the glades with the sound of sly laughter.

I had seen him too, my half brother, Klyton. I had seen them all, as I always did, those beautiful metallic princes, the Suns who were the inheritors of the Great Sun.

Taken out as I was, only for important events or festivals, this visual treat had assumed enchanted proportions. I craved it. I longed to gaze on them, the male gods I had been assured were my kindred. I saw few other than royal men there. Seldom men of any sort, anywhere.

The Demayia, the first celebration of summer, was marked by the carriage of the summer goddess, from her little house on the shore, to the Temple of the Sun.

I also had been ported to the temple, in my chair with golden clasps. I was dressed in saffron, for the goddess.

Truthfully, I do remember—oh, far more clearly than yesterday—that I looked across the vast space of the temple, into which, on these occasions, now clad as a princess, I might go. Through the curtains of incense and the rain of flowers falling from the solar chimney to the altar, I saw one of the Suns, golden, with eyes like dark emerald, and these fixed on me. I was seared to my bones, and looked at once away.

Never before had any of them, these lions, met my eyes. But I had not forgotten my first man, my glorious soldier, who had seemed despite everything I was told, to have rescued me of his own volition, from Death. He, it was a fact, had looked deep into my eyes on the road home, wrapping me in a fur against the coolness of spring, telling me I was pretty, and I would have liked his daughter. I had wanted to be his daughter. I had wanted to be his wife.

But Klyton—to my seven-year–old eyes, he at twelve years—was also a man. A hero, a deity, stepped from the paintings on the walls of the palace. And beside, him, my long-ago rescuer was only a flame to the Sun.

When Klyton looked, had he seen *me*?

I wanted so much to dream of him, but all I had that night were my waking dreams. Imagining I should meet him—but where, and

how? Would he mind, that I could not walk? She had said, the
they might not mind, if everything else were beyond reproach.

Fortunately, I had the sense to say nothing to my gu
Ermias was fretful and snappish all that day. Mokpor was long g
then, and her current lover had not appeared. She had gaine
weight, which she did not like. She would even shout at her
though it were some malign spirit which had attached itself to he
out her consent or knowledge.

She blamed me. *I* had restricted her. She must always st
me, was not free to roam, to dance with the other women, had 1
to pleasure her but sweets. I had ruined her life.

Curled in my bed, the luxury of which I now expected as
thing, I visualized meeting Klyton on a long stair. He paused ai
"Are you the one they call Calistra?"

The inchoate sexual excitement that comes before ui
physical impetus is strictly possible, flooded my body. For in m
my inner eye, he stood as real as in the flesh, his hair like
sunlight, and his body hard, spear straight, and utterly alien; a
a second race.

So he stands still, my brother. In my inner eye. He wil
change for me. Not a boy now, but a man. Thereafter ageless.
long as I shall live.

Annotation by the Hand of Dobzah

My mistress took up just now, her Muhzum. It is of hyac
enamel, bound with silver. She opened it, and regarded fo
minutes the contents.

She does not often do this now.

When she was younger, in her seventies and eighties, she
do it even once every day, usually at twilight. And then the colo
keepsake blended with the color of the sky, and so she seemed
the very sky in her hands.

Of course, the Muhzum contains all that is left of her b
Klyton. The first Battle-Prince Shajhima gave it to her, but she
yet told me when. It will be in the narrative, I expect.

The relic used to make her sad and then contemplative
she held it like a new and unknown object. I asked if I could br

anything. She said she would have the juice of a pomegranate. When I returned, the Muhzum had been put away.

2

A month and some days after I had first gone back to the palace at Oceaxis, I was carried into the presence of the Widow-Consort, Udrombis. I went in the arms of the same slave who took me about at the funeral. Even so, it drew some atteption; Ermias, walking by us, parried interrogation from those who approached. "I can't say. You must *wait* and find out." Doubtless that increased any speculation. I was only four, and felt bewildered, embarrassed even.

Of the Great Queen, I was frightened. Ermias had said Udrombis would have me hurt if she did not like me, which was very foolish of Ermias. If I had thought to blurt this out, she would have lost her guardianship, then prized, and maybe worse. Any way, she was left outside at an inner door.

Behind Udrombis's apartments was a terrace. It looked down on the gardens and so to the inner sea. The day was rather warm, the almost tideless waters silky. In the gardens I could see a statue of a boy carrying an urn, from which burst a bush of yellow flowers.

The Queen sat in one of her cedar chairs. She still wore mourning, as she was in fact to wear it all her life. But she had put on golden sandals, and fabulous glittering jewels. It interests me now, to consider that she must have meant me to be impressed, had known I would be—I, who was then four, and might mean nothing at all. Again, surely, not vainglory. My awe was thought to have use.

The man set me on a stool, and left.

There was no one else.

She looked at me a long while, and when I lowered my eyes in fear, she said, "No, child. Look up."

She wanted to see. And presently she got up and came over. As they do in the better slave-markets, she felt my hair, my skin, smelled my breath, examined, gently but inexorably, teeth and eyes. Last of all she lifted the skirt away, and explored with her eyes and fingers, the stumps which ended my legs.

Then she straightened. She clapped her hands, and a slave girl came out, graceful as a swan, which, then, I had never seen, and put a

dish of little cakes by me, and a cup of the honeyed juice I preferred to milk.

I had pleased Udrombis. And she had shown me, without a word.

Being too scared still to try the cakes, which looked very appetizing, I slaked my nervous desert of a throat with juice.

She watched this too.

"You have learned some manners. Is that Ermias?"

"Yes, madam." Ermias had instructed me how to address the Queen. Only on state occasions did all her alarming and child-unrememberable titles have to be employed.

"I must tell you, Calistra, the gods were unkind to you, but also generous."

I sat, speechless, confused. What had the gods to do with me? I was nothing.

Udrombis rested her head on her hand, bending her eyes on me. They were black as night. And I must not look away. I trembled. Then she desisted. She looked instead out towards the boy with the flowers. This was her courtesy, her tact, and to a child of four.

"You have been deprived of feet, Calistra. But you have great beauty. You're sweet and wholesome. There is only this one flaw. Understand now and for all time, you are a princess. Your mother was a Daystar queen, and your father the greatest man in the world, the Great Sun, Akreon. Though he is dead, he will live for ever in memory, and, my child, through you, as through all his children."

Somewhere near, a bird began to sing in the garden.

Udrombis smiled. She said, "Do you hear the kitri? You shall be taught to sing as prettily. You shall have every skill a princess should have." She turned one quick yet lingering look on me. It was meant to impress me, and it did. Her eyes were like black rays of light. "Your father has descended to the lower world. His immortality in this one must depend on us. You were sent away through an error. Your mother was foolish, but she's gone. I stand in place now of this woman. I tell you, Calistra, that you are, despite your deformity, a fitting daughter of the Sun House. But you must strive. Since in one area you're less than others, you must elsewhere excel them."

I sat. I looked into myself. I was nothing. What could I do? All my delicious month here, in this place of wonders, after Thon's hell, had been fraught with trepidation. An old woman, a phantom, had comforted me once, in a dream. Other than that, I had no reference.

I listened with my infant's ears to Udrombis, from whom a power flowed like the magnetism of amber.

"You will be our treasure, Calistra. Because you can make, once you are grown, through your beauty, a marriage to serve this house. And, by that marriage, you will bring your father to life once more, in your sons. Do you understand?"

I faltered something. She *knew* I could not understand. She knew I would never forget her words. Nor have I forgotten them.

One might say that my life began after this, and that Udrombis, Sun-Consort, Great Queen, the Mirror of the Sun, King's Mother, now a widow, gave it me. Hetsa had had no rights to dispose of me. But if Udrombis had not liked me, if I had been plain, if even, maybe, my fright had made too acid my breath, she could have had me killed, mercifully and painlessly, as she had killed my stupid, wicked, sad mother.

But I was a utility. The gods had robbed me and gifted me. I had use as a token of union and treaty, for the province-countries of the Sun Lands must always be secured. And beside, there were thought to be other lands, beyond the Endless Sea, which had—it seems—some end. One day, not Glardor, but one of the other Sun Princes sprung from Akreon's loins, might foray there, and bring home another world to add to our own.

More even than that I, being attractive, when grown, could entice from men their seed. I could make new men. I could restore Akreon to the earth in form at least.

I had been given the apartments of my dead mother. Perhaps obviously, I thought Ermias owned the large rooms with their painted walls and crimson pillars topped by snakes, and in the outer room, the little pool, where the turtle played. I thought Ermias owned the turtle too, and so never even asked to feed it. This was my first request, two days after my interview. Udrombis had somehow made me know, with everything else, that Ermias did not have all the power there, that was—*I*.

"She'll peck you. You may think she can't bite, not having teeth. But watch out."

However, the turtle was docile, and when I stroked her shell, that had on it a sort of shadow-map of some invented land, Ermias made a hissing noise, and went away.

Now to the rooms came new people, all women, but for one old man. He it seems had been a famous athlete once, at various sacred games. He instigated for me, through certain trained women servants, the exercise program that was to save my body from an utter distortion.

No more must I use canes, which might throw my spine awry. Now I must be lifted, and elsewhere learn to lift myself, and swing by a hanging bar, and, lying on the floor, curl and roll and twist, and, lying in the pool, juggle balls with the knees and calves of my legs. This at first amused me. Then I hated it and sobbed. The servants, thickset women who acted sometimes as assistants in the practice courts of the stadium at Airis, were patient with me. In their everyday role they were nothing, and might not touch, except in dire extremity, the body of a man. Having learnt the art of things from male tutors, however, they were in demand for work upon high-class women who had suffered any injury, or who had been harmed in childbirth. For this they were well recompensed.

They seemed not to dislike a child. They lured me with sports and confectionery to my work, and when I had mastered everything, to greater performance and better tricks, with promises of stories, and sometimes demonstrations of the most amazing contortionist abilities, which they had gained years before and never lost.

In two years, I would be nearly limber as a fish. Though I could not walk, I could twist and turn upon my bar like a snake off a column, and had all the agility of an accomplished child dancer—I, who could not put one foot upon the ground.

They were very careful nevertheless, that my muscles should not bulge or be overly stretched. Tasks done, they massaged me lightly by the pool, where I would lie, dreaming upon the image of the green turtle, who in turn gazed back at me with eyes knowing all things, or nothing.

Ermias was jealous. This must be true. Once she took to mimicking my antics, the fluid bends and turns of my arms and torso, screwing up her face as she did it. The older servant woman was there, the one with the scar along her cheek where once a charioteer had caught her, not meaning to, with his whip. She looked sidelong at Ermias and said, loudly, "Once there was a firefly saw a star. I can do that, said the firefly. But when the fly had done her very best, her fire went out. The star burns yet."

"You insolent sow," shouted Ermias. "I'll have you flogged."

"Been flogged," said the woman. Unlike a princess, they had had no qualms at building up her frame as large as a strong man's. "But I'd only take it now from the Sun Queen. Shall I go tell her you want that? Or will *you* try for me?"

Ermias grew red as a lamp. She went away, again.

The woman, whose name was Kelbalba, swung me round in a somersault from her big safe hands, catching my legs before any feet were needed.

"Scum rises to the top of the jar," she said.

Then she told me a story in her rough voice, about the Daystar, and how she was the sister of the Sun, and loved him so much she would never leave him, although she always walked an hour behind him through the sky, to console men at his going down. The Daystar was not worshipped, she said, accept among the peasants. And yet, how lovely was her light, in the last of the evening.

My education was taken in hand.

The rudiments of reading, writing and simple numbers, which had been thrust at me in the House of Thon, were now expanded into long tutorials, which sometimes fascinated and sometimes irked me.

Religion, too, was taught to me. I learned that the Sun had no other name and was only one. I was lessoned in the proper observances and prayers, and on how to conduct myself in his temple. To which, at the greatest festivals, I was carried throughout the year.

I was taught the ways of lawless, obscure Phaidix, the moon, who at certain seasons might be invoked by women, under the name of Phaidix Anki, as a sorceress.

I learned that these two gods, with Thon, the Death Lord, were current in all lands of the continent, and most of its islands. But that there was also a pantheon of slighter gods in Akhemony, some immigrants from Artepta, Bulos, Ipyra, and elsewhere. All had their places.

It was Kelbalba who told me of Lut, the Arteptan dwarf god, whose part it was to watch over any who came into the world at a disadvantage, or later fell to one, the very poor, the sick, those smitten in brain or body. "Those the other gods forget," said Kelbalba. I was nearly six then, when she spoke of Lut. She did not make anything much of the story, no more than of a hundred others. But when I said, curiously, that I supposed he would know about me, she said that she supposed he might. She had a charm of Lut, in blackened silver, and showed me it. She said, proudly, she had always been very ugly, and so adopted the god, although he lived in Artepta.

I marveled at that. I did not think her ugly at all.

Never, any more, was I allowed to walk, that is to use canes and swing about on them. At five or six, I often got in a temper at this. I had waited so long, perhaps expecting to get them back as another of my rewards for diligence at all my lessons.

It was explained to me all over again, that constant recourse to the sticks would deform my body utterly, because I had not finished growing, had scarcely begun.

So I had to be content, since they were adamant, with my chair with the golden clasps, which, as I grew, grew also, or rather was replaced always with a larger one.

The female slaves bore me to the cell of easement, even sitting me on the pot. I did not any more find this humiliating. They were, after all, slaves only, and lessons in my rights and worth as a princess of the Sun, had already taken hold. To move about, however, requiring always one other, and presently two, to bear me in the chair, was a cause of annoyance and frustration.

I would sit looking at the far end of the room, or the door to the room with the pool and my turtle—now she was *mine*—and chafe because I could not merely *go* there.

Dependency of any sort will rankle. A child any way is so dependent. It remembers worse. To be born helpless without language or any ability, surely we are all, at the commencement, the creatures of Lut, and at the end, with age, may go back towards him again.

Sometimes I was carried to a garden that ran under my apartment, reached by a small door. It was completely wild now, having been left untended since the time of Okos, for the moon goddess, who loves things untamed. Her shrine was there, black stone, and her statue, quite coarsely cut, but showing a lynx crouched at her side.

Once when they had put me there, near the outer wall under the vine, I saw a fox come through and a cub after her. They were in their summer colors, with a sheen like that on the Lakesea below.

I watched them gambol, and fight mock combats, springing at each other, hoping no one would come to frighten them. Then they were gone, away into some secret place of the garden, where the wild fruit trees had netted together and the grass stood high as I would have done, had I been able to stand.

Overhead, the Daystar was clearly visible, though it was almost noon, the hour when she is often shy of her appearance, so close to the Sun.

Looking up, I noticed, too, an old woman. She was dressed very darkly, but had heavy, dull-gleaming ornaments, a necklace of big somber stones, and a dozen bracelets. Although it was morning, she seemed to have offered something on the altar of the shrine. I could not see what.

Then she turned. I recalled her at once, she was the old woman who had soothed me that second night at Oceaxis, a century ago, when I was four.

She said, "Udrombis goes up to Airis for the hot months. But not you." I shook my head. I did not query why she put my deeds together with the Great Queen's. "They run the Sun Race soon. Have you heard?"

"To honor the god," I said obediently, "through the caves under the mountain."

"Yes, just so. Where have you been but Oceaxis?"

I shook my head again. Though a King might make military diplomatic progresses, and other portions of the court break off to travel, most of the household remained constant, in time of peace, by the Lakesea.

"You were once in the Temple of Death," said the old woman.

When she said it, I did not feel afraid or threatened, as when, say, Ermias spitefully mentioned my awful beginning.

The old woman pointed away, over the wall.

"Down there is the sea. Go far enough, you will come to the Sun's Isle. Have they told you?"

"Yes. Where the piece from the Sun broke off and crashed down. When the First King conquered."

"Who," she said, "do you think is the more powerful? Not a King? The Sun then, or the moon? Or Death?"

I puzzled. Such questions—not quite such questions—were put to me in the hours of schooling. But I did not know. The Sun gave life. The moon and Death took it away. A King could do both, but was also subject to both. She seemed not to want an answer any way.

She said, "Glardor is off again," like an elderly market-wife speaking of some nephew.

Even I had heard how Akreon's heir, the new Great Sun, was still, very often, on his estates. He liked the things of the earth. He planted, and tied vines. He would even take a turn with the plow. Glardor the Farmer they called him, out as far as Uaria and Charchis. For this reason perhaps, now and then, little eddies of trouble would stir, in Uaria and Charchis, in Ipyra, in Sirma. . . . What could a farmer know of ruling or war?

There was a silence then, but for the crickets in the grass. The Sun was lifting up high, and soon they would come to take me into the shade, for royal women had complexions like milk, unless they were ebony, as in Artepta.

"Did you come before?" I asked the old woman. I had forgotten the substance of our previous chat.

"Did I? When was that?"

"Years ago. I was a child."

She did not laugh. She said, "We are all children. Oh look, now. That butterfly."

I looked of course. And saw the butterfly, mint-green, with black eyes on its wings. And when I looked again for her, the woman, she was gone.

When the slave came, I said to her, "Who is that who comes in our garden and the rooms?" She stared blankly. "An old woman—like a queen."

The slave did not know. But slaves, I then thought, knew very little, not understanding they are like the mice in the walls of an ancient house, going everywhere, privy to all things.

In the afternoon though, Kelbalba entered, and when I had finished my exercises, and we were sitting with the turtle, I told her of the woman I had seen.

Kelbalba said, gravely, without any attempt to alarm or deny, "That would be the old witch, Crow Claw. She died in the snow months."

"Which snow months?" I gabbled.

"The last ones. They found her inside the door of the High Queen's chambers, lying on the floor, as if asleep."

"Then—it was a ghost." Stunned, I did not argue.

"She was happy here," said Kelbalba. "She doesn't want to go away."

"But Death takes—makes . . . Is there a choice?"

"Yes, if you're strong enough."

I dreamed that night I saw Crow Claw sacrificing a white hare to Phaidix, to whom no blood sacrifice was ever made. It was Phaidix who stole in by night and drank the life from the bodies of men and women, babies and beasts, but they died in a joy greater than any to be found on earth.

When Crow Claw had killed the hare, its soul jumped out of it, white as the moonlight, and she and it went away together, directly through the wall of the garden.

What was I, then, as a child? In wartime once, the pherom-steel, when hammered in the fire, was cooled by plunging into the blood of a living enemy. How had *I* been tempered? First miseries, then terrors, and so to a life which, if not in any way wholly carefree, was yet full of pleasures, and of boredoms, too. From *that* lesson, what was I learning?

At my seventh year, they began to teach me to sing, as Udrombis had promised, and to play the sithra, the little female harp which, being so light, was easily rested on my knees. I was not inept, but preferred to improvise, myself creating songs and melodies, not doing as they said I must. I made my songs from the history of the Sun Lands now being taught me, the stories of heroism and romance that caught my fancy. And I composed odes to geographical regions I had never seen, trying I think to bring them to me, since I could not go to them. When Mt. Airis was spoken of I longed to see it. I longed to sail across the Lakesea in a galley. I longed to sail the narrow winding straits at Artepta, and behold the monuments of smooth and shining stone rising out of the water, and the statues of strange beings, which spoke—a thing I did not know, even having lived there, sometimes happened at the Temple of Thon. In my head I went traveling, making up for myself these places and lands, reinventing them from what I knew, as they had told me the gods had done, at the very first.

For my arrogance I was reprimanded. Which helped me, for it made me worse.

Probably I should have been, after my start, a timid child. In some ways, I was. But I was forever darting out of cover. I was forever angry, sitting in my golden chair, beating my legs that had no feet against the lion-claws, until my calves were bruised and I cried.

It was I who wanted ghost stories, and then lay rigid through half the night. Oddly, I was never afraid of Crow Claw. If she had come then, I think I would have debated with her quite boldly on her state.

Then again, with certain adults I was stricken almost silent. A crushing rebuke made me shake, made me sick to my stomach, as did the dread of things not reckoned by others onerous—for example, the excitement of going to the temple, where I should see my beauteous male kin—before all those excursions, I vomited, until I was given a little wine, which would steady me. Even so, I would have died rather than miss the trip.

I had, too, unreasonable fears, or so they were called. Of a spot behind a particular pillar, where they must always leave a light. Of the sound cats made outside, fighting at midnight to honor Phaidix. Or a certain innocent food or drink. Yet—thunderstorms I loved.

Snow, however, made me melancholy, which was not so surprising. The bedcovers, shutters, and drapes of the palace had not yet blotted up the icy times at Koi.

What can I say of her then, this child?

She was a child. As Crow Claw forewarned her, now she is old; she thinks herself one still.

After Klyton had met my eyes with his in the Sun Temple, when I was seven, the world about me altered.

I did not seek Ermias, who was, apparently, my necessary foe. Nor could I talk to Kelbalba, who had gone away to her father's house in the hills.

Instead I discussed my life with the turtle.

"If you go *that* way after your ball, then it will be."

The turtle went the way I desired.

It was settled. I must work hard upon myself.

Not knowing that, only in Artepta, Charchis sometimes, here and there, now and then, but seldom, did brothers wed their sisters, I had decided that, when I was of the proper age, I would marry the unnamed boy-man who had looked at me. It was not I thought myself worthy of him—how could I be. Besides he was a symbol—I see it now—of something unknown, dangerous and alluring as the edge of a cliff. But I had been carefully tutored. There were gods. Their blood ran in my family. *They* would assist me.

I wove new stories, about him. I made him songs, not knowing this was improper. He was the Sun as a youth, going out to hunt the Sun-burned mountainsides. He lay sleeping in the shade, and the Daystar smiled upon him, and flowers grew into his hair to garland him.

Luckily, so solitary, wishing often to be private, I did not sing these songs in the presence of any but slaves. They were ciphers any way. Yet, when Ermias came, I fell simply to humming the tune.

"Twang, twang," said Ermias. "What discords. What a dunce you are, Calistra."

I put down the harp. My hands were cold.

Ermias seemed fatter by the day. How she hated it. There was a pouch under her chin, and a cushion at her waist. Despite her duties, she was infrequently, to my delight, in the apartment. Her lovers were liars, and she knew.

3

The year that Calistra was eight, and Sun Prince Klyton thirteen, war broke in Sirma. It was a matter of tribute to the Great Sun, which was refused. Conceivably they expected to be let off, having heard tales. But Farmer Glardor put down his pruning hook, and hefted his sword. With a thousand cavalry, many hundred foot, some siege engines and catapults, the troops marched south in bronze fall weather. Sirma was little. It would be a short campaign. Perhaps a farmer knew, weeds and tares must not be let come up, even in the onion patch.

"He swaggers too much. He doesn't need to. He's a prince. If Glardor stepped aside, it would be him. What does he need to show?"

Amdysos was watering his horse at the brook, downstream with the cavalry. At fifteen, he looked almost fully a man, magnificent enough, and he took his own advice, was modest and quiet-spoken where possible. His men liked him, and were not put out by his age.

Klyton looked less a man, more a wayward god in youth and armor. Something eccentric in the lines of him, something fantastic and magical, pleased. He was thought too young to be given a command, although Okos had apparently had one at thirteen, in the battles with Uaria. Some perverse idiocy had put Klyton too among the ranks of Pherox's detachment. Amdysos had tried to change that. As Klyton said, it was like the school, where they split you from your friends to make you conscious of new ones, which had not worked.

Pherox, at twenty, rode up and down the lines of men, mature man and warrior. He had fought before, small uprisings here and there, all called wars. Sufficient. His sword, as they said, had drunk.

Handsome, like them all, he had the darkness of his mother, black hair, black eyes, and an arrogance and coldness that made one bite the tongue.

It was a fact. If Glardor—not euphemistically "stepped aside," but *died*—Pherox would be the Great Sun. Udrombis had borne him on a night of tempest. It had been a difficult birth. You could believe it of him.

Klyton let his gelding have the water. He watched it. He said, "Do you remember when Pherox took the apple—"

Amdysos roared with laughter.

Klyton did not turn. He felt the eyes of Pherox on them both. Pherox did not like their friendship. He had said openly that they were not only brothers but lovers, which had never been true, at least not true in the carnal sense. To Pherox, male love—of any sort—was shoddy. He should have read the legends. The Sun god's many loves of every gender. But the strain that was, in Udrombis, burnished stone, and in Amdysos, pragmatism, was in Pherox—poison.

The incident of the apples had occurred when Klyton and Amdysos were boys, six and eight years old. Pherox was thirteen, Klyton's age today.

Stabia had been given a gift of apples, some country present, nice enough, but too many. Klyton and Amdysos ate their fill, and then had a slave cast the apples in the air so they could try to split them flying, with arrows.

Pherox appeared. He lectured them on this waste of fruit. They were children. What did they know.

Then he picked an apple off the garden bench. It happened to be the showpiece of the gift, a fruit of green and red stained marble. They watched him, and at his unawareness, neither spoke out. When he took it directly to his mouth and champed on it in righteous fury, it broke a side tooth, which, to this hour, might be seen flashing its repaired cap of silver.

They had been friends from the beginning, from when Stabia and Udrombis had leaned together in the cool, scented rooms, and Klyton and Amdysos had fought and played like foxes on the floor.

Pherox did not think quickly enough, or look properly at things. About the look and feel of an apple, whether it were flesh or stone, at friendship that had nothing to do with ambition. At his own stance on the black Arteptan horse.

He had two wives, and both had given him, already, sons. He called them, Pherox, his flocks and herds.

"The Sun's going," said Amdysos.

Far up the hill, thinly, the priest might be heard singing out the incantation. Arndysos tipped a few drops from his wineskin into the stream . . . *"Do not forget us."*

Pherox was gone. He had not bothered, as several had not, to salute the dying Sun. Campaign was different. The gods were not unreasonable. Still, if one could.

"It should be the first Sirmian town tomorrow," said Klyton.

"Yes. How do you feel?"

"I don't know," Klyton said. "Keen, I suppose. Very, very brave."

Brief but opaque, doubt drifted through both their eyes. Tomorrow they must, for the first time, kill a man. Or, they might— unbelievably—die.

Farmer Glardor gave a dinner for his captains, and for the Sun Princes who were in the camp.

Outside, the evening was gravid with storm. The thunder stumbled about the sky from north to south, east to west, banging against the winds that were rising. The trees bent, groaning, and dry leaves rattled between the tents like quills of thin metal. Those who claimed still to hear the beat of the Heart, mostly, now admitted they lost it.

When the strongest wine came, at the end of the food, Glardor gave a speech.

The younger men shifted uncomfortably, the eldest sat grim and unspeaking, drinking great quaffs. It was inappropriate, the speech. It concerned peace and the peaceful role of the Great Sun.

"He must bring life," said Glardor, red-faced, expansive, his mantle loose, as one or two said later, as a whore's dress. "Life to his fields. He must ripen the fruit and the vine."

Pherox sat openly sneering. But he, too, kept silent.

Amdysos said, afterwards, when he and Klyton were sitting in Amdysos's tent, "He wants his farm."

"No, worse, he thinks Akhemony *is* his farm."

"Well . . ."

"Didn't he guess the picture he made?"

"Evidently not."

Glardor clove to his wife, now the Sun-Consort, but she was seldom seen, and barren. He had too, a score of illegal sons who, if it came to it, might cause trouble one day.

It was hot in the tent, and hot outside. Klyton's own tent, over with Pherox's troop, was hottest of all. The autumn weather was perhaps unseasonally warm, and here and there they had passed, on the march, carpets of spring flowers nosing from the soil before their time. Winter would find them presently, and put them down again.

The first Sirmian town was two hours' march away in the morning.

Amdysos slept, no doubt, breathing deeply as he always did, as if slumber was a drink. Outside the tent flap here, a slave was snoring.

Alone, Klyton thought of dying. What terrified him, he found, was the length of his life that then would be unlived all that he meant to do, but which yet he had not *found* to do. It seemed to him that Glardor would not last as King, and in a curious state, between sleep and waking, he saw Glardor vanish, and Pherox too, somehow, brushed away like the too-early and unsuitable flowers. Then Amdysos was the Great Sun Amdysos, who would be exactly right, powerful and just, brave and self-controlled. Amdysos too would need Klyton, with his tinder-strikes of amusement and action, imagination, *fire.*

What might they not do then? King and King's Commander. They two.

But if I die tomorrow—Klyton pushed his mind towards the god, to the Sun. *I leave it with you. You must decide. If I am worthy, let me live and do bright and weighty things. Or let me go down into the dark.*

Calm came then. The gods were reasonable. And Klyton knew himself not so bad.

Phaidix stood over him at last, not to drain his valor, only to bring

"Is that how you sound in bed, Pretty?" he said to Klyton. It was conversational.

All around, the red noise of fighting, the oaths, yells, and cries of pain. The jewels of red horse eyes that gleamed and went out, the lightning slash of swords, knives.

Klyton brought up his sword and sliced open the man's cheek, so it hung from him like an ill-cut slice from a joint. The man had done nothing to him but jibe. Somehow he had moved so slowly, and Klyton, not seeming to, very fast. The man swung over and off his horse into the mud that was already, in places, richly scarlet.

Klyton was startled. He had not killed the man. He had an idiotic urge to search for him among the stampeding kicking hoofs. But then another man—another *enemy*—came hollering, and Klyton stuck him straight through, where the upper chest armor was undone at his ribs.

It was the press of horses now that carried Klyton in through the wall.

The buildings seemed to tower and reel over him, and he expected a further deluge of thrown matter, but nothing came.

Other riders were cantering after him. They yowled and yodeled, and echoes shot off the walls. Klyton did as they did. His voice did not break again. He sounded like the other men.

There was a barricade in the narrow street, barrels, an upturned cart. They jumped over it.

The other side, the houses clustered like honeycomb. Where there were doors, they were fast shut. No faces at the thin slots of windows. No sounds but for the insane cluttering of pigeons up on the flat roofs. And the rain.

Then more cavalry, their own, a surge of it, was thrusting through. The space was filled. A sea of horses, men, the upturned points of weapons. From all over the town came the noise, unmistakable now, of victory. And new screams, the screams of women.

"Gates have given," said one, unnecessary. At the louder howls of pleasure, their horses reared.

So, it truly had been—only that. So easy. Flat, and nearly foolish.

Someone was shaking him.

"Klyton—look at me. Yes, that's better. You're covered in blood. It's not yours?"

"No, I don't think . . . Wait, just this—" Someone, the man with the ribbon, or the other one he had killed close to, had slit open his right arm up to the elbow. A spectacular cut, not deep enough to be damaging. Just deep enough to leave a proper scar. "Most of it's theirs."

Amdysos studied him. "You've done all right, then."

"I think so."

"Pherox had no good reason to send you in like that. He should have waited. It could have been chancy."

"I expect he went straight in himself. He would."

Amdysos glanced about. No one was listening. The men were using the hoofs of their horses to splinter doors, or laughing together, telling each other what they had done. "He did, but at the gate, with his bodyguard."

Klyton said, almost idly, "I had a man's cheek off. I didn't mean to. I meant to kill him. He fell anyway."

"That happens. You can't always be tidy in this sort of thing."

"Did you?"

"Yes. At least three men. From the look, you had fifty."

"That one . . . he had a purplish ribbon in his hair like a girl, but he called me a girl—or a catamite—something. It wasn't that it worried me. You know, what the sword-master said, they do it to rile you. Don't lose a cool head."

"Oh," said Amdysos. "A purplish ribbon. Was his armor fine?"

"Yes. He had colcai on it."

"Don't tell Pherox," said Amdysos. "I think you did for the chief's son."

Klyton shook his head. He felt the same. Nervous now with, wanting to be doing something else. This must be wrong. They had told him of cowardice, ordinary fear, cold strategy, and battle-madness. What to do with each. This had been none of those. It was like sex the first time for a woman this—he had not been able to—to enjoy it. With some women, Amdysos said, they never could.

"So what?"

"You'll get his arms, sword and so on. You've defeated him. He's probably dead by now, if he went down."

Glardor the Farmer rode into the Sirmian town. He had imposed a certain order, stopped most of the rapine and theft. He told the defenders they would be fined, but they must come on to the next town, to act as envoys there. He wanted to save bloodshed. His soldiers were not too pleased. Akreon had always let them have the first town or city of a campaign, even a small one. It taught the foe a lesson. And it was a Fighter's just deserts.

As they were standing in the square, where the market would be in time of peace, and all this was being digested, Klyton, looking up, saw a girl appear on a roof, quite close.

She was an extremely lovely girl, with long, dark tresses and fiercely flushed checks. He thought her about sixteen, old enough to be married and to have lost today her husband, but she was smiling. She had a basket on her hip.

A silence came, as the sullen murmurs from the soldiers died away.

Into this the girl called in a high silver voice, "Will you have an apple, gentlemen?"

It was an incongruous cry, made odder by an uneducated Sirmian accent.

Then she began to fling the apples at them.

The soldiers dodged, cursing, partly entertained. They could get her down quickly enough. She was insolent, and surely even Farmer Glardor would not deny her to them now. Then a few of the apples struck home. The Akhemonians did not like the sting. There was growling, and men striding now, to get up on the roof. The omen too was not lucky. The apple might symbolize a woman's pelvis, but was also the fruit of Phaidix, whose silver apples were a gift that signified approaching death.

Amdysos said to Klyton, without expression, "When they catch her, they'll use her till she's pulp. He won't stop that, now."

Just then, an apple whisked over their heads. It was meant perhaps for the King on his roan horse. It slammed instead directly into the face of Pherox.

Pherox's head was punched backward. He arched on the black horse, letting go the reins. The gelding reared. And Pherox went flailing from its back.

He landed hard on the square, and there, between the legs of men and horses, his half brothers, like the rest, saw him spasming, cawing, hawking, clutching, seeming to try to vomit, violent—then feeble. Finally turning the color of cold ashes. Amdysos started forward. Already others were running, too late.

Pherox, blood and slime coursing from his mouth and nose,

was almost still. His eyes were wide open, standing out like those of a hanged man.

The square was full of roaring.

On the roof someone had reached the girl. She was squealing with laughter. Still laughing, as she was thrown down, still laughing as she was torn open.

To those who worshipped Phaidix, despite stories of sweethearts and mothers, it was no surprise a female might be vicious, ruthless, or courageous. And they had seen already, most of them, she too had killed her man.

Klyton was sitting in a side room of the chief's house. He was stiff and embarrassed. The women, veiled, had washed him and seen to his arm, under the direction of Glardor's own physician. This was the ritualistic sign of their servitude to the conquering Akhemonian men. No doubt, they were grateful Glardor had spared them rape. They did not overtly object to the Great Sun and his commanders talking over the battle, in the ax and knife hung, raftered hall, where last night their own little king, husband, father and son, had sat.

Sometimes they looked, slavishly, from the corners of their veils. They knew one of the Suns had perished, and that a Sirmian woman slew him. As a matter of course, any drink or food here would be tested for poison.

If there were any further attempt to insult, or take life, the town would be razed.

Amdysos came to the room in the late afternoon.

He admired Klyton's bandaging. He, Amdysos, had none, not a scratch, though he had taken five men.

In the end, they were silent for a long while.

"It was a freak—it was a prank of the god who likes to play pranks." One did not speak this god's name. Amdysos added, "I know you. You're thinking we talked about it. The apple that broke his tooth years ago."

"We did, Amdysos."

"All right. And she threw an apple. And the silver tooth got knocked out, and he swallowed it into his windpipe and it choked him. It could have happened, that same thing, a hundred ways in battle. We didn't bring it down on him."

"No."

"Maybe," said Amdysos, "we had foreknowledge."

Klyton said, in a cold voice, "Will you tell Udrombis what we did?"

"My mother? I should think not. She has enough to bear. It's only four years since she lost the King."

"Glardor's King."

"You know what I mean. Women mourn longer. She still wears the colors. No, I wouldn't tell her."

Beyond the window, the unending rain went on. The afternoon was dull, but in the puddles there still ran the galvanic red stain that had been the life of men.

Amdysos said, "By the way, that man was dead."

"Which man?"

"The man with the ribbon."

"I'd—forgotten."

Amdysos came and stood directly in front of him. Klyton looked up.

"Leave this behind you," said Amdysos. "We're not guilty of anything. I know that I'm not. And I know you."

"I didn't wish him dead."

"Of course you didn't. You're a prince. *Leave it behind.*"

Klyton got up. He walked up against Amdysos and put his head, for a second, on Amdysos's breast. It was the symptom of a sudden childish fright and hurt: the numbness of war was going from him. But, too, in the days of Okos, of which they both knew rather a lot, it had been the tacit symbol, this gesture, of fealty, from a lesser king to the Great Sun.

"They've stripped the Sirmian armor. It's with your gear. There was another man too, someone said you took him, and perhaps speared another. The men liked you. You were valiant and didn't mess about. Straight through the wall, they said, with a battle cry."

"Do you remember that pig at Airis?" Klyton said.

"The big she-pig? Yes."

"It'll be winter soon. She's fair game then. We've left it long enough."

Amdysos grinned. "That's better."

The rain ran on and on. It wore you away, that sound, but the worst sound was to come, the women keening, and Udrombis in her utter noiselessness of grief.

Klyton knew he had seen them pass in his heart, Glardor and Pherox, and Amdysos rise like the Sun. And he, by Amdysos. Two Suns together. No. One must not think of that.

4

For highborn women of the court, not actually royal, there were always ways. If you must finally wed virgin, and often a sophisticated man would overlook it, providing you brought enough money and status with you, a wisewoman could give you a mixture. Applied, it caused a temporary dryness and tightening. He would feel you were not easy, see that he hurt you, and perhaps you bled. That was what, in simple terms, virginity amounted to. There were other draughts if your courses came late, to bring them on. A pregnancy carried to term, if unwanted, was rare. This was women's business.

Only the highest women were kept sealed till marriage, for they made possible the treaties, and the marks of favor.

Ermias had had many lovers, and reckoned to garner an excellent marriage when her stint as guardian was done. She would be pensioned with enough goods and gold to make her an appetizing match. But she had wanted her looks too, to catch a husband who was young enough, and handsome.

Now, at just twenty-four, Ermias was a pillow, spillingly fat. Her neck was like a frog's, with only a crease to show the demarcation of her chin. Her breasts had grown shapeless. Instead of bangles, rings of flesh garlanded her ankles. She waddled.

All Akhemony, all Oceaxis, was prone to lament. As the rain rushed down, down rushed the tears. Pherox had died in Sirma. And though another three towns had fallen since then and the campaign was almost done, this could not restore his life.

So, the sound of Ermias, weeping, was only that other sound brought indoors for me. I sat in my chair, listening, wondering if I too must weep, if his soul might be lost if I did not. Though insignificant in myself, I had heard legends where such things happened.

But he was not Klyton. If Klyton had been slain, I would have died at once. For any unknown other, there could only be regret.

At last the weeping stopped or, as it turned out, paused.

The door opened, and Ermias came through.

In the lamplight, her eyes seemed bruised and the whites were red. Her puffy face was worse than ever, blotched with crying.

It was nearly my supper-time, and I thought she had come to say I must have my bath, now. Instead, she stared at me, stared on and on.

"Look at you," she said, eventually.

I shifted a little. She was not my friend.

"Oh the gods!" cried Ermias, "why have they done this to me? Why? *Why?*"

In that moment I thought she too had lost someone in the war.

Truthfully, I was not yet pleased to see her unhappy, she who was always so unkind, merely perplexed.

I said nothing.

Ermias said, "You filthy little monster, crouching there. Why aren't you all a mass of fishy blubber, like me? It should be you, you little beast." The tears came again, bursting out of her, sparkling like jewels in the light. "I'm so ugly. So ugly. But you—you—do you know what the women say about you, Calistra? Because they never see your legs, your *feet*? Eh?"

Now the full force of her malevolence bore in on me. I must give her some tribute or it was war.

I shook my head.

Loudly, she cried: "*Snake.* That's it. They say you've got a *snake's* tail under your skirt. Or you are a *fish.*"

The horror of this was dull. I was frightened of her, her vehemence, the strength of her emnity so massively displayed. There is too that terror which comes when civilized barriers, however flimsy, break down—perhaps children recognize this more swiftly than adults. Besides, fish, snakes—were beautiful, those I had been shown.

Ermias was drunk, I think, from a lot of wine.

"It's you—you're unlucky—you're a curse on me—"

She spun heavily about, and ran from the room, lumbering, knocking over as she went a small table.

The door between the rooms stood open. I saw her throw herself on her couch, the place where for years she had slept, and frequently done with her lovers that incomprehensible thing which made noises.

Now she noisily cried, in an awful manner. She choked and struggled for breath. It was a real agony, this, for her. One should never dismiss pain of whatever sort. The child who cries for a lost toy, the woman who weeps at the loss of her loveliness, they have their station, beside the greater tragedies of this world. If you have been brought down to tears, who may say you have no right to shed them.

Then I was mostly frightened in a new way. I wanted her to stop. To stop her. Yet I felt a wave of satisfaction, too. She had made me cry often enough. Let her suffer now.

But she kept on and on.

In one corner of the outer room, the water-clock dripped the seconds. The little silver galley had risen a handspan up the bowl, and *still* she wept.

A window curtain was drawn for night, not yet the shutters for winter. I heard the Lakesea, and beyond that, the Drum of the Heart, hearing it as one seldom did, and like a fresh sound.

I was, as I have said, trained to be very agile, and I wriggled around and down from my chair, something I never normally assayed. When I was on the floor, I began to crawl on hands and knees.

Probably my intention was only to shut the door, shut out her cacophony. But then, as I moved, it seemed I was not going to do that, but something else.

Just then, I saw the table, which Ermias had knocked over, was again standing upright. The warm lamplight lit, upon its top, a goblet, one I used, rather small and made for a child, of gilded bronze. It had not, I thought, been there before. But maybe it had.

Behind the table stood Crow Claw, who was a ghost. She looked solid enough, in her dark things, her dark gems shining, and her old eyes. She out one finger to her lips, and I glanced towards the outer room. Ermias was aware of nothing but her own wretchedness.

I looked back. Crow Claw indicated the cup with her forefinger, and nodded.

Did she mean I should drink from it?

She shook her head. She pointed now into the outer room.

I cannot say that I debated any of this. I suppose I did not quite believe in Crow Claw now; I had not seen her since that time in the garden. She could not be actual. Then again, she had done me no harm. She would not seek to poison me, or even Ermias, since that would be a murder at my hands. I trusted Crow Claw, that is the riddle, and its answer.

So I took the cup off the table—there was only, apparently, some more wine in it—and crawled on with urgent difficulty, through into the outer room, all the long way to the knees of Ermias.

When I touched her she sat up with a start.

"Keep away! How did you come out here?"

"I only crawled. I do it for exercise in the morning."

"Keep off. I don't want *you*—you're a curse on me." She reared up her head on its flabby column. "You *snake*."

"Don't cry," I said. "You're pretty."

Why did I say it? I loathed her by now. And yet, she broke my heart.

She gaped at me, and I held out the cup.

"Look, this is nice."

"What is it—what have you put in it?"

"Nothing." I took the cup back, and drank a mouthful. It was undiluted and went directly to my head. I felt soothed, consoled. No wonder people liked it. I held it out again.

Ermias took the cup and held it, not drinking. She looked at me, and her face peculiarly began to change. It was as if her true face was looking through, out through the fat, the spitefulness, the cruelty. Her true face, her true eyes, curious, considering.

After a long while, she spoke softly, her voice cracked and nasal from her tears.

"What I said—I didn't mean that. About a snake."

Then she raised the cup and drank it off.

She appeared very odd now, the true face fading back, but its knowledge still in her bloodshot eyes. She was exhausted, older, wiser.

"Come and sit here, by me," she said. She helped me pull myself on to the couch. Then she put her arm around me. It was as if suddenly she found how much simpler it was to like rather than to hate me. And I, after a moment, rested my head on her side. Her fat was warm and fragrant. She was comfortable. Her hair smelled of tears, like the sea.

"I know a rhyme," said Ermias presently.

She told me. It was a funny one about a monkey. We laughed. Then we lay back. There was no one in the inner room. We slept against each other until the slave brought my supper. Then Ermias got up and went away.

When she returned it was bedtime. She brought me a monkey made of confectionery.

"Don't eat it all now. Save some for tomorrow."

"I won't eat him."

She looked disappointed. I explained I thought him too nice to eat. I laid him on my pillow, which he made very sticky. I kept him for years, until at last he fell all to bits, hard and dry and tasteless as pieces of gravel.

By the time the army came back in victory from Sirma, with two hostage chiefs, and the mourning for Pherox, and a bride for Glardor who, they said, he treated with courtesy and never bedded, Ermias had lost a vast amount of weight. She was never to be again a slender girl, but became instead curvaceous and voluptuous, and light as a feather in the dancing on the shore, which I shall come to.

I have no notion, not one idea, of what if anything was in the cup.

To me, Ermias was never again seriously harsh. If she did snap, she presently followed it with a kiss. As a child I did not interest her, yet even so, she spent with me more time, if rather impatiently, seeing to my clothing, so I grew splendid at the festivals. Sometimes she took me with her, privately from the rooms, the slaves carrying my chair, to visit her friends, the Maidens of the court.

In this way, my world enlarged. And seeing myself, as I slowly altered under her guidance, had a fuss—perhaps false—made of me, and absorbed their chatter, I determined that, by the age of twelve, I must have found a way to be wed to Klyton. Although, of course, I could only be one of several wives, and although I did not think he could ever love me, or expect him to, I believed I would be content. I did not even fear for my cherished privacy. I imagined that, in the household of a prince, I could keep it just as well. Meanwhile I told no one my obsessional secret. It was magical. I held it near.

Before my attendances at the temple now I was cold and rigid. Sometimes I did not even see him there. Then I was sick of loss. He never looked at me again—had forgotten me. But I asked the gods to remind him. I had become aware I was not quite worthless. The praises of the women convinced me.

If there were any talk of war, I asked for news, though naming none. I named him at night. I prayed for his life every evening before closing my eyes—to visualize him better.

Otherwise, I studied more vigilantly with my harp, learned to sing many songs, excelled in my exercises, offered to Gemli on the wall, and reminded the green turtle—with the gods, my sole confidante in this matter—that only four years, three, two years, now, lay between us and an almost perfect joy. But, how to manage it.

5

Seated on her terrace, Udrombis, the Widow-Consort, looked down into her summer garden.

There, her youngest son, Amdysos, a tall, golden nineteen, was arguing quietly, concentratedly, with his friend, Stabia's son, Klyton.

On a second couch, Stabia sat, embroidering slowly, with great care, golden wool the color of the hair of both these Sun sons, into a mantle of dark orange.

Stabia's eyes were not so strong now. She made her way from practiced skill, and every so often, would hold the cloth her arm's length away, to be sure of the effect.

"He is very angry."

"Yes," said Stabia, "so he is. It's his impatience. He was angry last year, too. Next year—Sun protect us!"

She laughed low, and Udrombis, also smiling a little, took a sip of the tawny Ipyran wine.

Only royal kindred, the highest nobles, or princes of high stock from other lands, might compete in the Sun Race at Airis, through the caverns under the mountain. It symbolized, this race, the going down of the Sun into the Sleep of Night under the world, and his return in glory. To compete was a crucial and sanctified honor, and there were always many who wished to be considered. There might be only thirteen racers. They were chosen in the temple by lot.

At sixteen, eligible, Klyton had waited his turn—and got nothing. Neither, that year, had Amdysos.

This year—yesterday, to be precise—Amdysos had been chosen. Klyton, who had offered three white pigeons to the god beforehand, had nothing.

"I tell you, it's *not* luck," Klyton was saying, standing pale and set under the stone figure with the urn of flowers. "They doctor the lots. Didn't you *know*?"

"I didn't. Don't. It has to be random—the god chooses—or it would be a blasphemy."

"It is one, damn it."

'I know you wanted it. It's a chance to shine. You deserved it. It should have been you, not me."

Klyton checked. His face changed. "No, of course not. You. You had to be chosen. You'll win. Amdysos—it isn't I grudge *you*. I just wanted—" He stopped. His face of seventeen years, and several centuries of pure-bred beauty, broke into a boy's grin—became human. "Oh, there's always next year. You'll win any way. So I'd rather not make a fool of myself, coming in second."

"Second place is quite honorable."

"It's for mice.

Amdysos laughed, and on the terrace, Stabia sighed. "There," she said. "It's all over. That's how my son is. Like a summer storm. Frowns thunder. Then the sky clears. Mind you, Amdysos calms him. He has your trick of that."

"My trick?" Udrombis raised her brows.

"Yes. Remember, when I used to call you the Sorceress."

"That was long ago."

Both women paused, looking out through the garden now, seeing other times.

"I recollect when I could climb the stairs without stopping," said Stabia. "And I didn't need to hold my embroidery a mile from my face, or stand back a mile from the frame, to see it. And I was a pretty girl. But you. You don't change."

"I've changed."

Stabia glanced at her Queen. Udrombis still wore mourning, the most pastel brown. It became her very well. They had, these women, been lovers once. Those caresses had melted from them with the years, leaving them still each a little holding the other's inward shape. Stabia had no fear of Udrombis, although she knew, without a doubt, was it ever necessary, Udrombis would kill her. She admired Udrombis, had faith in her. Nothing would ever be done without good reason, or uncouthly.

Klyton turned now. He called up to Stabia, "Which flower shall I bring you, Mother?"

"Oh, something yellow, dearest," said Stabia, noting the convenient yellow flowers framing his head like a festal wreath.

"And for you, my Queen?" he said.

Udrombis said, "The smallest flower that's in my garden."

He bowed low, and went off, Amdysos laughing still at his shoulder.

Klyton, too, had been in love with Udrombis, when a child. Stabia had told her, not artless, nor untruthful.

Udrombis said, "May I be frank, Stabia?"

"With me, what else."

"Your handsome, valorous son. He is everything one hopes for. He has courage, and wit and brains. He shirks nothing. But these moods—tell me. Women. Has he . . . let me use the charming Orialian expression, *slaked his thirst*?"

Stabia frowned her brow worse than over the needle. "The gods know. I'd say not. He likes them. He isn't one for men that way. But if he's done anything—now, I'd be the last to know."

"From what little Amdysos has said of their adventures," said Udrombis, "I think, as you do, he hasn't, perhaps. My own sons were forward in that. Even Glardor." Here, a tinge of faintest distaste colored her tone. Glardor did not appeal to her. To her, he was not a King, not the material of which Kings were formed. Though who, in any case, could have followed Akreon?

"I suppose," said Stabia, "I've been lax. I should have put more of the tastier slaves his way. They all coo over him. I'd have thought one of them might have managed it any way."

"He may prefer free women. Your son is very fastidious."

"There are opportunities there, too."

"Possibly, concerned as he is with male enterprises, he may have missed them."

Stabia put down her embroidery. She saw, longsightedly, Klyton returning, with a yellow lily from a lower terrace, and a tiny white daisy—impudent, obedient, loving—for Udrombis.

"There are the summer dances in the groves, for the goddesses. Amdysos . . . knows." Stabia clasped her hands. "Men go there and spy. It's the tradition. The women are bound to accept only the most decorous overtures, but we know it goes further than that. In my day—it was different."

"I am older than you," said Udrombis. "In my day, it was exactly the same as it is now."

Klyton came and kneeled before her.

The Widow-Queen looked into his face.

"Is that the very smallest flower?"

"Yes, madam. I nearly missed it. A snail showed me."

"What reward will you have?"

"A kiss."

Udrombis beckoned him, and as he stood on the Stair, kissed his cheekbone. He smelled of Sun and health, male aromatics from the bath, of sexuality too. On his arm, the narrow white scar from Sirma. Four years ago the, gods had given him that badge, and to her another scar, all hidden, the death of a son.

But perhaps she loved Stabia's son, also Akreon's seed, as her own. And for this reason, Glardor had been sent to try her, and Pherox killed, and only her golden Amdysos left, the recognizable child of her womb.

The kitri, the honey-bird, often came to sing in the groves by the Lakesea. Even at night, she made music. Sometimes, there was other music too.

The shore below the palace had been planted with gardens in Okos's time, but then let go wild. The salt wind altered the grass. But the trees, cedar, myrtle, tamarind, the red marroi of the god, held fast.

By night, women of the court stole out there like the kitri.

There were the two altars on a rise, side by side. Clello, the goddess of love, white marble with lemon hair. And Daia, the goddess of love-desire, black-haired, ruby-lipped.

They held hands, these goddesses. The statues were quite recent. Everyone knew the women sought them, even slaves from the palace, or low wives from the town along the shore. Only the girls and Maidens of the queens danced there after dark, in long lines, their hands joined like the hands of the goddesses, to the notes of flute and sithra, and tiny shaken bells.

It was exquisite, the sight of it. The Sun had gone down inland about an hour ago, the Daystar was sinking. A lilac glow lingered through the sky.

But in the groves torches, the shade of electrum, burned ever more redly, picking out the lines and curves of things, the gathers and pleats of dresses, the flames of eyes and jewels, the small sand-flowers that had rooted in the salty turf. The leaves on the trees were black, then sudden brilliant jade as torchlight shone through. Between, in the shadows, might be anything, demons, spirits, or gods come down to see.

Beyond, a glimpse, here, there, the luminous near-tideless wash of the murmuring water, the slender waves folding over and over, rimmed with silver yet from the sinking star.

A certain light has still the power, near dusk, to bring me back again to that place, that hour, when I was twelve years old in Oceaxis.

I had never been invited before. A princess, I should not have been there. Had I known, this was how lowly they reckoned me, one of their own. Of course, I could not go off with any man, even if one had wanted me, a cripple, the girl with the tail of a snake or a sea fish, under her skirt. It was safe enough. She meant it kindly, Ermias; she had said I did not get enough fresh air.

She had put on me, too, my most elegant dress, the dark green web-silk with lines of silver in it, from Oriali, and borders of rosy pomegranates. From my ears hung the greenish pearls of the Bulos rivers, where men dive down for the quarter of an hour, or more, searching, sometimes dying.

For a year, since my menstruation began, my face was painted. I was a woman. There had been queens as young, younger, than I.

I watched them dance, the steady rhythm that wended in time to the always heard, unheard Heart, then quickened to play between the Heartbeats.

The women were laughing, had been drinking wine, crowned with myrtle and leaves of the holy marroi. There were faint flowers too on the tamarinds, filling the air with scent. The dresses brightened, saffron, orange, white, as they passed. Every face was the same—alight with amusement, excitement. Mine, too. I leaned forward from my chair, and clapped my hands in time to the little drum.

"Look—over there—do you see? *We are being watched!*"

This was the tradition of the groves by the sea. In the legend, the goddesses were dancing on a shore. Night came down, and Clello wore a dress of starlight, but Daia had kept the red of sunset for her gown.

Two mortal men, the sons of a king, and very comely, heard their music. Intrigued, and then aroused, the men spied upon the goddesses, who, seeing them, kept up some while the pretense, before drawing them in among the trees. The finish of the story is apt to their natures. Clello inspired a lasting noble love, and in the end took pity and gave the youth a human wife exactly in her own image. But Daia's swain went mad, and when she refused again to lie with him, hanged himself on the tree which took his name—the Saberon—which to this day has pendant blossoms in the shape of a hanging man. Unlucky, this tree—ironically—was uprooted in the groves.

Having caught the whispering, I looked in my turn.

Indeed, there was a group of men, perhaps seven of them, standing a little way back from the dancing ground. The torchlight found their faces under the hoods of their cloaks, and glints on their ornaments. One did this courting in one's best.

The women went on dancing, but now the line of them broke apart. They turned, showing their bodies in the thin summer dresses, their upheld arms with bracelets of gold.

A man laughed now, warm, and demanding.

It was a signal. Giggling, flaunting, the women left off the dance altogether. They fell away into groups, like flower-heads, waiting.

Who the suitors were, I have no reason to recall. Only one. Amdysos had been too tactful to come. A friend or two, I think. Others. Those who had walked to the shore on previous nights.

It was full dark now, the correct time. Fireflies winked in the bushes. I saw Ermias, big and luscious, tossing her curls, move out to greet one man who seized her silver-corded waist in both his hands, catching her, pulling her at once to his mouth.

He was standing back, but the torchlight described him, brazen upon his face that was a mask of metal. He did not look uneasy, bashful. I wonder what it cost him,, to be bold, there in that arena, taxing as any combat, to a man. At the time, I did not know.

It was a miracle to me. That Klyton was there, under the trees, the torches showing him to me.

But he did not look at me.

He crossed straight over to a girl with long, silky, lemony hair, like Clello on the slope above. He held out his hand, and she, blushing now, breathing fast, with bright eyes, went to him.

I had known pain, pain of many kinds. One reasons, it will pass, and then all will be as before, before the pain, kind days of nectar. But pain, once it has found you, will return. So life is.

What should I do? I could not even run away.

I sat in my chair, and in the centre of me, heart and viscera, the unrealized bud of my loins, the blackest agony and despair dredged down.

It was in this moment that one of the musicians, rising, carried his torch across the grove. Klyton looked up to see the light, and saw instead myself.

My dress—the color of his eyes by night.

Though I was stifled by my heart, I would not look away.

He glanced at the girl he had selected, said something soft, put a kiss into her open palm. When he came from her, she only bridled a little. He had promised her he would not be gone for long. She knew him a Sun Prince, the glamorous Klyton who, they said, was a virgin still. She would wait.

But he walked over the clover-grass to me, and when he was by me, he halted, looking down and on and on, into my face.

"Should you be here, little girl?" he said.

I said, "Ermias brought me."

"Who is Ermias? Your Maiden?"

"My guardian."

"Yes, you're very young."

Tears flooded my eyes at once. He thought me a child. And what was that girl's waiting to mine? I had waited for five years.

"You're a princess of the house," he said. "That's right, isn't it? Daughter of a Daystar."

He did not, unlike the waking dream, know my name.

"I am Calistra, daughter of Akreon."

"Good," he said. He nodded. "Be proud of that. I'm Klyton."

"I know."

He did not ask me how—all my furtive questions, not to stir unwelcome interest in my curiosity. Probably he thought we were born with knowledge of him, as such men—the beautiful, the brave, the god-inspired, the innocent—do.

"Well," he said. He was still looking in my eyes. He said, "Your eyes are like silver, Calistra. She shouldn't have brought you here."

I said, to protect her, "She wanted me to have the air. She takes care. No one insults me." I drew in breath. "It's because I can't walk."

His eyes left mine. They travelled down me, my slim girl's body with its breasts, that I had had almost two years, to my skirt's end, the pomegranate border.

I shut my eyes. I felt a wave of tingling and terrible unhappiness, such as I had never had, not even in the House of Thon.

I said, "I haven't any feet, my lord."

To my surprise, perhaps my horror, I was not certain, he said, "Yes, I'd heard of it." He added, "I asked someone, once."

I could not look at him now. Before, it had seemed we might go by my disadvantage. Now I felt the utter weight of it like stone tied to me. How could he *not* mind? He, this god, this Sun. I wished I was dead.

His eyes were on my face again. I felt them, like lights or heat, but I did not look now.

"You must miss it, not walking. Or to dance."

Of course I had missed it, but nothing was of any importance any more. I would die in the night of misery.

Then his hand came down and brushed my hair. It was like a healing touch. Flame flooded through me. I raised my eyes. My heart beat now so much I could not speak or breathe. I hung from him as the Daystar hung from the Sun, they said, by a chain of gold invisible to the eye.

"You shouldn't have been left this way," he said, firmly. "What were they thinking of?" I thought he meant the grove, Ermias again. I did not care. Could not answer, any way. "Calistra, leave it with me. I'll do what I can. Didn't they see, you're like—" he stopped. He said, "Akreon would have brought you out. You're not only a night–flower. You must be seen in daylight, too."

I understood none of it. I wanted him to stay, looking down at me, for ever. But my physical response to him, so close, so real, was overwhelming, nearly devastating. Also, I wished that he would go away. For a little while. Only a little. So I could breathe again.

And he did go away then. He smiled, and mildly tapped the earring in my left ear, so it swung. "Leave it with me," he said again. Then he turned and went back to the glowing girl, who walked away with him into the shadows, on two slender, arching feet.

Strangely, I did not die that night. Nor did I sleep until the dawn began.

Ermias thought I had a fever. I did not want to eat, to be got up. I did not want anything. Did not know anything to want. Only Klyton, who had gone away.

Three or four or five days passed like this, I forget how many. She was threatening me with the physician. She had not seen the prince talk to me, and those that had, had their own concerns. He was my brother. It had been courteous of him, to greet me, and either proper or improper, depending on how one viewed the scene.

A slave brought me his present. It was wrapped in silk, and when undone, found to be a bracelet, marvelously made, a dancing girl twisting about a ball of green pearl. The metal was colcai. It fitted perfectly.

He had written the message himself.

My sister, who has the name of Calistra.
Have you forgotten me? I hope you have not. I am sending someone to you. Do what he says. When we meet again, you will stand before me. We will walk together through the palace. Do your part, and I vow this to you.
Yours under the Sun.
KLYTON

Klyton, you brought me pain. So much pain. You took from me first the virginity of my soul. The omens were very clear, but I did not see them, as I ran upon the sword.

6

It was a month before my new teacher came. I had been expecting him daily, between trembling anxiety and overpowering anticipation. I was fearful too, afraid of failing in this. For if I failed, worse now than losing my own incredible chance, I would lose Klyton.

Kelbalba had returned, four days after Klyton wrote to me. She had been summoned to the prince—oh, her luck, the blessing; she shone for me with his reflected light—and she explained what was to happen. She seemed dubious, and was careful how she spoke. She told me at once it might be no use.

But I had only one verdict: Klyton had decreed it—it must answer. If it did not, *I* would bear all the black despair of unsuccess, the guilt of unworthiness. The utter loss of all.

As the month waned away, she put me through my paces. At everything I had been taught, on my bar, in the exercises on the floor, I was, she said, splendid. She praised me. But then she said, "This is a wholly new thing you must learn now. You haven't wasted, and that's to the good. But your muscles will need to go another way. And, Calistra—will *hurt*."

I already knew.

She had held me, and let me take most of my own slight weight on the stumps of my ankles. Presently the pain and vertigo made me cry out.

"Worse than that," said Kelbalba. "Much worse."

"I must," I said. "I'll bear it."

"You are all Sun children," she said. "In my village, I'd have been ashamed to be so valiant. But we were only clay." I do not know if she meant to imply her irony, or real awe. I think she only said what she thought.

She began anyway to make me do fresh things, working always with my knees, my thighs, the calves of my legs, my spine, and had me standing upright, minutes together, gripping her hands. She rubbed the ends of my legs with a solution that smelled of vinegar-wine and burned me.

The man, my tutor, arrived on a hot morning when the Lakesea was like a line of heated steel beyond the window, decorated above by two or three white gulls, and the red pillars of the room blazed as if also heated within.

Everything smelled of life. Birds were singing, the gulls calling, and I was feeding the turtle a salad of her favorite herbs and weeds.

Abruptly it had occurred to me, I do not know why, that I had been born in this very room, almost thirteen years ago.

But rebirth was hurtling on.

The door opened. Kelbalba walked through, and nodded to me. Then she let him come in. He was something to see, coal-black, with a black beard to his waist.

Torca, though more than part Arteptan, had lived in Akhemony for twenty years. Before that he had roamed the outlands of Ipyra. He had been a doctor with the armies of the kings of Uaria and Charchis. He had fought with Akreon's forces in several campaigns. He had a reputation as a man prized by the gods, having been nearly killed six or seven times, in war or by accidents, and survived.

He had a leg made from the knee down of solid wood. He had fashioned it himself, strapped it on to replace an amputation, and learned to use it. Once the master of it, he made himself serviceable to others. I had never heard of him, for such things were not common chat among the high women at Oceaxis. But in Airis he was known, for he had become a priest there, who served the shrine, and assisted at the Race.

Klyton had sought him out. If Torca took his time in coming, he announced afterwards, it was to test me. Speaking so many tongues, he was perfect in the accent of each land or region. So I could be in no doubt when he said he had left me the days in which to see that I was mad and in error, and for Kelbalba to frighten me into better sense. Finding me still insane, he scowled and said I should be sorry. How right he was.

Looking back, my impulse is to hurry through this section of my history. Even now, the injury, the awful doubt and dismay, scratch at my heart. Though she has become another, that one I was, Calistra, perhaps for this very reason, I do not like to dwell on her suffering and her humiliation. We say here, in Sin Dhul, City of the Moon, sometimes the potter, seeing the pot is taking the wrong shape on the wheel, must crush it again, to reform it better.

Probably I will be too quick, in my explaining.

I would get up, eat a little, take my morning bath. Then Kelbalba would soak the stumps of my legs in a solution of acid fire. After my new exercises, Torca came in. I would be lifted up and put down into two pits of agony. And in this way, through the days, I would travel. Often I fell. They caught me, or let me go down. Their hands led me, or betrayed. Or there were two traitorous sticks grasped with my own terrified fingers. My eyes were always wide, like those of a rabbit that sees the snake. I lost my virginity during this time. Actually and physically, I do not speak now by allusion. It tore open in one of my many tumbles, my legs sprawling so violently that, had it not been for all my work on my body before, I think both would have been broken. Feeling the other tearing, I knew, but did not speak. I could not care.

I was in pain, any way, from the first, all up my legs and into my crotch, into my very womb. Soon all of me hurt so much that, even after the bath and the massaging which came with evening, I lay weeping, unable to sleep unless hammered down into the dark with the strongest soporifics.

Even up my neck and into my skull, I hurt. And there was, too, the aggravation of the scarlet cord, which had been tied up my body from both my legs, into my hair. Torca had said this was to instruct my brain that as my legs flexed, it must respond. The cord duly wrenched and pulled. I cannot describe fully the mass of agony I became, but it was the thunder-colored pain described by certain poets, shot through with notes of sheerest razor white. And all this, to keep my feet.

My feet.

When I first saw them, I felt a mixture of delight—and revulsion.

They had been fashioned to Torca's specification, but in the silversmith's shop. I was no soldier, but a princess of the Sun House.

They were of silver, mixed with iron and pherom at the sole, then padded here with leather which would, as time passed, be resoled as with any shoe.

And, they were in the *form* of feet, slender and strong, the very ones I would have had if I had not left them behind in the chaos lands, in my rush to be born. They had toes, and every one a nail of gold. They had anklebones, slim and fine as a dancer's. They rose a little above the ankle, and here, too, was a rim of rolled gold. Inside they were hollow, holding each a sack stuffed with layers of down, into which the stems of me were inserted. The filling would need constantly to be replaced. You would think such boots soft and supportive, putting your hand far into them. Who made them did their very best. Others have not fared so well.

From the ankle-parts, four rods of silver rose to half the height of my calf. Between the rods, a mesh of silver wire. The lacings were silver ribbons, such as ladies had for their hair, or their most frivolous sandals.

When the slave put them before me, Torca said at once I would need all this to be done again, as I grew. There was a slight smile on his face. It did not occur to me then, the expense of such riches so often repeated.

They were strapped on as I sat. When I rose, for a moment I felt my power. I was upright. I was supported. I stood—upon my own feet.

Then I was dizzy. I remembered when the Heart had stopped— had mine? And beginning my first lesson despite that, sickened, bemused, I found the daggers in the softness.

That first night, my legs ran with blood. And for weeks after. Beyond the times of blood, were worse things, when my own flesh sheared from me. The unguents of Kelbalba saved me from further mutilation. I heard Torca tell her, frankly before me, that he would have her recipe if she would sell it to him. He had seen men lose a whole limb to gangrene from such labor as mine.

In my dreams, I was whirling through air, while beasts gnawed my legs night-long. They ate upward. They would have my center, they would rape me with teeth.

I woke screaming from what little sleep I had.

7

Perhaps it was still summer . . .

I think not—there had been leaves caught in russet webs across the garden trees—and now the leaves were gone.

I lay shrieking. I refused them. I refused the feet. Instruments of torture, they stood in their silver purity, with their toenails of sunny gold. And by them, new silver laces, and the red cord.

"No—no—I won't—no—no—"

Kelbalba lifted me. She held me hard, not the hug of friend or mother, but of the warrior in the thick of battle.

"Come on, girl. Don't you know how well you do? He says, old Black Beard, he says you are braver than any man he's known. Braver than he was, with the wooden leg. Come on, come on. Or I'll slap you. I have a bet on you with my sisters at the stadium. I said you'd walk unaided by Winter Festival. Do you want to make a mock of me?"

But I had a fever from my wounds. I lay, and feebly cried for my beloved, who had brought me to this pass.

"The prince? Your Klyton? What does he care? He's off at Melmia, with half the court. He's forgotten you. You must make him remember."

Later, when drugs and possets had washed me quiet, she told me the story of how Phaidix kills with pleasure, her lethal arrows tipped with sweetness. But life is bitter. To live one must put up with it. Then, taking my sithra, she strummed a gentle air of the hills. She sang to my feet, which she said I had, although they were not visible. She said they must make friends with the feet of silver. Then all would be well.

She had a hoarse voice, but it calmed me. I slept better than for months, and in the morning, stiff as a board from only a day without moving, got up and called for the silver feet, and put them on.

Then I walked the length of the room, using only the walking sticks, and not complaining once, though rivets of ice and fire were driven from my groin to my eyes.

It would be almost another year before I could walk unassisted. And rather more before I would walk in the halls of ordinary men.

She brought the god Lut to my rooms that winter I was thirteen, and garlanded him herself for the festival, with red berries from the marroi, the Sun's promise of summer's returning.

"Tell him you hurt," said Kelbalba, folding her big arms, the scar on her cheek wriggling like a snake. "You can say anything to *him*. He won't mind you whining or crying. He understands all that. And that you're more than that. He forgives weakness and despair, yet values courage."

He was in the form of a hunchback, with bandy legs and a bulbous nose. But his mouth smiled grotesquely. It was sharing a joke with his own, those such as I. He was made only of greyish wood, but they had polished him, and he was half a foot high.

I made my ruinous way, in the hollow feet, with one cane, and put him on Gemli's altar. The flame dipped, as if she were offended, but I meant to offend her. I said, "Give joy, Gemli, goddess of joy, to *his* kind." But then I poured her wine and sprinkled perfume. I asked Kelbalba what Lut would like.

"In my village, the dwarf girl put him between her legs. He likes *that*." She could be coarse enough, and I had heard plenty from her, which no longer made me start. "From a princess, just a kiss."

So I kissed Lut's brow. I gave him some raisins, too. The winter fruit that year was very succulent. Perhaps he was truly pleased, because before spring, I was doing rather better, though I had a great way to go.

It seemed to me I had certainly been forgotten by all the palace. Udrombis had spent no time on me after the first interview, and I scarcely remembered her, only her important name. Ermias was much away. For Klyton—well, I had no word at all. One day I took off the colcai bracelet which, till then, I had worn every hour, even in my pain. It left a green mark on my wrist.

Torca noticed quickly.

"Where is your bangle?"

I said nothing. Ermias, who sometimes attended me in the evenings when I was in my right mind, had tutored me too, in the hauteur of my rank.

Torca said, "You should wear his gift. "He gave it you to bolster your endurance and your spirit."

I shook my head. The cord had been dispensed with by then. But still, when I did such a thing when standing, a wave of vertigo might take me, and did so now.

As I stood at the floor's middle, on the tilting sea of pain, I heard Torca say, "It came from his first battle honors. The metal was taken from a foe's armor. A man the prince killed in war. Melted down and refashioned, for you."

Men killed each other in war. I had been told so. It was correct for them. Klyton was a hero, could be nothing else. I said, "I honor his present. I won't wear it again until I see him."

Torca, black and bulky, shrugged, and limped about. He did not dress as a priest away from the sanctuary, but in a gentleman's leather and linen. His wooden leg lunged like a cane, having no bending parts, as my feet did not. I had been shown I could only ever hope to shuffle.

I stood discouraged. The pretty bracelet had come from a man in death. Klyton, who sent me no word, had meant to help, but had no real interest in me. Doubtless, this was not unreasonable.

Across the room, Lut leered at Gemli. And she, royal and unflawed, her head poised high, looked away.

Winter passed like the moon. Spring spangle-veiled Oceaxis. I was steadier and walked with less pain. But I moved like a deformed old woman. I moved like a monstrosity. I had remembered my earlier name. Cemira—the *thing*. The bracelet lay in a box.

Late summer brought another small war, with the tribesmen in Ipyra, now. They said Glardor had refused to take another "spear-bride wife." Amdysos, Glardor's direct heir, was to have the treat.

Ermias went to watch the troops ride back into Oceaxis, I had declined to go. I would have to leave off my unmanagable silver feet, and be carried in my chair. I had torn my hair and wept, again. Lut crouched in the sunset, watching me, and from the town, once or twice, I heard the far notes of trumpets.

What can there be for me? My thought, in darkness. *Whatever I do, there is nothing for me.*

Still sometimes, my stumps sloughed off the wrecked skin. But for the rinses of Kelbalba, I would have stunk, to add to my horrors. Instead, the room smelled of medicine, as if for someone chronically sick.

If this is my portion now, how shall I live?

I thought I would die soon, and did not care.

Then in the night, I woke to silence but for the rasping of crickets beyond the window. Somewhere a kitri sang, as it had in the groves, but fitfully, a broken song.

A shadow bent over me.

I was afraid, as never before.

"What do you want, old woman?" And then—how cruel, how terrible these words: "Don't you know, old crow, you're *dead?*"

"Am I?" she said, indifferently, Crow Claw, who was a ghost. "Well, never mind it."

Then she painted something cool on to my legs, and—just as if Kelbalba had told her—all over my nonexistent feet, following their shape exactly.

The lamp before Gemli had burned very low. I could scarcely see Crow Claw, but yet I could not make a mistake.

"No one loves me," I said. It was not the cry of a child. I said it, in a way, to excuse myself. The rotting of my skin, my loneliness and inability.

Crow Claw said, "Then you must love yourself enough for two, or three."

When I woke in the morning, the light shone like silver all over the room—for someone who had not been there had pulled back the drape. The silver feet seemed to be dancing a little, in their corner, as if they had been skipping about all night, and only now settled to pretend they were still.

I had heard the whispers—Ermias—of how my own unattached feet were glimpsed in these rooms. Hetsa, my mother, who had not wanted me, appalled by such sightings, had grown ill and died suddenly.

As I looked at the silver feet I thought, *Not I, but they know how.*

Presently, after the morning rituals, I was put into them and I myself laced the ribbons, which were new again that day. I have heard of something like this in trying to master another tongue—though I did not myself find it so. All at once—it is in your hands, and under your heart.

I took my honey cup, half full, and walked over to make an offering to ugly, grinning, sensible Lut.

Kelbalba gasped.

She said, "Done!" And then, "Do you know? Can you do it again? For when Blackie comes? He's too clever, that one. I'd like to see his face."

"You lost your bet any way," I said.

"Never had bet. What do you think me? I was trying to make you spit fire, girl. But now you're *walking.*"

I was. It would need much burnishing. It would need great pains, of care not hurt, to get it right. I have heard them say, years later, that Calistra did not take steps, but glided, as if on runners, and pulled by some invisible uncanny creature to which she had harnessed them.

The feet slid along the floor. One could not raise them, or barely. They knew their way, my body followed, easy, in the dance. They made a faint *ssh-ssh*, the leather soles over the metal. So yet, I was a snake.

8

Annotation by the Hand of Dobzah

Seeing it is one of my tasks to lace on to my mistress Sirai, every morning, her Feet, I will repeat now that they are no longer of bright silver. She lets them stay tarnished black, though clean within, and refilled at intervals with down. Of course, her lowest legs are scarred quite massively, she calls these marks her "hoofs," and laughs at them.

I believe that if it cost many in the beginning such work to walk, they would crawl about till the end of their days.

She has seen what I write and says I must strike it out. She tells me all men, all women, are different from each other, what is simple to one may be a severe penance to another, and conversely. She says that in her walking she was motivated by her love, and since love has always motivated her, and is the gift of God, she cannot be judged, nor any other less fortunate.

I therefore pretended to erase what I had written, but have decided to let it alone. It is like her to say what she has said. But I would have no one think that she did not achieve a great thing. That would be to mislead and wrong those who read here, far more than my mistress.

The Sun shrine at Airis stood—perhaps still stands, for strangely, I do not know—above the town, but away, facing the mountain across the vineyards, grain fields and orchards of the plain. It is an hour's ride from the palace-fort, by a good road.

Steps cut white in the hillside lead there, to the sacred groves of marroi and pine. The cedar of the god's shade leans through yellow Maiden willows to a spring, which is reckoned healing.

The shrine is foursquare, a roof of gilded tiles on pale walls, with •deep ruby pillars. The priests' house, with its guest quarters and rooms of meditation, stretches down the slope behind, through the trees. You are meant not to see it, for the Sun, in his aspect of hunter and priest, likes solitude.

Red grapes wound around the lintel in summer and fall. No one stops them, they are the god's bounty, like all things that grow and live. You see, I cannot give up speaking as if the shrine remains. Like all things of a god, of course, even if brought down, it does.

Klyton tied his horse by the cedar, where a trough was filled up daily for animals to take refreshment. He drew out the bronze cup and drank from the spring. It was a day of heat. He was nineteen, soon to be twenty.

Going into the porch of the shrine, he saw it cool, and smoky with shadow within. You could just see the glimmer of the god at his altar. Klyton touched the bell that hung outside.

After a minute, a priest came up the hill, and surprised Klyton, jogging his memory out of place.

"Are you here, Torca?"

"My lord," said black Torca, approaching with his dragging walk, but a man of power now, in a white robe, the palms of his hands painted red, and a gold round for the Sun on his forehead. "Please be aware, sir, my service is here. However much I take joy in serving you elsewhere, when I may."

Klyton nodded. "I beg your pardon. I didn't mean to insult your vocation, Torca. It was any way a priest I wanted to speak to. But—since it's you—can you tell me how my sister does?" Torca stood. Below, the spring sounded its ruffling rilling music. A harsh bird called in the sky, and Klyton glanced up. "They said there was a giant eagle spotted over Airis. Is it true?"

"Perhaps, my lord. I've not seen it. Meanwhile, your sister has no need of me. I believe she's written you a letter."

"Has she? I haven't had it. Or—perhaps. The last fighting—you'll have heard. A horde of bandits under Koi. I've been busy."

"No doubt. No doubt your sister will have expected no reply."

"But you say she doesn't need you. What is it? Did she give it up?"

Torca stood on. Then he looked past Klyton, who was if anything an image of the Sun, into the plain below.

"No, my lord. She doesn't need me now because she's learned all I can teach. Kelbalba stays for her massage, that's all."

"Then—can she walk?"

"Didn't you suppose, sir, she'd learn? You were so full of hope and passion at first, when you persuaded me to go."

Klyton stared into Torca's black eyes. "Are you chiding me?"

"Yes, sir."

"Very well. I've been remiss. It isn't I hadn't thought of her at all. Is she as pretty as—what is it—two years ago?"

"My lord, there are no women of the line of Akreon less than lovely."

Klyton raised his brows. "And she *walks*?"

"Like a goddess. I don't lie. I never expected it, but I'm used to rough and ready men in the wars. She was trained like a dancer. She moves—like a dance. Slowly, you understand. She can never run, or hurry. She'll never climb a stair without her cane. But on level ground, on the floors of a palace, my lord—well. You should go and see."

"Is she in the life of the court?"

"No."

"Udrombis, then, knows nothing of it?"

Torca said no word.

Klyton, feeling himself to be a boy again, drew himself up, royal and tall and hard with Sun. "I'll see you're rewarded properly, Torca, beyond the fee. And the woman—Kelbalba, was it? She must have something, too."

Torca unnervingly bowed. He showed Klyton that Klyton was sacrilegious, reducing a priest of the Sun to a servant who had done a service.

Klyton worked a ring off his finger. It was heavy gold with a green beryl. "I'll give this to the god. To thank him. After that, can I talk to you, as a priest?"

"I should guess so, my lord."

"It's about the Race."

When the Sun declined and evening drew on, flocks of birds fluttered up from the plain, to feed by the spring, where the priests left grain and seeds. They were the creatures of heaven. One heard at this hour, over their twittering as they gorged, then settled in the groves, the voice of the white pet cat, sacred to Phaidix, meowing discontentedly, shut in the priests' house. At other times she might do as she pleased, but this hour was given safe to the birds.

Klyton, having prayed, and presented a young buck deer to the god, watched out the evening offering to the Sunset.

Do not forget us . . .

He frowned as he listened. What had he done that evening before Akreon died? He had been off somewhere with Amdysos, and later they had played the board game in Udrombis' rooms. And neither won.

Amdysos was at Oceaxis with his unwanted wife, Elakti. She was the bony, sallow daughter of some chief-king at Ipyra. Amdysos had had her; despite Glardor's performances, it would have been an insult to her and her clan not to have done so, and wars once had been founded on less. One year later, she had borne a girl, as skinny and ill-favored as she. Amdysos said she wailed at him, the mother, growing dangerously hysterical, something the women of Ipyra were famed for. He avoided her as much as honor allowed. Glardor the Farmer had been at fault here. For Glardor himself should have wed her. It would have been a greater honor for her kin, and the King would have more excuse to let her alone.

The problem was, any way, finding sufficient to do. By now some position should have come the way of Amdysos, the last King's last son. But he was only *there*. The bandits of Koi, a task really beneath them, had been a diversion, for such Suns as Amdysos, Klyton, and those others, children of the lesser queens, who thought themselves worth more than a seat at the tables in the Hall.

Klyton had put this by.

He wanted the Sun Race. For this he had come up here. Since sixteen three times he had been left out, while Amdysos had raced twice. And, once, had won. But it was more than that. You could not speak, even brother to brother, of what lay within the caves of the mountain. It was a passage into manhood, needful as war, and sex.

Now Klyton came to ask the god to relent, to select him, and if not, to tell him why.

Amdysos had said, "You take it to heart too much."

"It's my right."

"If the god doesn't choose—"

"Oh, and did the Sun choose Elakti for you?"

They had not parted friends.

Observing the priests, Torca as well, at their own measured life, and presently eating in the house at the long scrubbed table, with its earthenware bowls and cups, and he, a King's son, in one of the five princely chairs reserved for princes and kings, Klyton reasoned with himself. He doubted that the lots were connived at. Where would be the sense or gain? And besides, it would be a blasphemy.

Even so, coming here, making a lavish offering of gold, incense, and meat, gifts to god and priests alike, Klyton felt quite strongly the answer could not be cold.

He ate sparingly, as they advised, and went after supper with the old slave woman, who served the altars, the only woman allowed to attend there.

As they crossed the woods on the hill, the dark had roosted like the birds, folding down its broad inky wings, and stars blazed in patterns. Only the spring sounded now. The Heartbeat, unheard. And though the white cat passed, and the old woman saluted her for Phaidix's sake, the cat was silent as a ghost.

On the threshold of the guest cell where he was to commune with the god, through the night which was the shadow of his day, Klyton stopped still. The old woman pulled off his boots, strong as an ox, and looked into his eyes.

He had thought she was probably senile, but now, in starlight, Phaidix's moon not yet high, he saw the curious intelligence in her face.

"Ask him, and he will," was all she said, the ritual words. Before she went, he pressed a silver coin into her hand. Then she said, "Thank you, lord master. May it be a good dream." But then again, as she went up the hill to the house, he heard her laugh, short and sharp, like a fox's bark.

When he had shut the door, he undid his belt and took it off with the sword and knife. He stripped in the windowless place, and laved all his body with the chilling water in the urn.

Then going to the altar at the room's center, he lit, with the tinder, the single lamp.

Coppery light rose up, and touched the ceiling, which was only a foot above him.

Klyton spoke softly, wondering if any listened. Whatever else, the god would do so.

"My fourth time to be drawn for the Sun Race. Your holy number is five. But *now* I must have it. I *ask* it of you. Or tell me why not."

The flame curled over in the lamp. Klyton smelled a powdery, fermented smell. It was some drug in the oil. Well, the god spoke through a dream. If you did not sleep, how could he reach you?

Klyton went to the pallet and lay down.

For a moment, it was the cell, and dark but for the lamp. And then a gleaming copper column stood up through it, and through the room the priests were passing in their white robes, through the very walls, and next right through each other. And as this happened, sparks were struck body upon body, and hovered unextinguished in the air.

Klyton, Klyton, said a voice.

"I am here."

But it said nothing else.

Instead the ceiling dissolved, and he saw the sky of night, sequined with too many stars, each brilliant as a jewel, as the Daystar herself.

Klyton felt himself leaving his body. For a moment he fought this—and then he went up, and a power coarsed through him like nothing of the earth. And opening great wings, he soared out into the highest air, up among the stars, that were now each large as a queen's silver mirror, hanging, turning and chiming about him.

He knew himself. He was the great eagle above the peak of the mountain. He felt his goldenness, the wings like flame, the beak of metal, and the eyes that were suns by night.

He flew.

Below, Akhemony, but more—the other lands that lay about her skirts, Ipyra, Uaria, and islands that drifted out like pebbles on the glittering darkness of the sea.

The world was his subject. It was his.

Again the voice spoke to him.

Not before, since then it was not yours. Now is the time for you.

He turned, wheeling, and saw his shadow skim over the earth in the shape of a sweeping sword.

Fire buoyed him up. And then he felt the silken rope which hung from his claws.

He looked. Though free to fly through the roof of the gods, he was secured safely to the mountains and the land. A being that was partly a woman and partly a serpent, held him, her slim white hands gripped in and gripping his claws, her face upturned, stretched and exquisite, like the face of a girl in sexual ecstasy, which first he had seen at Oceaxis.

Her mirroring silver tail coiled down and down.

He might fly as he wished, and she would anchor him. Though he might touch the gods, become the Sun, she would keep for him the citadel of the mortal ground.

Fire and air. Earth and water.

A paean of glory and gladness roared in him and seemed to burst him asunder, just as orgasm had seemed to, that first time. But it was life, not Death. And the god had answered all.

Riding to Oceaxis, Klyton's two attendants found him unusually quiet. Normally he would speak, and joke with them, from time to time. He was one of those princes who, from his height, stayed gracious, even amiable and entertaining, when things went well. Upset or angry, he was seldom unfair, but often terse. They thought now this was the case, and let him be.

The road was excellent, and they only stopped once, for an hour, at noon. They reached the town at Oceaxis after midnight, skirted it, and went on to the palace.

They then expected he would lie in a little the next day, but he was awake before dawn. He went up to see the Dawn Offering on the East Terrace.

After breakfasting, he was gone, with only the slave boy, who carried, in a roll of parchment, the astonishing thing the old woman had found, on the threshold of the shrine at Airis.

A slave opened the double doors, and Klyton entered the outer room. It was not so very large, this former apartment of one of the lesser Daystars, but pleasant enough, with a pool, a tiled floor, and a big turtle lying dozing there.

From the inner room came a faint noise of a slow drum, playing between the Heartbeat.

"Tell her," he said, "her brother, Prince Klyton, is here."

The slave bowed again, very low. Then she folded her hands, eyes lowered, and said, "You can't go in, my lord. None of her ladies is here."

"Then fetch one. Go on, hurry up."

He did not speak roughly; the slave was pretty and had behaved correctly. She ran out, and he sat down on one of the chairs to wait.

Behind a screen of sea-ivory and oak, stood the bed of the chief lady, his sister's Maiden, who should be here. Probably, if she was absent at this hour, she was in another bed entirely.

Did everyone treat Calistra so carelessly? Only the slave had had decorum, and she was a child.

Then the outer doors opened and a short but massive woman entered. She had rings of copper on her bulging arms, worn quite bare like a man's, and a scarred cheek. She glared at him, making him want to laugh, to charm her.

He rose, as if for a queen.

"Lady, I'm Calistra's brother."

Kelbalba glared on. "Honor to you, prince, Son of the Sun. Which brother?"

He did laugh now. And through her eyes then flicked a glint of disapproving approval—a look he was used to from all sexes.

"The brother who sent Torca to her. Klyton."

"Ah," said Kelbalba. "My paymaster."

"I stand reproved," he said. "I gather I haven't paid you enough. But I heard you were any way beyond price, Kelbalba."

At her name, evidence he had recalled it, and once meeting her, she seemed slightly mollified, and stopped pretending she herself did not recall.

"The Maiden Ermias is away," she said. He noted, she did not gossip or imply anything bad. "But I can be your chaperone, if you wish to go in. My lady's at her exercise, but everything's quite in order. No harm." She moved towards the doors. "She glad will be you come here."

From the lapse of her syntax, he sensed a genuine feeling. Klyton said, "Wait. Would it distress her, do you think—not to announce me. I'd like—to see her."

Kelbalba frowned. "Spy on her, prince? Catch her out?"

"No. I fear she'll be angry with me, or cold. Or she'll cry. I've not been as attentive as I should. I'd like to look at her, once, before anything else starts."

"Oh, she isn't that way," said Kelbalba. "Still. Let me look first. Then, if I say, you can."

"Thank you, lady." He was mischievous. He glowed like the Sun outside.

"Who is this lady?" snapped Kelbalba. "I was born a slave and freed for the stadium, like a horse."

Then she went to the middle door, and undid it a crack. She peered in, and now he heard the notes of a shell-harp with the drum, and a soft, rhythmic whispering, as of a heavy silken gown.

After a moment, she removed her face and showed it to him, blank. She stepped back, and gestured him to do what she had done.

She said after, "Another, I'd have thought he only wanted to check his money well spent. But he was like a bridegroom with a chance to see the bride before they meet. A heat came off him. He smelled *good*, like new bread and oil of cedar. Who wants to say no to beauty?"

Klyton did as Kelbalba had, what women did, peeping round the door. But his self-irony at this was gone in one moment. Because, in this way, unseen, he saw Calistra *dancing*.

The inner room was finer. Akreon had always been generous, and Hetsa, who was Calistra's mother, was a stupid woman by all accounts. She would have thought to have the best in her privacy, not make an impressive show outside to visitors.

Snake-topped red pillars held the ceiling, and on the walls was a delightful sensuous mural, of girls and young animals, and Gemli in her golden shrine with something grey crouched before her, a sort of dwarf. They were sharing a peach and a cup of wine, it seemed.

On the smooth reflective floor, the harper sat with the great white shell, flushed pink and strung with red-washed strings, which fell out in tassels over his knee. The female drummer drummed, a black musician, from Artepta, probably. The harper must be sworn to Daia Donis, that is, proven aroused only by his own gender, or he would never have been permitted unwatched in the room of a young Akhemonian princess. Customs elsewhere, of course, were more slack, as if male artists had no weapons.

The girl moved over the floor, and light fell on her from the wide window, the flame of sunlight rising up on the Lakesea.

She had her back to him, and her hair was a sheet of quivering, glistening blond-whiteness shot with threads of gold, a substance that, if it could have been woven on a loom, would make rich the one who sold it. It fell to her thighs, glimmering and swinging, heavy yet weightless, flaring out a little at her movements, like frayed silk, or crystal foam from the morning sea.

Her white arms, sleeved in open pastel ribbons, were like snakes . . . turning, boneless.

All the while, she glided forward, away from him, *glided* as if on *wheels*—slowly, slowly, to the beat of the drum. And then, astonishing him—she slid her left foot to the side, her skirt rippling as it followed the silken action of her leg, and dipped over sideways from the waist down and down, almost touching the floor, brushing it with her luminous cloud of golden hair.

He would have believed at that second this could not be Calistra. He understood as much. But in the very instant he must have doubted, the light struck off a flash. She wore—not silver shoes—but feet of silver, the very feet he, Klyton, had discussed with Torca, saying she was too fair to have anything less.

And then, swimming through air, turning, her waist that swayed like a supple slender stem, the curve of hips, the line of her breasts, full for a girl's, high and pointing so the mouth went dry, and, so around, facing now the door, gliding now towards the door. The whisper of a mysterious robe was the susurrous of her feet upon the floor.

Serpents, her arms, her body, and her hair floating out behind her now. In the heart of the gold, a white throat, and poised upon it, a face so beautiful, so remote, lost in the dance—it was barely human.

He had meant to push the door wide and surprise her. A young man's trick.

But instead, he drew back. He let out the breath he had been holding.

It was this she heard.

Through the door-crack, he saw her stop quite still. She held up her hand, and the music broke off.

Then Klyton made out, as seldom consciously he did, the Heart beating from the mountain. And his own heart, going rather faster.

"Who's there?"

It was a girl's voice. Clear and musical. But from that alone, he could never have guessed. As he had not on the shore two years ago.

Then he pushed the door, drawing himself together, upwards, swelling, swaggering, to display his glamour, trying to ignore that another part of him was also doing exactly this, upright as a rod of bronze, to greet his sister.

Annotation by the Hand of Dobzah

She laughs at this point, my mistress, and says, "They will think it some silly old woman's fancy that once she was young and beautiful. Never mind. It's only as he told me, after. Unless he lied, which others might have, perhaps."

I will therefore say here, that since I am half the age of Sirai, I never saw her as a young woman, though as an older woman she was and is impressive enough. In my childhood though, I heard her spoken of by those who saw her, unveiled, in her youth. Women can be jealous, but she was seemingly too astonishing to inspire that. Instead, one likened her to a rose, and one to a star. The name he gave her, the Prince Shajhima—*Sirai*—means, as we know, The Risen Moon.

I say no more.

In the morning I rose early, because I would generally wake early. I bathed, and ate the fruit and drank the juices they brought me. Then they painted my face—only dark for my eyelids and around my eyes, some color for my mouth. It was the etiquette of a princess.

I dressed in something light, and then did my exercises. In the midst of these, as I was going about to music, he arrived.

When he threw open the door, it was if the Sun burst in through another window.

He was all gold. I could hardly see him.

I did not know who it was.

Within my memory, where I had kept him, he had grown almost faceless. The glimpses, now and then, at the temple, had not restored him. He had lost his features, like a statue, to the weather of my emotions.

In the middle of the floor I stood rooted. The musicians scrambled up, bowing low. He was a prince—a king—what did I know?

I bowed, I think. Perhaps not.

He walked forward, then he stopped.

He said, "You come to *me*, Calistra."

For myself, I moved like a fool. But when I was close he caught my hands.

"My beauty!" he exclaimed. "Oh, the God, oh Calistra. Best girl. If you weren't my sister, I'd wed you."

His face was full of fire. I mean, high-colored and also incandescently glorious. I knew him now, because he was all I had dreamed of, and if you dream of leopards, you know one after all, as it tears out your soul.

Presently he said, "Why are you crying? But I thought you might."

I said, taught by various rules, "I am glad you've come to see me."

"I was away too long. Forgive me. War—such things. But you, you've won all your battles."

I cried because he had said those words that damned me. From the women, in ordinary conversation, I had had my clues. Now he had told me. A girl did not marry her brother, here.

But he drew me close. The top of my head was at his breastbone. I heard his heart. It was the Heart of the World. I felt his heat, too, but did not know it for the lust the leather under his tunic kept from me. I felt also such power on him, as he did. He knew already, he was the chosen Sun—and yet, did not know.

Wishing to die, between joy and despair, I sensed his destiny in the same half-hidden way, the gifts which he brought from the shrine at Airis.

When he summoned his slave and gave me, out of the parchment, the eagle's feather, I was not surprised.

"There was a larger one, can you credit it? They kept that, of course, for the god. But Torca said this one must be mine. And I give it to you."

Set quill-down on the tiles, it reached to my breast. It was tawny, marked black at the root, with edges like raw saffron. The tendrils were like wire. When I touched them, they gave off a thrumming sound, like a ghost harp.

"For you," he said again. Then, "Calistra."

These silver feet were not the first he sent me. I had outgrown those. Kelbalba said my spirit-feet, those I had left behind, possessed each pair. Now as I stood before him, I felt them. They tensed and tingled.

I wished to die. I longed to live.

And I lived.

Soon after that—I do not think we said much more—Ermias returned. She was flustered, but Klyton showed her at once he was not out to disgrace her for her absence.

He said he would have people come to us after the noon meal, jewelers and those with cloth. He said she was to make me ready to visit the palace Hall tonight. And she must attend me.

"You're a lovely woman," said Klyton, to Ermias, "You're not only a guardian now, you're also her Maiden. Choose as well for yourself. Something fine. And some jewels. I expect you to be expensive, or I'll be angry."

Ermias was breathless. When he was going out, he caught her and kissed her mouth. I did not see this, although I heard her gasp.

She was as full of him any way, through the afternoon, as if he had had her, electric as storms. And she talked as if privy to his thoughts.

This would be a show of me, tonight. Even the Widow-Consort was still at Oceaxis. Only the Great Sun—Farmer Glardor—was missing, off, as so often in recent years, on his estates. Amdysos took the King's place at the Dawn and Sunset rituals. And tonight, I too, should be there.

She was also pleased with me, Ermias. Now I was bringing her to the Sun's center, where she had been meant to be. She said, not describing it, because to tell me now that once I had had to crawl on hands and knees, did not seem fitting to her—that she had not mislaid my kindness to her when I was a child.

I had no will to choose anything from the overwhelming display in the outer room. I sat stroking the turtle, properly indifferent, actually stunned. But Klyton had told Ermias she must try to match my garments to my hair, and so she took for me the white silk, and over that a skein of translucent Bulote web-gauze streaked with gold.

Cunningly, she chose silver ornaments for my ears and wrists, but for my neck a snake of rolled gold, with eyes of emerald. In this I think she was only naive—I, the serpent, and *he* green-eyed. Or not. Who knows now, and I cannot ask her.

For herself she selected a dark wine-red material. And for her jewels, only a necklace of copper flowers, set with tiny coins of garnet. It would be valuable enough to add to a dowry. She would assure him later, in the dark, she had wanted a token only, since it came from him.

Women stitched all through the afternoon. Sometimes they sang as they worked, as rowers do.

After they had bathed me and laved me with essences under Ermias's eye, after I had been fitted and dressed, my waist and arms cinched with silver, my ears hung with it, gold on my neck, my hair plaited, piled up, let down, and woven everywhere with little bees of green lapis, I sat in my chair, nearly as sick as I had been when a child.

"You must also wear this," said Ermias, and brought me a bracelet, the dancer of colcai he had given me before.

"No," I said. "Put it away."

It was the past. I was afraid of it. I must not love him. Yet, living, I died of love.

The strong wine of Uaria steadied me. Kelbalba, who stood by, told me a story to divert me, as they painted my face again, and put gold on my fingernails to match the gold nails of my silver feet.

"The Sun's Isle. There is a wine from there," said Kelbalba. She held one of my hands, careful not to spoil the drying paste. "But it poisons. There are monsters on the Isle and only heroes go there. There were priests there once, who guarded the piece of the Sun which lies there, in its temple. But they died. The strength of it was too great for them. It takes a hero, to survive."

When I stood up now, I was taller than she, though not quite finished growing.

Kelbalba gave me my new cane. She leaned up to my ear and whispered.

She said, in Artepta, in Charchis, brothers and sisters were sometimes wedded. She said her brother had slept with her for a year before they were found out. She said he was the only one who thought her desirable. He said she was a lioness and did not need beauty. It was he who gave her the amulet of Lut.

Ermias grew restive and told Kelbalba to stop muttering at me. But as we walked up through the palace, towards the Sunset, Ermias added I had a better color now, the women had done wonders with their cosmetics.

9

On the stairs, I was very frightened. It was the precipice flight of perhaps one hundred and seventy-four steps, that had winded Mokpor the merchant, up to the East Terrace and the great Hall.

Of course, I had become used to negotiating the stairs to Phaidix's garden, and certain of the women's apartments in the palace, where Ermias had taken me. But no stairway like this one. Besides, the cane was new—silver on pale wood, with a globe at its top of electrum. I did not trust the cane yet. It was too handsome.

Ermias walked behind. Her puffing kept my spirits up. We were both in difficulties and afraid of disgrace.

We paused at the landings for some while, admiring the forms of the Sun god.

At the top, we looked as if from a mountain, to the Lakesea. Ermias breathed in great chunks of air, and I shook. But it was a fine evening, and the water was flat and soft-looking, shadowy under a shadow-gathering eastern sky.

Two or three dozen people were on the East Terrace. They gazed at us, and gazed. When we were ready, that is, when Ermias was ready, we went on, she a pace behind me, haughty as a queen. Our slow gait attracted some attention too. For myself, I felt it painfully, but I soon heard afterwards that watchers decided me in turn intimidating. One who goes in dread and abjection hurries to get by. Who walks so leisurely must be proud, and cool.

I have let Mokpor already describe the Hall, but I was no less a stranger to it than he, and was filled by wonder, more so perhaps because it might also be said to be mine. The columns were gigantic, and the alabaster lamps of Artepta, already being lighted, and burning rosy on their stands of gilded bronze, lit every aspect, and every fleck of gold. The wall painting was of an old war. It had been done in the time of Aiton, who was the great grandfather of King Okos. They had not stinted on the blood, which one must observe all around, and fallen men stuck through, during dinner.

The floor, which Mokpor had not taken in—he was always a man for looking higher than he found himself—showed on the east side of the Hearth, the formation of the world; that is, the Sun Lands. One saw there how the continent, with its central sea and rays of islands, made, bizarrely, occultly yet overtly, the shape of the Sun.

On the west side, beyond the Hearth, lay open sea, with monsters in it and imagined lands. Certain things had come from the wastes of water beyond Artepta, Charchis, and the Benighted Isles. Curious beasts, the pieces of broken ships. Now and then, too, some traveler, lost by the will of the gods, who in ancient times was thought a devil, and put to death. The last of these had been shipwrecked on a float of wood, with one of their robes for a sail, at Kloa, in the year Okos died. They were two men, and it was said they had had skin the color of smoke.

Though the Kloans were barbaric enough, they sent an embassy to Artepta, so to Akhemony. It took a year, two or three years, depending on the version of the story. By the time Okos heard, the two men were dead by their own hand. They had pined, refused to learn more than a scatter of the words of the Isles, spat upon the altars of our gods, wept and lamented, raising their eyes to the sky in a tragedy beyond local comprehension.

So many people were in the enormous Hall. On the Hearth the wisp of magical fire burned, and above, the Daystars leaned to receive it.

A little dizzy still, I moved on, as I had been instructed.

The sky beyond the west doors was turning apricot, and there the buzz of a multitude turned my belly to ice—cool I was, indeed.

All this while I had hoped—and feared—to see Klyton. Now I did so, far off from me as the sinking Sun.

He stood with Amdysos, whom I knew at once from memory and description. He wore the crimson color of the Sunset Offering, and looked utterly a King, at twenty-one years of age.

But Klyton wore dark purple, black leggings, and boots of black bullshide, his tunic with a border of broad red and gold. He seemed a King also. Of all Akreon's glorious sons, these two shone out. But had Glardor been there, Glardor the Great Sun, they said now he would have looked what he was . . . a farmer.

I was on the women's side of the West Terrace, though some women mingled more freely here. I noticed the greater ladies, older and more weighed with jewels, had kept decorously to the left.

From the town, the gongs were sounding, a rush of noise like insects, carried by the amphitheater of the shore.

Everyone seemed to have come out. It was all at once quite still. I held my breath.

A boy sang: "Splendor of leaving—"

Amdysos took the cup of incense and poured it down.

The Sun, orange in a mulberry cloud, dipped away. The Daystar hung like a polished diamond, or a tear.

Klyton—Klyton—the lines of his body, and his face, standing solemnly by. I cut myself upon his beauty. Pierced to the quick, I missed the Sunfall, I missed the incantation. I closed my eyes.

When I opened them, everyone was stirring. The sky was an extraordinary color, between amber and amethyst—how many Sunsets had I properly seen? I had seen *nothing*. Two rooms, a garden, the shore, a few apartments of the palace women, a temple. And—the House of Death.

"Are you well?" hissed Ermias in my ear.

"Yes."

As we straightened, two young lilting women came to me over the Terrace. Behind them, the smoke rose from the altar. The priest was going away. Amdysos, Klyton, had gone.

"Princess!" They were two I had met before, with Ermias; now they bowed to me, pink as the pearls of the outer seas. "Our lady, the Widow-Daystar Stabia, requests you will approach her."

That was his mother. Stabia. They said she had been the Consort's lover.

I glanced across the Terrace, emptying now, but for the knots of persons who lingered. Against the mauve-amber sky, a fat woman bulged, with her greying blonde hair intricately done. I would see, in a moment, she had green eyes—from her he had them, Klyton.

I realized he had asked this of her, publically to notice me. I knew also, she would tell Udrombis. Udrombis who, widowed ten years, was still a fabulous goddess of the court's female life. She would punish me if she did not like me—was that still true? Oh, yes. Oh yes.

Walking to Stabia across the mosaic, I heard the murmurs. *Who is she? Look how she glides along. Is she real, or a doll?*

They said, too, I was—delicious.

Then, I did not absorb a word.

My ears buzzed as the voices did. I saw a round blot of light on the sky, which held stout Stabia, standing among her women.

But when I reached her, and had bowed, she smiled at me, not friendly, but as one warrior greets another, matched, so far respectful.

"Princess. My son spoke of his sister. Your mother was the Daystar Hetsa, I think. Your father, of course, Akreon, the Great Sun, before his death."

"Yes, madam." My voice seemed far away. She heard it better than I.

"I'm glad to see you at last. You must sit by me at dinner. And your Maiden with mine."

Ermias beamed. I felt her smugness as my hands turned to snow, as I hung weightless on the Terrace.

"You're very kind, madam."

"No. Come on, look happy, now." She leaned forward, and smackingly kissed my cheek. "There. Let them talk about that."

Although now, I can look back and see others wrapped in scenes where, at the time, I was not present, this is one of the scenes I cannot, looking back, see well at all. It passed in a trance for me. I was stiff with fear. Yet bemused and dazzled, I believe I did not often, now, glance at my brother. But once, I do recall, when I did so, Stabia said to me with quiet sharpness, "They're a fine sight, I agree. But to stare too much at the men's tables can mean you're forward."

So I looked at the walls, with their safely gutted men, and the yellow columns. At the floor, which showed the world—*our* world.

The King's place, raised up a step or two, was void, of course. But I saw his Consort, who sometimes now spent her time at the court, a big, blonde, ordinary woman up on the left of the dais, and also Udrombis, in her chair by a pillar there. The blonde Queen was greedy but well-mannered. Udrombis the Widow ate sparingly, and drank a little wine. When the harper came in, she called him to her. He bowed to the Consort, but to Udrombis he kneeled—he was from the Eastern Towns.

She was truly like a lioness. Oddly, so was Kelbalba, whose brother had compared her to one. But how unlike. Although I had grown taller, Udrombis seemed to have kept pace. She was still a tower, and her ebony hair, roped with greyish silver, even now with one strand of white—they said she woke with it starting three days after Akreon's funeral—was her crowning magnificence. Her mourning robes were the color of a lion's pelt, and edged like that with black. She wore a necklace I had heard of, called the Seven Daystars, all large diamonds, cut so that they flashed and blinded.

I saw Elakti, too, the spear-wife of Amdysos, from my mother's Ipyra. She made ripples all around her, complaining about a fruit with a worm in it, of the heat, once slapping one of her women in full view. Stabia made no comment beyond a crunching little laugh.

The many dishes of food were exceptional. I ate almost nothing. Stabia did not prompt me. She showed me I should take an occasional morsel, and, unlike Elakti, praise it. These things got back to the cooks. As Elakti should have learned by now.

Stabia stopped me drinking too much wine in my confusion, urging Ermias to fill my cup with a juice of summer roses. This perfumed taste brings back to me always that night I can scarcely remember.

There were dancers from Oriali.

When the harper began to sing, the Hall fell quiet. At first the music was only a delicate sound. He had the male sithrom and plucked it with a strong hand brown as wood.

Then I heard the words. They were of a princess shut in a tower of bronze, noticed by the Sun god and carried away. It was an old tale, girls had swooned over it for centuries. But as I felt their faces turn, like grass-heads against the wind, I came to see that it was my cipher, I the girl shut away, that the power of the Sun and of life had rescued.

I lowered my eyes and bowed my head.

When the song was done and other ditties were sung, the princes performing with their own harps here and there, to a high standard that did not match the harper's, Stabia told me very low, I had behaved well. "What a son I have," she said. She sounded exasperated, and impressed, and—unsure.

He had gifted the man to sing as he had; one did not bribe a professional artist.

In the end, they threw open both sets of doors on the warm summer night, and people wandered on the terraces to view the stars, and look where the moon rose on the sea.

Stabia got up, and bowed to Udrombis, the blonde Consort—who was still eating—then swept me out with her own.

That was the end of my first evening in the Great Hall at Oceaxis. If he looked once at me there I did not know. I was as exhausted as if I had run upon my silver feet for thirty miles.

In the half dark under the stair, at the west end of the Hall, in the lower Sun Garden, Amdysos said, "I have to go in to Elakti tonight. It's six months since I visited her. She makes a fuss."

"I'd have her poisoned," said Klyton.

"No, you've a soft heart."

"Something else would be soft. I don't know how—"

"Well, let's not talk about it. I wanted to ask you about the girl."

"Oh, which?"

"Don't play, Klyton."

"You mean our sister?"

"We have so many. I mean the girl who had silver shoes."

"No. Her feet are silver. Like her eyes, in all that pale gold."

"I thought so. It's the crippled one, isn't it? Cemira—isn't that her name?"

"*Calistra*. The other name's a curse her bitch of a mother put on her. I've learned a lot. Do you know, she was sent to Koi? To Thon's Temple—like some useless peasant brat they couldn't afford to feed."

Amdysos looked towards the mountains, just visible, painted in metal by a lifting moon.

"It was harsh. But this can't be right, not this."

"What?"

"The thing you did. Getting Stabia—and the song. Udrombis, I gather, had looked after the child."

"Udrombis left her to grow up in two rooms. Only her woman showed Calistra any life."

"And you, of course."

"You think it was a mistake. But you *saw* her."

"I agree, she's a pretty little thing. Maybe it will be of use. A good marriage—why not. But Klyton—"

"What *now*?"

"She's in love with you."

Klyton turned round and gazed long at Amdysos. Klyton's face showed nothing at all. He said, at last, "She looks up to me. Why not? She's hardly seen any men."

"She is in love with you. And—Klyton, her body's warped. Can you doubt her mind will be? It isn't her fault. Poor creature. But you've brought her on too far, and much too fast."

"You'd have left her with Thon. The *poor creature*. I recollect this conversation with you that day at Airis. You were in error then, and still you are."

Amdysos shrugged. "All right. We must differ."

"At Airis," said Klyton suddenly, "I shall have the choosing lot, and race.

"You can't know."

"Can't I. Watch it occur. And I'll take Calistra there. Yes. She can come to the Sun Games, and hold the Vigil with the rest, when we ride through the caverns."

"Don't do it, Klyton. You're making too much of her. What will happen when you lose interest, as you must?"

"Maybe you can't yet give me orders, Amdysos. Maybe you aren't yet King."

Amdysos stepped back. His face fell, and set. "What are you saying to me? You can't think that of me—that I dishonorably want Glardor's place."

"How do I know what you want. You get the best of every bloody thing. You've got your own command for battle. You race every year at Airis—"

"Not every—"

"And say not one word of what is in it."

"I can't. It's sacred. It's the god's."

"You can do anything. You can prod your ugly mad wife from the backlands, that would make any other man puke, at will. And you know my sister is an incestuous little poor deformed not-even-human whore, better left to die on a mountain. What can I know of *you*, Amdysos?"

"You'll be sorry you said this, when you consider."

"Who'll make me sorry?"

"We're not boys, to scrap over an argument."

"No. Not boys." Klyton turned and strode three paces. Then he stopped. And Amdysos, kingly and silent, clenched in his breathing.

Klyton said, "What you've said tonight, shows you to me. I thought you someone else."

"For the sake of the God!" Amdysos lowered his voice. "Be reasonable."

"I would rather," said Klyton, "shine."

He passed through the garden, brilliant by day with red and gold, the colors of the god, black now with night, spearing a path by the torch-glare of rage. He shone indeed, like arson through the dark.

After a few minutes, Amdysos, heavy as lead and conscious of duty, climbed to the apartment of Elakti, where the women were in tears, a mirror on the floor, and vials of scent broken. She shrieked and wept, and when he possessed her, later, sunk her nails into his back in hatred, not pleasure.

But Klyton found Ermias where he had arranged to do so. He complimented her on her dressing of Calistra, he asked two or three things about Calistra, before they lay down. He knew the hands with which Ermias stroked and clutched him, had run over Calistra's skin, and that Ermias's mouth had kissed Calistra's mouth in childhood. When Ermias screamed, he saw Calistra bent backward under him, her hair streaming, her face in ecstasy, a silver snake, the feather of an eagle, and broke inside the body of Woman like the boiling sea.

10

Udrombis lay sleeping in the wide carven bed. Four pillars run about by golden vines upheld a canopy and curtains of white gauze, to keep out summer insects. Beyond this filmy box, the room was vast, lambent only with night. At the tall gold shrine to the Sun in his form of a young man, a vague glow in the lamp of yellowish alabaster, cast off strange verticals of dim shape, the edges of a clothes stand, a chair, a vessel on a table. Nothing more. The doors were shut and the Maidens slept in small rooms of their own. Outside, the guard who stood, a story down, was silent at his post.

The Queen opened her eyes. She was quite awake. She had trained herself to such alertness from her earliest youth, having heard a story once of war that came in the night, and of a warrior's preparedness.

Through the curtains, only the usual, things, darkness, hints of color from the lamp.

But then the lamp flickered, and went abruptly out.

This was not a cause for alarm, only someone would need to be reprimanded tomorrow. There could not be enough oil in the lamp, and it was impolite to let go out the light before a god.

Udrombis sat up, and pushed aside the curtain. She would refill and relight the lamp herself.

At this moment, she made out, black on black, the form of a woman, standing over against the closed doors which had not opened, about twenty-six sword lengths away.

Udrombis knew who this was. The one who had always been able to get in, anywhere and at all times. Crow Claw. The one who was many years dead.

The Queen rose. She did not attempt to draw on her mantle. She said, quietly enough, "What do you want, old woman?"

Crow Claw shook her head.

There was in the dark a shimmer all about her, so that she had become properly visible, the same as always, ancient in her black and ornaments. She held out her old hand, and from it poured a trail of thick, black, gleaming dust.

It hit the floor, and a spurt of light sprang up, like flames.

From this, smoke columned upwards, blacker than pitch.

In the smoke, a tiny thing, turning and flashing, fiery gold, small as a gnat.

Udrombis stood still, watching. There were tales enough of Crow Claw's embassies. Being dead now, she must come from the world below. She crossed the unpassable River Tithaxeli, without trouble, and reentered the earth at whichever spot she chose.

This must be, Udrombis thought, a warning of her own death. She had had no symptoms otherwise, and rather than horror, she was prepared to receive and employ the warning. In this way she would have space to do anything she thought needful, before her departure. Death's kingdom, she suspected, was not precisely as depicted by priests, and the simply religious. But even so, she had nothing to dread. She had lived firmly in adherence to the tenets of her class and kind. After all, if Crow Claw had withstood it, she, Udrombis the lioness, would certainly survive the journey. And in that place, it was possible she might be young again, even as young as twelve, her age when she had married Akreon. Thinking of finding him, himself a young man among the dead, she did not hanker to remain above ground.

The golden gnat flickering in the smoke had grown larger.

She saw now it had a shape. It was—a bird.

This seemed dainty at first, this tiny delicate thing, passing in and out of the post of smoke.

But now it had enlarged again, and so went on enlarging. It was not a sparrow of the aviary or garden. It was, in miniature, an eagle.

It soared and stooped, it circled. The size now of a house cat—she saw it had gripped something in its claws and pulled it from the smoke. Now it hurtled free into the ceiling—it was large as a dog, and its wings expanded, touching the rafters. In its grip was a sun disk.

Both eagle and disk, both swelling on and on, seemed made all of gold. They glittered, blazed. And the eyes of it, the apparition, were molten.

Surely this could not be a forecast of *Death*?

The beak was like golden steel. It parted and let out a bellowing scream.

Huge now, the size of the room, it spread the sparkling pinnions of its awful wings, and dashed straight at her, bearing the roof upon its back.

She heard its harsh rushing, the boom of its wings. She smelled its poultry smell, the stink of old blood, the cold spice of the upper airs. Its feathers struck her face, her breast, spun her. She dropped down on the bed. It felt of metal, every feather fashioned on the anvil of heaven. Its claws scraped over her back and the golden disk burnt her with a heat that came directly out of the sun.

When it was gone, the glare of it gone, the noise and heat and stink and terror, Udrombis got up again.

Crow Claw too had vanished away, and only the yellow lamp glimmered, full of oil and undisturbed, before the feet of the god.

11

Traveling to Airis, with the Widow-Queen's party, took some days. I went with Stabia, in my own litter slung between two horses, and Ermias sat with me. She was full of anticipation, yet bored. Then she would remember her new lover, Klyton the Sun Prince, would soon be at the palace-fort there, perhaps ahead of us. I had gathered enough from her indiscreet sighs and hints—she spoke only of a highborn dalliance—to have guessed. My feelings I cannot describe. Who has ever loved very young, and seen the lover go willingly to some close friend or enemy, will understand.

In turmoil I rode towards the mountain. And all about, Stabia and her women, Udrombis and hers—they said the Widow-Consort was not quite well, no one knew how, she was so strong—and several others thought appropriate to the journey. Needless to say, Glardor's left-at-home wife came too, but not Elakti. She must have been with trouble persuaded from it, for we had already been told, Amdysos was to race again, and this year Klyton, for the first, had been chosen by the lots.

Along with us went the summer baggage. A favorite bed, chairs, dishes, ornaments and clothes, instruments and embroidery stands, and even one of the lighter loom-frames, in parts, for Glardor's blonde wife liked her weaving as she liked her food.

My own baggage was slight.

The days were all dust. The land went up on the left hand, to hills and forests, from which shy, affronted deer sometimes looked down on us. To the right descended a plain with skirts of barley and wheat. There had been a giant she-pig hereabouts, some years before, but she had disappeared, and no one claimed to have killed her. Currently there were tales of enormous birds, whose wings spread broader than the height of three men. They had been seen fighting above the Sun god's shrine, and feathers fell like spears of iron and gold. Having been gifted with one, I hid it and kept quiet.

By night we were put into tents hung inside with soft perfumed draperies. Stabia was often alone with the Widow-Queen. Even I heard a joke or two, softly murmured. But Ermias said, decidedly, they were now too old for any such nonsense. Love-desire was for the young.

She, almost thirty, had put in her corner of our tent, a pink soapstone Daia, on a little stand. Every night, Ermias offered wine to her. Once Ermias reached a peak of pleasure in her sleep—or some other way—and cried out. I knew the sound, and pretended I had not heard, as usual. My pillow was wet. Unlike my Maiden, I made no noise over my crying.

The palace-fortress was rocks, with large stones stuck upon them, plastered only to the front a ripe fruit yellow. The columns were red as rust, but a tower ran up, and the walls were notched for shields, and for slingshot, arrows and spears.

We were there five days before all the princes and men had come to join us. Nine days before the sacred Race of the Sun.

I sat playing my sithra. I had made a new song to him, my brother that I must not love as I did. But I gave him the name of the Sun himself, so I might sing it, over and over, never mind who went in and out of my stony little room.

"Is that the Daystar's dusk lament for the Sun? How sad it is!" cried Ermias. "One would think you knew. You're a true artist, Calistra."

But I recalled how she had been vicious when I was a child, and jeered at my playing.

When she saw the tears on my face, she came to me, cuddling me in her warm arms. She plied me with dates and sweets. It was not her fault. Why should I expect her to refuse him, when I would have died under the wheels of his chariot?

Somewhere in the town, the women they called the Spiders of Phaidix, were spinning the Web for the Race. I knew nothing of it, or barely, everything was spoken in a code. It was sacred, one must not say too much. But now, as Ermias tried to console, I saw I had walked through a web in that disused room. It clung about my unfeeling silver foot. I did not fathom any omen.

Outside the narrow window, Airis rose, green and brass, to a violet pane of sky. One saw the Daystar often, morning, noon and afternoon, for the air was very clear. Eagles wheeled over. But they were only birds, seven foot of wings, no more.

When I did not go to dinner that night, the first night he was at the fort, he sent me next day a present.

It was a brooch in the form of the Daystar, gold-washed silver, as usually she was shown, with the Sun's rays behind her hair, and a tiny mirror in her right hand, this one of dark jade.

His letter said he was sorry to think I might be ill. He hoped I would, by that evening, be better.

Perhaps I was a spoiled child, who thought, by avoiding the social dinner again, I could make him come to me himself. But at Airis, the hall was much smaller, and crammed by nobles, dogs, servants and slaves. Traditionally they roasted the hunters' kill at the central hearth. Fat splashed, flames spattered. Scents of meat and perfume and the beeswax candles and the oil of lamps rose, and hung in a thundercloud under the blackened ceiling. When the lights were bright, the room seemed all eyes.

I had been afraid enough, these alien women around me, watching. Stabia with her perhaps-kindly hawk's green stare.

To sit so, packed in, boiling and stifled, and have him there, not even able to look at him, as a *forward* woman would—I could not bear it.

The second night, I kept to my room. And the third. Nothing was said. Not by Ermias, who, enraptured, crept away after the feast—to be with him.

After the noon meal on the fourth day, there was an upheaval from my slave and Ermias in the annex. Unannounced, Stabia swept in on me. Though padded with her fat, she had a presence.

When not sitting to read or play my sithra, I would pace slowly, endlessly about. Twelve or more years of sitting kept me now, even when not at exercise, on my feet.

She slapped together her hands.

"So, you're not sick."

Not knowing what to say, I said nothing.

Stabia pointed to my chair. "Sit down."

"*No*, madam—you must sit."

"That's better. Always recall, manners before all things. At least until one is a friend."

I blushed, and she sat in my chair. She waved me to the stool, and I accepted it. She watched me closely. She said, "You move like water flowing. In a slave-market you'd be worth a few coins, I can tell you. What do you think you are? Don't know. I'll help you, then. A beauty and a rarity. The Consort herself—oh, I don't mean *that* one, Blondie, I mean Udrombis—has told me you are her treasure. After the first night you came to the Hall, she said to me how pleased she was, you were worthy now of a Sun King. You should put faith in her. She's a being of the highest order. Now, why don't you come to the hall here at night?"

"I'm—I find it—I—"

"You're scared as a rabbit. Poor fool. Look at you. Give me your youth and half your looks, and a quarter your grace, I'd have the place on its knees. Learn to see in your mirror, Calistra. What metal is it?"

"Silver, madam."

"Electrum's better. You shall have one. Study yourself. Gods don't give you a gift to see it pushed under the bed like the night-pot." She took a candy from my dish, ate it, and took another. "Two are all I'll allow myself when visiting." She said, "All the court knows what Klyton's done for you. If you shut yourself away, you shame him."

I stared, astonished. "But—"

"Listen to me. A woman is an ornament in this world of ours. More than that, naturally, but we disguise it. He has made them notice you, and now you make it as if he came to table with his latest war trophy left off. They ask why. Was it dishonorably got? Is it worth less than appeared. Is he a cheat. What is it—do you hate him?"

"Hate—who?"

"My son. My only son. Klyton."

I felt the blood ignite in me, up the column of my body, from my loins to my heart to my forehead. Even my hair seemed alight. But I stared her out. She let me do this, then she nodded. "So it isn't hate. What would you do for him then?"

Everything lost, I tossed my head. "Die for him."

"*Good*. By the God's own Knife, I began to doubt you had the ichor of our house. But if you'd die for him, then to come to supper is nothing, is it? Eh? Well, answer."

Despite myself, I smiled. At this, Stabia smiled too.

"No, madam. I didn't understand."

"Oh, of course not. Now you do. You've had no proper instruction. This other thing . . ." she paused, and ate her second sweet, licking her fingers to get all. She said, "You're too young for it yet. I don't hold with this bedding at twelve, fourteen. Some are fit for it and some not. Girls now need longer. Flowers bloom at their own rate, and when you force them they lose their petals to spite you."

I was at sea. I gazed into her face, but now she looked out of the window at the mountain.

Stabia said, "He wants you, you know, just as much. He has that curly hussy out there because her hands have been all over *you*. How do I know? Amdysos sent him off to the groves. That was the first time for him. Seventeen is late. I've taken notice, since then. It was the Consort put me wise." Dumbfounded—he *wanted* me?—I waited.

"Let him be patient. And you. In a year, maybe. You'll need to be careful, but I'll see you have a woman who knows what you should do and take. Yes, you're royal, but the most you can hope for in the end, my dear, is some lesser king of another country. And *he* won't quibble if he doesn't have to take a dagger and skewer to open a woman of the Sun House."

Was I shocked? I doubt it. She spoke as freely as some of the Maidens, coarse and to the point. The sentiments for which, twenty years before she might have been killed, were not startling because they went against nothing in me. I wanted what she told me I might—incredibly—have. The long-term future, with its banishment and sordid little marriage to another, in this fire, meant nothing.

"While you're with us, you and he—why not. You can be my daughter. Under my wing. That will make it easy."

Returning to this now, I see that shocked I should have been. For Stabia went against her true goddess in this one matter. Suggesting that Klyton and I might be lovers, however carefully, however much unknown, was as far from the rules of Udrombis as the earth from the sky, To the Widow-Consort, a princess must remain a virgin before marriage, as surely as a prince should not.

I think therefore someone had unlocked for Stabia the closet of coming time, a very little way. Searching, I do not see that scene, nor guess how it had happened. But half the court, half the continent, played at magic. Someone had read some portent for her, perhaps, and telling her, Stabia had known a truth.

She had no shadow, yet somehow, without shouldering her fate, she was aware that in this year where I and Klyton would wait, all things must change. And she herself sail down the River of the Dead, leaving him behind upon the raft of mortal life.

12

Now I have come to that place where I must speak of something sorcerous, harrowing, unthinkable. It is not I do not know how to tell it, for I saw it, and need only relate what I saw. Nor is it I think you will doubt me, because if you have read so far, we have trusted each other, a little. No, it is only some things can never be consigned to paper, nor even to the stone and clay tablets of the priests. Some things are too big, and too inhuman. They should be written once in fire, or water, and then left to smolder out, or wash away.

Yet, I cannot proceed unless I speak of this, from which after-events hang like jewelry chains from a hook of bronze.

Thus:

The caverns at Airis, sacred to the god, run through one side of the mountain's base. There had been mining there two hundred years before, until signs from the god forebade it.

You descend the plain on the western side, into a lower plain, a valley, where the mountain veers up into heaven, and everything seems above you, the glinting eastern dot of the shrine, and south, the defence tower of the palace.

Here, on the plain's floor, was a stadium, where at this time, for three days—one of the Sun god's numbers—horse races were staged, wrestling and combats with swords, shooting with bows, and other masculine arts. But there were shows also about the stadium, racing dogs, lions who danced, and men who ate fire. All around, a market was set up, selling horses, the white sheep of the mountains, who have horns like the crescent moon; silks and scents and foods of every land known under the Sun. There were even little botched-up temples of many foreign gods. Bandri was there, whose priestesses, black and white, all with padded bellies, sold amulets and statues to women pregnant, or desirous of being so. And Lut I heard of, too, though I was not allowed to go, represented by a herd of men and women who, it was said, were freaks, one having an enormous head, and another a tail, and two girls, lovely as swans, but joined at the waist with only two legs between them. Although apparently, a pair of all the other things were located below the waist, or so Ermias, horrified, mentioned.

I felt quite sorry for Ermias now. I was kind to her. Then again, I was not frequently alone in her company, but in with Stabia's flock. Klyton, despite my—now desperate—nervousness, I had seldom seen in the fort, and then he never turned my way. He was most often with the chariots and horses at the stadium.

Before the vast doors, Torca stood, torch in hand, looking down into the valley.

From here, the two-horse chariots assembling on the racing track, seemed of a comfortable size to pick up in his palm. From their metalwork shot flares of light, and off the bridles and headstalls of the horses, trails like sparks. There was, at the Airis Games, no chariot race but this one. They would take one turn, pacing around the track, then come out on to the slope that led to the base of the mountain, where they must pause for the litany.

While the Race was run, a period of, perhaps, half an hour, or a little less, or a little more, the crowd in the stadium, which included the Great Sun himself, would stand. Not until the first and winning chariot burst from the mountain's gut, upon the opposite ridge, could any man, or woman, sit.

He had thought of the girl. She had been told to see to herself, having extra padding put inside the silver feet. And she might need her cane, and the arms of her Maiden and her slave.

Strangely, Torca wondered how this would be for her when she had grown old. She would not, surely, be able to do it then. But he did not think she would live much beyond forty years—the deformed from birth seldom did. Even he had now, with his leg, no long expectations for himself, and each year was a bonus. He had been careful to let her know none of that.

He turned his mind back to the ritual.

The young men, Suns, and nobles of the House, and this year princelings from other lands, had been cleansed. They had watched since last night's sunfall until the mid of night. Then they slept. They were cautioned. No women must be even in their thoughts, or anything else.

Breakfast was hearty, the meat of a boar, the Sun animal, with summer greens and barley bread. So much wine, no more.

After that, another bath, and the oils and unguents. Dressing in their finest—each looked more gorgeous than the morning. Like a bride on her wedding day, no man who rode the Sun's Race seemed less than beautiful.

In the caverns, it was possible to die. It did not happen often, but it might. Those who perished there went to the Sun Below, to serve, him through the region of darkness under the world.

The man who won was, for the next three days, the Sun himself.

Torca thought it might well be Klyton. Though Amdysos had triumphed before, he was too steady, too wise. A race needed fire. Especially a race to honor the Sun.

Across from Torca, the other chosen Priest of the Doors, face masked in gold, and in the black robe fringed by red that marked the Sunset-like descent into the caverns. Torca, beneath his mask, had cut and shaved off his beard. It grew quickly, and in two or three months would be as good as the old one.

In the sunlight, the torches were transparent, but bright from the terraces of the stadium. Yet it was the chariots were made of fire.

The caverns, a system of wide caves, had been fashioned with walks and drives, in the time of Aiton. Earlier it had been more dangerous. Even so, the workings of the old mine kept it treacherous enough, and on the walls, the arcane paintings, which it was blasphemy to speak of, could startle a newcomer, and even shy the horses.

Nevertheless his money would have been on Klyton, if it had not been sacriligious to bet.

The sky was very clear, and the Daystar showed, following after the Sun like a gold-white hole in heaven.

The chariots were turning now, coming around to where the slope began.

Everyone in the stadium was on their feet.

He must direct his mind inward, to clandestine, holy things. But Torca thought, *Have I forgotten something?*

It was as if someone had whispered to him, during the night. He had heard, and meant to remember, but forgot. There was now no help for it, for time moved onwards like the Sun.

His chariot was of red marroi, the sacred wood, and inlaid by gold-skinned bronze. He had had it built last year, for this. Sympathetic magic—by making ready for a thing, you caused it to happen. But Klyton had not been drawn to race last year.

Now it was refurbished, polished, like a red, silken mirror. He wore its color, and ornaments of gold. Every man there wore the Sun colors, even the Charchite prince, who wore a color like colcai.

Klyton had slept only two hours. But he felt light and strong, his head as clear as the sky, and like the sky, with the two bright thoughts in it, the Race that was the Sun, and—the Daystar thought—the girl on the terraces of the stadium.

He had made her out. She wore the cloth he had had them send her. Not gold, but silver for her eyes. She shone like the moon amid the crimsons and ochres. But he had sent her a token too, a necklace of heavy golden disks. Ermias stood by her in dark yellow, which did not suit her. She looked better in her skin. But so Calistra would, and he must think of neither.

Klyton had lain with three women two days before the Race, to empty himself. Only one had been Ermias. All three had been . . . Calistra.

The thirteen chariots moved in the traditional manner, one rank five abreast, the next three, and the next three. In the last rank, as drawn by the lots, only two cars. Two was the moon number, given by Phaidix, the five and two threes being the Sun's. It was not that the two was an unlucky place, but those who drew it made the moon goddess an offering at her little outdoor altar beyond the shrine. She liked the open air.

As Klyton, who with the Charchite, had drawn the rank of two, poured honey and white wine, the white cat came and jumped to lick the drops. By the time the Charchite walked up, she had run away.

Amdysos was in the first rank of three.

They had not spoken beyond a few civilities. It had been hard on them. All their lives, since boyhood, they had grown used to speaking.

But Amdysos would not budge and Klyton would not shift.

Klyton thought, primed now with the flame of the Race, *Whoever gets this, we'll talk after.* Magnanimous now, because excited, unnerved, ready, Klyton wanted to be friends again. It occurred to him, too late, it would have been better to exchange warmer words before setting off. But after all, if there had been fresh anger . . . anger was as bad for this as sex.

Klyton thought, *He's almost unflawed. I have to teach him this. It's the Queen, it's Udrombis. Her codes. She'd sweep away a rock, why not a man. If I hadn't seen Calistra, I might have thought as he does. She isn't like the rest. That child in the market-fair, with two heads—not like that.*

Klyton's horses were close to the tint of the chariot. Groomed, they gleamed like water, more like red wine.

He thought, *Why does my pulse race for this, and not for a war?* He had felt no true fear, no elation in any battle. The notion came now, sudden, electrifying, as they turned up on to the slope, *Did I know then the god had me in his hand, and I was safe, for he wouldn't let me die?*

And then, as they stopped, the huge doors rearing, shut stone, carved with a terrible beast, all jaws, to swallow them, Klyton, his head singing, thought, *It's no use saying Amdysos may win. Or any man, but me.*

This is mine. It is all to be mine. All. All! I am the eagle. What I see belongs to me by right. From land's edge to edge of sky. The Race and the world.

"Who stands before the Gate of Night?"

"We, the children of the Sun."

"Beyond this place, the way leads into darkness."

"We shall take that way."

The ancient words echoed over the slopes of the mountain, and around them, in the stillness, sounded the faintly beating Heart. The hollow of the mountain carried everything to the stadium below. A cough could be heard from here.

The priest to the left—it was Torca—leaned and touched with his light the offering bowl on its golden stand. A comber of madder-red purled up.

"The Sun descends. You who descend, do not forget us, for the dark enjoins you to remain. But day awaits. Rise up. Return."

Each man said, singly now, one after another, "I pledge. I will return."

Klyton heard his own words, like another man's.

Two accolytes lifted the offering bowl away, and from the higher slope, boys sang in piping voices.

The song was old as universal memory. It spoke of the Sun beneath the earth. It was a dirge, but at the end, rose into a shining shout of joy.

As it ended, the doors of stone grated on their runners, and the mouth of the monster split slowly into two.

Beyond, within the mountain, Night awaited them, for an instant black as the waters of Death River.

But then the priests who stood along the upper ledges there inside, the first group of five, dipped their torches to the cups of oil.

There was a mumbled gush of combustion, and flame sprang out, showing, rocked by fantastic shadows, the vaulted intestines of Airis, ribbed purple and black, and with the fangs of stalactites depending, scarlet at their ends, as if recently fed on blood.

The girl stands on the terrace, among the women. The silver dress is cool, blood-heat only, the heavy necklace of gold is hot. She knows she must stand some time. Already this pains her, but she does not notice.

She watches, and sees the long slope to the stone mouth, and the chariots going up. She watches them halt, and hears, as does all the attentive crowd, the prayer and its responses. While some of the audience, soft as docile praying infants, speak them too.

Across the face of the mountain's lowest bulkhead, where for centuries they have cleared all but scrub away, she can see too, the figures of the waiting priests, and finally very clearly another great cave-mouth. From this the victor of the Race will, at last, emerge, his passage through secret night and death completed. And after him, the others, though not all still in their chariots, and seldom all the horses. Over the mouth of this blind-dark, wild and uncanny cave, goes a curious twinkling of the sunlight, caught there as if on strands of impossible dew.

No one talks of what lies between the two mouths in the rock. Or, if ever they have, never to a woman.

Calistra watches as Klyton goes into the maw of the mountain.

Ermias is breathing like a small scented hog at her ear. The little slave, Nimi, is still, as if changed to salt.

The dark has swallowed him, Calistra's beloved.

She believes it conceivable, she will never see him again, but over there too she hears the steady respiration of Stabia, her friend. He will return. *But if he does not* win—

Men of an era before time had come into this place. For these evidently, it had symbolized the same, the fall and return of the Sun. For in that way they had painted on the rock. Probably not sophisticated enough for chariots, if they had even had the wheel, they had run the whole route. It would be safer running, then.

At first, a channel went through, with the five priests, two on one side, three the other, standing by the bowls of fire, upright, masked in gold, like icons. The chariots folded into a huddle here, you could not ride more than three abreast.

Then the light flared up again, in a darkness ahead, and they came out into the first great cave.

On the high ledges, more than thirty priests were poised. The bowls they had lit had started up the bats which lived there, and which wheeled and flapped, dipping down low above the heads of men and the ears of the horses. But you trained your team to such things, with flags on cords, or tame birds. Not a secret betrayed; most caves had bats. The horses stood it, with lashing tails and jinking. Then the men were spreading them out neck and neck across the platform.

The floor was level, and a hundred yards ahead, a new mouth of blackness waited. Its lighting was the signal to start off.

There was no further ritual, and no jockeying for position. You waited where you were able, here. No advantage in it. And for many, no knowledge of what lay ahead.

The horses stamped, the bats swirled up towards their nooks above.

A trumpet sounded, deep in the mountain.

The entrance ahead burst to golden light.

New tumults of bats rushed instantly out of it, and to meet this streaming mouth of light and dark, between the shadows' leaping, every chariot tried to fling itself.

Klyton saw the Charchite slip back at once. A prince of Ipyra on his left went next. Lords of Akhemony, several known to him for years, were all around him then suddenly gone.

No one warned you. None must say. There was an old story of a prince who won by wringing knowledge of the Race from a Sun priest. But after his success a disease fastened on and killed him, and the priest was slain by a bolt from heaven. You did not ask. You did not tell. Perhaps, there might be a hint . . . but there had been none.

And so, whether to run fast or slow was a matter of choice, knowing nothing of what lay ahead. Except, there was this, you might study those who had raced here before. There were five. Only one had done it twice and been once the winner: Amdysos.

Klyton came in behind Amdysos's chariot. It was dark cypress and inlaid with cinnabar. He wore white and gold, himself like one of the priests.

They had been friends. Amdysos was his guide, going quite fast. After this, all would be well. After this, brothers again.

Beyond the first cavern, the way was narrow once more. Presently, two chariots struck together, collided, and Klyton heard the cacophony, rage, frustration, and the shrill of horses. But that was behind, and he, Amdysos, and five more, kept on. Those other six, left behind, must do the best they could.

Down the narrow way they galloped, the second Ipyran princeling now in the lead, after him, two together, Akreon's byblow, Uros, and stocky Melendor, and then Ogon, who was a boaster, and who had raced here last year. Then Amdysos, and a man whose name Klyton could not summon. Last, Klyton himself. As they went, one more chariot came rumbling up. It was the Charchite, broken through the muddle of the collision. He gave a scream as he passed Klyton, careering next between Amdysos and the nameless one. The four forward chariots parted for him, crushed to the walls, and then the Charchite and the Ipyran were gone into the fading of the light ahead.

The bats, which had withdrawn, dived again. They ripped through Klyton's aura, the nerves of his body now stretched beyond the flesh, through the physical strands of hair that had come loose from their clubbing. One bat brushed his temple, another settled a moment on the left-side horse, fluttering like a black ribbon in its mane. Klyton saw the wink of red eyes in its rat mask. He sprung the whip and cracked it just clear of the bat. You were not permitted to kill them, they were the creatures of Thon, allowed here by the Sun god as a reminder. But the bat dashed up and was gone.

Amdysos, though far enough back, was checking his team.

Guided, Klyton checked too.

Away behind there was a crash. A man's voice raised in grief, perhaps in pain.

Behind, too, the lights were dimming down.

Ahead, new light—a new entry—the channel opened abruptly wide.

Klyton heard the leading Charchite scream again, not from triumph now. And hauled harder on the reins.

Even so, erupting out into the second cavern, he was not prepared.

In front and above, caught in the fresh flush of light, a lowering wall seemed to bar the way. On it was the huge picture of a thing painted apparently in blood and night, which uncoiled its curling tongue to clasp the disk of a crimson Sun. Enormous, it seemed you must run into it all, and be lapped up too.

The Charchite had clapped his hands across his face. His team bolted to the wall, and stopped there, the chariot swerving round and going over. He had been lucky. Two yards more, there was a drop of twenty feet.

The Ipyran screeching prayers, rushed at the wall, and went in through a tiny hole below, which had also now come to light.

The terror of the wall painting poured over.

Klyton saw the priests who stood like stones along the walls. Here their faces were masked in black. How could you be sure they were only human?

Amdysos was going faster, and Klyton too urged on his team. Coming to the opening, instinctively he ducked his head, and drove under the thing on the wall.

Before him—far before—the Ipyran, sole leader now, ran howling still, his yellow horses snorting and prancing.

Ogon, Uros, Melendor, Amdysos—the nameless one dropped back—Klyton passing him. Bizarre, the man's name surfaced as he did so, but was left behind.

The need to gain ground, as in any race, felt paramount, yet must be subdued by will. The Ipyran was maybe not clever, snatching first place so soon—this much already one saw.

But others too were closing from behind, a roar of hoofs and wheels. No time to look. The bats had flown up again—you did glance there, and saw them clustered like black bunches of grapes with scarlet beads that were bunches of eyes. Venom dripped from their mouths. Echoes now went through the skull. The head spun. *Clear* it. Again, the way narrowed.

More painted images—what now? On either side was the Sun's disk, colored a dreadful dying red. It fell in stages, depicted always lower, behind the bars of the stalactites, seeming—as they ran—itself to fall. And then came a steeper slope ascending, and on the walls were the awful bulbous shapes of men who had lived once in the world, men with the heads of stags and foxes and lions, and over all the black clutching form of Night, whose mouth, like the bats' mouths, slopped poison down. It stank here, of death, and the light faltered, and the echoes drowned—

Klyton was cold inside his heat. The sweat felt thick on him, and the fine hairs stood along his spine, the strong hairs crawled on his scalp. Just so worms would feel, that went through and through if you were left, when dead. For this they burnt you, to save you such dishonor.

But all men die. All men, high or low. Happy or accursed. Even the King, in his sleep, like a woman or a child—

But not the eagle.

Ogon had got a bat in his hair. It had flashed down on him as if called. He was shouting, cutting chunks from his locks with his knife, to get it out. His horses floundered; he went to the side, and trundled out of control down a mysterious side passage, some old working of the mine.

Seeing it, Uros, his friend, set off after. Do friends do this? In battle I would, Amdysos. But not—here. This is nothing to do with life. It is the fight with Thon, knee to knee, for the Sun must rise, and to lose my brother and my friend is nothing to the safety of the world—

Now, all at once, a swerve in the track—and chaos. Walls rushing in, or chopped away—

The track was thin, in parts less than the width of two chariots. He saw the priests stand aloft, far spaced in groups of three, two on one side, one man another. They lit their fires as the riders approached, as before, but now the light was murky and greenish, and their faces were masked in silver, and their robes were grey, the color of mourning . . .

Either side hung the ancient workings, crumbles of stone ballasted by poles and shafts of oak, with great pherom stays. Drops of a hundred, two hundred sword lengths. Veins of metal left alone, gleamed transparently, like tears or saliva.

The paintings on the walls had in some areas disintegrated, flaked off. But one saw enough. Things with huge white eyes, the beasts of Night Below. They leaned to dead men, eating of them, pulling out the ropes of their viscera, and like flowers, their hearts.

The Ipyran was slowing, he was weeping. There was madness in Ipyra. Their vaporous caves, where skeletal women sang of horrors—he should not have come here—all at once he stopped his chariot, drew rein, and got down as if on an avenue. He walked to the rockface, under the picture of a snake that had men in its teeth. Here he kneeled and wove to and fro, crying. While his horses stood champing, and shaking their feet and heads, spraying foam like cream.

Someone would have to come back for the Ipyran. The priests would see to it.

The remaining chariots curved round them.

Now Melendor was whipping up his team. He had raced the Race before—it must be safe to do so. Yet Amdysos kept firm, his horses going only at a pouncing trot.

As Klyton went by the Ipyran in his ecstasy of madness, he

saw the man had clawed his face, the way women did there for a loss.

And from behind now too, the nameless man, his name truly left behind, for Klyton could not again recapture it, was all at once thundering up again, with others at his back.

The echoes rolled about in Klyton's skull. It would be easy to fall down, to lie there, in the green dark-light.

Although Amdysos, the guide, trailed a little, Klyton cracked the whip again, lightly, over the backs of his team.

The chaotic route was leveling, and ahead another cavern loomed, its lights rising from night.

But the bats as always were coming out again, as if signalled.

One huge red bat, with eyes as white as those of the hellish things on the walls, hurtled straight at him. Klyton swung himself aside, and the horses bundled together, unwieldy as a pair of carter's ponies. And then the red bat was by, and Klyton heard behind him an exclamation, not even loud, after which there was the unmistakable crunch of a chariot wheel going over a dip.

The unnamed lord fell with a cold call that was not even properly that, and quickly over. The chariot, wheel-lodged and tilted, stayed sideways on the track, the horses still as statues, washed by torch-green sweat. Vague as ghosts, other chariots rammed together, trying to steer aside. A shambles. The cursing and grinding faded like a dream.

For here again came breaking light, and the next cavern—Melendor and Amdysos spilled over in to it, and now Klyton, who flung up his head, while the horses reared in terror, nearly jerking from his control.

From the ceiling of the rock hung down the robes of Night, the long, black, rusty chains of Night, and caught in them, the masks of a thousand grimacing skulls. Jangling and clattering, and the bats swooping, and the sound of laughter—but whose?—and along the walls the unhuman priests, garbed at last as they said that Thon was garbed in his crypt, white faces and red manes and purple lips and disks of metal on the eyes—

Melendor, who had done this before, had even so lost the mastery of his team. They circled, jounced, bucked around the space, setting the chains ringing worse, and Amdysos pulled hard back, and Klyton saw the chance before him, the long, up-swollen sweep that sprinted for a hole of jet black ahead. The priests ahead would light the darkness as he came up. They had done so every time, hearing the riders come on. And the other two could be got by here.

Anything might be beyond, *this* had been here, something worse than this—but Klyton did not pause. He had been patient. Now in the lines of Amdysos's body he had seen a sort of answer. The Race of the Sun was won not necessarily by speed, but by endurance. But one must have more than that.

Here, *here*, the *chance*; Klyton knew himself in the hand of the gods, who, however many they might be, had one hand only, and that larger than worlds.

And so he raked with the whip across the air, and his horses bounded forward. There must always come at last a time to take the risk, and to jump the chasm of fate. After all, they had shown him. He was the eagle, and had wings.

Passing Melendor and Amdysos, they *ran*.

13

Each time they lit the torches, Ermias cried out. She clutched my arm, as if I might not have bothered to see.

"Look: The first cavern's passed. Look: The second cavern!"

The passage of the leading chariots in the mountain was communicated to the priests on the rock outside by some unknown method. As torches illuminated the stages within, so they did outside.

Now at each spangle of white light on Airis, the crowd shouted. Its noise was growing. They were dancing on their feet, clapping, crying out names and prayers, and the people below, from the town, were bawling like one huge bull with several thousand throats. Though to bet was blasphemous, no doubt there had been a few.

I think, at the third lighting, I began to turn cold. It grew in me as if from a seed. I blossomed with ice, and thought it only fear for him.

The torches had lit up far along, I cannot recall the number of them, when the shriek sounded above, deep into the sky, and between us all and the Sun was brandished a flail of cavorting, awesome shadows.

Every head must have gone up. Ermias was one of many women who screamed. Even little Nimi let out a yip of fright.

Over our heads, three eagles fought. Two were very large, but one was a monster. It was the being that had let fall its feathers by the shrine.

They were black against the high Sun. As they thrashed and soared, and dived and rent, between the claws and beaks the Daystar glittered on and off like a startled eye staring in heaven.

All about me, men and women cowered. Most were crawling beneath the benches. On the stadium floor below, men had thrown themselves flat, and horses had slipped their tethers and were galloping away.

It was Nimi who tugged at me, and made me kneel.

"Before the gods—" she said.

She put her arm round me. She was little more than a child, about ten. Ermias had curled up tight as a snail, moaning.

But I could not help it. I continued to look up, abject, but caught in fascination. So one gazes at the drawn sword which comes to make an end—yes, I can swear to that, too.

In this way, though, I noted Stabia had been put into cover by her women and that, some distance off, Udrombis sat like an effigy in her chair, not stirring, while her maidens were face-down on the terrace.

The eagles ripped at each other. Some spots of blood splashed quite near me. It was almost black, and it smelled of fire, and of ordure.

Their shadows shut together, and broke, and the interrupted sunlight splintered like lightnings everywhere.

Suddenly one bird veered away. It slid sharply down the sky, as if along an invisible hill, then righted itself and flew raggedly off. A feather drifted from it, along the line of the air, bright as goldsmith's work. But that was the smallest one. The other two fought on.

Bronzen men were running up the terrace, the guards of the King's House. I could not now, in the confusion, see the men's side, nor Glardor; it was as if the very noises of alarm and avian war had blocked him away.

A man had positioned himself with a bow.

I heard Udrombis then, her smooth voice carrying, itself like a shaft.

"Put that down. Are you mad? They have their own business, and belong to the Sun."

He did not know what she had been shown, at Oceaxis, but

shaken by her censure, where he had been prepared to face the might of the eagle, the soldier put down the bow.

After the green light of death, the witch shawls and chains and bones, Klyton plunged into utter blackness. He had expected momently the torches to light there as, in all other parts of the caverns they had. But no light came. He rode now, fast as in battle, and in pure Night.

The horses were whinnying, and he called loudly to them, letting them have at least his strength on the reins, his known voice: "We're with the God. Trust the God. In his hand."

And then the way sloped steeply up. Rushing, racing, all things, time and life and silence, they tore upwards on its back.

When from the dark—came light.

Now. Unlooked-for.

Light like the levin-bolt that had slaughtered the blasphemous priest.

Here on the last stretch, the priesthood awaited the novice, and all men, since to gods, all men are novices. And as he ran night-blind, they struck the tinder and flung it in the bowls of oil, as always they did. And outwards exploded brilliance, as for the child newborn, a dawn not kind but unbearable and searing, after blind-dark, the sheer killing white blindness of the Sun.

Klyton half glimpsed those priests, only five again, in gold raiment, gold-faced, but everything was one thing. For he could not see. Not even the exquisite woven net of silver and gold thread, which the women, the Spiders of Phaidix had spun quite unsecretively, to close the exit from the mountain in silk.

As he reeled there, only twenty feet from it, and the horses, all to pieces, shrilling and bursting against each other, and the chariot crashing against the rock, hopeless—some merchant wagon on the road in the hands of an idiot—as his dream and his faith gave way, *then* came Amdysos, his brother. Pouring past like a wind of flame.

And Amdysos laughed.

Perhaps it was only delight that once again he would win the Race of the Sun. Or it was, for once, malice.

"Damn you—*curse* you—" Klyton's mouth let go the words— he had been betrayed by the gods, so what did kinship or mortal love matter? "You bloody trickster—you never told me—some hint would have done—damn you down to all Thon's hells—"

But Amdysos was gone. Like a golden vision, he rode his horses straight at and through the flimsy tinsel Web, out on to the flanks of Airis, in victory.

The brain of the giant eagle, carved by the gods from amber fury, burned, as he gouged out the eye of his adversary, and clawed through his wing.

Seeing this one, like the first one, turn over, and, better, cascade in a storm of feathers and blood straight down, crumpling, spinning, to the mountain and the river beyond, the victorious eagle screamed his champion's scorn.

He, too, had won.

Did he know then, that in that instant, another had won his race with life and death?

Does destiny touch even birds and demons with jealousy?

On his enormous pinnioned wings, the length of three tall men or more from brazen tip to tip, the eagle circled over, and bending his head, his lion's eyes glared down and saw the glittering thing spring from the mountain's belly in a spray of silver and gold.

There can only be one king. All kings know this.

The eagle gripped the day, gathered himself, and like a spear, he *fell*.

All those who had got under the benches came struggling, scrambling out. Most were on their feet. Some were shrieking and some pointing. So many hands and voices, thrust towards that place upon Airis's purple flank. Even the priests were moving, running.

A great cry would always greet the victor. Not like this.

As the thing of gold gushed, beating and roiling, in on him, like a wave spewed from the heart of the Sun, Amdysos dropped the reins of his chariot, tried to pull the knife from his belt.

No sound came out of him, and even the knife did not come from its sheath.

Next second, the eagle had hold of him.

His hands smote it two or three times, as a baby's fists smite the great arms and body of a full-grown man. Then it had him, and had lifted him straight up. Reins snapped, the horses, wailing, went pelting down the fair paved track that would return them, and the chariot, unharmed to the stadium floor.

In the air, Amdysos shouted only once.

None heard what it contained, the shout, an appeal to gods or to men, anger or despair or only human panic. It was already too little.

The eagle rose as if weightless, and carrying what was weightless, up and up, into the peak of the dark violet sky.

As they dwindled, they sparkled, beautiful, the gilded feathers, and the golden man.

Udrombis, the Queen, had finally stood. Oddly, her body had shaped itself like a bow. Her veil had fallen from her hair. She did not raise her hands.

No one now made any sound, not the tiniest murmur. Although from the Mountain of the Heart, the Heartbeat of Akhemony went ceaseless on, and on.

3rd Stroia

The Eagle Grips the Sun

I

Annotation by the Hand of Dobzah

After her last dictation to me, my mistress Sirai was called from the tower. The Prince Shajhima, son of the Battle-Prince, took her to the bedside of his dying mother, Lady Chot. Sirai remained for the obsequies, which lasted seven days.

When Sirai returned here, she was exhausted, and even once it seemed she was recovered, did not for some while feel able to resume her history.

She said to me, sadly, that life is exacting. It is easy, she said, to forget this, when one is happy or secure.

She sat long hours gazing out across the empty waste. The powder of the sand blew strangely, forming dancing demons, as sometimes it will. Sunsets of red, and purple on the wings of storms, these she observed, and the brilliant stars by night.

"Dobzah," she said, "perhaps I am meant to say no more. Perhaps I should not have begun."

But I laughed and said she had done enough that to go on was only sensible. I have seldom seen her cast so low, not since she was very old.

At last she said, "Every word I speak will be like lead. But only for a while. Then the words lighten and become like stars. Yes, even when they turn in my hands and hurt me."

She has been eight elahls without working upon her book. That is, for any who do not know, eight periods of four days; in all, the thirty-two days of the month of Muur.

As I took up my pen, she said, "The past seems strangely altered to me now. As if I saw it in a different way than ever I have. Even the palace at Oceaxis looks changed to me. Am I forgetting?"

I said, "It has *been*, as you yourself say, and so it *is*. Who will mind if something is misplaced, if only the heart of it is true?"

This was bold of me, but now and then, even with such a woman as Sirai, firmness and common sense are needed. She lives now half out of the world, and cannot therefore be expected to understand it.

Rain poured on Airis. It had come suddenly, turning the clear sky white. The mountain was glass in a cloud of smoking trees. In the fields, crops were flattened and the vines broke, the rain trampling the unready grapes so the air smelled strong of young and bitter wine.

Night came like an unloved guest.

There was a great silence. A priest had spoken, saying that there should be no mourning—the Sun had sent the eagle, and taken Amdysos to himself. Or so the whispered story ran on little dark feet about the fortress house, about its gloomy twists of corridors, its leaning stairs.

In the silence between the rain and the night, human things huddled to their wavering lights. For summer, it was very cold.

Either the god had chosen, or he had punished us. Best be still then, stoop low, speak softly or stay dumb.

The Sun-Consort, Glardor's blonde wife, had quite properly assumed the royal apartment at Airis. Udrombis, the King's Mother, had therefore been given the second greatest of the womens rooms.

It was a stone chamber, hung with heavy woven curtains to keep out draughts. In the fireplace, a brazier dully burned, but rain came in gusts down the chimney. Then the coals sizzled bright like angry eyes.

The Maiden who bore his message in was frightened. Serving Udrombis, she almost hid it. When she came out, she bowed.

"She says you may go in."

Her eyes were wide.

But Klyton only went past her, off the bleak black stair into the chill and half-lit room.

She was in her cedarwood chair, which had been brought to Airis for her, as always. She had changed her light robes from the Vigil and the Race, and now wore something else, something made of a dark grey silk. There was even a necklace of pale stones round her throat. She sat upright, her head raised. There was no mark on her face, though even stone will take a mark, if cut deeply enough. But the face of Udrombis was like iron.

"What is it?" she said.

She spoke as if to a boy, someone in her care, whom she would notice and do her best for, even in this insane extremity.

Klyton shivered, and wrenched hold of his psyche not to cry out.

Hard nearly as she was, he walked over the floor, and cast at her feet a thick, shining, brazen rope.

"What—" she hesitated. She said, "I see. Your hair. An old custom. That is very generous. Won't you save it and take it to the temple for him?"

Klyton looked into her eyes. His own were stretched wide like those of the girl at the door. Like the eyes of an animal caught by lightning.

His hair, untidily lopped off where the plait had been clubbed for the Race, reaching now only to his shoulders, had seemed to stand up on end. It was like a raft of Sun rays behind his face.

Udrombis saw he had not changed his garments nor washed off the dust and dirt of the Race. He smelled of the sweat of it, unbathed, and under that an odor like metal in a fire. It did not offend her, it braced her. He was a man. The very best of the men of this house who remained, now all the best was gone.

"Why are you here?" she said.

"Madam . . . "

She waited.

Klyton at last looked down. He drew a knife from his belt. He held it up for her to see. It was new, the pherom blade incised with gold, the hilt—a golden eagle. Light caught all of it, stayed on its edge which had been honed like a razor.

"What?" she said again.

Klyton dropped to his knees before her.

His voice burst out of him, rough and stumbling.

"I cursed him. I cursed him. Your son. Amdysos. It was in the caves. The Race—I thought they meant it for me. And then he went by to win. And I *cursed* him."

She stirred. It was only like a coal settling in the brazier.

"Here's the knife," he said. "Tell me to use it. I will. I would have seen to it any way, but I couldn't go—without telling you what I'd done. So you'd spit on my name not weep for it. I don't deserve—"

"Wait," she said. Her voice stayed his voice. He grew silent. She said, "When do you say you cursed him?"

"In the caves—just before he broke the Web—"

"Then your curse was nothing," she said.

He threw back his head and glared at her. If she had been any other, he would have ranted at her that she was a fool. He swallowed and said, quite flatly, "No, madam, I cursed him. And *that* came at him. It's mine. An eagle—"

"Hush." she said. There was a slight impatience on her. She put her hand to her necklace and touched the stones, as if to chide them. "Listen to me, Klyton. I had warning of the eagle. I foresaw it, sweeping down. That was before we came here. My son's destiny was already set. And the eagle—you suppose it yours, do you? You're arrogant, Klyton. The eagle is the Sun's."

She saw plainly how he began to shake. He lowered his head once more. The knife dropped out of his shaking hand with a clatter from which the shadows of the room seemed to rear away.

"I meant to be done with myself. He was my friend—I loved him— I'd have given my life for him—to speak those words and then—"

"You think the gods are harsh," she said softly, clearly, "but the gods are neither kind nor cruel. I think these emotions are unknown to them, or have other, lesser, names. Do we weep for the fly we swat away?"

"Udrombis," he said.

She let his breach of etiquette and courtesy go by, as she would let go by all the rest.

It was not his work, what had come to Amdysos. Klyton loved him, would maybe have preferred to die in his place. Crow Claw had shown her, and perhaps for this, the future.

He was weeping now, the sobs rocking him, like a child.

She had seen Akreon weep, when their first son had died. And she had smelled this smell of labor, sweat and flame, on Akreon, just the same, after a battle when, unable to wait, he had tumbled her, and she had gloried in him, in his *life*. As if—as if she had known.

Udrombis rose. Klyton had slashed off the marvel of his hair. He had brought a knife so she might order him at once to die. He knew her well enough. He had trusted her with the fact of his sin, believing she would construct his death. So honorable he was, and clear as water.

"Stand up," she said.

He got to his feet, taller than she, larger than she, the tears of his green eyes red-jeweled as the coals in the fire. He could not speak and she put her arms about him. Then he lowered his head and wept into her neck, into her black hair now all turning grey and white, as she felt it do, under her skin.

"You must go to the shrine," she said, "and be absolved there. Make my son the correct offerings. He will be across Tithaxeli now, and ready to receive them. Don't doubt he'll forgive you. What are a few harsh words against a life of loyalty? You were like two brothers from one womb." He nodded, burrowing in her shoulder, his tears so wet, his hands upon her arms so strong. "Trust no one else with it but Torca. He will be discreet. Tell him, the Queen asks it, too."

She thought, here after all remained one son. The one she had not borne but loved, with Amdysos. Glardor was nothing, and Pherox was gone. Though Pherox had left boys, they were children. But now in her arms, Akreon's strength made flesh. Akreon. Her lord, her love.

She did not acknowledge what she had thought. It was sloughed from her in a second.

She held him one further moment, then put him away. She said, firmly, "Stop this, now. There's no darkness between us. Go directly to the shrine and make your peace with my son."

We returned to Oceaxis in the rain. Mudslides slipped to the road. The storms were fearful. Such weather at this season had not been recorded for a hundred years, or more. No one was astounded. A terrible thing had happened, and would be attended by terrors and mishaps.

Men searched the northern borders of Akhemony. A man who had a vision of Amdysos, lying unharmed and as if asleep in a fiery nest, in volcanic Ipyra, was examined by priests. But even so, crossing into the north, no sign, no sight was, found. The giant eagle had itself not been seen again. But it was known well enough what such raptors did with snatched prey. They killed it, and fed.

For the younger son of a King, only forty days of mourning were given. We observed them.

I was brought two new garments, one the color of soured cream, and one dappled like the skin of a fawn. The court women went barefoot—and I, who always did so.

Of course, he had forgotten me. I expected nothing else.

Since Stabia did not invite me to the Hall or to her rooms, I stayed in my own place. I paced the chambers back and forth. That sound, of my silver feet, that whisper, like a snake—

It was Ermias, who went about among her friends, where, now, it was not suitable I go, who brought me the stories. Klyton, it seemed, had stayed behind at Airis, making offerings for the dead. Awed, Ermias was also sulky. She wanted her lover back. She sensed what had happened would annul their affair. Just as I, in secret, sensed it, for myself.

Glardor came back to Oceaxis for the funeral ceremony. There was no body to cremate, as it had been with Pherox.

Instead we remained in the temple for three hours, as offerings were made and prayers spoken for the shade of Amdysos, so young and fair, a warrior and prince, the son of Akreon, Sun of a Sun. For Pherox, as a child, I had been spared this.

I sat in my chair; that was allowed me. I watched the beautiful animals, two pure white cows, and one crimson, a black bull for Thon, five snowy rams, brought wreathed and proud to the altar, and there immolated, for the benefit of Amdysos's soul.

So much death, for a death.

Women fainted from emotion and standing. Udrombis stood like a statue. It was Klyton who spoke the oration. I had not expected this, not known he had returned.

He did not take very long, no longer, I suppose, than custom demanded. I heard no word he spoke, and cannot now recall them, but they would have been ritual words, of Amdysos's valor and worth. Klyton was steady. His hands were steady as he poured the wine for his half brother.

Klyton's beauty, which now must be lost to me for ever, was unreal, like a painting or a gem set into something rigid. He was like a god. And gods, I knew then, were never to be touched. Yet too, he was hollow. Had his spirit followed Amdysos down? Left only the body—

His hair was trimmed, and I missed its length. I think he saw no one.

And, as I say, I knew that he had forgotten me. I watched him without any fear, without any excitement or even quickening.

Ermias put her soapstone statue of Daia out. Although I did not question this, she said to me, "She played with and used me ill." Amdysos might have warned her, you should not, whatever the provocation, be sharp with the gods.

Torca stood just inside the shrine, listening to the bees.

Something strange had happened, although after the events which went before, this strangeness seemed very mild. The unseasonal rains must have ousted the bees from their house among the orchards and fields of the plain. They came up the hill in an angry swarm, depleted and small, for they had lost many members in the downpour. Into the shrine they went, and took refuge among the rafters behind the altar of the god. Here still they clung, murmuring, crawling on the beams. Now and then two or three might buzz about the space. They were sacred to the god, and also to Phaidix. No one had touched them.

The bees had been in the sanctuary through the night, when Klyton stood here with Torca.

Torca had heard Klyton's confession. At first, Torca's tough heart had ached for Klyton. The gods knew, such a curse spoken to a friend before battle, if the friend should then be lost, was a stone to carry always, however far from the mind you pushed it. But then Torca saw that Klyton had accepted his cleansing, risen from it washed and whole. This surprised Torca. He had not thought the prince shallow. For though religion should console and heal, it was not to be in one split second, save for the most devout or naive. Klyton was neither.

And, though he seemed restored, Klyton did not quite come back. He was not entirely present. Even when they gave for the soul of Amdysos the ghost's nourishment of blood and honey, milk and wine.

At the end, Klyton had thanked Torca, taking his hand. He made a handsome gift to the god, as before.

Torca thought then of the eagle feathers scattered by the cell, where Klyton had slept for his dream. Klyton had not revealed the dream—one did not. It was between him and the god.

As Torca considered the feathers of the eagle, reminding himself of the coincidence that they had fallen there, and of the monster which had next sprung down on the Stadium, plucking Amdysos away, several of the bees flew out and circled round the altar.

"They like the honey," said Torca. "A good omen. Their kind will form a comb of sweetness for Amdysos in the Lower Lands."

"Yes," said Klyton. He watched the bees.

In the dim, dark light of the night shrine with the rain lashing outside, they had shone gold and silver, the sheens of the Sun and the moon. While in from the outer world, wet and shaking herself, walked Phaidix's white cat.

When she meowed, Klyton turned. Looking at her perfect face with its silvery eyes, he seemed to have some thought, and then he was closed again, complete.

Klyton said, after a moment, "When I had the dream here, it promised me something. The Race—but I didn't have the Race."

"No one had the Race."

"That's true. But then, I was promised, I seemed promised —more."

"The God doesn't break faith," said Torca. "But you must always be sure you haven't misheard him."

"Yes," Klyton said.

Torca left him towards dawn, to see out the last of the watch for Amdysos, and went to his own cell, where a paper had come from Akreon's Consort, Udrombis.

Her language, as he anticipated, was subtle and polite, but she told him she entrusted him too with the task of questioning those priests from the caverns of the Race, who might have overheard any words Klyton had spoken. No other chariot, it seemed, had been near. Torca was glad. Udrombis would have wished to be sure. And this . . . might have meant other things. He did not think she would have insulted him by asking him to become her assassin.

But neither did he relish work as spy. Unlike Klyton, she had had no qualms in putting service on him. For Udrombis, one knew, the Sun House rose paramount. And she valued Klyton, it seemed, like her own.

The priests when he tested them were ignorant. Half tranced by the ritual and the drugs of the caves, they had heard nothing above the pound of hooves, the clash of metal and thundering echoes.

Torca wrote to Udrombis in careful terms—being very certain she should behold all of them as unknowing. He wondered briefly if he was in any personal danger, seeing he had undertaken Klyton's purification. But that was not her way. She had trusted him, and thought him, therefore, useful—*retainable*.

For the bees, they would perhaps make their comb again inside the shrine. It might be inconvenient, and soon enough it was. As the rain dried, and hot days returned with a lion-like ferocity, a priest was stung on the arm, which sting swelled up like a bladder and sent him delirious for three hours, a sacred number of the god.

2

Days went by. The rain ended and an awful heat began. Soon even the palace noticed its effects. The fruit that was served was overripe or withered. There was a dearth of milk, or it was too thin and tasted bad. Insects burst out where the flowers and fruits had been. My slave, Nimi, ran to and fro all day till she dropped, wielding her swatter and fan. By night, the filmy curtains were drawn fast about my bed, beyond which I heard the whine of poisoned things seeking me.

The Lakesea looked so still, as if partly thickened, like a sauce. The gulls called with raucous mocking laughter.

There was a sickness in the town.

Stabia sent me a letter. She reminded me, for my own sake, I must be seen in the Great Hall at dinner, and at the Sunset Offering. I perceive this was her thoughtfulness for me, and she was good to recollect it. At the time it seemed to me she only desired me to suffer worse. I had though enough sense left to go, forcing my way up the enormous stair, with Ermias behind, gasping in the oven-hot cinders of each day.

In the Hall I saw nothing, only looking stupidly about, trammelled by Stabia's old cautions against "forwardness." Trying, nevertheless, to find him. I did not even know why. Perhaps only as sometimes the blind hanker after the Sun's light, although they cannot anymore witness it. I knew I could now mean nothing to Klyton.

In fact, he was not there. He had gone with a force to Melmia, on Glardor's command. Once-restive Sirma was Melmia's neighbor.

At the dinners, I did everything Stabia had inculcated in me that I should. I ate a little, though I did not want it, and praised the cooks who had been able to contrive sweetmeats from the difficult fruit, drank sparingly, seemed to attend to the important harpers and dancing troops.

One royal woman certainly did not come to the Hall. I had heard her extraordinary keening once—lament was not done quite in this way in Akhemony, the crying never so loud. I had thought her voice to start with was that of a gull.

Elakti, Amdysos's spear-wife, who had caused him so much mundane trouble, performed alone the noisy prolonged rites of Ipyran widows, rending out her hair, ripping her cheeks and bared breasts with her nails, even cutting her left arm to let blood fall for him to Thon's country below. There began to be another tale, that she was pregnant again and had been shown early by a sign. Amdysos had left in her his burgeoning seed.

Kelbalba came for my massage, as she had always done since I started to walk. Sometimes she worked longer and hurt me, saying I was neglectful of my exercises. I was. She brought me little treats to eat, cakes bought in the town market, sound apples and ripe figs from pockets in the hills, which almost no one else could get. I did my best with them.

"Don't be so sad," she said. "He'll be back."

"No," I said. "Everything has altered."

"*That* doesn't alter. That undone thing between a man and a girl."

She took to oiling the turtle, and made me rub the shell to a mirror's gleam.

Ermias accepted a new lover. He was a youngish noble and gave her outrageous gifts she should not perhaps openly have worn, a gold necklace with a polished diamond, a ring with a rare black pearl. He had heard she had belonged to a Sun Prince.

Glardor hurried away again to his estates.

They had sacrificed a white horse to the Sun, as they regularly did in Ipyra. Here it was, like Elakti's rites, not usual.

I did not see the sacrifice, I am glad to say. It was performed at night, under the moon invoked as Anki, so Phaidix also should take note.

In my little garden, rogue roots and fierce weeds had almost obscured her altar. Brown ruined apples lay in the grass, devoured by wasps and flies. Nimi had found a dead cat among the trees.

A curious sense of waiting, as if for the sunset sounding of gongs, lay with the boiling dregs of summer on the land.

Like any sensible farmer, Glardor spent all day now, sunrise to set, tending to his scorching fields and vine stocks.

A large, bronzed man in a sleeveless tunic and straw hat, he was as ever most at home there, working among his freedmen and slaves. It had been related they called him only Father, as servants did with the master on the farms of nobodies in the back hills.

His Sun-Consort had also absented herself from the court to go with him. That big, blonde, greedy woman, who seemed to find no fault with anyone, had had enough of Oceaxis. She had no time for the extended ceremonies, the gossip and games. She preferred her loom. The outcome of the Race had upset her, too—someone reported she had exclaimed such things did not happen to ordinary people.

Some cows had got loose and in among the grain. It was an old story. Glardor and three of his freedmen went into the field and ushered them out. The grass was so burnt up now, they were already bringing the cattle fodder, but the blackened corn had enticed them.

As they got through, the cows and men, into the pasture, four or five bees flew up from a bush by the gate.

No one thought anything of it until Glardor clapped a hand to his neck. A dead bee tumbled away in a powder of saffron and black.

The senior freedman came to look, but Glardor waved him off. "It's nothing. Poor bee, she lost her life for that."

Five minutes later, Glardor said his throat was sore. He breathed very quickly, and the freedman saw his neck had swollen abnormally on the right side.

Glardor climbed on his donkey to ride back up to the house, but presently he turned very red and began to gasp for breath. They held him up and beat the donkey till it trotted. By the time they reached the farm, he had lost consciousness.

Glardor's wife had been singing with her woman at the hearth, cooking the midday meal. Now she rushed out, and kneeling in the dust on the track, where they had laid him, she held her husband's hand. A physician was brought from the village, and said the beesting had swollen up Glardor's windpipe, and it must be pierced with a reed to let Glardor breathe. Glardor opened his eyes and somehow whispered the man might try. Then he indicated to the freedman the physician must not be harmed if he failed.

The reed went in, but either it was too late or missed the vital spot. A few minutes after, Glardor went into convulsions and died.

Only when he was quite dead did the Sun-Consort begin to weep. She had stayed dry-eyed not to inconvenience her dying husband nor alarm him further.

In Oceaxis she was, until then, generally sneered at behind the hand. Silly tales were told of her stupidity and bucolic preferences. Now they said she rose up stonily weeping, like an ancient queen, and spoke over the King at once a prayer of farewell, commending him to the god Below, binding herself with a vow that she would never love or turn to any other man, until she and Glardor should meet again, beyond the River.

3

Because he was swimming under the coolish water, for a while he did not understand there was a commotion up above. He took it for the water drumming in his ears.

When he surfaced, he thought the fat captain had been chastising—unfairly and again—a slave: the dropped tray, spilled wine, and nuts rolling on the green marble perimeter of the bathhouse pool. Then he saw the faces.

Klyton gripped hold of the rim and pulled himself out. He was naked, but most of them were. All but the messenger.

"What's the trouble?"

The fat captain, who was pallid under his tan, said, "By the gods—by the Sun—"

It was the messenger who spoke. "Sir, the King is dead."

Klyton felt something fall from him in a wave. It was not water. Perhaps it was all his days, until this instant.

"The King. You mean Glardor, the Great Sun."

"Yes, prince."

Klyton said, reasonably, "The Heart still beats."

"Yes, sir. It took some while for the news to reach Oceaxis. The Heart will pause at Sunset tonight."

Klyton experienced a ringing in his head. But it went off at once. He stretched out his right hand over the marble, an antique gesture. As the blonde Queen had done, he said, "Thon, receive well and with honor, a mighty King."

Glardor had sent Klyton to Melmia with a few hundred men, part of the battle command which had belonged to Amdysos. In this there seemed some muddle-headed patriachal hope to find them all something to do to take their minds off what had happened at Airis. But Melmia, with its pleasure gardens and hot springs, lay against Sirma, from which, as elsewhere, notions of unrest floated like the geyser smokes.

Klyton had had the men drawn up for him. He addressed them from horseback, smartly but not showily attired, his cloak a washed-out grey for mourning.

He told them they had lost with Amdysos what could not be replaced, and he had lost that too, a peerless battle leader and a true friend. He now would do his best for them if they would do as much for him. They were his brothers, and he knew they would understand his pain was also great, for Amdysos had been his brother in blood.

What they had been watching for he was not sure, but they cheered him, rapping spear-butts on the earth and clacking on their shields.

Klyton did not predict much for Sirma, and in Melmia, which also had wineshops and prostitutes, whose high standards were matched only by their numbers, the difficulty would be in not letting his loaned troops go soft.

The garrison there proved the point. The last big skirmish, in which Klyton had participated, his first war, was long over. The garrison captain bulged with food. And by night, the stairs were busy with boys and girls going up to his apartment. Klyton organized drills, parades, hunts. Once or twice, Amdysos's men came to him, as he had told them to, with their worries. They liked him, as Amdysos had always said, and as he himself had seen. Now, they began to be proud of him. Klyton had wondered if Glardor would have the sense to gift him, at last, a command, preferably this one. But he did not think about Amdysos, save in a ritualistic way.

The soldier who visited Klyton, detailing a dream of Amdysos, a golden prince in the Lands Below, Klyton rewarded with a golden coin. But in Klyton's heart, now, it was all a blank. Too much hurt, the too-swift passing of guilt—and that other omission—which he would not think of either, his sister. As if, by the sin of lusting after Calistra, he had betrayed them all and brought down the death of flaming feathers. He bolted the door of his thoughts against them both.

The morning the messenger arrived had been nothing special. Klyton swam every day, for the bathing arrangements were primitive and the pool electric. Sometimes after it you wanted a girl, and now and then he let himself have one. He selected black-haired girls currently, tall and laughing, with strong, sandaled feet.

When he had dressed, he called the captain in. A combination of the overly sophisticated and the superstitious, the man declaimed at length.

" . . . It's a catastrophe. Is the God trying to destroy us? The mighty Akreon—then all his sons—"

"Not quite," interrupted Klyton.

"Excuse me, sir. Pardon me. I meant, of course, by her Majesty Udrombis, the Consort. There are countless others."

"Yes, we're like a plague of rats, aren't we."

The captain again apologized, and bit his nails.

"The awkward thing is," said Klyton, "they must go to the God now, to elect the King's successor."

"Indeed," said the captain. "Will you wish to hurry back?"

"Hardly, Captain. You seem to miss the mark."

The captain looked at him uncertainly. He admired, perhaps fancied Klyton, but did not like him. Klyton was not of the same breed. Having some royal blood, the captain would have favored being familiar, but a Sun was a Sun, and in these circumstances, who knew what he might ascend to.

"You see," said Klyton, "those places which are somewhat unquiet may grow boisterous after this. For a while there'll be no Great King in Akhemony. Some may try to—grab."

"Sirma," said the captain, intelligently at last. "Or—Charchis— Ipyra—everywhere, by God's Knife."

"Everywhere perhaps," said Klyton. "But I am *here*."

"You'll take your troops, make a show of force, the crush

of conquest," declared the captain, happy now to have the turn of things.

Klyton smiled. It was the first time anything had amused him since Airis.

"Less a conqueror than a bridegroom."

He took, nevertheless, all of his command out of the town. They were on the road south by midday. When the sky started to flush, they had already made camp among the dry woods.

Klyton walked round the tent lanes. He spoke to the soldiers. They were tense as bow-strings. He had wanted them out of the town when the Heart stopped.

The west deepened beyond the hill slopes. The older, wiser ones planted their spears and leaned on them. Some knelt. It was so quiet, the sound of a bird in the trees, oblivious to the themes and duties of men, shrilled loud as a bugle.

Klyton could hear the Heart. It was faint, almost supernatural, as he recalled from other journeys away from Akhemony. Some, he knew, could not hear it now, with their ears. It was in the bones.

The sky was like wine mixed with sulphur from the springs. Then a darkening came, like a veil across the land. And the Heart— was gone.

Klyton leaned a little to one side. That was all. Righted himself. Some of the soldiers sent up a noise, and their officers quietened them, like babies, these courageous and war-heeled men. The bird called again in the wood, and someone cursed it, then wept.

Klyton thought, *I wonder what she*—and pulled himself back from the thought as he had from the leaning of his balance.

His sister, forewarned, would be well enough. It was Ermias, doubtless, who would palpitate and swoon. But he would not think of any of that.

Up from the void that was death, the beating suddenly came again. For a moment, you were not sure. But it always came back, as nothing else could be relied on to do.

Red shadows crept down from the hills.

He thought abruptly of Amdysos by the stream, the first time they went to war, in Sirma. How they had jeered at Pherox, who had died. Klyton turned the eye of his mind away.

He went round the camp again, congratulating the men. The Heart beat, life went on.

It was afternoon, when they reached the Sirmian town. When he looked at it, it did not seem as he recalled, but that had been in heavy rain and the onslaught of battle. And they had repaired the walls.

He had brought only forty men with him, polished up, with a few fall flowers tucked into helmets and bridles. The rest were left above, where the town scouts could see them quite clearly, if they chose.

Sirma shared a union, in a half civilized way. What one town did, the rest would concur with. They had no high king, but called a council of their chiefs, when necessary. Their fealty, any way, was supposed to lie with Akhemony.

Glardor had not let the army raze these towns. Klyton acknowledged now that had been a fine and useful thing.

Nevertheless, it was nearly seven years ago. He would have to hope his luck was in. But when he thought this, it was as if he only played a part. Luck was not his to question.

The Sirmians let in the little force from Akhemony, the polished, apparently jaunty men, who acted well. The Sirmians looked sullen, and maybe disturbed.

At the house of the chief, Klyton and his officer were welcomed by a steward. Without a word said, the, steward brought forward a boy to taste the wine.

"That's all right," said Klyton. "I know you wouldn't so offend the Great King."

The steward's eyes flickered. They had heard here the stopping of the Heart, or been told of it. But nothing else was said, until the chief walked in with his sons.

The former chief had died seven years back, along with that son whom Klyton had sliced, almost his first kill.

Klyton made sure they knew his title and worth. As the officer recited, he stood, looking the Sirmians over. The men wore embroidered tunics, and were barelegged for the heat. 'The young ones had their long hair braided in side-plaits and twined with silver wire and ribbons.

The seven-year chief was about forty, lean and grisled, and with a moustache. He let the officer finish and then said, "Are you here to make war?"

"Nothing like that."

"I remember you from the last war," said the chief. Klyton had learned, these outland places reckoned a hundred years ago like yesterday. Ipyra was the same.

"You do me honor to remember."

"You killed the chief's Spear Tall Son."

"I regret that, but it was in the fight. He died nobly." And Klyton had a vision of the man, his cheek off, falling down to be trodden to death in the mud.

But the chief only grunted. "Akhemony rules us. Say what you wish."

"I am a Sun," reminded Klyton, "my father was the Great King, Akreon."

The chief said stiffly, "You shine brightly upon us."

"When I was here before, I was a youth. Now, as you see." He held out his right arm, showing the old white scar. "Your women washed my wound clean. I recall a little maid. She was about six or seven then. My heart warmed to her, her gentleness."

The dog-grey brows of the chief went slowly up. He pursed his mouth.

"My brother had many daughters."

"She was, as I say, very young. She'd be about thirteen, fourteen, now . . ." Klyton waited. It was a gamble for he did not remember any such thing, some dear little veiled female child. There might almost certainly have been one, however. Or one near enough in age they could fob off on him.

The biggest of the chief's sons spoke.

"Father, Bachis was in the house after the battle. She was a child then."

"Is she unwed?" asked Klyton, looking radiantly at them. If she was, his luck—the luck he played he must hope for—was in. For they married them early here, earlier even than Akhemony.

They were not beyond, maybe, disposing of another husband, presented instead with a prince from Oceaxis. Or they might refuse. If they refused, then they had war very much on their minds. Marriage was surely better. A tie like this did not come their way every hour

—a free asking, not a war-taking. And if they wanted it, they were bound. They would be his kin, and their daughter a princess. They could not, under any ordinary provocation, raise swords any more against Akhemony, which meant that probably neither would any other town of the region.

Glardor had not properly seen to it. The wife he took, though from Sirma, had been from another town. Unbedded, so disgraced, she had any way died inside a year of homesickness or overindulgence, in which a lover may have played some part. No new alliance with Sirma had been fashioned. But then, who would ever have thought a season like this would occur, without a Great Sun.

"Unwed. Yes. She's timid," said the chief.

"I'm charmed. I shall be very gentle. But, also I must have her today. I'm sorry the wedding has to be so canteringly done. That's possible?"

The chief gnawed his moustache.

"Customs are to be observed."

"Of course. Everything. But I must ask, quickly."

They were all scowling. But they knew what was offered. Besides, perhaps they were sick of skirmishes they could not win, the flower of their men cut down, their women weeping.

"Let me present a handful of tokens, poor things," said Klyton. He nodded to the two slaves, who undid the saddle-chests. Some attractive silks from Melmia were got out, some carved boxes, and a jewel or two. He explained there were wine casks outside, leathers, some weapons they could delight him by accepting. It seemed quite lavish, on the spur of the moment. Klyton had ransacked the captain's hoard, much to his distress.

As they picked over the barter, the chief moved close to Klyton. He looked long into Klyton's face, and one had the impression of a dog again, which sniffs to scent the vigor and nature of a man.

"You have to come to our temple. We worship Perpi here, the marriage-maker. And someone must go to the womens side and tell the girl."

Klyton felt sorry for her. But not very much. He would not harm her, and she would have a glorious time in Oceaxis, out of this dung-hill.

The temple of Perpi seemed made of dung, its color, and slight tang, overlaid by the incense.

Once the offerings had been seen to, and they had garlanded him, and requested he utter various religious sentences, the bride was brought. She was small and slight, reaching only to his breastbone. Under the veil, he glimpsed a darkish fall of hair. Her hand trembled when they put it in his, but she had been staring at him, off and on. Perhaps it was not from fear.

It was a proper up-country marriage. After the wedding, he must go around the town with her, in a rickety chariot drawn by two white oxen with gilded horns. The crowd gaped and gurgled, and threw flowers, looking astonished. They wanted their money's worth of him. It was their right. He stayed good-humored, and when one stone dropped in the cart with the half-dead flowers, only drew in his escort a little.

He refused to spend his honey-night in the town. He sorrowfully explained he had business elsewhere and had indulged his whim too long. They had some tradition of a bride being carried off to her husband's house, so allowed him to do so.

She brought with her an entourage of one thin slave girl, and the slightest baggage. They had not bothered with a dowry, for peace with Sirma was that, and they had no reticence about showing him they guessed.

Klyton did not see her unveiled, his wife, until they had rejoined the camp. Then in his tent, when he suggested it, she instantly put off the covering. She was not pretty, but neither displeasing, with a white skin and pale tawny eyes. Her hair was brown, and had been washed and braided with mauve beads. Around her neck was a necklace of rough silver discs, and these were all the riches she brought.

He had had them bring some things from Melmia he thought she would like, some decent fruit, and a cake in the shape of a ring. She picked at the food, and gazed about her and at him, in rushes, then looking down at the floor. In the coppery lamplight, he began to note she was very frightened, worse than he had suspected.

Klyton saw it might be difficult to reassure her. She was not one of the free girls who yielded to him from desire. They had said she was timid.

Eventually, he lowered the lamp, and led her to the bed of rugs. He could not spare her, because to have her was all part of the treaty he had made. Not to penetrate her would be the worst insult of all, and could leave the union invalid.

He made love to her as tenderly as if he had genuinely yearned for her all those seven years. But in the end, finding she would not or could not soften her nerves, he parted her body and sought her out. Then he found what the impediment was—or rather, that there was none. She was not a virgin. She had been properly deflowered, and in Sirma, it seemed, they knew none of the herbal arts of court women.

At once, she burst into tears. He stroked her hair, tried to recall her name, recalled it.

"Bachis, it's all right. I'm not angry."

"Yes, yes, you'll strangle me now."

"Why would I? Only you must tell me when it happened. Does your father know of it?"

"No—no—oh, no—he would have strangled me."

So much strangling for such a little matter. Despite what he had said, however, he was raging, and held the rage away from her, as he would a feral beast. If the Sirmians had thought to cheat him—make a laughing-stock of him—for what pact could hold on this?

"Calmly, Bachis. See. I won't hurt you. Tell me who knows."

"Nursey," said Bachis, childishly, clasping her hands, "but she died."

"No one else?" Of course, they had not bothered to check her virginity, there had been no time for such age-old barbarisms. And he had made no demands.

"No one else."

"But the man? Bachis, that I do insist on knowing."

"He died, too."

"How?"

"There were bandits and he fought and his horse threw him down."

"And who was he, Bachis?"

She buried her face in her hands. Then, through her fingers, told him. "Arpon."

Klyton sat back from her. "Who was Arpon?"

She said, only a rustle in her throat, "My brother."

After a time, when he did not speak, the bride sprinkled her story on the air, in quick, tiny drops. She was a simple girl, not much above a child, even in her fifteenth year. If she had been given to Klyton in the expected condition, she would have lain here wild with joy. His beauty daunted her, but then all men were meant to daunt her, and he was like the god.

Since she was ten, Arpon had discovered a way of sneaking in to her. At first, he had only caressed, invading her mouth with his tongue. When she was twelve, he commenced to use her as a woman. She had stretched in fear beneath him. She had wished him dead. But when the death-spell she and Nursey had, years before, concocted, seemed at last to work, Bachis was stricken by fresh terrors. Would the gods punish her?

"No. Your virginity was sacred to Phaidix. You were raped. She'll protect you."

Bachis relaxed somewhat. All at once she sank back on the rugs and drew up her skirt with an awful, sly, placating, false lasciviousness, just what she must have employed for her brother.

"It's all right, Bachis. I won't bother you tonight. We'll pretend we have, shall we."

And down in the wells of her pale brown eyes, he saw a slither of disappointment, which now disgusted him.

He left her to sleep, and went to sit in the other end of the tent. Quite soon he heard her softly snoring. She had had a busy day.

When he slept himself, he did not know it. He stood in a dark place, and said over and over, "Her brother, her brother." Stars glittered and shot by, tipped on Phaidix's arrows.

Had he been shown the mirror, himself and Calistra?

Was he in some hell, sent there to atone?

The stars flashed past and on, and were no more, and then he saw he had immovably reached the bank of a river, which was black and very still.

On a rock which jutted from the water, a static flare of gold, which was a man, stood waiting for him.

Amdysos carried no mark of any mishap. He wore the clothes from the Race, gleaming and perfect. But his face—his face was closed behind a golden priestly mask.

Then he spoke. His voice was recognizable, though pure and far off, as when he had officiated sometimes in some religious rite.

"Klyton," he said, "don't you remember the bees at Airis, in the shrine?"

"The bees . . ." Klyton said.

"Glardor," said Amdysos through the priest's mask.

Klyton thought in the dream, how Glardor had died of the sting of a bee.

"And Pherox," said Amdysos, "dying of the silver apple. And I of the eagle of gold."

"I was afraid," said Klyton, "to remember the bees."

Yet through him, like a tempest of fires, some splendor came, returning. And in the dream he retraced the other dream, when he had been the eagle above Akhemony, and the world was his.

"What you felt before the Race," said Amdysos.

"I—feel it now, again."

"Your way," said Amdysos, "is made certain."

"But I thought that way was for both of us. For myself, and for *you*, as my King—"

"I was the sacrifice," said Amdysos the priest. "I have gone down into the dark that you may soar up into the sunlight."

"The God—is too harsh—"

"No prize is given for nothing. We are gone from your path. Take your trophy, Klyton, or you demean my death."

At his table in the tent, Klyton woke with a leap of flame. Blazing, he stood, and all the space seemed swirling, burning, till it settled, and only the golden light poured on through his brain. He had become a ghost, but now the web tore from him.

And hearing the girl snore on the rugs, a million miles below the height of his fate, he laughed aloud.

He recounted this to me later, all this, as a true dream, sent by the god. But I do not think it was.

I, Calistra, was in Oceaxis that night, as I had been, night on night, day on day, left like a shell upon a shore.

The Heart had stopped, and begun again. Prepared, I had only waited out the interval. It felt of death, as in the whirlwind of Thon's temple it had. But what had stunned me then seemed now far less. I had learned of other separations. And I did not die.

That night, this night. As Klyton dreamed his true dream, I lay awake.

The lamp does not show a circle of rose red on the ceiling, as once it did. They have changed its position. Lut crouches by Gemli.

They have an understanding now. Lut, like the others, has forgotten me, since I am no longer quite a creature of his band.

In the morning I will wake, and day on day, night on night, time will pass. Kelbalba will scold me and make me dance and exercise before her. I will do it in a dream unlike the dream of Klyton.

And a morning will arrive, and Ermias will appear, wearing the jewelry her noble gave her, yet angry, scornful, showing her teeth like a cat.

"Well. He's *wed*."

Uninterested, I will glance.

Ermias will shake her curls. "The precious Prince Klyton. Some slut he's wanted seven years in the flea pits of Sirma. Couldn't wait, they say. What tastes he has, for a Sun. And she brought no dowry. He was so *eager*."

And walking to the window, forgetting all the dictates of policy and alliance, how treaties are made to hold nation to nation, I will see him for one second in the arms of a lovely goddess-like girl. And the Lakesea will turn green before my eyes and stream into a narrow, fiery line, as I loudly weep my soul from my body, and Ermias, in horror, clutches me back from the brink where already I have tumbled down.

4

Winter came. I see again an early morning in Phaidix's garden, when the last tall brassy flowers were black, burnt by frost to sugar, crumbling at a touch. Snow bloomed on the mountains and closed the higher roads. Hot stones put into my bed, and under my silver feet, to warm them before I should draw them on. And Ermias, she too I recall, very straight and still as she stood behind me, reflected in the electrum mirror Stabia had sent. Ermias and I said nothing to each other of that other morning when I, like a frost-burned flower crumbled into my tears of blazing glass. It was not like her, to be so reticent. And she was kind to me. She brushed my hair herself, sending Nimi away. What went through her mind? No doubt that I was simply a poor dolt, inevitable victim of unsuitable obsession. Yet she treated me with dignity.

For myself, I did not cry again where any could see me. And now there were no helpers, no one came to tell me it was Calistra he wanted, none other. Though Stabia had delivered the costly, promised mirror, she did not add any message.

I went to the Hall one night in three or four. I stayed until the harpers were finished, or if there were no harpers, until the men's singing began. I sat among the women, but not close to any of the queens. Of course, I must have seen them, Stabia with her amiable brisk ways, Udrombis, with the new tide of white breaking through her black hair. Even Elakti, who now was present, sitting with one hand pressed to her stomach, which still looked perfectly flat. But they were not real to me, as he had not seemed real. And if I saw him, he was less real than anything, now. I marvel at myself, partly for the remoteness I felt on seeing him. But this Klyton moved behind a pane of crystal. He was further from me than the sky.

Events, naturally, had happened, although I paid them no attention. Returning to Melmia with his borrowed troops and the little Sirmian wifelet, Klyton had been ridiculed on one hand, praised on the other. The general story went about that he had lusted after Bachis all those years, and swept her up without dowry. Then put himself to total shame in the rubbish heap town, stones thrown, and oxen and chieftains lowing under the window, as he did business with her body.

Presently the tale changed, as his strategy was pointed up. To the town in Sirma, Klyton sent, at his own expense, some extra, very handsome gifts. He summoned the chief and his Spear Tall Son—that is the eldest—with two or three other relatives, to Oceaxis, and made a fuss of them there as his kin, for five whole days and nights.

They began to say Klyton had the wit King Okos had had, willing to make a firm strategic wedlock, and then cementing it in. Such niceties Glardor had never bothered with. Soon enough rustic Bachis, strewn with trinkets, had—unlike Elakti—a round, hard, budding belly. Her suite was small, but in a pleasant part of the palace. There was nothing to complain of.

And Sirma lay quiet, well stroked down and purring.

By then, Glardor's funeral rites were long past. No spark had come for his cremation. It had been an overcast day of the drought, though lacking rain. They had had to use the priestly trick with the chimney.

Following this, from among Akreon's sons, a Great Sun was chosen. He was selected by means of ancient precepts that must operate,

should the descended Sun and all his foremost male offspring of age die in battle. Omens and signs, supposed to attend the process, were duly fabricated. The new High King was twenty-five years old, in the prime of his health, the son of a Daystar Akreon had turned to, they said, only that once.

I have not until now spoken of Nexor. Nor do I summon any scenes of him, before the first ceremony of his Kingship. He was an effulgent, mighty prince, like them all, standing forward to receive the Winter Diadem, since his crowning could not come till next summer, the time of the Sun's waxing. His hair was reddish, they said from his mother, a Uarian woman. No doubt the compliance of Uaria was considered, in electing him.

He had been in many wars, performed hardily, though never shone. He was said to be a forceful man, not weighty in Glardor's manner. And Nexor had no hankering for the fields. He was, besides, young.

He stands up in my inner vision only like a puppet. I see no further than the bold face with its glimpse of Akreon. Their beauty, in those days, my half brothers, the lesser gods of Akhemony, was a weariness to me.

For Klyton, he was waiting. He had had two dreams. Besides, Udrombis had forgiven the single terrible transgression. And one night she called him to her after supper.

He found at once she had dispensed with all her power games, unless this was another played by default. A chair with golden lions' heads on arms and feet had been set for him. Her chair of cedar-wood was not one of the larger ones. He did not at first quite believe, but came to see, the golden chair was that which Akreon had used, when in private with her.

It was strange there, that evening. The winter dark not quite dispelled by the soft lamps of Arteptan alabaster, her lion desk crouching in the blue-black shadows. Before a shrine of the god, a flame fluttered redly. Klyton knew all her apartment at Oceaxis, all save her sleeping chamber. With the years the rooms had grown smaller, as had she. Tonight they had, peculiarly, the feel of an open place—not especially cold, yet peeled wide somehow to heaven, the watching eyes of other beings.

"I have something for you, Klyton," said Udrombis. She brought it to him—she had sent the women away. As she put it in his hand, he saw how the white had flooded her hair since Airis.

"A ring—"

"It was Akreon's ring. His hands enlarged with age, and work. He said it was a pity to alter the gold."

The ring was a knotted round of golden leaves, holding one searing cat's-eye, an unflawed, greenish topaz. By the richness of it, the gem's quality, the workmanship, he knew it was worthy of a King.

"I wish you to have this, Klyton," she said.

"I'll treasure it, madam."

"You were clever in Sirma. I was pleased with you. A little matter, but such little pebbles, laid all together, make a hill."

"So I thought."

They sat down, and he drank the wine laid ready. She had poured it with her own hand, as she had brought the ring.

"I've something less happy to say."

"Have I offended?"

"No. You've been busy at a prince's affairs. Your mother, have you noticed, has lost some weight."

"I hadn't, but I expect she's pleased. The stairs have been annoying her."

"It is an illness, Klyton. Your mother is sick."

He put down the cup.

"Why didn't she—"

"She doesn't know it, not quite. But I've spoken to her physician."

Klyton frowned. A boy's affection, a slight, half-sinister sadness, brushed him. He had gone far from Stabia, as a man must. But she was yet his mother.

"What should I do?"

"Nothing. Will you leave it with me?"

Klyton said, "Stabia has always loved and trusted you utterly, lady. If you will assist her, I'd leave it nowhere better."

Udrombis inclined her head. For a while they sat in silence. He thought of his boyhood, but could not keep hold of the past. The shadows flowed in the lamps' pulse. Drapes moved, as if figures shifted behind them. The god seemed on his stand to smile, and then

to frown as Klyton had; it must be a new icon, Klyton did not remember it from before.

At last, her voice came up from the night. "I have lost my sons. You will lose Stabia. Now, you are my son."

Klyton rose. He went to her and kneeled at her feet as he had that time of the abyss.

"I dreamed of Amdysos," he softly said. "When I was in Sirma. He glowed in the darkness of Thon's land. He seemed—to give me the life he should have had."

Looking up at her, he saw she had become old, but she had achieved with age the glamour of the mystic Hag, the dark of the moon, when Phaidix herself became old, and walked in disguise unseen across the world.

Her black eyes gleamed like the topaz in the ring, as she gazed down at him.

She said, "We know, you and I." That was all. *We know.*

One man did not, could not wait.

Melendor was the friend of Uros, Uros the friend of usually boastful Ogon. Uros did not have legitimacy on his side. But then, while Uros had been got by Akreon on a Daystar's wild-haired Maiden, Ogon and Melendor belonged to the outer kindred, nobles, not sons of Akreon at all.

"I lost the Race for you."

"That was your choice. Any way, if you'd won—that *thing* was out there. The God punished the winner." Ogon, his hair just growing straight where he had chopped his locks askew, freeing himself of the bat in the caves, turned from Uros. "It isn't a debt."

Uros shrugged. He had followed after Ogon, down a side-working of the old mines. In the dark there they had miserably joked about the mishap. When they came up, the world had changed—Amdysos was in the sky.

"The gods are trying to lesson us," said Uros.

"You're wrong. Anyway. I don't want this."

"All right. But the line of the Kings is stale," said Uros stubbornly. It was his stubbornness which had made him track Ogon into the working, to be sure he had survived. Like this, you saw Uros did not have the fineness of most of Akreon's sons. One shoulder was set too high, his nose was thick and his mouth too thick in the upper lip.

"It's a madness on you," said Ogon. And walked off.

But stocky Melendor said, "Go to your folk in Ipyra? Stir them up? What are you aiming for?"

"What do you think?"

"I think," said Melendor thoughtfully, "the priests' law makes this happen, by delay. According to the law, Nexor has to wait for summer, to be full crowned. It's as if there's meant to be this time—for someone to step in." He looked lovingly at Uros, with whom, indeed, on cold campaigns, he had shared more than the blanket. "They say, the man who risks nothing gains nothing." He was like a huge boy off on an adventure. But Uros wanted what he always vaguely had. Aiton had taken the crown in just this fashion. That was long ago. But so was last year.

Perhaps it was madness too. The drama by which the three direct heirs of Akreon had been removed. Akreon's own finish. The gods offered a cup of gold. You had to reach for it, or always wonder.

Uros, Melendor, their households and men, these last numbering jointly at nearly one thousand, rode north. They managed it, surprisingly, with some secrecy. Reportedly there was a local trouble, a feud in the hills, where Uros had a farm. He was heading there. With the real journey, despite the increasingly hard going, they got to Ipyra, and over the partly frozen river, inside a month. Uros's rough-haired mother had been, in her turn, the illegitimate daughter of an Ipyran Karrad, a little king. So to the Karrad, Uros went.

Ipyra, like her restive mountains, seemed always ready to erupt. In the stone hall with its roof of beams and thatch, above the mud-village city of the king, Uros declared the hour was right for conquest, that Akhemony lay luscious and helpless as a fallen peach, soon to be rotten. Nexor was no use. All the strong sons were dead.

Among the torch smoke they cheered him, it seems, while the dogs scratched for fleas. The Ipyran royalty ate a roast of mountain lion, which sour meat was reckoned to make them proof to all ills, and valorous in battle.

Meanwhile Ogon, though he had sworn otherwise, boastfully betrayed Uros to Nexor, the new Great Sun.

Ipyra had her own inner alliances. She had never been very quiet. Though winter might now hold them back, spring would come, unlocking the ice of the rivers, unlocking the roads and the hearts of warriors.

5

My mother, Hetsa, was the daughter of a Karrad, an Ipyran king. I was half of Ipyran blood.

I did not think of it, ever. I had been taught early to regard my other side, the blood of Akreon.

The talk in the palace at Oceaxis was of war again. I knew Klyton would be going to fight, as generally he did. What could I do, what could it mean? Nothing, nothing.

I dreamed three or four times instead, that someone had stolen my silver feet. Again, as in childhood, I must sit hopeless in my chair, at the grudging mercy of those who would carry me, but all of them had gone away.

Kelbalba often remained in the evenings. She brought chestnuts to roast at the hearth or in the brazier, while the turtle slept under my bed—which had been changed, apparently at the order of Udrombis, to a large platform on clawed feet.

I hear that voice still, Kelbalba telling me her hoarse tales of the hills, and of an earth before recorded time. Sometimes I would forget, minutes long, the slough of misery in which I had sunk, the ache so deep I no longer felt it, even as it crippled me.

The Winter Festival was past. One night, when I thought Ermias away with her lover, she scratched at the door and came into the inner room. She wore a dress of warm, flaming yellow, and seemed herself like a live flame, her hand uplifted, and the pink of blood showing in it, her face flushed and eyes contrastingly so dark and still, like a messenger of mysterious extraordinary news. She was.

"Madam," she called me that now, "the Sun Prince is here."

I turned my head. She seemed to have spoken in an unknown tongue.

It was Kelbalba who disjointedly said, "The Lord Klyton mean you, is it?"

"Yes," said Ermias.

I stood up. I now felt I burned, but inside myself I was cold and heavy as the snow. I did not know what to do.

Then Klyton was in the doorway, moving Ermias gently aside with his hands.

"Kelbalba," he said, "I hope you're well."

"I'm well, prince."

"Let me speak to your lady alone."

Ermias said, flat as a slate, "That's not proper, sir."

"Oh, isn't it?" He glanced at her. I wondered how she could bear his gaze. She could not. She stepped away and out into the other room.

Kelbalba said, "We'll wait by the pool. That does." And strode past him. She shut the door, and he and I were alone in the red-pillared chamber, which had only the fire and the brazier to light it, and chestnuts scattered on the floor.

"Calistra," he said.

Though his clothing was dark, every gold thing on him glimmered. And his hair, which was already growing long again. His face looked no more unreal and far off. It shocked me by its humanness. In his lustre he was almost ordinary, come down from the height to earth. And it seemed he remembered my name.

He told me later I was pale as the ice. He said I stared at him, and he had met such eyes across a shield. But I did not know what I did. I had ceased to be, and drifted there, an atom, in the air.

"You're displeased at my neglect. I deserve that. And now I can't even stay, only a few minutes. Nexor wants to march on Ipyra before the spring. It's original. And there are things to be done. He's given me Amdysos's command, at least. But I don't know if any of that interests you."

I moved my head. I said, foolishly, "I'll pray for your safety, my lord."

"Yes. I'd value your prayers." With no prelude he walked across and took hold of me, not by my shoulders, but his hot, hard hands on my waist. "You're taller," he said. Then he raised one of his hands and ran it behind my neck, up into my hair, cupping my skull. He bent his head and put his mouth on mine. I had not expected it, yet from all my dreams of long ago, it was familiar to me, this second, as my own body. His lips were warm, they parted mine. As his mouth possessed mine, my flesh, the room, the world gave way, and I hung from his hands and mouth in whirling space. I had never known such fear or divine delight. Had never, in my most profound dreaming, imagined it.

When he lifted his head, I lay against him, folded into his body, safe for ever and for ever lost. I heard him breathing, and felt as once before the thud of his heart which had become my own.

"Calistra," he said. My name was a star. I had no thoughts, had forgotten all things and might have been dead, so extreme had become my life. "Listen to me," he said, "my brother said you loved me. Is it the truth?"

Somewhere I found a voice which whispered that love was the truth.

"Oh, the God, Calistra—I've wanted you I think from the first, when you were that child in your chair. But now this woman made all of silver with hair like a sigh out of the Sun—"

"You have a wife—"

"I have Sirma, not a wife."

He kissed me again. He held me pressed close, and bent me in his arms, and on my breasts his lips and hand came knowingly and known, and through me a river of ice melted away into the wine-hot torrent of desire. It was so sweet, tears ran from my eyes. He kissed them up, drank them.

As he held me again inside him then, grown into his body, he said, "It can't be, Calistra. Only just this once. The gods aren't unreasonable. Just this one time."

And then he put me back from him and let me go, and now I was alone in space, and round me howled the cold of empty millennia, and the whine of broken stars.

"Do you understand?" he said.

"No."

"You're a woman. A creature of the wood. Phaidix rules you. Lawless. But there *are* laws, Calistra. This isn't for us. Do you blame me for touching you, now?"

"I love you," I said, very low.

"Your love is sacred to me. That's all it must ever be."

I felt the old vertigo of standing, but stayed rigid, upright. There was nothing I could say. I was fifteen, and he a prince, and a man.

But he had wanted me.

At the door, Kelbalba struck with the palm of her hand. "Someone has come, prince, from the King."

"The King," said Klyton. He laughed shortly. With no other farewell, he turned and left me. In the outer room, I heard him pass like fire. The slam of the outer doors.

When Kelbalba entered, I said, "Not now, Kelbalba," and she went away.

6

That night, Elakti, the spear-wife-widow of Amdysos, ascended into the hills above Oceaxis. She too was Ipyran, all Ipyran, and any alliance value in her was gone with Amdysos. Moody and snappish and discontented always, there had been some notion, since she wished to leave the court, that the back of her might be the best side.

She had wished too to practice certain rites of her homeland for her husband. They were not smiled on in Akhemony, where the priests stood before the people with the gods. Already there had been some talk that Elakti had summoned a crone into her apartment, where they slaughtered a black dog. Phaidix, in her witch form of Anki, would sometimes accept blood.

The pavilion in the low hills was meant for summer, but slaves had been sent ahead to make it useable.

Elakti rode there in a litter between two mules, uncharacteristically not once complaining at the day-long, bitter journey. Her Maiden, her two women, and the pair of female slaves, shivered and wept at leaving the comforts of the palace behind. The Maiden had, by nightfall, a dripping cold, and went about the new domicile voiding her nose and sneezing dolefully. Even to this Elakti returned slight heed. She was changed.

When presented to Amdysos, and conscious he did not want her, Elakti had given vent to all her sense of misuse. She had had recourse to the crone quite early on, wanting love-potions to bind Amdysos to her. They did not work. Elakti knew she had no beauty, but she had a curious pride, and a great awareness of wrong done to her. The awareness of wrong had caused her to nag, to censure, and to blame. The pride made her fierce and vicious, and in her own way, brave.

The first child she bore was a girl, an ugly, skinny infant, with her own sallow complexion and dark, unshining hair. It had no look of the

Sun House. To no one was it a wonder Amdysos did not like it. Nor did Elakti. Leaving for the hills, she had presented it for keeping to its nurse at Oceaxis.

The second child, within her now, sown on a short night visit of her reluctant polite husband's, had been slow in showing. Now Elakti evidenced some signs. Unlike the first pregnancy, and most pregnancies Elakti had seen, her belly had not swollen particularly outward, in the normal, apple-like roundness. Rather, her body seemed to have been filled, like a loose sack, with fluid, from just below her breasts to the mound of her sex. She appeared more fat than fecund.

In early summer, she would bear the child. It would be a son, this time, the crone had assured her, a son like the Sun, metal-fine as his father.

When they came from Airis and told her Amdysos had been carried away by the giant eagle, she had fallen on the floor and screamed, tearing at her hair and cheeks. In Ipyra, this was what a woman did, on losing her lord; Elakti saw no reason to adapt. And because she was so often overlooked, she made her outcry especially loud, she keened on and on, although forbidden to do so, to remind them all she had been a prince's wife. She had not even seen the dreadful event, since they had also left her behind in Oceaxis.

Now Elakti glanced about at the pavilion. Shutters were attached to its many summer windows, heavy wool curtains hung for warmth, braziers and fires were everywhere, giving not much heat. There were only three rooms, and a kitchen across a yard. The cells of easement were also outside. Only Elakti and the Maiden could have an indoor pot.

Everyone but Elakti was in despair. She alone seemed not to mind the cold, the snow across the hills, the three dead rats lifted from the frozen cistern.

They ate a makeshift meal, Elakti, the crone and the Maiden, before the one central hearth, while smoke puffed up to a ceiling hole above, through which, in return, snowflakes drizzled down.

The Maiden sneezed. "I'll be glad of my bed, madam. Though it's a hard one."

"Not yet," said Elakti.

The Maiden gazed at her lady in dread. Phelia had royal blood, but only a drop. So they had sent her to wait on this unjust and insane barbarian. Already Phelia carried two thin scars on her arm from Elakti's former tantrums. Elakti did not strike out now very much. Maybe this was worse.

The women huddled at the brazier had also caught Elakti's two words. They did not look at her.

Elakti said, "The moon is full tonight. There's an altar here, isn't there, Mother?"

"Yes, yes, altar, altar," mumbled the crone, her wizened old tooth-less face buried in her gruel. She alone found this service better than the back alleys of the town.

"Tonight, madam—?" questioned Phelia, her heart a stone.

"You must understand," said Elakti, straightening herself suddenly, and raising her right hand in an uncouth and primal gesture, some religious signal of Ipyra, "Amdysos is not dead."

None of them spoke.

Whatever her craziness before, she had never gone so far to the brink as this.

"Amdysos," said Elakti, "my husband, will return to me. They're all in error. Those fools. He lives. He will come back. But I must assist him."

The altar, which was dedicated to Phaidix, stood in a grove of pines. The snow was thin on them, but thick on the ground, in places slippery as a glass goblet.

In itself, the altar was not much. A rough hewn slab, without carving. The moon fell full there, however, like a spill of milk, and beyond, above, the hills lifted up and up, and the height of the air was bordered by the white teeth of the two mountains.

In the pristine quiet; the Heart Drum sounded shakingly loud.

Elakti stood some time in her furs, listening to this. The Heart did not sound for her, but for Amdysos it did, and so eventually she matched her chanting to it.

To Phelia, and the young women of Akhemony, Elakti's wails and screeches were like the awful noises of a savage animal. She did not feel the cold, and threw up her bare arms out of her wrappings. Soon her face was mad and blind in a sort of ecstasy, the eyes rolled back. They had never thought her genteel, or fair, but now, through all their unease and wretchedness, they began to be awkwardly impressed by her. Unconfined by foreign walls, she grew dominant.

Surely she had loved him. Decidedly, from her, streamed a sort of ragged power.

The crone scampered about the altar, strewing herbs, and liquids from vials. At length, out of her robes, she pulled a dead and bloody rabbit—the god knew where she had procured it—and slung it down.

"Anki!" screamed the crone, to match the howling of Elakti.

No wonder they did not take cold, the two of them, so bustling were they.

Phelia thought she would perish. She closed her eyes. Shut in this way inside her head, she started to hear a dreadful extra noise. Above the beat of the Heart, the crackling of the winter night, the slender whistle of the stars—a rhythmic, appalling booming—

Thinking she was fainting, Phelia opened her eyes. She saw Elakti's women, the slaves, the crone, all but Elakti herself, staring upward, to the tops of the pine trees.

Phelia looked too.

The moon was enormous and searingly pale, freckled with uncanny faint blemishes. Now across its face there flew a gigantic bird, firstly black, next flaming white as it cleared the lunar disc. From the unbelievable wings spread out a booming gush of sound, like waves from the core of the ocean. Phelia thought she saw a flash of eyes, each circular and blanched as the moon itself. Snow blew from the trees at the downsweep of the bird's passage. Its shadow covered them in darkness, and slid away.

"A big owl," muttered one of the women. She made the circle sign for protection, the circle like the circle eyes of the bird.

But the crone shrilled from the altar: "It was eagle! The ghost of eagle. Anki sent it! To show, to show."

Elakti lowered her arms.

"My lord," she said, "Amdysos, the Dead Sun."

Phelia drew in her breath too sharply and began to cough. The phrase was blasphemous, yet almost holy. The Sun descended under the world to regions of sleep and umbra. The Sun could not die.

The sky, but for the scalding moon, the stars, was vacant now. The moon also had moved a fraction to the west.

Elakti went to the altar and stood over it, oblivious. They would have to wait for her, however long she dawdled. It had been, had it, an owl?

Before a hearth fire at Oceaxis, Stabia raised her eyelids. She was drowsy. Now and then, she had started to have a little pain, and Udrombis, her Queen, made a draught for her, that took it away. Udrombis. She sat like a lioness in her chair. When did her hair go so white? Was it only the firelight? How terrible old age was, to dare to mark even her.

"Rest, my dear," said Udrombis. And when Stabia slept again, Udrombis said, more softly than the ash shifting on the coals, "Your son will be a King."

7

"Who heard of a campaign in winter? Apart from in a book—or in extremity?"

"Perhaps he thinks this is extremity."

"Ipyra isn't that eager. She'd have waited for spring to start."

"That's the plan then. To take her unprepared."

Klyton shook his head, and woke. He would not have needed to question and discuss this with Amdysos, as he had just been doing, in the dream. But in the dream they were boys still. They had been hunting, and were cleaning their knives. Even so, Amdysos had been masked in gold. It seemed quite natural in the dream. Probably the charitable dead always partly concealed themselves; they would have changed so much—

He sat up. Outside the tent, a wind yowled, its voice thick with cold and rage. Through the leather walls came the wind-flickering grey gloom of predawn.

Klyton's servant brought him hot beer from the brazier, with a little spice mixed in.

"That's good, Partho."

The servant grinned, pleased at recognition. He was a Sirmian, a gift to Klyton from his father-in-law. At first the boy had been awkward, but Klyton was patient; goodwill, once won, was worth having, particularly in war.

Father-in-law, and his other-town kin, had sent a thousand warriors, too, to bolster Klyton's command. He had asked the chief graciously if it might be possible, he would understand if not. But his new
relatives were still eager. Doubtless the men sent here with him were
not of the absolute best, but Klyton's drill captain had got them into
some shape in the days before they marched.

With Amdysos's command, now his own, Klyton's battalions
numbered three thousand men. Nexor had said nothing to this. Klyton
had anticipated some word, even of displeasure, but Nexor did not
bother. He wanted, it seemed, only to go headlong at Ipyra.

They crossed the border under Airis, in a blizzard. The river, that
was so green in summer, became a different thing with the snow. The
ice at first held up, a white table in places split by black and silver rock.
But above, to the west, the rapids never entirely froze, there was always
the chance of motion. Suddenly, with a warningless gush, an area of
plates broke up in the ice. Men and horses slipped away into ink black
water, in seconds too numbed even to shriek. Most were hauled out.
The army began skidding in panic to the farther shore, or pushing back
to the shore it had come from. Beasts bellowed, and men swore and
screamed. A shambles.

Klyton, already safely across, looked up and saw Nexor sitting
his horse above, in the snow-clad forest, gazing back, not moving.
Klyton went down the line. Finding a trumpeter, he got the signal
sounded for standstill, then rode to the river's edge. In the stampede,
more plates had broken. A long crack, like a crack in a white dish, ran
for twenty-five sword lengths. At the trumpet, most of the floundering
had stopped. Klyton shouted the most distant men off the ice,
and ordered the nearer sections to continue over. To show them it
could be done, he took his horse back down, and stepped it out into the
middle of the river. There was a rock there, and he knew well enough
he could take hold of it if the worst happened. But it put some sanity
into the men, who then came on quietly, cheering him once they were
safe on shore.

Other commanders had come down by then. Soon the sun would
set. It was agreed the rest of the army should stay on the far side of
the river, make a bivouac and wait for night. An hour after sunset,
the crumbled ice froze hard again, and men and beasts got across
intact.

Klyton had done no more than had been there to do. But it was effective, even showy. He saw this, mostly, later, when he heard how his own men were vaunting him round the camp. The Sirmians especially.

When he went to the King's tent at dinner, Nexor said nothing. The King did not seem put out, or even interested.

Finally perhaps someone must have spoken. Nexor took Klyton aside as he was about to leave. The tent, hung with crimson, and heady with Orialian gums and wine fumes, seemed to have heightened Nexor's reddish gold. Nexor spoke.

"What you did: pretty fair."

Klyton said, "Anyone, my lord, could have done it."

This was so true, it was insulting. But Nexor, who had not bothered with any of Klyton's titles, or his name, and maybe did not recollect it, only nodded. Insulting Klyton in turn.

The early days of the march were uneventful. The weather shut down, white as sweetmeat, but not sweet. Within the vaulted forests, they progressed through an eerie pale shadow. Nothing else moved, as if all life had died, but for the black crows that came sometimes, and circled over gaps in the trees, watching them. The mountains jutted from the forests, blacker than the crows, with marble snow-scarps gleaming like mirrors. Into the null odor of winter cut sometimes a tindered sharpness. Soon enough, where the forest thinned, they looked up and saw a mountain that was awake, a pillar of brown smoke standing straight up from its cone. On the slopes below, a few maddened trees, nourished by the laval warmth, had broken into forward leaf and blossoms.

They passed a handful of ruins. The first fortress town was due on the eleventh day. The night before, Nexor addressed them in a jovial and, offhand way.

"We have nothing to fear, as you know. The rocks are sheer, but we'll use catapults. I might ask for volunteers to climb up. We'll see."

The older commanders, the princes, glanced about at each other. Lektos, son of Akreon and a Daystar queen, said, "Sir, perhaps it should be thought out now. It will—save time tomorrow."

Nexor smiled. "Don't fuss, Lektos," as if to some old nanny. "This is just why we came now. They don't reckon to see us yet."

"Sir, the Ipyrans know their own country. You can be sure they know we're here."

"You'll be saying next the crows are their scouts and will fly back and tell them."

There had been some superstitious talk among the soldiers. Lektos said, without inflection, "The scouts *we* sent haven't returned."

"Holed up in a cozy cave," said Nexor.

Klyton scrutinized this elected King, for whom the omens had been manufactured. He must be intent to seem valiant, and impervious: he was the Sun. Nothing could oppose him. Not an enemy, not his own kind. It had appeared he wished his initial act to be bold and decisive. For that, he had brought them into the snow, over the ice. He rejected all obstacles, had no personal nervousness, was not a coward. Nexor had no imagination at all.

Outside, Lektos had paused, quiet and grim under the stars. As Nexor's gold was of a red sort, Lektos inclined to paleness, which lent him now a glow like blond pherom. Friends, his half brothers, stood round him, calming him, not speaking ill of the King, but explaining Nexor had not meant to dismiss or demean. Nexor was simply fixed on victory. Their eyes said other things.

Klyton thought how he and Amdysos would have digested all this. But all this would not have been, had Amdysos lived.

In the night, a band of men, conceivably only four or five hundred of them, galloped from nowhere into the camp, on their broad-backed mountain ponies, hacking down the sentries, and the soldiers who came out, half-armed, to meet them. The night changed from dark and pallor to a fitful scarlet, as flung torches set tents ablaze.

Klyton saw the faces of masculine Ipyra, as he had in a previous year, wolf faces without fur, but blotched by war paint, and embroidered by the incredible traceries of tattoo, pierced by teeth and firelit eyes. He killed six of them before they plunged away. They went up through the thinned out forest into the mountain skirts. As if to approve their action, a distant crag let off a sudden plume of muddy flame. Black ashes smelling of vomit floated down on the wind, with the retreating yells and yelps of the foe.

Next day, they got to the fort. Of course, it was halfway up a mountain. There was a shepherds' path, treacherous as a slanted version of the river. When it was tried, the Ipyrans on the walls catcalled, and picked off the climbers with their bows and javelins. In return the catapults flung stones and burning straw, some of which at last lodged. Then the fort began to resemble the fiery, distant crag that they could see better from here. Under the fire's cover, more men got up to the fortress gates. Before they could do anything, the Ipyrans had killed them.

So they sat ringed round the snowy rocks, watching the town and fort escalate in flame, and then put it out.

Klytan remembered the former wars here, and what he had noted from his time in them. In summer weather, the mountains had some overgrowth, plants and bushes. These gave shelter, and a means to climb more safely. Even then such high places as this one sometimes needed to be starved out. That was simpler in the hot months, too. Now the besieged food would last, the water stay clean.

Having put out their fire, the Ipyrans danced on the walls.

Nexor came amongst his men, on his large red horse. He said, Well, they must sit and wait.

That night the snow dropped again, with the little black flakes mixed in.

Klyton walked through the camp with a couple of the others. The soldiers looked up from their spitting bluish fires. Some of the men had frostbite, and most were chilled to the bone. At their posts the sentries craned, ready-armed, staring at the swoops of a land indomitable above, robed over in pines below, which could hide almost anything.

In the dark, the luminous volcanic mountains gave a misleading witchlight that stained the stars.

Lektos said, "Even Glardor would never have pushed us into this muck."

Another one shook his head at him. "Nexor is King."

Klyton felt for a moment like a boy, that boy he had been on the first occasion, at Sirma, split off into Pherox's command, the army sweeping him along like a torrent in spring. But he had not felt enough, then. Now the power of this very night took hold of him. The Sun journeyed beneath the earth. But the Sun would come back.

He said, "Men make mistakes. But the God is with us."

Nearby, soldiers at a fire heard him, and looked up. One soldier rose. He was a bear of a man, flaxen-haired. He laughed at Klyton with pure joy and said, "There speaks a Sun. Akhemony is the God's own."

From all the nearest fires they were raising their wine bottles, their old leather cups, toasting Klyton because he had spoken shining words, here in the black ice of alien winter night.

Partho, still burnished from the accolade of the beer, dressed Klyton, and brought him a piece of bread kept warm from the oven. Eating it, Klyton heard the wind had dropped. He went out. He gazed straight through the camp, up the mountain to the fortess town.

It had sounded like a filthy day, starting, but no. The yowling wind seemed to have been caught and caged. The sky had opened its doors to a flooding dawn. The Sun was rising free, over the camp, hitting the mountain face with strong yellow rays.

Klyton observed keenly the blackened walls, the seam where the catapult bolts had done some harm. And the glint of spears.

There was a low sonorous noise, more than the mumble, clink and clatter of the wakening camp.

A pane of white snow peeled abruptly from the mountain and tipped off and away, falling into a northern gorge with a strange soft crash. Klyton felt the earth grumbling under him. He braced himself like the men outside Melmia, when the Heart had stopped. In the camp there were cries and exhortations. A standard leaned over, a tent collapsed. From the burning crag, one tuft of copper phlegm shot up. Then the rumbling ceased. The volcano had cleared its throat with a small earth tremor.

But up on the Ipyran walls they were howling. Klyton looked and saw some of the damaged wall had gone, like the snow.

The Sun was behind Klyton. He could feel it like a supporting, pushing hand, the hand of a proud father, thrusting him forward to achieve some potent enterprise.

All around him the Sirmians were standing up, staring at him, as if they guessed now he would want them for something. And the men who had been Amdysos's command, they were crowding over too.

Klyton raised his voice. "The God's spoken. He wants them out of there."

Worse than Nexor, surely, with his story book of warfare in winter. To go up the bare rocks now—but the Sun was in the defenders' eyes, and they were apparently afraid. Perhaps their walls had always stood firm. Perhaps they had been given other omens.

"I'd like to see if I can get to the top," Klyton said, almost casually. "I don't ask anyone to come up with me. Unless he'd like the fame."

Ten minutes before, even discussing matters with Amdysos in the dream, Klyton would not have thought he would say any of this. But the gold hand pushed at his back. The hand promised to thrust him on, but to hold him, too.

He did not know how he looked to them, the soldiers standing before him, or what they saw. He heard only later.

The Sun blazed about him, giving him an aura of wild fire. He flamed, his hair, his eyes, the wings of light. But more.

One cloud had come up with the Sun, the color of honey, edged with brilliance, and it had taken a curious form.

Klyton heard one of the Sirmians murmur, "He is in the hand of the God."

For the cloud had the image of an enormous hand, holding, supporting above, the disc of the Sun, while with the lower fingers, flexed like those of a man, it seemed to curve about the body of Klyton.

Klyton partly turned at length, and saw this too. He was not startled. The men who watched said that he smiled.

Already Partho had moved up, and was arming him, the light body armor, the helm and sword.

The men of his command struggled into their gear.

Over a thousand followed him as he ran lightly down and away from the camp.

Luck was in it as well. The catapult crews, not waiting for any order, but seeing the state of the wall, had loaded up and begun a bombardment. The Ipyrans were involved with that.

Others on the rock, noticing a Sun-flash stream of men pouring up the dangerous steep path from below, flung out their spears and stones.

But the clear sky of rising Sun was in their eyes, and the fulvous cloud swung down, casting a shadow over the climbing men.

Of the more than a thousand who followed Klyton, nearly a thousand escaped serious hurt.

The outcrops of the slope offered peculiar holds.

When they came to the gates, poor rough things, which any way the quake had loosened, it was not so hard to break in. Hand-o-hand then, on an Ipyran floor, they fought.

But the Sun had come in with Klyton's band. They radiated light and hooted with happiness, cutting men down with their morning swords.

When they stopped for breath, the Ipyran prince had already arrived to surrender, holding out his hands for chains, his women clinging, weeping around him.

At first, Uros's grandfather, the Karrad, had been welcoming. He seemed to think Uros had brought an embassy from Glardor, who, it transpired, they still believed in these backlands to be alive, and King. Uros explained. He said, with Glardor gone, a nobody had replaced the dead, someone thought safe. But the gods had punished Akhemony, and she was ripe for plucking.

The Karrad was an old man. In his riven face, the faded tattoos had crumpled together, so his skin looked to have been made of brown leaves. But he had sharp sight. He glared at Uros.

"What are you saying, boy?"

Uros said what he was saying.

The Karrad thought. For a moment his bright eyes flashed. Then his mouth drew down. He said, "I got your mother on a village woman. My legal daughter was sent him," he meant Akreon, "as a Daystar spear-bride. But he preferred the servant, who whelped you." Uros stood impatiently, fiddling with his rings. "We are always at war with Akhemony. We hate the Sun Kings, but also honor them. It's a rite between us, our wars. The gods made us like a pin to nip them, lest they get too comfortable. Now this," said the Karrad, "your notion, goes too far."

But there was a murmur then from the men about the stone hall. They began to shout at the Karrad. It was an eternal law in Ipyra, the king must always listen and give weight to his lords. In the end, they cheered Uros. Antique legends of outland Sun Kings, made from just such situations, were rehearsed.

However, though the messengers went out from stronghold to stronghold, though fervent replies came back, the Karrad looked sidelong at his byblow grandson.

Uros, actually, was more wary of the Karrad's wife.

The Karrad had taken her late, when the other royal women had died, and she was a great deal younger, and had borne him one son. This boy was still a child, black-haired and handsome, yet with ancient eyes. They whispered the soul of a long-ago hero had come back in him. Evonissa, the queen, was herself a priestess of Anki. Although she deferred, of course, to the Karrad, she had power of her own, and was said to foresee things.

Uros had inquired why she did not foresee the death of Glardor in Akhemony. Someone told him, hushed, that looking in her sorcerous mirror, she had told the Karrad an interval would come among the Great Kings. That was all, and not everyone had understood her, till Uros appeared.

She said, Evonissa, nothing against Uros, but now and then in the cold, smoke-choked hall at night, he felt her eyes on him from the womens' place. She was a good-looking woman, small, firm and strong, with lively crinkled dark hair falling to her waist. She had pretty eyes, but he did not like them much. For when she looked at him, he felt something—not conniving or even antagonistic—he did not know what it was. But then, she was only a woman, an upland queen. So what?

There came an afternoon Uros was fretting at one of the great open balconies of the Karrad's house, which in summer must be pleasant and scenic, and now was scenic and direly cold. Melendor, wrapped in lynx furs, stood grumbling at his back.

Outside, the mountain walls fell through white-striped ebony stands of larch, to the white bear pelt of the pine forests. Far down in a gorge, a frozen glass waterfall hung fantastically, from boulders that seemed made of opal. Above, on a dense sky, achingly pregnant with oncoming snow, other mountains lifted in grave processional ranks, capped with niveum, their bastions changing with distance from sable to lavender. Only a single western peak had raised its eruptive cloud, but the early-dying winter Sun, a bronze plate, had now passed into it. The Sun would sink in the volcano, or seem to. They must, here, be used to the omen.

Melendor, less enthusiastic now, was complaining and grieving about their own men, forced unhappily to shift as they could in the ramshackle village-city. Then he broke off.

"Look, visitors."

Uros, who had been peering into the sky, peered down. A trail of about twenty men was coming up the bad road from the gorge, leading their horses. They looked done up, and soon were near enough one could make out some bandaging.

Uros and Melendor rattled down the uneven steps to the Karrad's hall.

Another Karrad had sent the men, sent them with their wounds to show, to prove his communication.

The Akhemonians had crossed over in winter and commenced battle. Five strongholds had given way, two surrendering. There had been alarming portents—dead crows falling in a rain, Anki's moon divided by a cloud in the shape of a sword, a weird voice that had been heard on the wind, seeming to call out to the Ipyrans, *Yield*.

Uros blinked. He reckoned himself too sophisticated to be moved by such stuff. He thought that his Karrad-grandfather probably was not. Uros strode forward.

"Karrad," this was all one called them here, "clouds take odd forms. The winds in these crags can say anything one thinks of. My men tell me they cry out the names of girls they've left behind."

If he hoped for a laugh from this, he got none. The grandfather sat pulling his sidelocks.

"As for the fortress towns—they were unprepared. We've had other word here, haven't we, ten strongholds at least willing to join with us. That's many thousand men. If Akhemony wants a snow fight, let's meet them."

The grandfather said, bleakly, "The Two Mile Valley is the only place."

"Yes, sir. I've been hunting there."

Melendor grunted behind him. "And it's a rotten spot. Gulfs and topples, trees everywhere. All under seven feet of snow."

"We can smash them there," said Uros brazenly. He had not known boastful Ogon for nothing.

"You're a brave warrior," said the grandfather. Some of the men about the hall stamped and offered a yell. "I give you that," he added, when they were quiet. "But wait a moment. Let Evonissa the priestess sacrifice, and take the reading. The gods may have something to say."

Uros saw no harm in this, save that Evonissa would do it, and he did not trust her. Most women were against a war so near to home.

But they all looked solemn. The Karrad sent word to his wife. Then everyone attended while she went off with her girls to the mud-wall temple in the yard. She was not seen again until the night had settled black.

She walked in, with her tame crow sitting on her wrist. All crows were sacred here, but this one had a white bar on its wing that made it Anki's own. They said, Evonissa could speak its language to it.

She went to the king and bowed. She wore a dark robe from the sacrifice, with the silver knife still hung at her belt. Although generally women were not tattooed in Ipyra, she had on the palms of her hands, and at the center of her low, wide, intelligent brow, the Eye of the goddess, done with a green iris.

"Husband," she said. This was all a queen called a king in Ipyra. "There is a balance, both cups equal. On their side and on yours, weakness and strength."

"Did you read the entrails, the organs?" ritually asked the Karrad.

Evonissa replied, "The aspects were unusual. Something's strange. I would guess the gods are at play."

The hall went silent. And in the silence, its iciness seemed worse. They heard the moaning of the wind, which would outlive them all.

"What should be done?" asked the Karrad. He looked abruptly sly, but her face was unshadowed by anything other than knowledge.

"If I were a man," said Evonissa, "I'd make a truce. I'd ask the Akhemonians for pardon. If we're in a god-game, husband, who knows how it will go?"

Uros lost his temper. He shouted, "Yes, and present Nexor my head on a tray, to say you're sorry."

Evonissa glanced at him. She said, "The prince shouldn't fear men before gods. What we do is nothing and soon over. But after life, who knows?"

Uros thundered, his thicker top lip making his speech unruly, and causing him to spit, "I want my time *now*!"

The Karrad said, "You can go away into the mountains, to some obscure hold. Winter there till your Nexor King has forgiven you."

But Uros knew Akhemony did not forgive such sins as his. He did not want a life of squirreling about, ducking under walls and behind curtains, roused before first light to race from one concealing midden to the next. The awful life of the exiled fugitive.

"*Give me my rights!*" he roared at his grandfather.

The Karrad shrugged. Uros had about a thousand men of his own here. The Karrad said, in his old voice, "The gods are playing. You might win. Whoever wants to fight beside you shall go. For my allies, they'll take their personal augeries and their own decisions. For the sake of that girl who was your mother, I make truce yet with the Great King."

Evonissa bowed her head. Her face showed nothing now, but a slight color in her cheeks. That night she sent her son away to the north, that was all. The Karrad must have agreed to it.

As for Uros, he would have to make do.

That valley named for Two Miles was far larger. On every side the mountains went up, dressed in trees, confirming the valley floor as a stadium. Here Ipyrans had fought with each other their most primal battles, while gods sat on the mountain tops to see.

Passes came in through the crags at three junctures. All were bizarrely accessible, even in the worst winter.

But the ground itself, as Melendor had stated, was unreliable, and in the heavy snow like a third adversary, unkind to either side.

The Akhemonian troops, when they heard from the scouts the Ipyrans had put a force into Two Mile Valley, were scornful and outraged together. They thought they had got the hang of the winter campaign, which till then had been sieges and sudden attacks. The size of the Ipyran rabble was also disconcerting. Banding together in this way, they were reportedly ten thousand strong.

Nexor's southern force had lost men. To the weather and the terrain more often than to skirmishes. Now they found themselves less in number than the savages of Ipyra.

When they came out on the wide natural terrace beyond the south pass into the valley, they saw, across the huge spoon of snow, deceptive and innocent as a sheet of white silk, the Ipyran camp. Perhaps only a hundred feet below, miles down it looked, in the glacial, crystalized, motionless air. The Ipyrans were black on the snow; where the mountain shadow spread, the enemy fires spangled. The scouts had not lied about their mass.

The Akhemonians extended themselves along the terrace flanks. In three hours it would be night. The stoical soldiery laid its fires. The few women who had struggled up with them, the pages and boys, set cook-pots on.

But in the Great King's tent, Nexor was saying, "Let them rest an hour, then we'll get down. The descent's easy. Startle the foe."

It was Lektos again who said, "My lord, you mean go straight down and *start*?"

An older man, a noble, said, "Great King, it will be dark in an hour or so."

"We'll be done by then," said Nexor, beaming and hearty.

Klyton had just come in. He had previously sent a band of his Sirmians off to hunt. There had, for some reason, been a lot of deer sighted in the forest along the pass, fat deer despite the cold, and not shy. Now the men were coming in with glossy carcasses on the saddles.

He listened to Nexor's words. Then spoke.

"No, my lord."

Nexor looked round at him.

"No? What did you say?"

"They've been on the move all day. Yes, it wasn't such hard going, but they need to get warm and to eat. If you like, we can go down in the hour before dawn, and be ready for the Ipyrans at Sunup."

Nexor smiled. He looked away at another man. "Can *you* get your fellows ready in an hour, Adargon?"

"My lord, I—"

Klyton walked by Adargon, and stood a hand's breadth from the King. In height they were matched. Nexor was a little heavier, but it did not give him psychic weight. Nexor met Klyton's eyes, and stared.

"Great King," said Klyton, his voice not raised, held level as a pherom blade, "I won't fail you by sending on to the field of battle men too weary to serve your honor."

"You're disobeying my order. I'm your King."

"It isn't a game," said Klyton, who had not heard the witch-priestess Evonissa speak in the Karrad's hall.

Nexor's eyes slid away, returned, slid away again. A King must have settled Klyton then and there. The tent was full. Nexor had argued. And no one had made a move to rectify the moment, for not one man was ready to scramble unneedfully to a fight in half an hour.

Outside, the shouts of Klyton's command, crowding round the fat deer dinner his god-blessed luck had ordained for them, reached the tent like the notes of a turning tide.

"All right," said Nexor. He was not even enraged, more . . . sulky. "Have it as you wish."

Adargon's men came over to Klyton's campfires soon after the moon rose, Phaidix Anki riding above Ipyra.

The battalions brought wrung-neck chickens they had had from the last village, and their ration of beer and wine.

At first Klyton's men, particularly the Sirmians, beat them off, softly enough, joking and laughing. Then Klyton walked out and said, "We're brothers. Come on. The enemy is over *there*."

A feast began, and further men moved in from other stations, Lektos' troops, and more. They brought what they could, and the roasted venison was shared with the rabbits, the chickens, and the drink. There was not enough wine to get drunk, which was as well, with the fight tomorrow. But by the light of the torches, some of the soldiers' women danced, their faces and arms flame-polished gold. The men sang songs from old campaigns. Klyton sat with Lektos and Adargon, and one or two other commanders—most of the leading lights of the army in Ipyra.

From the smoke, maybe, the moon blushed rosy.

In his tent hung with crimson, Nexor dined with a meager scatter of sycophants.

They heard the songs.

Over the valley of two miles, the Ipyrans heard them, too. A joyous bridegroom sings before his marriage day, they said, in Ipyra. They listened to the joyous brideroom singing, and wondered if marriage would mean, for them, something else.

In the mid of the night, as the soldiery bedded down and slept, Adargon said to Klyton, under the ice green stars, "Akreon had your luck. Your hunt. That mountain you climbed. He would have done this as you have."

"I aggravated the King," Klyton remarked, lightly.

Adargon, it was sometimes said, of all the royal Suns after Amdysos, had most the likeness to Klyton. Yet they said, too, there was always with Klyton some other touch, the others royal from their blood, and Klyton royal as if from the breath of a fire.

"King," said Adargon. "That one in the red tent?"

Pale Lektos said, "A ship with a buffoon for captain, sinks, or runs aground."

They could not quite see Klyton's face. His smile they saw. In those years, men and women both liked always best to have pleased him.

"Good night," said Klyton. "We meet again, the hour before dawn."

8

The Sun rose unseen in the morning. The sky was dark as a dusk. Far brighter than the sky, the snow looked back, staring white, between the clumps of trees, virgin and unmarked, dividing the two armies. This was soon changed.

The Akhemonians had got down the graded mountain easily, as their King had said, their weapons and harness muffled. When the part-light of day came up, the van was already forging forward over the valley.

The Ipyrans, who had been making offerings, left off and sprang to arms. This could not auger well. Afterwards they blamed it, their unavoidable impiety.

I see the battlefield from the air, as a bird would see it. I have no desire to go down. Though I have heard Klyton recount these events, this is the only view I truly have.

And so I behold the meeting clash of men, the advance, so tidy, like a parade, cloven and wrecked. Lightnings lit from swords. The cries of men coming up to me, so small they cannot mean very much. Udrombis had said, the gods would seem to regard humanity in just this way. Such little noises—of fury, terror, agony, despair—what can they matter?

The Akhemonians were outnumbered, but superior in their training and their tricks. Foot soldiers progressed, slewed away, returned, and cut out the center of the Ipyran force. While Nexor's cavalry closed in the sides.

As Klyton rode over the snow, his men poured at his back, cheering him, and Adargon's men after. Others followed. The whole army in Ipyra had rallied to Klyton, as to something gleaming and worthy of trust. So he looked, golden, infallible, if I could go near enough to see. But from the air he is only, my great love, my lord, another tiny glittering insect.

They fought. Then a rift came in the sky. On the Akhemonians' right, the east cracked wide, and the Sun flared through. It was the Sunrise, coming late from the cloud, a blazing guest to the banquet of war.

The Akhemonians took it for a sign of favor, and the Ipyrans, the enemy of the Sun King, their sacrifices interrupted, were dismayed. The Sun seemed always in their eyes, as had happened at the first fortress, when Klyton scaled to the gates. The Sun beat hard on Ipyra. They said after, the men who fought and lived, that the heat of the Sun was stupendous, too much for a northern mountain day in winter. From the trees in the valley, icicles snapped off and darted down. The ground turned queasy. Foolishly, Ipyran men and horses slid, and before they could adjust themselves, Akhemony was always there, steady as if moving on a well-paved floor.

Probably it needed no more. But there was more.

As his allies grouped in about Uros, ganging to him, shouting out to him to triumph and save them, the wonder was worked that ended everything.

No doubt the sun had slushed the snow. The valley in winter was known to be treacherous.

Even from the air, as I wait now with the circling, optimistic crows, I see the huge, invisible hand punch downward. The sight is so curious, it makes at first no sense.

It is the snow, packed under the horses and men of Uros's massed battalions, which has given way.

As it caves inwards, slowly, more swiftly, too fast, like children at sport the little figures slither down, and are gone into purple dimness. Sixty or seventy sword lengths, the measure of the Sun Lands, the funnel in the earth has opened. The waving arms, the sunny splash of falling spears, all these are part of the game. The game of children, flies, or gods—

The ground roared as it took them in. Uros, bellowing again as he had in the Karrad's hall, Melendor, too astonished to cry out, went down with it, and after them, the snows rushed, and washed over, to bury everything in pillows of white death.

When the roaring stopped, a silvery column of ice-spray rose high from the place, like a beacon.

The battle—faltered. It was finished. Half the Ipyran force was gone. Akhemony gathered itself, watching, as the Ipyrans scratched for their dead, piled one on another seventy sword lengths down, under a bank of snow once more pristine, but for the marks of their digging.

Having unveiled himself, the Sun burned on. The sky was fantastically clear now, pastel as the youngest violets. From the mountains round about, slips of snow gracefully sailed down with the noise of mild sighs, booming in the gorges.

Nexor had accepted the surrender of the Ipyrans. He allowed them to continue digging out their dead.

The priests of Akhemony were making offerings now, on a makeshift altar in the valley. The smoke rose white on the colored sky.

The Great King's army, tranquilized by its uncanny and abrupt victory, waited in silence, watching the smoke.

Nexor was ruddy and merry. He turned red-handed from the sacrifice. And made out, as his commanders did, a line of chariots and men moving carefully along the valley. They came from where the Karrad's fort would be, Uros's grandfather's hold, but there were too few of them to suggest aggression.

The Great King raised his arms at his soldiers.

"The old dotard's coming. To make peace. We'll hang him here, from that handy tree."

The men of Akhemony murmured. Nexor, as always, had misjudged their mood. When he should have courted them, he had stayed aloof. Now he was familiar. A rousing win against dire odds would have left them rowdy and still thirsty for blood. But what had occurred in Two Mile Valley had laid on them the shadow of an ultimate respect. In the prescence of gods, they had had the wit to lower their voices. But here was their High King, bawling and showing off like a nasty boy.

Adargon said, his voice carrying outward to the men, who repeated his words among themselves, "My lord, the Karrad's old, and his son's a child. He won't have wanted to go against Prince Uros, who brought his own troops with him."

"Yes?" said Nexor. He did not grasp what Adargon was saying. He turned and volleyed at the men, "Sack the town, eh, lads?"

Again the men murmured, and stepped from foot to foot. Someone called out, "They've paid their dues."

And a grumble of agreement sounded.

"What? I give you a town to sack and you don't want it?" Nexor chided them, ridiculous and inappropriate. He was like some uncle joshing with a squeamish infant. The army did not like this.

Then Klyton was standing by the King. There was a spray of blood like rubies on his breastplate, and a thin cut which bled across his cheek. Nexor had been somewhere in the fight. Where, they wondered. He was very neat and clean.

Klyton said, so they could hear, "My lord, let it go. There's not much worth taking in Ipyra."

Someone else called from the crowd, "I'd like to take a yellow-haired girl."

Klyton glanced. He said, "But you don't need to *take* her, soldier. You can charm her, surely?"

At that, the crowd went up in laughter. You could see them slapping the caller on the back, tipping his helmet forward over his eyes, since the Sun Prince had got the better of him, and quite right.

Klyton let the mirth die off. They had needed it. Then he said, "Show mercy, my lord King, to the Karrad. Even the God spared him."

The two or three chariots, and the men who had entered the valley with them, had now been taken possession of by Akhemonians. They were being brought towards Nexor, on his high place, by the smoking altar.

Nexor pushed Klyton aside.

"I'll do what I think proper."

A cloud went over the Sun.

An impossible dark bloomed, muffling the valley. It was like that phenomenon which is known in Pesh as an eclipse.

The soldiers made sounds, staring up, gesturing signs for protection. Nexor, too, put back his head to see.

It was not a cloud, but a bank—of birds. The crows of Ipyra, jet black, hundred on hundred of them, and in the midst of them another bird, far larger, which seemed to pull on the rest by the storm of his wings.

"Nexor," Klyton's voice rang out, speaking the King's name without title, "pay attention to that. If you won't hear me or any man, *listen to the sky.*"

He said to me that as he uttered these words, the hair stood up on his head. In the deep cold of the mountains, no longer warmed by supernatural Sun, a comb of ice passed through the hair, the nerves and bones, of almost every man present.

The edge of the Sun tipped free of the bank of flying birds. But the light of the solar orb was lax now. And the colossal shade sank in over the Akhemonians, clustered to the altar; over the Ipyrans, who had ceased scraping out their dead.

It was a moment for stillness, but Nexor shouted again. He shouted those words of his he should not have had, ever, to use. "I am the *King!*"

The giant within the raft of crows was an eagle, they said. It was very large in size, though nothing like the monster at Airis. Nevertheless, seeing it, the soldiers began to cry oaths and prayers. Many fell on their knees.

And the eagle dropped from the cloud of crows. It beat downwards, and on its wings came all the dark heart of the sky.

Now must be given the answer, for Nexor had proclaimed himself what he was, the chosen of the god.

The Sun disc was all free now. Light broke over them. They saw, every man who dared to look, something pure white burst away from the eagle, and descend.

Shining bright as a pail of milk emptied from heaven, it dashed directly upon Nexor's head, bared for the sacrifice, over his face and shoulders, down all his unsoiled armor. Anointed, he stood, spluttering, blinded, wildly wiping at his eyes and mouth, while his priests and servants, horrified, stayed rooted to the ground.

But from the army of the Great King another music began to rise, low at first, then boiling up and over.

The eagle lifted away. The birds of omen flew northward. The army rocked in its lines, squalling with joy, telling itself through its tears of ultimate amusement, the news, until several thousand voices took up those words as a lawless, bronzen chant. "The God—the God—the God has shat on Nexor."

When the old Karrad had his interview with Akhemony, on the cold road, Nexor was not to be seen. It was Klyton who spoke to the Karrad, with Adargon at his side.

The Karrad had dignity. With dignity he held out his hands, in the traditional manner, to be bound.

Klyton said there was no need for that. He understood the Karrad had been threatened by Prince Uros, his grandson, and had had no choice.

With these sentences, the Karrad concurred.

All this while, his comely, deep-breasted wife stood in the chariot with him. She had put on her priestess's black but, around her neck was a copper ring set with milky green agates. She gazed at Klyton without insolence or modesty, from her two smoky eyes and the third eye embroidered on her brow.

Finally Klyton spoke also to her. "You can bring back your son, lady. There's nothing to fear now."

She said, straight out, "Make sure alliance with Ipyra, lord. Then we shall be safe."

Klyton nodded. "I think so. But there are no daughters in your house.

Just then from across the valley, the soldiers' chant, which they were still lovingly indulging in, drifted. Adargon grimaced, but Evonissa turned her head, listening.

After a minute, she looked again at Klyton. She addressed him clearly.

"The gods disdain to bring down a little man. They like to make him tall before they break him, as we make beautiful the beast for sacrifice."

Klyton added to me, when he detailed her words, "I wasn't certain, whether she spoke of Nexor, or of Uros."

Of course, he could not know, as now I know too well. It was of Klyton himself that Evonissa spoke. Her third eye had seen through his shining day fires, to the greater spire of night beyond.

In the following month, most of the lords and Karrads of Ipyra came in, wrestling with the winter passes, to give homage to Akhemony, in the person of Klyton. Nexor had been put away like a poor knife in need of mending.

Among the Karrads, there was one who brought a small army with him, declaring them as loyal to the Sun Kings as the Akhemoian troops. This man was, like dead Uros's kindred, old, yet he rode by horse to the meeting, and had walked over the passes. Though his hair was white, it had been golden, and the beard he kept showed this still.

He had brought a present for the King. Klyton received it. The gift was a book, a marvel, with pages of stone inscribed by a silver chisel, and polished with the dust of diamonds. The covers were also of stone, clasped in bands of electrum. It took two men to carry it with style. The contents, said the bearded Karrad, concerned legends of Phaidix Anki. In other words, here, it was a tome of sorcery.

Klyton was impressed by the book. He said the King would be given it, and would not quickly forget such a token. The bearded Karrad chuckled. He must have heard new-risen Nexor was having an early sunset.

"I never broke my faith with Akhemony," the bearded Karrad announced. "In my mind, I'm bloodkin still to mighty Akreon."

Klyton bowed. "I didn't know it, sir. How is that?"

"My daughter was a jewel, a rare yellow-haired girl of Ipyra." If Klyton considered the portent of the soldier's called-out words, he put it by. "King Akreon beheld my daughter and wed her. She was some while a Daystar of the Great King, but her flowers withered of sorrow after his death. Her name was Hetsa."

9

Happiness comes sometimes in dark disguise. As sorrow comes now and then hidden in a festive dress, with garlands in its hand.

I see, from time's vantage, down that long cliff of my century, they walk together now, in my fifteenth year, and each is masked as the other.

Annotation by the Hand of Dobzah

When Sirai had said these words, she paused some minutes then told me to set the paper by. Two days elapsed before she instructed me again to write.

* * *

From Oceaxis, winter withdrew itself. Moist days of cool Sun had tempted the buds on the trees, miniature flowers under dead leaves. The Lakesea was enamel smooth. Even the turtle roused herself, waddled from under my high bed, and sat in a gem of sunlight by the little pool.

I had heard of the successes from Ipyra. Ermias had garnered too the story of Nexor's disgrace. He had proved a ruffian and an idiot—and finally the god sent a sign of disapproval too exotic to ignore. She did not tell me what it had been.

Klyton and the Sun, Adargon, led the army now, though Adargon, it seemed, stepped back somewhat. He was nearly thirty, and had said, reportedly, everyone had seen in Glardor's day what happened when men of his age took on leadership too late.

Had Nexor been full-crowned, all this might have been more difficult. But, as dead Melendor had declared, the time from winter to summer seemed to have left a space for trial. For Nexor himself, with a small entourage he had gone to consult the wisewomen in Ipyra's most volcanic heights, far to the north. He knew now, at least and at last, when to be absent.

"The certainty is Klyton will be made Great Sun," Ermias said. She looked straight at me. Then lowered her eyes.

"Yes," I answered idly. Why would I care? He was my brother, one of many. He had never held me as a man holds a woman, lit fire in me with lips and hands. For was it not Klyton who taught me afresh that he and I might never be lovers, undoing all the house I had built upon my longing, tearing even my fantasies in pieces.

How had I lived since that night? God knows. I cannot remember. I lay deep in a sea of somber cold that made any winter midsummer noon. And in this hell, I had turned him about, my brother, my beloved. I had reviewed his thoughtless cruelty, his irrational and sudden strides towards me—then, forgetful, away. He had his life, where every second counted like a link in some endless gleaming chain. A woman was, as the saying went, a rose upon the way. Ornament, passtime, comfort—nothing of moment, ever. In my newborn cold, cold anger, I would not curse him. But I withheld my prayers. And see, he had done well enough without them.

Ermias reined her tongue, chose her words. She had often had to do it with my mother, Hetsa.

Nor did Kelbalba anymore broach the subject of my love. No one had had to inform her. She had seen my face that night he came to me and left me. She talked of other things, and sometimes told me her tales, but not very much. She knew I had far less tolerance now for dreams.

By her garments and bearing alone, I knew the woman for one of Udrombis's Maidens. She bowed slightly to me. She said, "The Queen-Widow of the Great Sun Akreon, wishes you to present yourself at the third hour of afternoon."

In my inertia, I was not immediately very unnerved. But I thought, once the woman had gone, that I must have erred in some way. How? *I* had no scope to commit any crime. And then I thought perhaps Udrombis had discovered Klyton's unchaperoned visit to me. This did frighten me. I had learned much of her. She was severe, ruthless, uncompromising. And I—was nothing, easily swept away.

Of course, I had agreed, as I must, to go to her. I dressed with care, also putting on two or three jewels; for one of my rank to appear slapdash would not earn her approval.

Apart from the Hall, and here and there at various ceremonies, I had not seen Udrombis all those years.

I recalled, as I glided at my slow pace through the walks of the palace, how she had leaned in the shape of a bow when the monstrosity, the eagle, ripped her son up into the murderous sky. Even at such an instant, she did not evoke pity. She was a woman of power and marble.

In the passage that led towards the Queen-Widow's rooms, I saw Crow Claw. I knew it was she, a thin, black-clad figure, coming out as it seemed from a doorway—but no door was there—and turning into an alcove from which, when I reached it, she had vanished.

What this sighting could mean I had no idea, nor was there time to ponder. Or to question Nimi, who was following me.

The doors of the royal apartment lay ahead, and a waiting woman, not Crow Claw, hurried from the alcove to usher me on.

Udrombis received me in the room with the hearth, an intimate room, for friends. Her garments were impeccable, as ever, and muted, though her rings blazed, and she wore a cache of emeralds at her throat.

The cedar chair she sat in was one of her smaller thrones. At first I did not reason anything from this, being too anxious.

I bowed to Udrombis. She watched me and watched on when I had straightened up. Then she rose, without one word, and moving up to me, inspected me from head to toe. She felt the stuff of my dress, too, and a piece of my hair. Inevitably I recollected when I had been brought to her as a child, and she had gone over me as they did in the slave-market. But she was still the Sun Queen, Glardor's wife had counted for nothing. Perhaps no other could.

"Calistra," she said. "I hope you're well?"

"Thank you, madam, yes."

"Sit there." I sat in a chair only by one stage smaller than her own.

"The promise of your infancy has blossomed," she said. "I've long admired your ability to walk, and the elegance of the performance, which vastly exceeds that of many born with two feet. You have spirit, and cleverness."

Again I thanked her. On the hearth the fire fluttered over scented logs. My mouth was dry, as it had been in her presence when I was four.

"But," she said, "you dress too plainly. No, I don't reprimand you, Calistra. That you're modest has done you credit until now."

Now?

She sat down. She gazed into her fire, giving me an interval to collect myself. But I lay scattered in bits, and could not do it.

In these very rooms she had administered poisons, so I had heard over the years. Or she had crushed with some more merciful blow.

"You will have heard," said Udrombis, "Ipyra's settled. More firmly settled than for several years. That's Prince Klyton's work." My breath clenched of itself. In a motionless maelstrom, I stared into the hearth. "Klyton has written to me. He has suggested to me something that I've meditated on." I was glad I was not standing up. Dizziness passed through me in a wave. I heard her say, "I will read to you a few words from his letter." Then came the rustle of the fine Arteptan paper lifted from its box. She read me the few lines in a calm, almost inexpressive voice.

When I looked up, I saw as if for the first time: the fire quivered on the white strands of her hair, which now, like snow on obsidian, had almost obliterated her darkness. And for a second I did not know who she was. But she was Fate, as Ermias had been, entering in her yellow dress, and Crow Claw too, manifesting, vanishing.

Klyton had put it to the Queen that my mother, Hetsa, had been the daughter of a strong king in Ipyra, a man who disdained to take up arms against Akhemony. I, therefore, half loyal Ipyran, and half the blood of the Sun House, possessed unique worth, should I be taken to wife by any Great Sun crowned this summer.

"Evidently," said Udrombis, "the incestuous marital union of brother with sister goes unrecognized in Akhemony. However, Klyton points out that, should it be claimed instead that you are the daughter of Hetsa by Glardor and not Akreon—for which reason you were concealed briefly by your mother when a baby—you would remain the progeny of a Sun King, and the next Great Sun, when chosen, would stand as your uncle and not your brother. The union of uncle with niece is credible, in certain circumstances." I sat like a statue, or one dead. Udrombis said, "Of course, it offends your honor to accept bastardy, where you are the legal daughter of Akreon. You must forgive me that I request the sacrifice of you, to secure Ipyra."

My lips parted. Having lost my mind, I got out one name. "Elakti—" Even though I had forgotten who Elakti was.

"Elakti's kindred raised the sword in this war, against Akhemony. Besides, the woman is crazed, running about the hills like a wild cat, with a train of servant girls, rending live rabbits with their teeth." I shivered. She thought, or pretended to think, it was for that. "One is disgusted. But she carries the seed of Amdysos, it seems, and must be safeguarded, as best we can." There was no mark on Udrombis's face. I suspected, disorderedly, she believed Elakti's pregnancy a lie, or some hysterical sterile swelling. God-like Amdysos could have had nothing to do with it.

Someone came in, just as when I was four, and brought me a reward, on this occasion premature. Wine in a fragile goblet, slices of candied winter fruit, transparent, too exquisite to eat.

To manage the cup without spilling it took all my skill. The wine tasted bitter and cold, like the milk of iron.

"Well, Calistra you must reply. To be the Sun-Consort, wife of the Great Sun. This is an enormous mountain all at once before you. But to a woman who has learned to walk without feet, perhaps, a little thing?"

I said, or some creature inside me used my voice to say, "Whatever you want of me, madam. Whatever is best."

"Answered wisely. I expected no less."

To this day, I judge her dealings with me then were as simple as she had presented them to me. But even I had seen how she prized Klyton, and now I know that, without admission, she prized him also as a man. Yet she had no jealousy, no edge. For Udrombis, the honor of the house came first. And I truly believe she did not know I loved him—she truly could not imagine that one such as Calistra should so have *dared*. Note then, this strand of naïveté woven in her robe of dominant power.

But I was not, even then, quite unaware. I saw her sip her wine, and I wondered, what was its taste for her? Doubtless also bitter, always bitter now, as her hair now always would be white.

10

Again, everything alters, in Calistra's world.

We are to be moved. We rise.

Lost to me, the garden of Phaidix, the room with the snake-topped pillars in which I was born. Lost to my turtle, her pool.

And to Ermias, her status as Maiden. She is to be only a lady attached to a princess, for Udrombis has selected and sent me a new Maiden. Ermias says nothing to me. Does it not matter, after all, seeing that she will come to be the lady of a Sun-Consort, all of whose women are named Maidens, higher than any ordinary Maiden could reach?

There are so many women, now. Women to see to garments, and to see to bathing and anointing, to the hair and the nails. And slaves—countless girls—to wait on every whim. I search for Nimi in their crowd, and locate her, finely clad, with little jewels in her ears. We have all gone up, lifted by the Queen's disinterested hand.

But no. She has an interest in our value. We serve the House of the Sun. For the diadem of which she has chosen Klyton.

We are physically higher too, in the upper storys of the palace.

I have five great rooms which open off the central chamber, and a set of luxurious cells to content my chief women.

This, the central chamber, amazes me.

A terrace looks towards the Lakesea, between long, mulberry pillars. At night shutters and draperies are pulled close, but on the fine days, this side of the room is all a heaven of atmosphere and light.

Below, the palace gardens, and then those other ancient gardens which cascade to the shore, where long ago, as a child of twelve, I sat, and Klyton found me.

Because my turtle is mine, they make for her a new pool. This pool is much larger, and its floor is laid with leaf-green tiles. A statue of Gemli, taller than I, poises on the rim. She is painted and lovely, and nearby is an enormous cage with six pale pink doves. Once the doors are secured, the doves are let out, and fly around. Any droppings are wiped away at once by one of the slaves, whose name I have not learned.

Somehow I keep Kelbalba. I have explained it was she who helped me to walk.

She and I, then, one afternoon, staring, in the room with mulberry pillars. From the gardens beneath breathe the scents of tamarind, the myrtle, the marroi, on an orchestra of crickets, and with that, the sea, which has now a louder voice.

"Whose rooms are these?" questions Kelbalba.

"Calistra's rooms."

We smile. My smile dies the first.

I have new dresses. One a ripe, deep red blood-color, the blazon of the Sun Kings. There is, among the ornaments, a headdress like a great wreath. It is formed from the petals of gold flowers, the gold traceries of leaves, and golden wheat-ears, symbol of fruition, of the earth mated to the solar sky.

In this gown and this crown, I go first to the Hall, and sit, as she has told me to, close by Udrombis.

I see myself like a beautiful doll, near to the Widow-Queen's chair. And how, every so often, she confers with me or sends me some sweet or fruit to try.

None of this is overlooked.

Disgraced Nexor had taken no High Queen. Glardor's widow is gone. I notice instead, Klyton's Sirmian wife, Bachis, her tawny hair plaited with Bulos pearls, her belly like a bladder under pale silk. Once she raises her eyes to me, flits them away.

She is to be my little sister, if I am to be his . . . I think you are looking at me now, asking of yourself, and me, what then I felt. From the air, I gaze down and see Calistra. For her heart, imagine the constrained turmoil of a waterfall. Her mind is the river in spate. Nothing stays.

In my land of shadow I had began to debate. Now I was woken

quite roughly from my shadow, into a brilliant dream. There was no place to find my balance. I felt a strange terror, and more than glad, I was finally rebellious. If I, so little, was to be made Queen of the World, I was at last entitled to anger.

He returned in the late spring. He had been busy in Ipyra, settling her in his own fashion, visiting the chiefs and kings, taking them gifts, and letting them see the smart soldiery of Akhemony for themselves. But what had started as a war had become a progress. Adargon went with him—Lektos had come home to speak volumes of Klyton's worth, in the councils at Oceaxis. The Karrad, my grandfather, Hetsa's sire, traveled with Klyton, too. Ipyra had not often had so much trouble taken with her. Like a groomed horse or a human cunningly flattered, she began to show her friendly side.

The blossoms of the gardens had made way for green. The troops marched in through the town, and the first roses were torn out to award them a carpet.

No one said I must go to shower Klyton with flowers. As once before, I stayed in my rooms.

Akhemony had by then decided. It was all settled. From the Sun Temple uncurled the thick pall of the offerings, visible to me from my terrace over the trees.

I had a new tutor. He was a skinny, squeaky-voiced priest; his task was to teach me the manners of my ascension—the religious duties and day to day behaviour of a Sun-Consort.

But I was used to learning. I had learned such a lot.

Klyton, his formal reception over, went first to see Udrombis, and next, his mother.

I was conscious Stabia must be ill. She had not come to the Hall for more than two months. Ermias no longer gossiped to me, and my Maiden was a perfect icon, her slim mouth closed on anything but the platitudes of her service to me. It was Nimi, burnishing my turtle's shell, who whispered that Klyton had only just been in time, for Stabia was near to death. An exaggeration, as it happened. Or rather, a prediction.

Even in my tumult, this checked me. Stabia had been, for a moment, a guide in my desert. More, she had seemed my friend. There was a shrine for the most royal women on the upper roofs, that now I had access to, and so I went there and made an offering of perfume for Stabia. Squeaky, my priest-tutor, had told me exactly which substance must be employed in every circumstance. But as the jam-sweet odor of the scent drifted with the smoke, and melted in the sky, and birds sang carelessly in the gardens, I knew how useless this was, and how redundant. Never before, I think, had I detected the true distance of the gods, their inattentive quality. Passionately, in all my tribulations, I had kept some faith. Was it perhaps curious or apt, that as my wish came home to me, I lost it?

The Squeaker had decorously hinted that I would be the next person Klyton should call upon. My closemouthed Maiden also intimated that I must get ready.

So I, like the offering, was laved in perfume. I was dressed in white and wound with gold. Over my hair, they set a golden net with silver stars, and into this were fastened flowers pink as the caged doves. I thought of the flowers cast before Klyton on the street. I, too, was to be his carpet, something fragrant and pliable for his glory to step on.

The day had passed. They were kindling my lamps. This procedure had taken a few minutes in my former apartment. Now it was a great business.

As the hollow familiar caves of rooms blushed into light, Klyton arrived at my door.

I received him in the outer room, where all the lamps were burning. Two of his servants appeared first, and put down a pinewood chest bound with brass. This they flung open as though before a market crowd, to reveal a heap of shimmering cloth and tinsels, while ropes of purple gems spilled artfully on the floor.

Then came another servant, leading forward a milk-white hound on a gold leash, which moved daintily up to me, ignoring the turtle, who drew in her head under her shell.

Perhaps he had chosen the time, the hour of the lamps when our eyes find the color again which a fading Sun took away.

As two more servants approached me and put down a tall electrum mirror on a stand of gilded bronze, a third undid a cat-shaped glass flagon, and let me sniff the balsam of Ipyra's forests. It was utterly unlike the stuff I had offered the gods for Stabia. As if he had known.

By then, he had walked through into the room. And the lamps did their office, too, for him.

I got up. I bowed. The women were rustling all about me like half-settled moths; fluttering for his beauty, ritually, but it was only partly pretence.

Now I must face him, and see him.

He had dressed himself richly for our meeting, a proper courtesy. In the lampglow the armlets and collar of gold, the golden borders of his tunic, and his hair, made him one with the light. He was winter-tanned from wind and sun on snow. And against this frame his eyes took a metallic gleam, like the surface of swords.

What had I ever seen when I looked at him? A god, of course a god. And the gods were far away, unlistening, their kindness incidental, *accidental*. If they should speak of love, it was only as a man would caress the neck of a favorite dog.

I withdrew my eyes from Klyton, and godlike, smoothed the neck of my living present, the milk-white hound. Its eyes were black, reflective, two more valuable jewels.

Klyton had somehow come right up to me.

He said, "I thought you'd like that the best."

"He's very fine. Thank you, my lord."

"I've heard the view from your terrace is pretty. I have never seen it. Show me."

He was moving me, his hand on my arm. We were going through the room, the women, to the pillared terrace, which had not yet been shuttered for the night.

My Maiden, the women, followed us. The slaves at the lamps, the shutters, hesitated, and turned to mellow carvings.

Klyton left me. He strode to look down from the terrace into the gardens. The moon was rising, little more than the shaving of a white pearl. Two stories down, guards passed at intervals. Klyton hailed one of these and there rose up the clank of a salute.

He is so handsome, so miraculous, he means nothing at all, this King-to-be. I remember when he was a boy. He was only a prince, and I—I had come from the House of Death.

He retraced his steps to me and, bending, ran his hard, golden hand, stamped with a fresh black scar, over the head of my milk-white, moon-white dog.

"I'm glad you are well." he said to me.

He did not touch me any more. Without any further words, he turned and left the room, passed through the group of women, Sun through cloud, was out of a door which careful servants closed.

I went to the dinner in the Hall, as Squeaky, had I asked him, would have told me I must. Klyton was there, feted like the god he now was. The harpers rendered songs of sublime heroes hidden from enemies on mountain sides, disguised as mortal, revealed in youth by valiant deeds.

The more I watched Klyton—surreptitiously, of course, the less I knew him. But I never had known him.

After the most important harper had sung and Udrombis had sent me some fruit to try, and I had done so, I left the Hall.

Once able to dismiss the butterfly flock of women, I stood alone by my terrace, one shutter pulled back.

The pillar where I rested my hand was chill. The night was a luminous pane, and the warmth of summer had not yet come. The Lakesea resembled endlessly folded silk under the slender hip of Phaidix's bow. All the gardens were black, composed of secrets. There would be dusks when the women danced there. I would see lights near the shore, a fringe of fireflies.

I then, felt old. It is strange. With age has come the knowledge that what I felt was accurate enough. Save I was old within a young skin.

Down from the high raised Hall, a great roar rushed, extraordinary, like fire. Probably the princes were harping now, and the wine poured over among discarded garlands.

Sleep was softer than the fur across the bed. And then it lifted like a lid. Calistra lay, her eyes wide on the darkness. A door had opened, closed.

Over the length of the room, on Gemli's shrine, the apricot-colored flame stooped, and straightened. It showed half the outline of a tall male figure, the roped drop of a cloak. The girl in the bed did not speak, and the man moved to her over the floor of night.

Her attendants, that host of them, slept in their own apartments away across the outer room. One slave must keep watch by the doorway but presumably she had slumbered—or been bribed?

The man trod noiseless as a leopard. From him came the scents of bruised garlands, wine and heat, and of the tindery tamarinds in the gardens. Shadow hung on him. Yet Gemli's flame described his hair like gilding. He still wore his own garland—ormis, myrtle flowers.

"Don't be frightened," he said. "Do you know me?"

"Klyton," Calistra said.

"I won't harm you. I wanted to see you—out of that swirl of women. Udrombis has told you. You and I."

She said, "You are to be Great Sun. I am to wed you."

"Sun-Consort." he said. "You talk as if it were nothing." She heard him laugh, very low. "But it isn't so much to us, is it? Only like the air. We were meant for this, Calistra."

Calistra sat up slowly. Her filmy garment she kept within the cover of the fur, pulling it round her to conceal her arms and breasts. But farther down the bed, she noted, as perhaps he had not, the lapse beneath the blankets, her ultimate nakedness. Had he remembered? She could not spring up to run away.

Klyton sat on the bed's side. He seemed at ease. He said, "You mustn't be upset. I haven't disgraced you. I saw to it Adargon's man has the watch below. I climbed up when he was relieving himself. For decorum's sake. But if he saw me, he knows who it was. And your slave girl is one I know as well. There was even a shutter left ajar."

Calistra shook her head. These facts were irrelevant. "Why?" she said. She heard her voice, an isolated, glassy note.

"Why do you think?"

His hands reached her in the dark, slid over her and *through* her— she was drawn out of her wrappings into the warmth of the shadow. And the shadow was clean breath tinctured by wine, smooth flesh and muscle, and his tasseled hair brushing heavy on her throat. She turned her mouth from his. At this he sat away, releasing her. "Forgive me. If you don't want to. I'll wait, of course." He had been so sure of her, still seemed so. He did not breathe quickly, was not yet urgent. Not even disappointed.

Who was he? He controlled so much, yet climbed up the wall like a boy . . . The faint light gave her nothing, only the line of his cheekbone, his brow and nose and lip. His lashes, one sequin in one eye. The wide shoulder and the costly gem that pinned the cloak and had a heart of scarlet.

"You told me," she said, "we must remain apart."

How small her quarrel was. Why speak of it?

But he said, "The gods showed me otherwise."

I love you, she thought. The words were only the echo of another cry. Inside herself she turned—like a fish, a serpent—seeking to find the way back to him.

And thought, terribly, *He is no longer that same one I loved.*

In reply, oddly, he said, "The gods have changed me, Calistra. I was almost afraid of it at first. The power, this *power* they've given me. I can *take*, and *make*. I'll see Akhemony certain, and then stop the Sun Lands fighting one with another—I'll give them something else. Have you heard of the other mythical land? The place beyond the outer ocean? I think now it does exist. It's there for us, and I shall have it. Calistra. I'll have all the world. Ah, darling girl, how beautiful you are."

He leant forward. The garland dropped away.

She realized the lamp shone only but fully upon her, illuminating her for his inspection, her face unpainted, sheer, her hair loose in a sheet of paleness, her throat, her breasts distinct now under the gossamer nightrobe. She seemed soaked in luster, and felt her own loveliness as she had never done. She had never seemed to herself so actual, so present. And where the dark hid her, from the ankles down, where she was not, even at her *feet*, as before, she tingled with liveness.

"You're mine," Klyton said. "You know this, Calistra. You knew it before I did. Won't you give yourself to me? In two months, you'll be crowned my consort. And we've *waited*—"

She belonged to him. It was true, she had always comprehended. And in the somber mirror of his unseen face, she glimpsed the vision of her own profound mystery, for the first.

Stretching out her hands, she put them on his chest, pushing lightly against him, not to thrust him off, but to contact the reality of his flesh.

His breathing changed. He leaned to her once more.

"Let go of yourself, Calistra. Give yourself to me. I won't allow you to fall."

It was as if, deep in the well of self, she sensed the dawn, and swam upward towards it. Not understanding, not even in desire, but primitive instinct. No other thing had any importance.

He took her face in his hands like a silver cup, and drank from her mouth. And she became only wine that gave itself to be drunk.

Klyton was to have the world. She became the world. He had filled her with his soul, his power, his splendor.

And as she clung to him she beheld him now, as if the lamplight shone suddenly through her, on to him. She met his fire with the torch of her surrender, through every surface of her skin.

Pressed back into the bed by his weight and his body's near-metallic hardness, she flew, suspended from his strength, as he bore her up on wings as wide as Sunrise.

Her virginity was gone already, torn by the accident as she learned to walk. The first pain of the storm-strokes of human lust altered, in an incandescent spasm, to a bursting sweetness that turned her inside out. Winged with light, as he was, she soared through illimitable inner space. In the grip of an eagle.

Klyton was the Sun.

How had she ever doubted the gods? They were her kindred.

11

Along the shoulder of the hill, the shrieks came now almost continuously. It was afternoon, but no birds sang. Crickets indifferently drizzled. A cloud sent down its ominous indigo shade, which ran from hummock to hummock of the high grass, like spilled water.

The summer pavilion had improved with the coming of warmer months, and some cartloads of necessary luxuries brought from Oceaxis. With the settling of Ipyra, Elakti's status grew less suspect and more cherishable. There was still a spy in her makeshift household, however. Through this woman, one of Elakti's two lesser attendants, the news filtered back that Elakti stayed both mad and heavy with child. Other details of her life also, more fluidly, reached the court. How wonders were supposedly performed at wild ceremonies in the hills, huge animals and spirits manifesting. That Elakti had been joined by a band of lawless girls from nearby upland farms, even from the town, females who had been disowned or, alternatively, were thought touched by divine unreason.

It seemed the insane acts at the pavilion did no harm. Elakti, who might have become quite unacceptable in a palace of the Sun Kings, was for the time being permitted to go on in her crazy career.

Last night, as the spy had this morning duly reported to her messenger, there had been another frenzy under the full moon.

The women had caught and killed a deer, not with their bare hands and teeth, as the rumors had it, but with spears, for the girls of the farms often learned hunting perforce. This meat they roasted on a fire in the pine grove by the altar, allocating a raw portion to the goddess Anki.

Then they danced and sang to Amdysos and to Phaidix and pregnant Elakti screeched and jumped, though by now enormous, her black hair whipping over the moon's face.

All the women, Elakti and the spy included, got drunk.

Also with the wine had been chewed peculiar herbs of the hills, which Elakti's witch crone recommended. The spy secretly avoided the herbs, pretending to take them or spitting them out. She had informed the Widow-Queen Udrombis that it was undoubtedly these herbs which caused the appearance of huge, snow-white lions, gigantic tarry foxes, for she herself never saw them. The one appearance she had witnessed, she did not mention. To tell of a supernaturally large bird, possibly an eagle, in the winter after Amdysos's loss, had seemed tactless.

The spy woman came back from her walk with the messenger, and began ordering the preparation of food in the yard kitchen. Presently Elakti's first shriek cracked through the morning air. Until now Elakti had never screamed by day.

The other slave flew in from the cistern, having broken her jar. About the yard, the uncouth farm sluts sprawled to sleep off their drinking, roused and gaped, from round peasant faces and greasy disordered tangles.

The spy turned contemptuously, but Elakti screamed again.

Phelia, Elakti's Maiden, hurried into the yard. She was vivid and horrified, as she had been all winter and much of the spring.

"Where is the old woman?" demanded Phelia of the spy.

"I don't know, lady."

"Find her. Find her at once. The mistress is in labor."

They found the crone gathering her dubious simples along the hill, and brought her back.

She cackled and prepared a brew. Elakti gulped it and slept for an hour. Then she woke up and resumed her screams. Under the sheet her belly heaved, like a tempest in a sail.

Phelia stood dithering, twisting her hands.

"She should be at Oceaxis. The child's too early. The last birth was difficult."

The spy, seeing her chance, piped up. "Shall I take a mule and ride down, lady? The roads are all passable now. I could be there by evening."

Phelia sent her. In this way, the spy missed a good deal.

Through the day, Elakti screamed on, and kicked the sheet in buffets. Her face was deadly yellow or bright red, and sweat streamed from her. She cursed with words Phelia shuddered at, but had heard from her before. She snatched Phelia's hand, which had tried to rearrange her pillows, and bit it.

Clouds rolled in across the Sun, amethyst, and languid slaty plum. From the upper hills there was no sound beyond the crisping of the crickets. Everything, but they, stayed dumb before Elakti's strident agony.

"*Why* must I suffer this? *Why* must a woman suffer *this*? The gods— *the gods*—I piss on the cruelty of the gods—" railed Elakti, and then she screamed for Amdysos, wailing how he would have held her, bracing her effort with his strong arms. Unlike, apparently, the first time.

"He's behind the moon, he lives there, in the dark. My husband the Dead Sun—who will return—look down and pity me.'"

Phelia bound her bitten hand, from which the blood streamed. She had not eaten the magic herbs either. Like the spy she always pretended. Phelia had seen none of the sorcerous creatures who circled the altar.

Now, observing Elakti, writhing and tumbling on a birthing couch unfit for any royal woman, Phelia clasped her heart in a new fear. For the thing in her mistress's belly churned and bulged, bestial, abnormal and obscure. It had no look of anything natural. Indeed, it never had, for Elakti's burgeoning shape had always seemed grotesque.

It could not get out this being, whatever it was. Would it work its escape with claws?

In the coils of an incredible fright, Phelia rushed from the room.

Above, the cruel gods might have heard Elakti's vituperation. Lightning split the clouds, the thunder crashed and guttered through the hills. No rain fell.

Nevertheless, Phelia was quite wrong. The child would soon be born.

The spear-bride-wife Elakti leaned on the chaos of her bloody, rumpled bed. The room was in silence. No one made a noise. And she, cleared of all her screams, pointed at the crone with one blunt wooden finger.

"*What have you done?*"

"I? Done? Done nothing."

"Those herbs—some wickedness."

"*No*, lady. Done nothing."

"You shall be skinned alive. My girls will see to it."

The crone crouched low. She hid her face in her robe. Elakti's women whispered, and were still.

Elakti sank back. She shut her eyes.

"They punish me. Always. Amdysos, cry to the gods, for me."

The room was full of shadows, also turning the color of cinnamon as the storm lapped up all light. Even the bloodstains had lost their cheerful red.

In one corner, a rough stone image of Bandri, goddess of birth, smuggled there by one of Elakti's girls, watched indifferently. She seemed to say, All things may occur. Even this.

"How have I deserved it? What shall I do?" Elakti asked, but of no one in the room.

The crone crackled, "Child comes too fast. Too eager."

The child lay on the bed. It was wrapped in a piece of cloth. But still, despite Phelia's care, it was partly visible.

No one looked at the child.

No one spoke.

Outside, the swarthy lightning flashed, the clouds were mute black with nightfall, in the dying afternoon.

> *How are we to live?*
> *There is no sorrow unknown to men.*
> *Birth sends us to a house of shadows,*
> *And at the end, to Night.*

KEPSTROI

The verse spoken between the dances

CONTENTMENT MAKES NO STORY, as they say in every land, even here, in the Moon City. Tales of heroes end with bliss, or with death. But for me it was as if death had died. Or, it was the lot of others. For Klyton and for myself there stretched forward the pathway of destiny. And we were young. There was to be more than a year, much less than two. In memory this time floats, a lucent bubble shot with colors. Who would not ask, after, was it for this I paid in my heart's blood? Was it then worth its price? The gods were kind, hiding the future behind a veil. Or they laughed at us, thinking, how high they fly these mortal things, up into the Sun which will destroy them. Unless such gods as those do not exist, and random chance rules all. Chance which is blind and deaf and crushes worlds under its feet, unseen, unheard.

That summer, I was crowned Klyton's consort in the Temple of the Sun, some days after he had been diademed as the Great Sun. Udrombis, the most important woman in Akhemony, far more than I would ever be, stood for my mother. This honor did not go unheeded. I was garbed in gold on gold, and the heavy golden crown, with its dazzles of ruby and diamond, made me dizzy, but I did not care.

The King wore robes of lions' skins, fringed with silk stained red from the marroi. His golden diadem masked over his eyes also in gold. That he was a stranger in these moments did not count against us. The god had filled him. I knew him also as the stranger.

Could I see anything aside from Klyton?

We went about Akhemony, greeted everywhere with flowers and songs. I recall a landscape made of precious metals, gems and dyes, scented with summer blooms, like Paradise. The edges of Bulos received us, and three hundred pearls as large as the paws of my white dog were heaped before me. From Oriali they brought us gums, ointments, and silks. Later we went north into Ipyra, and the old Karrad, my unknown grandfather, greeted me, once Klyton had carried me in his arms up the awkward stair of his fort. In a raftered cavern baked primrose with sulphur, and mostly floored by fire, two ancient women, with the faces of lizards, told Klyton he was a true-born King. They did not prophecy, I remember. He did not ask it of them. He knew, and doubted nothing. Besides, they were always ambiguous.

I recollect nights with stars so thick the sky itself was like a fretted lamp. Great windows which opened on these skies, the sound of rivers, acres of wheat sighing, and a coast where Uarian ships lay in reptilian lines, sailors bringing the homage of copper ingots, coral and aquamarines, and horses whose manes had been made green, like the scales of the water.

But all these sights, this jewelry of the earth, has become one with Klyton. It is he that is their center, like the Sun, holding them out to me, pouring them down on me. The taste of the delicious peach is not more yearned for than his mouth. He is my temple, larger than any country, the golden pillars of his body, the altar of sex, the sword of pleasure with which he cleaves me. In a torrent of sights, I watch only his eyes sea-green. Or the faultless choreography of his limbs at exercise and riding. He seems tall, to me as the sky, and at night, his hair rays through all the lamped stars as he possesses me, I am obliterated and reborn.

No longer do I make any songs to him. I have become the song itself.

I suppose he was not continuously with me. He was the King. He moved in the sphere of the male universe. Yet I was at anchor, held to him even in absence, lost in the daydream of him, until he returned to me, and the wonder of reality brought back the perfect light.

Nor was it solely with me, this abundance. From the land itself richness teemed out. The harvests overflowed the ending of that first year. Beasts bore two-fold, or three. And so I see a tapestry of sheaves and fruit, young animals, the beaded grapes on malachite vines, the honey dripping amber from the comb.

Stabia, his mother, did not stay for the harvests. She had died that summer, in her sleep, before we came back to Oceaxis. For a queen, even a Daystar, the mother of the Great Sun, the priests did not bring flames from heaven. Embalmed, she lay in one of the granite tombs, her hands folded, on every inch of her the precious stones of her royalty and her years with Akreon. Udrombis had mourned her, in the ordained manner.

Klyton told me of his mother's death in three sentences. "How I regret I wasn't here, but she knew her days were done. She had courage. She'll be glad to be with my father."

I was all in all to him of womankind. I did not hear any murmur which said, *What will he say of you?* Because I did not remember I could ever die.

The winter was mild, the air so clear Koi and the Heart were usually visible, touched only with two wreaths of white.

Klyton had drawn the lands together. No longer a game-board for war, a challenge and testing ground.

Nevertheless, the army of Akhemony trained, turning a field of spears like silver corn in the wind. Sirma had added her battalions, and Ipyra. A corps from Uaria cantered on their ocean-maned horses. Embassies marched in from Charchis. And from everywhere came men, scholars, poets, any who would speak of the other land, which lay across the Endless Sea, the legend which now seemed to be coming into life, far out beyond the Benighted Isles. How curious it is. I remember the harpers now began to sing of it. And I recall not one word.

Through the dark, between lovemaking and brief sleep, he would talk to me. I learned all his plans. I heard of the past, of the years of pause, and of Amdysos, brother and friend—everything of *him*.

Klyton had had made a portable shrine to Amdysos. It went with us wherever we journeyed. It was of white crystal, plaited with gold, and within stood a polished marble statuette of the man, handsome and proportioned as he had been when alive. But the statue also was winged. Being now in the Place Below, Amdysos had forgone most human limitations, and might be thought of as a lesser god, since he had almost been a King. Klyton offered to him, giving him wine and incense, even portions of a kill when he had been hunting. Memory brings me the image of a beautiful bird, lying on the shrine, with turquoise feathers slowly growing dull. My husband told me he had consulted and spoken always with Amdysos, until their quarrel—the quarrel which had foretold, as does the dusk the night, Amdysos's end. Now, still, Klyton spoke to Amdysos. In those separate kingly rooms, once or twice, I had heard Klyton conversing with Amdysos. There were silences too, as of listening to Amdysos's answers.

"If he had ruled Akhemony, I would have stood beside him. All this I do—I believe he showed me the way of it. It's only right, to keep him informed."

Love is unreasonable, therefore was I jealous? I think I was not. The male universe, I had always seen, was separate from my own. That Klyton spoke also to me was joy enough.

Of course, it was he who talked. What had I to tell? Sometimes the charming dog did some trick and amused us both. Klyton would stroke the turtle under her chin. He called her Old Lady. She had become remote from me as he drew always near. I was sorry for it, but had not time, every second filled by him, to rectify or lament. I could see nothing but him, I have said.

In the fall of the first year, amid the harvests, Bachis, his little spear-wife from Sirma, gave birth to Klyton's son. This was a fine boy, with hair like the gold plaiting on Amdysos's shrine. Again, I had no jealousy. Klyton visited Bachis prudently, once in every month. As the mild winter stepped on, I knew that he must also, then, lie in her bed. That was merely propriety. Similarly he had made her uncle a commander in the Sirmian military ranks. Now and then, though not often, I would meet with Bachis. She was always obsequious, bowing very very low. Udrombis had ascertained, she posed no threat. After all, Bachis had been lucky. She was a Daystar. And I—I was the Sun-Consort.

For Calistra, no idea of pregnancy interposed, for sexual delirium seemed everything in itself. No one chivied me. I was just sixteen years, and had, no doubt, time to prove myself. Even Udrombis, as she brooded on the edifice of our dynasty, must have thought so, for she left me to my idyll in peace.

I swear I felt nothing of my temporal power. The Widow ruled, and I had no wish to assume her mantle. I wanted only what I had. And very few petitioners sought me, most deduced where they must try, for favors, justice or advancement. Nor was I jealous of Udrombis.

Oh, love. Love is best of all. There is no such total element, not even pain. Who has ever loved, knows this. I need not say more.

But in Oceaxis that winter, among my now colossal train, I caught sight of Ermias.

I had forgotten her, as I had forgotten everything. Even Kelbalba
I had mislaid. She had lessoned another girl in her work, got me accustomed to her, then gone away to the hills. I had tried a little vague dis-
suasion. She jokingly refused me. I let her go. Sometimes I wonder, if
Kelbalba had still been by me—but I shall never know.

Ermias wore clothes a princess would not have spurned. Her skirt
border, which swept the earth, was a hand's length thick and sewn with
silver nuggets. Her face was haughty. I discovered she had another
lover among the Suns. Something prompted me and I called her to me.

She entered the room carefully, and glanced at me, sidelong. She
knew as well as I that Udrombis wished her neither elevated nor cast
down. Did she ponder what I had become?

I asked her how she was. Ermias said she was well. I said I had
been thinking she might like to own a small estate, one of several
Klyton had given me to use as gifts.

Ermias flushed. "You're very generous, madam."

Did she ever think of that night, thousands of eons past, when she
had wept and I had gone to her, and given her the drink Crow Claw
seemed to have prepared. The night Ermias had ceased to hate me, and
so taken me to the groves.

I said, "Ermias, you've been a friend to me. I regret I can't do
more for you."

She put back her head and stared into my eyes. It was unnerving,
suddenly to be conscious, in my gleaming exclusive happiness, of
another life that was not his or mine.

She was thirty or more by now. She kept her attractions, her curly
hair prettily dressed, her form voluptuous and graceful. I recall, she
wore earrings shaped like moons.

"Another High Queen." she said, "might have killed or banished
me, because I went with him when she could not."

Astonished, I felt a blush of shame in turn rush up my throat and
face. I lowered my eyes, and ran my finger over the head of the white dog.

I said, diffidently, "Don't you want anything? Ask me, perhaps I
can see to it."

Ermias stared on at me.

All at once she said. "You're in the sunny mesh of fortune,
madam. Oh—be careful."

I met again her eyes. They were wide and dark. I thought of her
in the doorway announcing fatefully Klyton, and her yellow dress.

"What are you saying?"

"He—may not love you always," she faltered.

Until then, I had never thought of that. It had been a task of many struggling, frantic years, to reach him. Now we were one. Tales of heroes end in bliss. I did not think to chide her.

"Why do you mention such a thing, Ermias?"

"What's come to you—it burns too bright—" she cried out.

Had I called her in for this? I had learned with time a few forms of behavior, and now recalled them.

"I shall forget you said it. Ermias. Now go away. It seems in fact I must banish you. Go to the estate I've given you. Remain there."

She fled me. She had cause. Another Queen, as she herself might have added, could have repaid her with much distress. Naively, I did not assume she had spoken from malice. I think she did not. She had done well, and might have done better, keeping my friendship. What then, oh what, seizes on us all, at such times, to make us speak what is not in us, like a bell struck by some unseen hand.

The lamps had been lit, and far beyond the pillared terrace, when I parted the shutters, the Lakesea lay winter-dim. In the gardens mist had gathered like ghosts. All I considered, was how Klyton had climbed to me up this wall.

I was young, I was young, and soon enough, marked as always by the flurry of our servants, he would be here, the trumpet note, the Sun's rise.

I folded Ermias away in my mind. Deep in that chest I buried her cry, *It burns too bright*. That cry the wisewomen in Ipyra had been too wise to utter.

One scene does come to me, all at once, now, delineated more intensely than my coronation, than the first time even Klyton lay with me.

It is my bedchamber, in the earliest of some summer morning. I see the sunlight, pink as a cat's tongue, on the high blond bed with its frame of citroen wood, inset with ivory, its ivory stems and feet, its patterned linen, and gauze curtains drifting like thin glass become smoke. The designs on the floor I see, the tiny squares of russet, mauve and rose. Gemli's little shrine, with an electrum bowl of straw-colored flowers, that have filled the air all night with the cool aroma of pale fruits. The small flame there flickers, and makes each flower seem to stir, as if about to flutter away. The dog lies stilly sleeping at the bedfoot, and the sunlight through the drape finds also pink in his alabaster coat. On the walls the never-moving women are gathering unfading tamarinds. But they are motionless and sleeping too, the man and girl. Their long hair has mingled in the night, his bronzy gold with her fairness, which he compares to topaz. Yet, in slumber, their bodies have dropped quietly apart, like two halves of a broken shell.

And she has no feet.

Soon they will wake, turn thirstily together, and be one again. The dog will shake himself, and the birds sing. Akhemony will ring with sunshine.

And when the second year sweeps in, we will gallop through its arch in our chariot of victory, behind the starry horses, the world running after with ribbons and music. Up, up, towards the scorching Sun.

4th Stroia

Thunder, and Night

I

UNDER THE SLOPES OF AIRIS, herders had pastured their flocks. They came up also from Ipyra now, to the thick summer grazing, and mingled mostly freely with the folk of northern Akhemony. Now and then there might be a spat, boys fighting over a patch of clover for their goats, or a ram that had mounted another man's sheep. These things were put right usually before the Sun had set. It was becoming another lush summer, after quenching, full rains. There was more than enough for all.

By afternoon, the land stretched beneath the sky's warm bowl, showing slight movement, and purring with bees. Below, the fields were flushing to their green, and above, the trees that circled the lower mountain, had gained a green as dense in color as blood. The crag rose, cut clean as if carved from marble. Birds flashed down, and upwards. Sheep lazily grazed, or lay under the trees with thinking, watching faces.

A boy, having eaten ewe's cheese and raisins, sat with his pipe, making a tune. If he had any awareness beyond the tune, his flock, he did not know it. And so, as a shambling unhuman figure crested the slope, he viewed it a moment with apathy.

The bright wall of the sky was at its back, undimmed by any cloud. The shape of the figure seemed all jagged edges, darkened, flattened, and uncouth, having no purpose in the day.

The sheep nearby under the tree started, and got up, and came trotting towards their keeper. Rising then in his turn, the boy let out a warning yell. Though he had barely seen what this thing was, the hair now was lifting on his neck. He wanted others, the men from farther off, with the herd dogs.

But the figure stopped quite some way from the boy. It had the semblance of a head, and used it, to look about, as if only just now had it evolved there, from some other country that was not like this one. Some country perhaps that had no sky, and no land.

"Keep back!" shrilly shouted the boy, standing in the white huddle of the sheep.

The figure in fact had not come on. Now it turned its head, such as the head was, in the direction of the boy. There sounded a breath like a punctured bellows. "What say?"

It, too, could speak in a fashion. The voice on the wheeze of breath was rough, breaking across the words—oddly just as the boy's voice sometimes broke at the approach of manhood.

"Keep back—keep off—"

"Is danger?" asked the thing, which possibly *was* a man. And then, gently, in those tones of crunched shale, "Don't fear, will help."

At this moment two men dashed down from the higher pastures, with three big dogs. There were boar in the upper woods, and sometimes lions, one took no chances with a frightened call. Knives glinted. One man rushed straight at the creature, and the dogs bounded with him. All pulled up three feet or four feet away. But it was the dogs, bred for their fight, and who had tackled wolves only this winter gone, who went down belly-flat, showing their teeth, ears back, growling, not moving one inch closer.

"Came over the hill—" cried the boy.

The man who had got close to the figure backed off and the dogs backed off with him, slow, like stones moving.

"What are you?" shouted the man. "What do you want?"

The figure looked, as it seemed, aimlessly now. But the nearer man saw it had only one eye, a muddy watered black in a bloodshot and terrible, staring, bulging eyeball. Where the other eye had been was a pit, like the crater of a burned-out volcano.

Braver, and impatient the second man strode up and struck the intruder across the head. The creature reeled, and then peculiarly whipped back. Taking hold of its aggressor as he tried another blow, it had him at once over, and down on the ground. The thing stood above him, watching him with the repulsive eye. Even at this the dogs did not fly for its throat.

But it made no further attack, not pressing its advantage. The man presently struggled up, and limped aside.

"Leave it be," he gasped, no longer so valiant.

The thing, unmoved, gazed up now at the sky. It would have been easy enough, as the herders said after, to have flung one of the knives, or a rock, at its big shape and so bring it down. But some new mood had begun to come over them, more than anger, or superstitious unease. Like the dogs at last, they felt themselves in the presence of something—not only uncanny, but crucial— something that had been seared by gods.

"Where this place?" the creature finally asked.

The men stupidly shook their heads. The boy shook away the sheep. The dogs lay belly-flat, and one, the mightiest, had urinated from fear. This sharp smell mixed with the stink of the holy and unholy figure, which other stench later they named as being like the reek of a butchered fowl-yard.

In a few moments more, the thing shambled away, as it had come, but going on now towards the south, and downwards in the direction of the fields and farms. When it was almost out of sight among the violet shadow of the lower woods, the men thought they had better follow it. There were women about below at their usual domestic chores, and cattle, and the vines.

They did not ask themselves why they had not answered the thing that this was Airis, under the mountain. It did not occur to them that they too, in that instant, had mislaid the country, and were lost, as if in alien climes.

Only seventy men made up the garrison now, in the Sword House at Airis.

It was a fort of ochre-plastered stone, built up into the rock. On one side, the sweep over to Ipyra, and its jade green river, from which came recently, of course, only friends. On the other side, rustic Akhemony.

The young captain had been bored enough that day, holding the fort while others went off hunting. King Klyton did not come up much to

Airis now. He preferred to keep the summer months for battle training, or for inspections of his outer empire. Even Udrombis the Widow had not yet visited this year. Later there would be the Sun Race and games, but that was not yet. The captain found Airis fairly dull.

When he heard the commotion below, he went down because it was his duty to look into such matters. He expected the same as it had been the last two times, a feud between drunken farmers, an Ipyran sheep-stealer.

"Well?" he said, walking into the courtyard. There were two peasants who had ridden here pell-mell on ponies, animals and men steaming from their speed.

The soldiers looked bemused, or tickled.

"They say, sir, some—ah—*demon* has walked into the town."

"A demon? That's quaint. Of what sort?"

One of the soldiers laughed.

The shaggier of the peasants said firmly, "He came down from the hills under the mountain. Just appeared there in the meadows—"

"In a smoke-cloud?"

The peasant scowled. "It was like he'd come from the Ipyran country, but no one saw him come."

"That's a fact," said the captain amiably. "None of us saw anyone cross, since herders yesterday."

"He's no demon. Not like a man, but—a man," went on the peasant, brazening it out.

The captain nodded, and made a brisk gesture to a couple of sniggering soldiers to be quiet. The captain had recalled suddenly that, although he himself had seen the light in Oceaxis, and fought in the ranks under such Suns as Amdysos and Adargon, the captain's granddad, whom he had liked, was not much different from this hairy peasant here. "What trouble is he giving you?"

"We're afraid," said the peasant simply.

That sobered the captain properly.

He could see this man was no fool, nor a coward, he had the courage-badge of scars on his arm, plainly written by a mountain leopard. Despite his garments and sweat, he stood straight and had not lost his temper, or his nerve, before the soldiers' mockery.

"Why fear?" asked the captain.

"His body is broken all out of shape, but he still walks. His teeth are broken, and his nails long, like the dead. He's strong. He threw Gol down, and that's the first Gol was ever bested. The dogs and other beasts act oddly around him. Even the cocks started to crow when he came up, as they do for fire or an earthshake."

"All right, a cripple. What's he done?"

"He went up the path to the gate of the summer palace. There's no guard there now, only the steward, and a dozen men, and slave women. He stood about there, then sat down."

The captain said quietly, "Someone should feed the poor devil. Give him some slops and beer, and send him on his way."

"One did," said the talking peasant. He stood more straight with his news. "We'd put the women inside the houses, but old Thistle came out, and brought him a dish of softened bread in honey. He took it and sat looking at it with his one eye, which has no proper upper lid. He didn't eat, and Thistle—someone's trying to pull her off, but she struggles and squeals. And then she kneels down in the road and sobs."

"And you should be kinder to your women."

"It wasn't that, sir. She was crying over and over about the Sun—"

"Wait. I don't understand you."

"I mean a Sun Prince, sir. One of King Akreon's sons."

Heat, then chill, passed over the captain's shoulders and spine like swiftly tossed water. The yard was silent as a grave, and high up he heard a hawk scream in the iris of the light-clear sky. A hawk, but not an eagle.

"You tell me she was confused," was all he said.

"Sir, she was crying like a little child. She's old, but not silly. She sees to the womens' ailments, and they get well."

"So she was calling for protection from the Sun House. And you came here."

"Sir, she wasn't calling for help. She said this one—this thing—the broke ruin that slouched there over the honey-bread—she called him Amdysos, son of Akreon. The Sun come back from under the world."

He left fifty-five men at the fort, and left them alert. Astonished, the captain had even had some notion Ipyra, forgetting her radiant marriage to Akhemony, had somehow staged these antics to draw off watch from the pass.

With fourteen of the soldiers, therefore, and the two peasants trailing after on their weary ponies, the captain went down to see for himself.

As they went, the road through the fields curled round above the descent to the lower plains, where the games were held, and so to the caves under the mountain where was run the Sun Race. The captain reined in, and gazed to that direction. Among his men, other heads were turning.

The spot was defined somberly in the end of afternoon, for the sun was going over beyond the mountain, the Daystar cool as a zircon. A pool of bright shadow, the Stadium lay below, where the chariots paraded before each Race. The holed rocks above were dark, mysterious, and shifting, against the mountain and the deepening sky. There was a marker on the mountainside, quite new. The gold showed redly at this hour. King Klyton had had it put there. Before the Race, a boy would go and pour wine over the mark. That was all.

Who could ever forget why. Who could ever forget that Race not two years gone? Even if you had not witnessed the event, in your mind you had seen it, not once, but many times.

The golden charioteer, the gem-work of team and chariot, bursting free of the caves—the thunderhead of gold which axed down to meet them—

And then the sparkling vision borne high, the prince of men caught in the talons of the god—a Sun god who was also the god of Death.

Some of the soldiers were right now making religious signs, ward signs against the power of Thon. If a man had escaped from Thon, would the god not be enraged? But no one came back from there, save in songs and stories.

When they reached the town, the Sun was still fingering sidelong the red columns of the palace. As they climbed up the road to it, they found the people from the deserted streets, the women at the crowd's edges, children clinging in their skirts.

He was standing in the street now, with the palace looming up into the rock behind him, its face the color of warm curds, and the pillars bleeding. Even up there, were a handful of people on the terrace, servants from the house, and probably more were looking from the old war tower.

A crone—who must be Thistle—sat peacefully now in the dust.

The captain realized he had been avoiding looking at the crippled man. Now he must do so.

Though he stood upright, his posture was of one asleep, the torso slumped forward rather, over the legs, which were of unequal lengths, the arms hanging, also unequally, and the head drooping, with what there was of its hair frayed forward over the face.

A soldier cursed softly. Another let out a bitten-up cry. The captain did not know if this man believed he saw anything recognizable before him, or if he cried only at the idea of such a recognition.

One must be unheated and still, as water in a deep well. One must take one's time, over this.

Yes, it was, or had been, a man. And he had been badly injured. You might see, in the outer lands, sometimes, victims of private or ritual tortures, who ended in such an approximate form. But generally they did not survive long enough to be gaped at.

The right leg was a good five inches more in length than the left, the right arm about the same in relation to the left arm. From the look, both had been broken in several places, and healed without benefit of doctors, or any assistant correction. The gods only knew how.

The body, where it showed through a patchwork of ragged stuff, that might well be ancient skins, was sunburned like mahogany, and demonstrated scars so awesome and vile, one did not expect to see them, save occasionally in war, and then not normally all together. The ribs had evidently been broken, mostly on the left side. There the body was like a stairway of loose jagged stones, just covered by the thinnest flesh. The feet were splayed and strange. The hands had lost fingers.

The scalp was all scars, a ridged tumulous of white and purple and black, with, in one area, a little space that seemed even to reveal the grim nudity of the skull-plate. From this medley hung out irregular clumps of hair, very long. The hair was mostly grey, or thin white as skimmed milk. But here and there, as sometimes happened in the old, there ran a skein of bronzed gold, shining and harsh with strength.

In his own chest, the heart turned, and thudded against the

captain's windpipe. He coughed, composed himself, and dismounted.

Reaching the crone in the dust, the captain leaned down. "Has he hurt you?"

"Oh no," she said. She looked sad but not insane. "He wouldn't."

"You can't know that, mother."

"I can. He was always fair."

The captain did not argue. She was senile and fragile, and he, a young man with his wits.

He went forward, and only stopped three sword lengths from the cripple.

Here the horrible body-stink was enough to bring up his gorge. But the wheezing breath was worse, hitting him in gusts.

Controlled, and ready, the captain spoke.

"Old man, I won't harm you. Look up."

For some reason, he did not think for an instant the crippled man would understand speech. Even though the peasants had also assured the captain that the prodigy uttered.

But the torn and rendered head tipped slowly back, and the shoulders, unequal as all else, partly straightened.

The captain saw the watered black eye, like scummy ink, shorn of its lid, fixed on him. He saw the decayed mask of the face, itself burnt almost black by a pitiless Sun. The nose had bent. Only the mouth, though the shade of dried blood, was whole over the wreckage of the teeth.

The eye looked, and seemed to take in the armor, the metal and gilt, the white plume, the undrawn sword. The captain was aware, as seldom in battle, he had begun to tremble.

A breath went in at the puce lips, down through the twisted throat to the ladder of twisted ribs, and the rib-pierced lungs.

"Like," said the crippled man, "an eagle."

And the captain felt the thongs of his sinews loosen. Felt the hand of a god push him. He was on his knees. Behind him came the sharp rattle of his troop, the low wails and whispers of the crowd.

Somehow the captain spoke.

"It is Amdysos."

2

Daibi sat on the earth floor, grinding nuts with the smaller stone.

The farm was, in a way, hers now. She was mistress. Her old father, who had been god-struck two winters back, and had the use only of his right side, and no use at all for his brain, she tended dutifully. But his decline had left her free to run over the hills to Elakti's band. She had been entranced by the talk of magical elements, but also by liberty, women on their own without the tyranny of men, only the dead god—Amdysos—to watch out for.

Daibi had spent all her former life in service to men. In the beginning there had been her father, and his two sons. But the sons were lost, one in a war, and one at a boar hunt under Koi. Meanwhile, Daibi watched her mother dwindle, ground away by hard work, like the very corn and nuts of the farm. The other daughters had been married off, but Daibi was the youngest, and finally evaded wedlock with some rough upland neighbor, being left to serve her rough father instead.

A month after his stroke, she was away with Elakti's girls. Mostly she had stayed with them, only returning to the farm when she must. At such times one or two went with her, to assist, strong girls like herself, with round arms and tawny hair.

The father would have had something to say, if he had kept the use of his eyes and his speech. But then.

Grinding the pine nuts to flour now, Daibi sang very low under her breath. She had been made conscious of the shadow side of the magic, and did not want to attract worse fortune.

The morning mantled warm on her shoulders, and there was the aroma of the yellow peaches ripening over the door. But beyond the sun-rinsed yard, where the sacred marroi rose up, stem the color of red copper in its sheaf of vivid leaves, she could see the wall of the barn. And now and then, above the cluck of her hens, she would hear a funny little cry. The hens had become used to the noise, and resumed laying long before summer came again. But the half-wild cats, and the dog, avoided the barn. The dog sometimes snarled at anyone who came from there.

* * *

The previous summer, that spy Udrombis had positioned in Elakti's makeshift household, had hurried back to the Lakesea, her pretext to fetch a physician for Elakti's labor. So intent was the spy on her role as messenger that she left well before the birth.

At Oceaxis, she was astounded and filled with trepidation, on being hurried by a back way into the apartments of her patron. Although the spy had guessed her information was passed at once to the Widow-Consort, the spy had cautiously pretended ignorance. Never before had she met a true Queen face to face.

The storm which had wracked the hills was also here. Through high windows shone a deadly lilac glare, winged by darkness, cracked by flame. The room seemed lofty as a mountain cave, and in it there burned only the garnet mouths of a pair of braziers. To the tempo of the storm, filmy draperies crackled as if with sparks, the reflections and shades of furniture jostled. All the atoms of the chamber seemed alive and sinisterely changeable.

But Udrombis stood nearly immobile, her pale gown of hazel silk massed about her, her jewels gleaming like ropes and bunches of eyes.

"Tell me what you wish to say," said Udrombis.

The spy wished to say nothing. She had given her message below. But she said it again.

"The spear-bride Elakti is in labor. It's a difficult birth, and long."

"I believe the birth of her other child cost her much effort."

"Yes, madam. They said it was dangerous. And this is worse."

"And you were sent for a court physician."

"Yes, madam. The Lady Phelia sent me. I'd offered to go."

"You were diligent." Udrombis turned, and the brazier light drew her profile in fire. She seemed made of polished granite. She said, quietly, looking aside, as if from some curious courtesy, "You will await the physician. But there will be a delay. If you discuss with another this delay, you will die. Do you believe me?"

The spy hoped the storm and the darkness hid her, knew they did not. "Yes, Great Queen."

"Expect nothing. The gods favor modesty. Good things will come to you."

Outside the room, the spy's bowel loosened, but luckily only let out a loud clap of gas. In the empty passage it echoed, ribald token of her mortal terror, to the glassy walls of godlike Kings.

She scurried away, and waited on Udrombis's physician. She waited through the stormy night, the unsettled morning, until midday.

The ride back to the pavilion in the hills took some while, also. Not all wrung out, the storm wavered and boomed. The physician, an elderly and irascible man, journeyed in his slow litter, with two guardsmen, and a boy assistant on a mule. Rainless clouds cast gouts of purple, lightning burst behind trees. And the mule shied constantly, and once threw the boy, so they had to stop and pick him up. Perhaps it had been elected for its temperament.

A wine-red Sun was setting, dragging the storm away with it at last down into the Sea of Sleep: only then did they reach Elakti's pavilion.

The spy, becoming an attendant again, slipped from her mount, and raced up the hill ahead of the rest. She must now appear eager and distraught. But in the fluctuating madder Sunfall, the pavilion seemed odd to her, morosely unwelcoming, threatening even, a ghost-place she had betrayed, and so aroused its curse.

Near the wall, the spy lessened her advance. She walked. There were no sounds but the herds of the storm wind, following the Sun downwards.

She went round, and entered the building through its kitchen yard. No one was there. And now night ascended, and filled the court nearly black. There were no lamps burning in the pavilion.

Frightened despite herself—since, after Udrombis, ordinary fright seemed redundant—the spy hesitated, for the physician and the guard to come up.

So, in the end, they entered together, by a door which hung open.

The rooms chimed hollowly with their voices, abrupt questions and calls. Then torches were lit, and, by the flare the pavilion was found to be deserted. They had gone in a rush. Here a lamp had burned, which had gone out. Here a bowl of soiled water stood. Here, there, crocks had fallen and been smashed. Clothes and hairpins lay scattered on the floor. Where the main bedplace was, they all saw plainly enough that something had gone on, a birth—or a murder. The mattress was daubed with blood. And twitching his nose, the physician declared he could scent the unique smells of parturition.

But nothing remained of Elakti or her child, nor of her women, nor the girls who had formed her lawless train. Only the remnants they had left behind, sudden, abandoned, spoke for them, as if of some eruptive flight from merciless enemies.

* * *

Through the months of summer then, as the Ipyran Queen Calistra traveled with her lord, the Sun King Klyton, men rode about the hills, from Oceaxis to Koi, from Koi over towards Melmia, or north to Airis.

These men were from the guard of Udrombis. They wore her lion badge in gold and silver. She had some rights, as a grandmother if nothing else, to search out the pregnant wife of her last son, Amdysos.

Up the hill, down to the valley, through the ripe green woods, along the fields, that even then were turning to the triple harvest home that marked that first year of a new King. The mobs of workers, little men and women on the apron of Akhemony, showed no fear of these lustrous guards. No wrong had been done. It was a time of reward and plenty.

So, there were no lies. No unwisdoms. And still, nothing was found.

The day came that five men, brilliant with inlaid bronze, the plumes floating scarlet and snow from their crests, rode up into the poor farmland somewhat out towards Mt. Koi. They saw how beautiful the farm had become, even this wretched hovel, its walls glowing like a rouged cheek, and hung with rosy peaches and grapes, and the red marroi, the tree of the Sun god, tall in its fans of heavy leaves, near the yard.

Their mood was not unkind. When the girl came out, they laughed and let her bring them wine cold from a pitcher, with butter stirred in. They picked the peaches off the wall, favoring her, and one of the men leaned over and gave the girl's own peaches a squeeze. They were in a friendly mood.

She said, when they asked, she was called Daibi which they knew was for the goddess of carnal love. She glanced down when they whistled. But they showed they meant nothing too much, not dismounting.

Her father, she said, was old and struck stone-side. Some of her female kin helped her with the farm.

One of the soldiers said, as they had said to others, on the chance. "Is that a baby crying?"

Her brows were straight, her mouth serene.

"No. There's a queer bird sometimes, sounds like that."

Because they must, they searched the farm, the big lower room with its earth floor and grinding stones in three sizes, and the area for the animals in winter. They looked at the two upper rooms. In one, the sick man dozed, in the second were only the wide mattress, and a loom, hung with cobwebs—but she would not have much time, and Daibi might practice her weaving at a kinswoman's house.

The two barns were empty, only the tethered cow by one, seeming not quite comfortable, as if she did not like the barn door. But the cow had a calf. Perhaps she was wary of strangers.

Of the little earthen cellar Daibi did not inform them, nor the trapdoor into it, over which stood the largest of the grindstones.

She and the others had sworn an oath to Elakti in the pavilion. Her spirits had told her she must stay hidden. And most of the girls had seen these spirits, telling her.

And so the guard rode away, not knowing that down there, in the cellar, all that while, Elakti had sat, her Sun-baked face flat as a slate. Holding in her lap the thing which sometimes did cry, but which the soldiers had not heard. The thing which, to Daibi's mind, was not, anyway, a crying baby at all.

As she was scraping off the last of the flour into the jar, Daibi felt a shadow fall between her and the Sunlit door. She looked, and Phelia was there, the court Maiden, who normally seemed by turns nervous or haughty. Now she was both at once.

"My lady says you're to come to the barn."

Daibi stoppered the jar and stood up, brushing off her big hands on her coarse skirt. During the more-than-a-year Phelia had been here, her garments, too, had gone for rags. The Maiden now wore homespun with badly cobbled darns.

They crossed the yard through the scurry of the chickens. Against the Sun, the leaves of the marroi looked russet as plums, and the stem like blood-filled bronze. The barn was very ordinary, beyond it. Daibi's mother had said the sacred tree brought the farm luck, but rather than any luck at all, it appeared to have brought Elakti here, magical and possibly accursed, for how else had she borne—

Daibi saw the women were coming out of the barn, as if to meet her. As last year wore, the band of girls had dwindled; Daibi had wondered if any had blabbed. Both slaves had run away, too, and probably been taken by wolves. And one attendant had gone to Oceaxis before the birth, and not returned in time to join their flight. All in all, Elakti was now served by twenty-one women.

Elakti moved out first. She wore a cheese-colored linen dress that Daibi's mother had had for holidays. On her bare arms shone still the bracelets of a royal wife, colcai, silver. She had lost only one of her coral earrings.

The crone, bent over from two winters lived casually, came out pressed close to her queen. The crone's mouth was turned down. She smacked her lips in unvoiced irritation over almost toothless gums. But she still found the herbs for Elakti's court. The herbs that helped to bring the magic.

Daibi had stopped, and Phelia beside her. Elakti had her awful face, the face she wore when something was *coming*. And Daibi's hair shifted at the roots.

Where was the child? It was often drugged with a posset, left in a hollow of straw in the barn. When they danced, up the hill under the moon, the child lay beer-stunned on a wolf pelt, fighting slowly with the fur.

Daibi even now, even so near, did not want to think about the child.

Elakti raised her arm. She had been thin before, now she had got plumper on the heavy food, the breads and porridges of an upland farm.

She pointed, away beyond the barn, towards the pasture where the few sheep grazed.

"See—see—fallen from sky!"

And the crone jabbered, dancing like a rheumaticky doll.

Into those fattening porridges went the herbs. But Daibi forgot this. A veil seemed lifted from her eyes.

There, on the rim of the shorn grass, something writhed and tumbled—claws and wings—

"The eagle," Elakti cried. "Fighting with a leopard."

"Eagle," shrilled the crone. "Eagle with leopard."

Daibi saw, as did nineteen others. They saw, in various forms, the same picture. A great bird with feathers of yellow flame and soot, that had snatched at a meal too big for it, a mountain leopard like turned cream, spotted, and scored with rents. The hooked black beak opening like two knives against each other, and the crimson oven of the leopard's mouth. Then as they rolled, one huge paw wrapping speckled velvet round the neck of the thrashing raptor. The snarls and screams in a crescendo, a whirlwind of wings—the crack like a breaking sword—

Phelia with her hands pushed to her lips, shuddered and averted her eyes. Avoiding the herbal porridge, she had grown thinner for Elakti's bloom. Devoid of the crone's simples, Phelia saw merely this, one of the farm cats with a dead pigeon in its jaws.

"I've waited on this sign," said Elakti, moving like a shade among them, touching them, a wrist, a shoulder. "The eagle must give up its prey. The victim rises in triumph. The Sun comes from under the world, reborn."

Phelia perceived, beside herself, only one who was mostly sane: the crone. She squinted sidelong, muttering carefully, "Triumph, triumph, born again."

Elakti now stood before Phelia like a clammy hot nightmare given flesh. To Phelia, Elakti said, boldly, gladly, "We will wash ourselves and our hair. We'll make garlands. We'll go down. Now is the time. My lord and husband Amdysos has returned."

3

It seemed unlikely they could mount him on a horse, so no one tried. Instead the captain walked at his side, guiding him a little.

The captain felt embarrassed at his self-appointed task. This was a prince. More, since the thought could not be put aside, this was a high King, the Great Sun.

Over two hours it took them, to gain the shrine. By then it was evening. A bow of new moon was strung far up on a peach sky. The pines and marroi of the groves were darkening. When they reached the willows by the healing stream, their charge walked immediately away from them—until then he had been docile as a sleepy child. Amdysos, Sun King of Akhemony, bent over the horse trough, and using mouth and hands, gulped up great draughts of water.

One of the soldiers let out a sort of praying oath.

"Shut your noise," said the captain.

He waited until Amdysos had finished his drink before leading him on, about the shrine, to the buildings down the slope.

Someone had been sent ahead. The patriach of the shrine was waiting. He was dressed in white, as all the priests here were, palms hennaed, the gold Sun symbol on his head. But he was a big, grey, oldish man. The insignia of his rank weighed on him, easily to be seen. The captain had noted him about, two or three times, at priestly works.

He sat frowning as the captain stood, and Amdysos stood, the ruined blackened face tilted a fraction, to clear the one eye of the lighted lamps.

"This—you say—"

"Sir. I know him. I served under Amdysos, a year or so back."

"But I knew him too," said the Chief Priest, without emphasis. And then, "My lord—will you come closer, and sit here with me?" Amdysos did not take a step. "Does he not recall his name and titles—"

"Sir," the captain said, "we have to remember what came to him."

They stayed quiet, remembering.

"This seems—incredible. Almost two years."

The captain said, flatly, thinking of war reports made to civilians, "It carried him high up. It would have a nest—a stinking nest of twigs and boughs, full of old bones and rotted pieces of meat. And it would have attacked him. Somehow he killed it—he had a knife from the chariot. The God knows how long that went on, how long he had to wait for the chance. Then he must get down from the height—some sulphur mountain perhaps. He was torn and bludgeoned, and after, maybe he fell. No one to help. He'll have wandered. Memory at last brought him this way. But his brain still rings to the ordeal. He'll be better presently, among his own kind."

"Presently—his own kind—"

"I mean the court, sir. He's King. After Akreon and Glardor, before any other,"

Then wine was offered, a dish of mixed fruits, grapes, apples; pomegranates, and a section of honeycomb. There had been bees in the shrine some months, apparently, then they went away, leaving the comb behind them like a gift of thanks. But when the captain took a little, and tasted it, the honey was stiff, and sour in flavor.

They brought in other priests, who had formerly spoken with Amdysos son of Akreon. A couple said that the Arteptan, Torca, should have been there, he had sometimes spent time with Amdysos, as with the King—with Klyton, that was.

Some turned pale and said they saw it was Amdysos. Others peered, and one even lifted up the lamp, and held it to the arrival's flinching, skewing face, as if looking at a painted wall.

"I protest, sir," said the captain.

The Chief Priest told the other one to desist. It was this other priest who said, "It might well be the prince, captain. What's left of him. If such a thing were possible."

"It was a bird of giant size," said the patriach. "There are feathers here, which it sloughed. Enormous."

"If the god willed he survive," said the captain, "it would happen. And it has."

A silence dropped.

Amdysos spoke. "I am near the Sun."

The Chief Priest rose, and his chair screeked on the floor, going backwards.

"My lord," said the captain, gently, urgently, to the wreck that stood, foul and unreasonable, beside him, "my lord, speak to us. Tell us what we must know."

But Amdysos lowered his head. His one eye went horribly opaque. It occurred to the captain he must have to sleep with it open, like a snake.

That night, Amdysos was taken by the priests, bathed and salved. They were used to the disturbed and unwell, and he gave them, anyway, no trouble. They investigated his wounds, both old and new. Hie had been hurt much as the captain had deduced— breakages, punctures—possibly exactly as had been described. There was another thing. Under the crippled man's arms, and in the hair of his loins, was found a rash, which the priests treated, and claimed they could cure. It had been found before, they said, mostly among traders who sold, or kept as pets, such large birds as owls, or eagles.

"But there is another thing," the Chief Priest said to the captain. "I can hardly keep it secret. Anyone can see how he is—whoever— whatever—he is."

"What thing?"

"The ribs were crushed, and ripped inward. The left lung is healed, but severely damaged. It won't ask very much to kill him. In any event, his life can hardly be long."

The captain said, "All the more reason then, for going quickly to Oceaxis."

The escort the captain organized was made up of thirty men. No longer did he think much of a plot in Ipyra. He did not even—

curiously, he was not a fool—think how this must seem, what he did, in the reign of another King.

Amdysos rode in another litter, he was royal but wounded. Sometimes he soiled it; not always. Sometimes he would get out while it still moved, squat, for both functions, at the roadside.

How long had he lain in the hell of the nest? The captain did ponder this, as he rode along the sunny, pleasant route to the Lakesea. Some while, maybe, for the eagle might have wished to store this succulent, muscular young meat. Months, off and on? Perhaps he had fought it off a hundred times, and still been himself. But in the end, winning his race, himself no more.

He stank of it still, of the nest of the monster bird. How much would it require, of water, perfume, time, to wash him clean of the taint?

But also, it was his proof.

Perhaps then, he would reek until men acclaimed him.

And in Akhemony, among his own, his mind could be made whole.

The captain recollected, Amdysos, seventeen or so, Sun-born, flawless, a man, the sound material of Kingship.

At noon they halted. Among the roadside woods they ate some food. Amdysos did not stir from the litter. It was as well—he ate like— like an eagle—tearing, stuffing his mouth of snapped fangs—the men were not talkative. The horses were restive. Birds—small ones—had flown from the trees in sprays, and not come back. The woods were now empty, here, of birdsong.

During the afternoon of this concluding cumbersome lengthy journey, the green woods broke above, and sunlight ran down towards them, laughing and calling—local girls crowned with ivy and flowers, Sun white and brazen on their arms and molten on their ale-brown hair. One darker one ran first. She was not so toothsome. She had, you saw too, a long, plate-like face, and two wide, wet-black eyes.

But it was she, this one, who stood in the road, holding up her arms in the gesture of a primitive priestess, to halt them. Authority incarnate.

The captain had never seen Elakti, or certainly never seen her near enough to identify. But he knew the name, and that she had been missing.

He could see too that there were now others up the incline, men and women of the farms and villages, watching, waiting on her word. Not everyone had disapproved of her mad career. Foremost stood a slender and aristocratic woman, and an old hag. The woman carried some object, closely wrapped, and he thought it must be a baby, yet surely it was too bundled up for that—and the woman seemed not to like holding it much . . . an animal?

"He is with you!" the woman on the road sang out. "I am Elakti, his wife. And he, the Dead Sun."

Then the captain understood her rights, even accepted who she must be. And something in him cringed; not only a crippled and stinking lunatic to escort, but now this insane hussy, and all to be kept with honor. For that very reason, disciplined, he got off his horse and went directly to her.

"Not dead, madam. Alive."

"Risen," she said.

He put her up on his horse. Followed now by the other women, some barefoot, all garlanded, conceivably drunk, and in tatters, and by the staring folk from the hills, the captain and his soldiers went on towards pristine Oceaxis, capital of Kings.

4

I see her distinctly, Queen Calistra. Only for a moment. She has risen from the bed where the pink cat's tongue dawn has flicked her awake. White limbs, slender firmness, waist circled with light, her high white breasts with their two sweets, like peony buds. The shower of golden hair, down, down to her thighs, sun-silvered on one side—the silver feet into which she has eased—with all the forgetful nonchalance of repeated things. And now she bends to lace them on. Beautiful young girl that I was. Beautiful young crippled girl who has unremembered.

Only a moment. Then I become this being once again. I am Calistra. Great Queen of Akhemony and the Sun Lands, Sun-Consort, Mirror of the Sun, Jewel of the Heavens, wife to Klyton the Great Sun.

The silver feet are laced on. I pace to the side table, and pick up the cup of juice they have put ready. The dog comes, and rubs his white silk on my side.

"Do you miss him too? You should only love me."

Klyton has been gone a whole night. The training of troops out beyond the town, discussions with his leaders, dreams of foreign conquest . . . He will be in the King's Apartment by now. Soon I will see him.

The dog raises himself, putting gentle paws against my thigh. I kiss his head. He licks fruit juice from my fingers.

The shutters were thrown back and between the pillars I could look to the shimmering Lakesea. The water dazzled my eyes. Three gulls circled languidly, then another joined them. I glanced away, and saw their afterimages imprinted on the scroll of poems I was reading.

It was almost noon, and Klyton had not come to me yet. Business of the court and the world detained him. My impatience was heady, hungry for the reparation I would be given.

Some of my women were grouped about the room, rustling and chattering, playing board-games, embroidering. I was so used to them now, I barely noticed them.

I wore white sewn with green. The golden earrings in the shape of kissing birds tapped my cheeks and neck as I leant to the book.

These words meant nothing.

The white dog got up, and turned to stare across the room— Klyton?

But the door opened and my Chief Maiden entered. Her shut-lipped correctness now almost pleased me. At her arrival, the women grew quieter, as they seldom did for me, the Sun Wife. Yet the Chief Maiden had no urgency at all, which indicated this, whatever it was, had nothing to do with my husband.

The Chief Maiden—her name was Hylis—bent to my chair. "Madam, a person has been escorted to the palace. She has begged an audience with you."

I said, careless, "No, she should plead with Queen Udrombis."

"Madam, the woman is a priestess, From the Temple of Thon."

Sinking, the four bright gulls turned black on the sequined sea. Thon's number was four. I saw at once the four black pillars in place of mine, the bone capitals, and the drearily smoking bowl of ancient bronze.

Coldness sluiced down me, and as I rose, my legs felt leaden, attached by silver shackles to the floor.

"No one must ever leave the temple—"

But I myself had left it, rescued by order of Udrombis, twelve years back. Demonstrably there were special circumstances, on occasion.

"No, madam. But it seems they allowed it. She's gone blind, has some wasting illness."

"What does she want with me?"

"She says she was helpful to you and was a favorite of yours at that time—when your mother left you for safekeeping . . . in the temple."

It was not that I had any terror or any real premonition. I had been taught superstition along with everything else, here in these palace-houses of Sun and air and light.

But I recalled the old priestess, vaguely enough, like a sort of fleshly ghost. Now, it is a fact, I remember her far better. A dim memory came that she had held me that day when the Heart stopped beating and all things quaked in fear and horror. Afterwards she had given me sweet porridge, and then the soldier came to take me away forever.

Had I thought of her since? I believed I had not. And taken up into the Sun, nothing had been further from my mind than she.

I looked round at the women. "All of you go out." They obeyed, chattering again, offended, questioning. Perhaps they did not grasp I meant not to be embarrassed before them.

I told Hylis to fetch the woman.

Quite quickly, Hylis returned with her. The priestess was muffled up in her black, but unmasked now. Her eyes had a film over them, and she lent heavily, despite her thinness, on the shoulder of a thinner girl, a child about ten, also, evidently, from Thon's Temple. As her black sleeve slipped, I saw on the child's arm, the marks of a rod. And could imagine her back.

That House—that Death in life. I *smelled* it on them. I was glad that Hylis stood near me, immaculate and scented with perfume.

Using the child for leverage, the old priestess got down on her knees.

"Oh, shining lady, it does me good to find you in your high place. I have dared to entreat a kindness for a kindness. Pardon me."

I had not recalled her, but even so. I had seen her in the temple, that moment when her mask had slipped. Those twelve years had passed, and she had been elderly then.

Not from arrogance, only from bewilderment, I failed to speak. She filled up the gap like an anxious spring.

"Have you forgotten how I sheltered you, after the terrible hour when the Heart Drum paused at King Akreon's death?" .

Her voice came to me. I knew it suddenly.

"I remember," I said. "And then you gave me a salty soup to warm me."

"Yes, yes," she cried, grinning, clutching the child's shoulder in a wrenching grip. The child's uncovered face—should it not have been covered for traveling?—was white and sodden, the eyes downcast, hoping for nothing.

"You were so kind." I said. "you allowed me to call you in secret by your name, though it was forbidden."

"Oh yes," she said, "what else. You were only a poor little scared girl."

"I regret, I've forgotten your name."

She told me promptly. I forget it now. In her case, I have expunged it.

"Well," I said.

I watched again in memory, faintly yet surely, her sharp thin shape, poised like a pole, as she made the tiny boy lie down in the snow, while she counted slowly to four hundred

How desolate and shameful it seemed then to me that I recaptured her so completely, because she had been wicked, where the gentle priestess I had almost mislaid. Not quite entirely. I knew this face was not hers. I had never seen this face, for it had never been, till now, unmasked before me. It was porridge not soup, and I was never told any name. The gentle one would not have broken such a taboo, even with me.

"Wait outside now," I said, "someone will see to you."

Thinking she had won her prize, she gabbled on, but Hylis made an abrupt gesture and the child began to heft her up.

When they were out of my rooms, I said to Hylis, "Did they come with anyone?"

"One guardsman from the temple."

"Have someone ask him the price I must pay for that child. Let him be paid the price. Give her into the charge of—" I thought and regained another human thing "—of Nimi. She will stay here, with my women."

Hylis's arched brows became octagonal. She did not often show surprise or disapproval.

"And the priestess?"

"She can go where she wishes, providing it is away from here. Whatever she wants and Thon allows."

Hylis opened her lips. They stayed parted.

I said, "She was a liar. The one who helped me must have died. Udrombis would have this one flogged, but this is better. I'll give her nothing, not even a punishment."

My Chief Maiden drew her dignity back about herself like a fold of silk.

"Very well, madam."

Cruelty summons cruelty, save in the weakest or the most strong.

Before that day there seemed to have been no rancor left in me, but now I had been made to glimpse again those wounds of early pain which never quite mend.

Thon's Temple, bizarrely, had reckoned to please me, giving up to me this one friend. Well, I had saved the child. That was my answer to Thon, and conversely my gift to the gods of joy and safety.

I did not know they had already turned away their eyes.

As Hylis crossed the chamber, I began to hear a noise. Probably I had heard it already, and not considered it. Hylis, too. She halted and turned back.

"Is that shouting?" I said.

"I don't know, madam—yes—it might be."

"A crowd," I said.

It was like the sound of certain festivals. And yet, not quite that sound. A mass of throats calling, *demanding*—

I walked on to the terrace. The gardens hid, with their wild arbors, the view of the town and the road. But something seemed to rise beyond them, some quiver in the air, smoke or dust, or maybe that disturbance which sometimes happens before a storm.

"Shall I go and ask, madam?"

How patient Hylis was with me. I instructed her to do so.

I stood then in the center of the room, and I felt as if for the first, its largeness the gleaming rarity of it, that had nothing to do with me.

Had I not just been reminded thoroughly of what I was? Cemira, the serpent-beast. Cemira who had gone on the crutches of canes.

The sound was louder, but no more identifiable. Not anger—not fear—but neither gladness, nor praise.

Some momentous thing had occurred, and they had rushed to the palace to bring news of it. Perhaps the perfectly happy are above the sense of unease. I had believed myself perfectly happy, and invulnerable, too. But the shouting, lessening and building, ebbing, swelling, like some chanted song—seemed buzzing upward through the feet of silver, into my vitals and my heart.

I dreaded nothing. Yet my hands trembled a little.

Hylis was gone half of one hour, so the water clock told me. She came back unimpaired, not hurrying, her head held high. On her slim cheeks, the soft powder stared. She was pale. In her hand was a paper. She brought it to me without a word.

Taking it, I thought it was from Klyton. But before all else I saw the Queen-Widow's seal.

"Udrombis," I said.

"The Queen's messenger met me in the passage," Hylis said.

I read quickly. The words refused their meaning to me—someone had made some error—a crowd of people—I must stay in my apartments.

"Why did you take so long?"

Hylis said, quite trenchantly, "I asked what was the matter. Not from her messenger, who wouldn't have spoken."

"*What* then?"

"Madam, they say a man came from Airis who claimed to be the Sun Prince Amdysos. The soldiers have brought him to Oceaxis. The King has been fetched."

"That shouting—" I said.

"People from the villages, and some from the town. And some women are there calling out that the Sun has come up from under the world—the ritual call, as you know, madam, at the Dawn Offering. And some of them are saying Amdysos is the High King."

"How could it be?" I said stupidly.

My white dog followed me as I paced to and fro. Hylis observed me gliding, accustomed to it.

She said, teaching me how to behave, "You should pay no attention, madam. The King will see to it."

I sat in a chair and the dog moved to me, and put his head on my knee. I took hold of him softly, but not letting go.

Invisible, the shouting grew very rough. Then died choppily away.

Amdysos was dead. Even I had seen it happen. A tremendous mythical Death, supernatural and without chance. Who could come back from Death?

Yet I had had my omen. Thon would let go some.

I sent Hylis out. The scroll of poems had dropped on the floor. Klyton would come, at last, and then I should know it all.

The day was passing. Sometimes I heard the shouting chant come and go. It never now kept up for long. The soldiers must be stopping it.

Refreshment was brought me, though I had requested nothing. I drank some wine but did not touch the food. Later, a slave came to remove the dishes.

I slept a few minutes in a chair, and dreamed I was back at the base of Mt. Koi, going on my canes to drop blood in the noxious summer inner sanctum of Thon. The god reared on his column, but his face was only a skull, like all the skulls spread at his foot. I wondered when he had died, and if any other knew; whether I should speak of it or not.

Later still, Hylis came in with women to dress me for the evening. A gilded cast of light was on the sea, not a single gull.

"What is happening?"

"I can't learn anything, madam. I did attempt to." The palace was hushed, not in its usual late afternoon murmuring, fussing tone. Outside the birds sang as always, and flitted over the terrace space. Nothing had upset their kingdom, beyond the stalking of a cat or the passage of a slave.

But with evening came the Sunset Offering, and then the dinner in the Hall. A pang of revitalized blood shot through me. I thought that now I must hear and see. But I did not know what to expect.

Hylis brought me out a gown. It sparkled, a sky shade folded with rose red, the veins and tucks petalled by gold spangles. And the necklace of hammered gold, and the coronet of gold made like the spokes of the Sun.

"No, not those." I said, as if they would scorch me. Hylis said to me quietly, "Queen Udrombis has expressed a preference."

I was to be garbed then for display, and she had ordered it. One did not go against her, of course.

The women dressed me. On my left arm was clasped a coil of silver and electrum set with one turquoise the size of an ox eye.

As they were finishing my face, there was a flurry at the doors, and feet. Klyton had arrived, I thought, and stood up quickly. But it was not Klyton at all.

Udrombis surveyed me, and nodded her head. In turn, I must look at her. She had gone in mourning since Akreon. I could only recall her in such clothes. Nevertheless, she had not given up her superbity. The robe was of a grey dark almost to black, with borders of silver, and pearls stitched as lilies. Her jewels were the colors of suns and stars. Was she sixty? They said so. Her badger hair had been hidden away complete inside a headress of Artepta, a golden helmet set with chrysolitcs and jet, that had two scaled flaps falling down onto her breasts, each ending in the golden head of a lion with amethyst eyes. She had worn it at his coronation, Klyton's, and to my coronation and wedding. The weight alone would have made another woman weep. But her eyes were smoothly dry and black as a summer night.

She raised one hand, and all the women flooded away, were gone.

She said, "Don't ask me what I know, for I know nothing except what I have written to you, and your Hylis has discovered."

No point in quibbling. Or asking. She would know if any did, and if she did but would not say, it must rest.

I said, "What shall I do, madam?"

"Sensible Calistra. Act as always. Nothing from the ordinary."

Amdysos had been her son. But oh, one did not wonder if her heart beat.

"One thing," she said, "show no dismay. Klyton won't make the Offering. He is detained. Adargon will do it."

"Yes, madam."

My own heart, weighing like her helm-crown, wore down through my body, turning all of me to iron.

Then she said, "Once, when I was with Akreon the King, in Uaria, a madman broke through the guard and leapt against him. Akreon slew the man himself, with his own sword. After that we went on to the house where we were to dine. Neither of us spoke of it, either to our host, one of their little lords with a green moustache, or together. The danger wasn't discussed, and so it withered. Do you understand me, Calistra?"

I said that I did.

For a moment I saw her, young then, slight, and more malleable, yet still unbreakable, stronger than a pherom spear.

Now even in her shadow on the floor, some of her jewels glimmered from the gathering sky.

Up the stairs to the East Terrace I climbed, my women behind me. I recalled Ermias, panting as she followed me. Ermias, exiled to her estate. And then I dwelled a second on Kelbalba, who had left the trained girl for my massage, and gone away, saying not much, wishing me well. I had not bothered with it. I was Klyton's wife.

Tonight, not myself, the steps winded me somewhat. I paused on the landings, before the golden altars of the Sun in his disguises, the horse with chariot, ram and bull, the eagle—yes, the eagle. The boar. Behind me, a Lakesea like melted steel under a sky that kept the savor of brass.

The air was fragrant with flowers, with subtle smokes. I could hear music, a sithra down in the Garden of the Sun. No longer any shouting detectable . . .

On the East Terrace, the young god presided in his marble marvel, hiding his loins in a Sunburst. Though reverenced at daybreak, a trail of smoke simmered up from some gum left burning there. I had never seen this before, at Sunfall.

There were people on the Terrace, as on the landings. They bowed, greeting me with several of my titles.

Was there tension, like that of the string of the sithra, in their faces, their spines?

I did not offer to the god. *She* had forbidden anything abnormal. Besides, I felt it once again, and so deeply now, what, after all, was *I*?

Through the east doors I went, as so many times since my exaltation, a princess, a queen, a woman walking on two feet.

The Hall, with its oval of dark yellow stems, slid by me, the fighting walls of battle, the gigantic lion skull, large as a man's torso, an animal killed by King Okos in his boyhood. At the Hearth, the god knelt twice, back to back with himself, black on a heart of fire. Smolders rose up to the waiting Daystars in the ceiling. Old King to Hag, Young King to Maiden. The Kings had eyes, the Queens none.

But Mokpor told you this, long ago in my book. Did he inquire if women, then, should be made blind?

I stood on the women's side of the West Terrace, my girls and Maidens about me. At Hylis's order, two of them arranged the folds of my gown. Was *I* blind? I recall not a single face, only the blur of skin and hair and raiment and gems, in the Sun's ending light.

He was low, the Sun, but not this evening spectacular, Amdysos had been seized by an eagle of gold and thunder, but this Sun would sink merely in drained afterglow. No mass of dyes was on the skyline, where Koi rose, and behind Koi, the phantom of the Mountain of the Heart of Akhemony.

The gongs were sounding in the town, a mile away.

I found I had braced my body and my mind—it was for the shouting to begin again below. But there was nothing other than the gongs. Even the sithra had been set aside.

Like diluted butter, the western sky.

The boy chosen tonight to sing the Sun down, piped up. His voice cracked a little on the first note. This had happened before. He was nervous, but at nothing more than his role. No one responded, and now his voice was pure as the light.

> *Splendor of leaving,*
> *Beauty of going away,*
> *We stand powerless at the Gate of Night.*

I had heard these words on so many, many evenings, as I had often heard the welcoming ode of dawn, brought there with Klyton from our bed, where we had scarcely slumbered.

The words—meant nothing.

> *Do not forget us, O Greatest God.*
> *Do not forget.*

Adargon faultlessly offered to the Sun.

Incense was ignited, a drift of pinpoint lights, the musky steam rising as the pastel Sun sank down. The mild Sunset reminded us that death might be a simple matter.

Klyton came in late to the Hall, with Adargon and some of the other Suns. They were elegantly clothed, jeweled, fresh from the bath, laughing together. It might have been any evening when they had been kept behind on the business of war and Kingship. Save Klyton would have broken off, to make the Offering.

Klyton walked up the Hall. He gestured graciously to me, and to Udrombis, who sat a few feet apart from my own chair, but, no lower.

"Excuse my tardiness, ladies. There was work to do. But now I'm here. The sight of you makes me glad to have hastened."

A courtly speech, playful, and light.

The laughter in the room was also light, and might be false.

It came to me that perhaps he had not officiated at the Offering because it was deemed ill-augered. To reverence a *sinking* Sun—as now things stood. My heart beat its slow hard iron, but I smiled and let him take my hand. He leaned down, and muttered in my ear, "Thank the God, not long now till bedtime." He was warm. His hair had a scent of thyme and myrrh. His lips brushed my cheek, and at the touch my skin crinkled like the sea, tingling at proximity, to be stretched beneath him, and in my loins the twang of desire, out of rhythm with the heavy heart that beat too slowly now to match the Drum on the mountain.

As he walked to the King's place and sat down, I gazed at him for a scatter of moments, never too long, for even in a wedded Queen, it must be thought forward. He had put on dark red, with a border of gold deer running. He had not overdressed, had not needed to. He was the Great Sun. His presence, his gracious, graceful lightness, were enough. Nothing had disturbed Klyton. Nothing had caused him an instant of doubt.

I had come to know him, not thinking that I did. This was a show, careful and clever, not a chink left open.

As I sampled the meats and conserves, the egg dish with its pretty decorations, the fruits and sugars, complimenting the cooks, drinking from the goblet sparingly—all Udrombis and dead Stabia had taught me—I, too, kept an uncreased surface. I, too, had not experienced one second of unease.

The harper sang. He was a man from Ipyra, with a special song for me about a golden flower that with its fragrance unified two lands. I barely heard it, but he was much applauded, and Klyton gave him a ring set with an emerald. So I sent to him, all across the floor, a yellow flower from the table and my armlet with the turquoise. He bowed very low. But I had seen, even missing most of the words of his song, how his eyes now and then darted. *He* had heard things, even if we were so inured to them.

Soon I could get up and leave, and presently Udrombis would also. Klyton would stay to drink a while. But Oceaxis knew he cared for me. They knew a King's work had detained him all today. How natural then, that he should seek early the couch of his young wife.

For myself I did not know if he would then come to me. What he had implied might have no relevance to what he must do.

I thought that, even if he did visit my rooms, he would go first to her, to Udrombis who had made herself his mother.

In my apartments, I had myself prepared for bed, as on every night. Then I sent my women away. Some went to their own beds, some slipped off to others. I had never seen a need to reprimand them.

Hylis was last to depart the bedchamber.

She came and combed out my hair, in exact strokes that had no involvement in them, no interest, and I thought again of Kelbalba and of Ermias.

Hylis was faithful, reliable and without fault. She cared nothing for me. If I had struck her she would have dismissed my act as that of a royal woman in a rage. If I had kissed her, or clasped her hand in terror, she would have soothed me, and going out, forgotten me.

She said, "The King will come tonight, madam."

For the first, it seemed, I saw how often my servants would give me these personal fragments. When he would be with me, if he would, even, sometimes, the hour he must leave—or that he was already gone.

"Thank you, Hylis. That's enough."

She put down the comb, anointed with saffron and myrrh—she had chosen perfumes to match with his. Her eyes were lambent and void as glass. She said, "Shall I see to your shoes, madam?" My *shoes*— the silver feet. Tactful, impervious Hylis.

"Don't trouble. Good night, Hylis."

She bowed and left me.

The lamps burn low. In the chamber with the pool, Gemli stands and palely gleams on the air, again in the water. The turtle is swimming, by night. I see her pass like a dark sigh through Gemli's reflection. And in their cage the pink doves are nestled, two by two, to sleep. The white dog pads to my side. He stares at what I seem to be staring at, sees nothing in it, goes away back into the outer room.

Just so I gaze on this world of my youth, my Queenship, I Calistra, wife of the Sun, and as the dog did, I see nothing that makes, suddenly, any sense to me. And like the dog I turn away.

The door opens, the outer door. I glimpse the well-lit corridor, and hear men laughing, and then the clank of the sentry's salute.

My husband enters the room and the door closes. The dog trots up to him. He bends and affectionately, gently, pulls its ears, just as he whispered his promise in mine.

Annotation by the Hand of Dobzah

Sirai stopped at this point, and clapped her hands. I looked at her, I suppose, aghast. She said I was like a child when the storyteller falters. But she did not smile. "Put down now," she said commandingly, "what the Muhzum is. Yes, here. You see, Dobzah, I don't want to do it. Say what the Muhzum is."

And so I dislocate the narrative to describe the Muhzum, which is perhaps anyway familiar to you.

In our land of Pesh, the Muhzum was at first a keepsake of the dead. It was intended to retain a tangible momento. And so into a box would be placed a coil of hair from the corpse, perhaps a fingernail, a small bone even, or a tooth, or perhaps a drop of blood kept in a vial. Even now one may come on an old widow lady who has kept such a box by her, or see the lovely boxes kept in great houses, that are many hundreds of years old, boxes of silver and enamel, or poor little boxes made of wood or parchment, or out of two hollow stones. These keepsakes are mostly crumbled now, when one examines them. One wonders, how many tears are dried up in their dust.

In recent times, although that is before I was born, the Muhzum became also a battle object, a thing of power. By obtaining such trophies from one who had been slain, a warrior could take dominion over the spirit of the deceased, which then could not afflict him after. They have been used too in magic, to summon up the dead. We may know many such stories.

The first Battle-Prince Shajhima took death tokens from the brother-husband of Sirai. But later he gave to her the Muhzum box, of hyacinth enamel that is like the sky.

Sirai says now to write the holy words, *Sharash J'lum*. She tells me

I must also say what is their meaning. I finally protest that in Pesh, we know. But Sirai says, "Pesh is not all the world." And though, now, surely Pesh *is* all the world, I will explain. *Sharash J'lum* is spoken at the end of a prayer and means, *So it is through God's will.*

5

My husband is made of gold.

He has flung away the mantle, the tunic, the jewelry, leggings, boots, leather and linen. His groin lifts a fire to me, one shaft of fire from the golden fleece.

Klyton puts me gently on the floor, and keeps one arm under my head. He penetrates me almost at once. But I burst to a blossom of lust—his scent, his skin—his hair rains gold on gold and I am molten and I die. His own cry is low, muffled in my breast.

Soon he releases me, then picks me up and carries me to my bed, pushing aside curtains like thought. Once we are there, he begins again.

A frenzy. Lovers. Stars explode and perish in our bodies or the night. It seems an act of Death, not life. Is Death so wonderful? Or more wonderful—

"What can I tell you that you'd understand, Calistra? It doesn't make much sense. Yes, a crowd came and they shouted. Some dolt from Airis had brought him, this wreckage of a man. A soldier, a captain—he should have known not to. And that bitch Elakti was there, prancing about with a trail of women, filthy and half out of their minds with some drug. The soldiers dealt with that. Then the temple sent to me. They wanted him, this—*thing*. Presumably human once. *Amdysos*," Klyton said. He gave a short harsh laugh. "*He* would have been the first to say, Put it out of its misery. It shouldn't go on living in that state. How do I know this? Well, we had a conversation, once." He had left the bed. The night was hot, thick with the nocturnal taste of flowers, the peppery scent of sex and skin. He paced back and forth, naked. His strides were swift, and the dog, which had jumped up to keep in step with him, drew away and sat down. "But it isn't Amdysos. God's Heart, I'd know. He's Below. I've had—true dreams of him there. I'll keep him in my brain and thoughts, I'll do him honor. But *that*—that—God knows what it is. Some crippled felon set on in a mountain village down in Ipyra. Wandered to Airis. Taken up. Mistaken. A fluke of fortune. Yes, I glimpsed it—him. It wasn't for me to go and *inspect*—Anyway, the priests want to and so they can decide. This is beneath the King, or beyond him. And Torca is there—do you remember Torca—of course you do. He was in the Sun Temple on religious business. He has a level head. And he knew Amdysos at least as well as he knew me."

I said nothing. I had not spoken, nor asked him anything. He had simply begun to tell me.

"The Queen," he said. Then he said, "I mean, Udrombis. I had to go to her of course, and explain what went on. I've never known her fumble. She was magnificent, what I'd expected. That's good. It's enough to make her ill, such a tale, this madness. She mourned him and knows him to be dead. I wish Stabia were alive," the first I had ever heard him say this. "Udrombis loved my mother, and confided in her, I think. It would have been a consolation. She's like a goddess in metal, but under it—this must make her sick."

He stopped. He stood in silence, not moving. The dog wagged his plume of tail, then left off. Some minutes passed. I said, softly, "Won't you lie down, and sleep?"

Why did I say this? Oh, my training, I imagine, as a virtuous and careful wife. As a woman. Adjunct and servitor, the rose upon the way which must have no thorn.

He only said, "Sleep? Yes. Later. Could it be, Calistra, that it *is* him—are such horrors conceivable? I had my signs, Calistra, portents of pure gold. The God showed me it would all be mine, but not how— would I have tramped up over his back to get it? He would have been the King and I his right hand. That was enough—I thought it was enough. But how could I serve—*that*—how could the Sun Lands hold together in the grip of *that*?"

I said then, "Did they ask it of you? To give it over to— Amdysos?"

"He is not Amdysos. If he were, do you think I could resist? But no, the priests took him out of harm's way, to examine him. By the light of the God. By use of their tricks and sorceries, too, I suspect. They can only reveal he isn't Amdysos. I'm content with that. Let them do it. Then the crowd can see. Would you believe—enough people for a festival—most of the town it looked to be. Were they so ill-content with me? Yes, those very ones that threw you flowers and brought you lambs. Howling about the curse of the God. As if I—*I* gave him to the eagle."

He turned. The lamp fluttered and I saw, lit on the buckle of his belt which he had tossed aside, the eagle of red gold that had been his blazon since he was a boy.

He said, "I dreamed I was an eagle, Calistra. Before the Race. But he forgave me all that. Could I speak openly at his shrine, if he wanted vengeance?"

Klyton sat down on the bed. "My brothers, the princes, how they argued. Only Adargon kept steady. A few others. They can all see some stake in it. It would tear Akhemony apart. Lektos gathered five hundred men and went over to the temple. To guard the doors. But what does that mean? I let him go. To make a rumpus could do worse. Calistra, it wasn't Amdysos."

"No," I said.

He lay down beside me. He said, his eyes hooded and untransparent, "How can I sleep?" And, slept, gone as the dead sometimes are, before the lids of his eyes could close.

I lay next to him, and the dog stole up light as a breeze, and rested along my side. I stroked the dog, but in my mind saw only the temple at Oceaxis, the under-room where I had been taken before my coronation, to swear my oaths to darkness, to the shades, to Thon, for a Queen remains a Queen even in death. They were strange chambers, those, not hideous as Thon's Temple had been at Koi, yet filled for me with ominous mysteries, and a weird shiver like black wings.

So intrusive was my picture, on that night, of this spot and what went on there, that, even from the landfall of my old age, I can fashion or detect no other.

Ancient stone, pillars ringed by gold and brass, a floor painted with the maps of the Lands Below, into which Tithaxeli flowed, the River of Death. By a leaping brazier like a fever, I saw the priesthood, black clad there, interview the smashed thing from Airis. Even Torca I saw, in my imagined vision intransigently clothed as when first I saw him, in my youth, in leathers, his wooden leg clacking, coal-black, the black beard grown again down to his waist.

But the deduction of the priests I did not conjure. So abruptly it had come, this storm. It was not real, and could alter nothing.

When I woke at Sunrise, Klyton had left me already.

6

The room was not of great size. A prince among the priests sat to one side, and nearby, with his slate, a scribe. The light was artificial, from tall open lamps, fitful therefore, yet not really misleading. Less so than daylight, for one took more care. The Ipyran had come in, Elakti, in her hill dress. She had danced about, and then one of the brown young women had led her aside, and the guard got both of them out of the room.

Then Torca was able to concentrate upon the man.

Torca had previously asked various things, to none of which had the man—and a King, too, was a man—replied.

His stink was horrible, reminding one of rottenness, even after all the salves and bathing. Torca had breathed it in, grown used to it. It was no worse, probably, than a tent of the wounded in war. These, too, were injuries which would kill. A wonder they had not already done so. In itself, you could say there was something in that.

The man's one eye had not fixed on, nor followed Torca. It seemed to gaze inward, perhaps did so, to some unnatural sight.

Torca touched the man lightly, on his right arm. Torca was prepared for any reaction, even to having to defend himself.

But only the eye revolved now, and looked full at him. In the eye was a core of lucency. Before it went out.

"Tell me," said Torca, "about the eagle."

To his surprise, the man spoke at once.

"Eagle is God."

"Why is that?"

The man sat back in his chair. Everything was changed. His face was grave and thoughtful. Torca made himself keep very still. The priests had administered herbal tinctures and these too might mislead.

"Up to God we go," said the man, "on wings. On anvils of fire God beats at us. To smooth us. Then plunged in flesh and blood we are, to cool the fire."

Torca held his breath. Not from the stink.

The man said, consideringly, "Fell before done."

After a long wait, Torca asked, "You fell, before the God was done with you?"

But the being had lain back in its chair. It stared upward at the ceiling of the chamber.

Torca felt time washing over him in waves, minutes, hours, days, years. He coaxed now, almost a mother's tone. He took hold. Once he lifted the inert element of the being into his arms, held it eye to eye.

But *its* eye was asleep now, perhaps. And it would not speak again.

After many hours—days, years—still would not speak. It had said all it had to say.

These words Torca read again and again from the slate, afraid the scribe had scribbled them wrongly, or that he, Torca, was forgetting.

The higher priest, standing up, spoke to Torca.

"Cease now. It's enough. We know. We have the other evidence."

Torca shook himself. Yes. They knew. There was other evidence. But almost, this did not matter. Lord or offal—truth had been given voice. It was truth that counted.

Yet later, waking from brief slumber Torca put all that away. God had sent them to live on earth. And there was enough in hand.

The tall room was as Torca recalled, not from his own experience but the descriptions of others. The Widow-Consort had not given over her apartments to a now High Queen. Udrombis kept her state here, as she had since her thirtieth year, when Akreon first had these rooms furnished and painted for her. Perhaps, although they said he had stayed faithful to her for longer, he had lost some of his heat. In the years before, she had slept always in his bed, having only a tiring room apart.

Torca composed himself. He had put on ordinary dress, not clad himself as a priest. She had summoned him. He wanted to display he did not, with her, have to represent the temple, that he had chosen to. Nor for that matter, was he solely a priest.

She in turn, when she entered—had she delayed for a purpose? Most of what she did had one—was dressed very simply. She wore only one jewel, the circlet of peal that supported the mass of black and white hair. She seemed to acknowledge he would not be impressed by glamours, and that this she knew.

They sat.

She offered him wine. A young woman poured it then left the jug and went away.

Udrombis, even at sixty, reminded him of the basalt lions crouching at her desk. The reality of the world was very real.

"You were thoughtful," she said, "to attend me so swiftly."

"Naturally, madam, I've come as soon as I was able. I would have sent word to you, in any case. As I have to the Sun, Klyton."

"The Great Sun," she said.

Torca put down his cup.

"Yes, madam, the Great Sun, Klyton. But there is this problem."

"The creature taken to the temple. What are the priests doing there, to be so long over it?"

Torca said, "They're working to be sure. It would be unforgivable to fail this trial the gods have set us all."

Her face was very still. In her eyes he saw the tips of swords, and black drops of fatal medicine.

"Madam, I knew Prince Amdysos—as well, that is, as I have known Prince Klyton, before his coronation."

"Then you can have no doubt," she said.

"I have none." He waited. He met her eyes, knowing that she would read him.

"What are you saying?" she asked.

"I have no doubt, madam, or rather, as slight a doubt as is inevitable, given the circumstances. His appearance and condition, the fact," he paused, searching selected the words that would do, "the fact that his wits are tainted, perhaps only temporarily. We must hope so."

"Torca, I think you find something in this that makes a joke."

"No, madam. He is Amdysos. I am as sure as I can be of this, or I wouldn't burden you. For it must be a burden of great grief and immeasurable distress. To see him so brought down."

"I haven't seen him," she said. "I have never seen this man." Her face remained still.

"Perhaps you would know him too, better than any other. He is your son."

Then she rose. She moved away two or three steps. Her robe hissed as it passed over the tiles, like a warning to be wary, but wariness had no part in this, could have none. He, too, got to his feet.

"My son was blessed, mighty, clean, and wise. He would have made a fitting King. But he died."

"The gods have sent him back to you."

She turned slowly. His belly grew cold from her gaze, but he held her gaze.

He said, "Pardon my words, great lady. I can't lie to you. You wouldn't thank me for it later."

Then for a second, she put her hand up over her mouth, and through her hand he heard her say the name of her last, lost son . . . "*Amdysos.*"

"I have to tell you," Torca said, "the temple will give voice as I have done. Yes, many of the priests are sceptical. Some have even railed against the others for bringing a deformed man into the holy precincts. But most have seen—"

"How are you certain?" she said. She had no expression now. "How can you be? I was told of his state."

Again he must pause. The god revealed, but also silenced. "A sword, bent and blackened in a fire, may still bear its insignia, which, if one knew it quite well, can be deciphered. A turn of the head, a way of standing, yes even as now he must stand. There's an authority about him that comes from old training, and out of history itself. How else did the captain from Airis know him? And then, there are—the things he says. He talks . . . of an eagle, and of a high place. He speaks of the Sun."

"A madman!" she cried.

She had lost all her boys. In her youth, also, three male children died in the birthbed, one before she had borne Glardor. Did she see ghosts, the greater, and the smaller, all pulled in with this one? However she appeared, whatever her strength, she was a woman, too. But never had he known or heard of her without control. It was only for a second, as before when she spoke the name. It was enough. She, too—she, too, had a *belief* in this.

"He has let go the full grasp of language, madam. But his remarks are pertinent, to the miraculous facts."

"Someone has somehow taught him then," she said, "how to speak, how to go on."

"The God," said Torca.

Udrombis flashed her face aside. She resumed her chair and waved him back into his. He was not quite sorry to sit down. His leg of wood was hurting him as if it gnawed at him to run away.

Torca hauled himself the other way, up on to the firm and rocky ground.

"Madam, allow me to tell you why I know it is the God. Allow me to excuse to you my avowal that this is the Prince Amdysos, your son, who should have become High King."

"If you can," she said. She put her arm on the arm of the chair, and rested her chin on this hand. Was it possible she trembled? Her eyes bored into him.

"You recollect the spear-bride Amdysos took, Elakti, the Ipyran."

"Yes. She vanished in the hills."

"Elakti bore Amdysos a child, a girl, who I think has been cared for here in the palace. This child was quite normal."

Udrombis raised her brows. "Yes. An ugly girl, but without other blemish."

"Elakti was again with child at the time of the Sun Race, in the year Amdysos was lost."

"She was. But I have said, no one could find her since she ran away. The child may have been born dead, up there."

"The child survived. She brought it with her when she returned to Oceaxis.

"I heard she had returned. I heard nothing of a child."

"It is barely that. Barely a child. The women hid it. Only in the Sun Temple did it come to view."

Udrombis said, "What significance does that have? You imply this child is deformed? Amdysos needed a woman of beauty to make for him fair children."

"Elakti's second child, Amdysos's child—Madam, the child is deformed in the same way that the sire is crippled. Its arms and legs are of unequal length, its body twisted, and though it has both eyes, one is malformed, the same one as is missing in the man. The child is a mirror to the ordeal your son has undergone; the gods have forced the child to stand as proof of it." Udrombis drew in breath. He heard this. Torca said, "But there is another thing, a difference." He waited, but she did not speak. He said, "Tufts like feathers grow in places on its body. And it has a head like that of a bird. The head of an eagle. This is no exaggeration, lady. I saw it close. It had the smell of an eagle too, as he has, now. What has happened is a hideous and awful event. But there's no avoiding it, no chance to escape from it." He got up again and bowed low. She did not move. "I'll go from your sight, madam. You will be glad to see me gone."

"Yes," she quietly said. "Yes, Torca."

He went, limping the sweat clinging on his back. But it was not *she* who had made him afraid.

Akreon.

He had been, as the Great Sun must, without flaw. Amdysos also he had formed in this mould. But if Amdysos truly lived on, half destroyed, the shambling parody of a god, human decay, corrupt and earthly mortality—was it not *this* which would draw the wrath of heaven upon them? And the House of the Sun, gold and cinnebar, thewed marble with blood of flame, the hearts of lions—besmirched, spoiled. What else could come to it but the plummet to the abyss.

Udrombis went into an inner room. From a chest she took a mantle of dark orange, embroidered by golden thread.

Stabia's women had woven it, Stabia embroidered it with great skill, despite her then increasing long-sightedness. How old had Amdysos been at that time . . . nineteen, surely. And Stabia's son, his friend, his brother, Klyton, seventeen years.

This mantle, Stabia had offered to Udrombis. It was a color she had worn in youth, the female orange that was the handmaiden of a King's scarlet. She had not divined that Stabia was working this for her, the elaborate stitchwork the softness. "Oh, no, my dear. I'll never wear such a color again. You know that." And Stabia, sadly saying, "But, your looks. Always to wear mourning—why not for the Summer Festival?" Udrombis shook her head, and seeing Stabia's face, took the mantle in her arms. "But no other shall have it. It will lie on my bed in winter. It will remind me of him." And Stabia had laughed: "He was a King."

Udrombis took the mantle now and sat by a window, which looked out across her garden, the garden meant for a Sun Queen, that Calistra had not thought to request, and that Udrombis had not thought to render up.

Stabia had eventually begun to feel the pain to be more than pain, to be what killed her. She had nevertheless feigned ignorance, blaming a greedy, aging woman's poor digestion.

There came the night, some while after Klyton's crowning, when the royal pair, god and goddess, were away in another land.

"Do you know," Stabia had said, sitting in that room with the almost matching chairs, where Calistra had sat, and Udrombis had told her she would be Klyton's Queen, "do you know, I feel so very old tonight. I think I'm near the Gate."

"Which gate is that?" Udrombis asked her, calmly.

"Oh, Death. What else. But the path's too hard." Stabia had lifted up her face, and in the lamplight of that dark, Udrombis saw the memory of Stabia's girlhood, a Stabia only voluptuous, and lively, her bright eyes and, tangled hair, and how their hands met on the comb, and their lips over the goblet. How long ago, far as some distant shore to which the boats no longer traveled.

"Let me prepare something to help you sleep."

"And to take off the pain," said Stabia, astutely. "My Sorceress. Only you can do it. But always it comes back, like a lean black dog with knives for teeth. This morning I cried. I cried just from the pain. Silly old woman." Stabia had shut her eyes, as if she feared to see pain also in the eyes of her Queen, or else not to see it. "I always thought," said Stabia in a stubborn small voice, "an hour would come you might need to be rid of me. And I never minded that, because I knew you'd have a deft hand. You'd never make me suffer. And I loved you, I love you so. Don't be angry, my darling one—I loved you more than him, yes, more than our Sun King, Akreon. Much more."

Udrombis took her hand. In remembrance now she seemed to take it again, among the folds of the mantle.

"Do you see," said Stabia, "what I'm asking for?"

Udrombis had risen. She mixed the draught without subterfuge. If Stabia recognized the ingredients she did not say. They were only those which Udrombis had employed before, to kill the pain and bring sleep. In a greater quantity they would end pain and sleep together. As now.

Stabia had accepted the glass of thin, greenish crystal. She kissed the brim, rather than the lips of a lover.

"Thank you."

"It will take a little while," Udrombis had said. "The pain goes first, then comes serenity. Time for you to reach your rooms and prepare. To offer and to pray, if you wish. I will pray here for you and make the offering. About two hours. Is it too quick?"

"Of course," said Stabia, "if I had life. But life's already stolen. Two hours are exactly all I need."

Udrombis kissed her forehead, and went on holding her hand as Stabia drank, and said, "It tasted very nice. You know how I like my food."

Udrombis said, "Your son is King. His children will rule this world."

Stabia sighed. "May the gods watch over him. And over you. I'll see you in a hundred years, my Queen. I'll wait for you then, by Tithaxeli, with a garland of the black roses they say grow there."

When Stabia had gone, Udrombis offered to the Sun at the altar in her rooms. She gave him a rare incense of Artepta, wine, and drops of her own blood. Into the offering flame, the last she let down a golden collar that Akreon had gifted her. So great was her respect for the woman she had assisted to depart.

And Klyton would rule. His children would rule after him.

Was it then for *this* they had dwelled here, and suffered and stayed proud and strong?

For a creature like a smashed, brainless bird?

And was it her own—her son—No. *No.* An apple, a bee, an eagle—these had taken her sons. Phaidix, and the god.

Klyton, too fastidious to go and see, knew this.

And Akhemony, which had feasted on nectar and wine, should not be made to eat the leavings of the jackal.

That night Crow Claw was seen by many about the palace at Oceaxis.

Calistra, the Queen, did not see her.

For several she glided, Crow Claw, across some thoroughfare, vanishing through some wall.

In the wild garden, a slave beheld her at the altar of Phaidix, but Crow Claw stood motionless, and the slave took her only for some lesser noblewoman of the house.

Nimi, the Sun-Consort's slave, was sitting with the new attendant, the child from Thon's Temple, for whom Calistra had expressed a fancy. This girl, almost ten years old, was yet mostly dumb and breathless from her sudden flight. With huge eyes she watched as Nimi, accustomed now, set out the figures of an easy game, in her little cubicle, and a dish of delicious sweets.

Then Nimi glanced up, her earrings twinkling, and saw Crow Claw standing *in* the wall. Indeed, inside, among the painted figures there.

Nimi who was more of a nurturer than a slave, had care for the unnerved child. And so she did not shriek. Nimi too had now and then heard tell of a deceased wisewoman of the palace, who wore crow black and rich gems.

Crow Claw's face was neither benign or malignant. But in her hand she held a narrow alabaster vessel, and upending it, poured out a stream of fiery embers to the floor.

Nimi, not unaware of symbols, recognized the sequence of a death.

Then Crow Claw smiled at her and said. "It's nothing, girl. After, is everything."

With this she faded, as a shadow fades with the coming of the moon.

Nimi looked away, and seeing the little Thon child two years her junior, had turned and seen and was frightened—despite or because of her origins—Nimi said. "She's only a guardian of the house. It's all right. She often goes about. You'll get used to her. Now, will you play yellow or red?"

7

Night lay always inside the hill. Above, the three tiers of the temple, white and hot with color, stretched to the glittering chimney that by day enticed the Sun. But in the rock beneath, as in the sea beneath the world, was darkness.

Calistra had rarely heard of the Precinct of Night. It was a secretive place. In the sumptuous euphoria of her coronation and marriage, it had enfolded and left her like a cloud.

Those that saw the guarded litter pass, imagined some woman of the palace went through the town. Those that noticed the litter borne up towards the temple paid some attention, for armed men stood about the terraces now and a Sun Prince, Lektos, son of Akreon by a Daystar of Akhemony, kept the main doors. But the litter and its guards were muffled and had no device. Maybe the young Queen had sent someone, or the Widow had sent another.

There had been some confusion and noise in the town a day or so before, when the rumor spread. Dead Amdysos had returned. Women had danced and screamed, throwing flowers upward to the Sun. Soldiers dispelled the women and the crowd. There had been three women they took away. They must have been peasants, from their clothes. One carried a bundle that seemed alive and made a hoarse, mewing sound—some animal perhaps, meant for sacrifice.

The town of Oceaxis was uneasy. From Sunrise the Sun had beaten on it, and at the wharfs the fish market began to stink even before noon. A Sunset, thunder-red, lit by flickerings over towards Mt. Koi, ushered in a night like smothered velvet, smeared with misty stars.

Inside the temple hill, Night was also close and airless, and set with uncanny stars, but it had a roof and walls of stone.

Lektos, standing in the upper temple, before the altar, had called aside his men. A woman alone did not much alarm him, until he saw who it was.

He wore full armor, as if for a battle, and the sword had been drawn, gleaming, in his hand. He bowed. He knew, she had never thought much of him, but he was not privy to her other thought, that she might need to have Lektos dealt with now. Udrombis's spies had told her, he was not quite content, less jealous of Klyton's Kingship, than eager for action. Lektos was happiest in times of strife. But he knew to be cautious of her.

She had put on her almost-black, and at her throat blazed the necklace of fabulous diamonds, the Seven Daystars. There were rubies of three shades on her hands, rose and purple and crimson. Her hair was roped with gold. All this the litter had obscured, but now the lamps of the temple showed it off. Near by, the enormous altar under the O of the fire chimney, dwarfed Lektos to a shiny toy.

"I regret you felt obliged to come here, madam."

"Please," she said, "don't trouble yourself."

Brushed aside, he bridled up like a girl overlooked in her best dress. He had been this too, had he, in Ipyra, going against Nexor?

"Why are you here, lady?"

"This is between myself and the priests. I won't rob you of more of your time."

She sailed by him, and the priests came and took her away. Leaving him biting his lip and wondering. He would have said to her, as he had to Klyton in the palace, that he was here to keep safe the honor of the temple, to prevent riotous mobs arriving. At no single moment had Lektos so far claimed the man-thing which had been brought to Oceaxis, was anything much. And yet, if pressed, passionately Lektos would have declared that, if the man were indeed Amdysos, the sword of Lektos was ready drawn, to defend his inalienable rights.

That Udrombis had not bothered to question him and so receive such answers, demonstrated she already knew them quite well, and thought them irrelevant.

Udrombis trod down into the black Precinct. Behind her the great door thudded to, but this did not unnerve her. She was not easily upset, had never been. Sixty years had taught her, too, that most omens are nothing, or intended for others.

The stairway ran down into the hill, lighted at intervals by brazen bull's heads that spouted fire from nostrils, jaws. The bull was the Sun creature that linked the Sun to the earth. Once the solar god had been driven underground to fight with this bull, which was both himself and his foe, the deity in two aspects, of patron and of ravisher.

The pair of escorting priests kept at Udrombis's side. They were masked in bronze, in the faces of old men.

Under the earth the Sun went, and the old. Udrombis moved fluidly. She did not have the stiffness nor the tread of an aging woman.

At the stairfoot, the Precinct of Night opened, chamber upon chamber, circumvented and enmeshed by numerous passages, slopes and steps. It was a labyrinth, not quite impenetrable to those accustomed to it but to any other a wilderness. There must always be a guide.

In the third chamber, vast squat pillars held up the black-stained roof. From black beams hung the fretted lamps of Artepta and Oriali, letting fall pieces of light like silver coins.

A black-robed priest was waiting. He bowed to her as Queen, and she to him. He was not masked, being a keeper of this place, his features nondescript, yet banked with priestly power.

"I greet you, once Mirror of the Sun, Wife-Widow and Mother of Kings. Your messenger informed us you wish to regard him, the man who is your son."

"Who is claimed to be," she corrected.

"Great lady. The testing is done. Though not as you recall, this is Amdysos."

Torca, now this one. Soon all Akhemony would hear it. And that toy warrior in the temple above, pale, inflammable Lektos.

She had been driven here, as the Sun was driven, to meet an enemy who was—perhaps—part of herself. For she dreaded it might be a fact, as Torca had told her. This thing—Amdysos. The parody, the crumbled effigy.

She meant that it should be put to death quite soon. She would have herself the power to see to it, without defacing any other god. And if it were the remnant of her son she was to kill, she was determined now to know her sin. How else could she wrestle with it? How else be absolved?

Udrombis said, "Then you have decided. I have yet to do so." She had served a King. These priests were only men. "But let me see him, certainly." And the priest bowed to her once more.

She sensed conspiracy among them, but it was the plot of those who thought themselves right. Torca had written to Klyton. She guessed Klyton had refused to come here, look for himself, and this might well be fear, not aesthetics. She could forgive Klyton this. He had wished to retain the other picture of his friend. There had been times, too, when she had assisted Akreon, sparing him. A King must not bear all.

Given this creature's physical condition, what she had been told of it, not only by Torca, it would be simple enough to remove—though all the priesthood, all the little Lektoses, stood against her. It was the woman god, Phaidix, who had made shadows.

They walked on through the labyrinth. Udrombis made no special note of the way. She did not need to. Some priest would guide her back to the great stair.

And she saw no portent either in her descent to the Underworld, which this domain symbolized, her descent that anticipated a going up again.

Actually she recognized the vaulted passage, the swoop of the vast door-mouth and the cavern of chamber beyond. She had come here once, to make her coronation vows.

Thus, Calistra, too, had seen this room, which was hardly like a room. The walls were lost behind the streamers of rusty smoke, rising out of silvered tripods. Above, the ceiling curved up, held, it seemed, almost randomly by groups of pillars, whose capitals were the heads of horned beasts. In the uneven dome of the ceiling, stars sparkled, hard as daggers. They had been set in constellations resembling those visible in the lands overhead, but thicker, and more luminous, as the dead were said to see them, though far, far below and under ground.

The priesthood of the Precinct was stationed everywhere here.

They tended the braziers, and the several altars, all of which dripped black.

The air was very dense, breathless and cloying. It smelled of dark aromatics, and entrails from the immolations.

There was no sound but for the high singing that the ears supplied.

Udrombis stopped when the priest indicated that she should. He spoke low to her, his temple-trained voice resonant and theatrical, not touching her at all.

"I ask, madam, you don't speak to him, as yet. Recall, in spirit he has come up from the country prefigured here. Therefore, he rests. There is some way to go towards the light."

"Very well," she said. She was impatient, but did not reveal it.

He went in front of her now, and led her on, and she saw there was a curtain, a sparse silvery net, which went gliding up. What was then displayed did check her.

A travesty. In a tall, ebony chair, a man was sitting. And at his side, in a chair of ivory, a woman. Who held on her lap a child.

The red-grey light, the coins from the lamps, the blast of the torches, gave them over strangely to be seen. But they were like the murals of Kings. Friezes that showed Kings, with their Consorts and foremost heirs. Just so Akreon had been depicted, and she beside him, Udrombis, holding the infant Glardor.

She was affronted, but she said and did nothing.

The priest said to her, "You may go to that marker on the floor, madam. The golden line."

She thought how arrogant they were, and that their power was too big. If Akreon had lived, this one would not dare say any of this. But if Akreon had lived, there would be no need. Or Glardor even. Or Pherox. Or . . . Amdysos.

Was it Amdysos in the ebony chair?

Udrombis went forward to the golden chain they had stretched across the black marble of the floor. She was perhaps eight sword lengths from the group of King, Consort, heir. She focused her eyes, which were acute, upon them.

Who had put them out like this? Was it for her sake? No, surely not, some part of the ritual they had conducted.

It was Elakti, the spear-wife, the insane woman, who had taken the place of the Consort. She wore a sable gown in keeping with the

Precinct, and a ring of creamy stones held off her swarthy hair. Her eyes were large and brightly mirror-blind; some drug had been given her. The child was wrapped close in white. The silver border of the cloth sank heavily in, over its face. It sat, or maybe slept. Udrombis could not make out the horrible deformities Torca had spoken of. But the child was of no importance. Neither Elakti. As with the man, when needful, it would not be so taxing to be rid of them. If Torca had not lied, they were an offence upon the earth.

Udrombis turned her eyes to the man who took the place of the King.

She had made certain of the rest, before she did so, not from reluctance or dread, but in order she could dismiss everything else from her mind.

What did she see?

Seated, he did not look very unusual. They must have cleaned him, calmed him, drugged him too, no doubt. His hands lay on the arms of the chair, and it was not particularly apparent that they were unmatched. The legs, one foot supported on a footstool, gave a similar effect of the normal. His head drooped a fraction. But he was not disgraceful. Not even unregal, but like an actor taking the part of a king. A small king, of course. Not the Great Sun.

The face was raddled, and as she studied it, through the freckle of the lamps, where the torch fire did not reach, gradually she made out the eye which had gone, and the dirty white leer of the other eye, shorn of a lid.

In repose, the face was unfrightful, but sad. A poor creature, definitely mortal, but brought down, and with a broken nose.

It was not Amdysos. Her womb had not carried it. Whatever woman had brought it forth, it had not been of the glorious seed of Akreon.

But then—they were chanting, and nearby a gust of fire brushed up. All lights, all shadows altered. And for one moment she saw—she saw—a face she knew—a face of flame and gold, of judgment. And tenderness.

She had made a sound. The priest turned to her. But next second there came another noise, across the distance.

The child was wriggling, as young children do. It was struggling. And suddenly the mother, mad Elakti, had let it go.

Straight to the floor it dropped, the child, and—not human, unhurt—righted itself at once, as an insect might. As it did so the shawl of white and silver unraveled from it.

Udrombis stood, imperious. She gazed, not flinching, at the demon-beast which had somehow grown in Elakti's curdled belly.

It was the priest who drew away.

The demon child began hopping forward. Hopping—yes, like an ungainly bird better at flight. But it had no wings, only the two stubby and unequal arms.

Its legs were skewed. The head—the head was held forward also, pointing at Udrombis. The nose, if a nose it was, slanted downwards, and the chin angled steeply up. A beak. Between, a sort of squashed, lipless mouth, that now, again, let out a high, hoarse, meowing screech, and a black tongue like a worm.

One eye was a slit, a slash of costive yellow. The other stared. Wide open, round, seeming lidless too, the color of a baked egg that *burned*.

The skull was flat. Something grew on it. Fur, feathers—

As it hopped on and on, Udrombis did not move.

It hopped right up to her, and with a hand like a wooden claw, took fierce, almost pleading hold of her skirt.

"Well," she said clearly, "what do you want?"

All her days since she had been a Queen, others had done, mostly, what she required of them. Where not, she had dealt with it. And always she had been guarded. That day the assassin leapt upon Akreon in Uaria, a circle of ten men had instantly thronged around her.

But now the priesthood hung back, either in amazement or simple slowness, because their time was now different from her time, her time and that of the demon imp which was an eagle.

And grasping her skirt in its claws, it climbed, it *raced* up the stone figure of Udrombis. Before she could push it away or hurl it from her, it had reached her waist, her breast.

And then it stared up precisely into her, eyes, and in the stare was all the unreasonableness of utter chaos.

As the claws went into her, they lurched it upward again, and it was face to face with her. Udrombis made an attempt at last to strike it down. But it was fixed, fixed in her flesh. She screamed spontaneously yet belatedly from pain, and then the claws thrashed up.

Some of the priests sprang forward now. Before they could reach her, the demon had torn her open. Amid a pandemonium of pummeling, ripping, flailing—her eyes vanished, her hair seemed to explode—blood spurted and hanks of gold-plated black rained down on carmine roots.

Udrombis wore a butcher's apron. Her face was a mask unlike any other, a torrent of red. This turned here and there, noiseless, sightless, seeking. But she fell heavily, the demon still attached, still busy. As the running priests surrounded her, the demon jumped aside. It darted out its tongue. And the chamber paused. It was so *little*, there among the sprawl of limbs and silk and sprinkled pearls, only the size of a child not much more than a year old.

However, Phaidix's shadows must have reached for it. It slid between robed legs and was reeled off into nothingness.

Udrombis knew she must push off the agony and blindness, and rise. But Crow Claw was there, the old witch from the palace at Oceaxis. Udrombis remembered the vision of the eagle. After all, it had returned for her.

She was angry. She was not prepared. But Crow Claw had always been insolent.

The pain wafted to a distance. Lifting from it, she saw the pain lying on a floor as dark as a River by night.

The priests stood over the body, knowing it only by its dress, what remained of the hair, the well-kept hands glittering with crimson blood and rubies.

8

Once more, events begin with a sound. It is the cry of grief common in Akhemony. I had heard it when Pherox was killed in Sirma, though with Glardor's death I do not recapture it at all. Now it is loud and immediate, and the walls of the palace throb like a lamplit shell.

Presently, Hylis came in.

Her face was dusted white. She bowed.

"The news is terrible, Great Queen." I waited, suspended. She said. "Udrombis the Widow-Consort, is dead."

This was surely impossible. How many others must have reacted as I did? I shook my head. But I said, "When?"

"At the temple. Something unspeakable occurred." Hylis made a sign against evil or wrath. She said. "A creature—tore away her face."

I thought she meant the monster supposed to be Udrombis's son. But I could not believe in her death, so colossal her presence and her status had been. And so the manner of her death was itself a myth.

Something made me dispatch Hylis to Klyton's rooms. I had been taught long ago, by the squeaky priest, that even I did not go to the King without first sending my courier.

But Hylis came back and said Klyton was not there. He had gone at once to the temple.

I visualized his courteous regrets at the death of Stabia, but Udrombis was perhaps much more to him.

The wailing was dying off. They did not keep to it long, here, unlike Ipyra.

I sent Hylis to her bed.

The night was nearing its cusp, when it passes over into morning. I had been sitting in my retiring gown, but now I threw it off, and dressed myself again, not calling in the women, who would sob and chitter, their eyes glaring on me to see what I would do.

It seemed I must be ready.

The white dog followed me about. Finally I sat and took his head between my hands, but caressing him my mind was working oddly, as if before a journey, when things must be prepared.

After the dinner, Klyton had left the Hall early, and he was in his rooms, the King's Apartment. Perhaps a strange moment to describe them, but to me the image is intrusive. The walls were plastered the purest white, with white marble, and pillars of red marble that had Sun-ray tops of gold. On the walls were depictions of the Sun god hunting, the gold leopards and albino lions leaping joyfully to be speared. Around the ceiling were painted patterns in thick purple. In the floor was the mosaic of a procession of the god. The bed was of marroi wood inlaid with nacre, and the hangings were the Sunburnt yellow of apricots, the bedcover the purple-red of the flesh of grapes. What supported the hangings were six white marble horses, the height of two men together, carved rearing. There were other rooms for reception and bathing, and for study, with books and scrolls on shelves from the floor to the roof. But I remember this bedroom. I had slept with him in it now and then, and the horses had watched with unbridled mouths over our lovemaking. A lamp large as a six-year-old child hung from the ceiling. It was pure gold over a frame of pherom, and when it was refilled with oil., three slaves were needed to bring it down and raise it on its chain. I know it hangs there no longer. I saw it drop.

Akreon had not used these rooms in his last years. Perhaps uncharacteristically, Glardor, when in Oceaxis, had taken them. They came to Klyton with their paint touched up, everything fresh and in order.

At the far end of the bedroom was a screen of pierced sea-ivory. Behind this stood the shrine Klyton had made for his brother, Amdysos.

The garland from the Hall, tamarind and ormis flowers, was on Klyton's head still; he was a little flushed by the wine.

He had made an offering to Amdysos with a priest to assist him, pouring shavings of a scented resin, an exquisite bird with tarnished feathers letting go its blood.

The priest made no comment upon the living possibility of Amdysos. When he was gone, Klyton stayed, talking to his friend.

The oil was low in the wonderful lamp and he had called no one to refill it. The flame at the shrine hung still and bright. The doors of the shrine were thrown back, and Amdysos gravely smiled and gleamed, his wings outspread.

"I did give you those," Klyton murmured. "The wings of the eagle. Do you remember, in Ipyra, I shot an eagle and dedicated it to you? What have I done wrong? I had my omens—the Sun, the cloud like a hand. The dream when you spoke to me. You don't do that now. Have I offended you? What did you want me to do, sit by and let Nexor play at being a King? I don't believe you grudge me this. Then why has this—this *cretin* been sent against me? For the sake of the God, Amdysos, why did that idiot at Airis think this was you? And that bitch Elakti, that you loathed, with a child so deformed, and in such a way— it makes a *mockery* of your death. A mockery, Amdysos. Give me some sign. Come in a dream if you won't speak here. I've asked you to. I've begged you. What must *she* think, your mother, Udrombis. It must tear out her heart, all this. And there should be some method to be rid of it all, something quite easy. But as things stand—" Klyton raised his voice. "What are you meaning? That you've nothing to say to me? That would be like you, turning your back on me. Why do you think we quarreled that bloody day? Your silence, your stubbornness. Not now, Amdysos. *Give me a sign—*"

There came the crash of a fist upon the outer doors.

Klyton turned with a curse and left the shrine standing open, the sweet smoke going up. A slave met him at a doorway.

To the news, Klyton listened. Reaching up, he took off the garland, and let it go. To the slave he said only, "Get out."

From beyond the closed doors they heard his roar. They had never known at any other time, in triumph, in anger, in war even, Klyton to give out such a sound.

Presently, he came like a flung stone through all the doors. He shouted for an escort of fifty men. Some of the younger slaves were crying in terror, at Klyton's rage, at Udrombis's death—not from any love, but as if the world had given way. An old slave man came and spoke quietly to them. At any other time, Klyton would have turned to him—"Thank you, Sarnom."

Klyton whirled them all off with violent gestures. He grasped a mantle round himself and buckled on his sword. As his hand met the pommel, a carnelian incised with an eagle, he gave a laugh. But his face was as they had never been shown it. It had no mind behind it, only this fury, and the green eyes were stretched wide, with a kind of blood-lust one sees in animals, as they take their prey.

It was Adargon who came, armed and running, the fifty men gathered ready below.

"My lord—God's Heart—the Queen-Widow—"

"Yes, I know," said Klyton, so light it only floated on the boiling surface of him. "They told me."

"You're going to the temple."

"It seems the priests have barred the inner door, the way into the Precinct. And Lektos has let them.

"Lektos," said Adargon.

They ran down through the palace, which was making now its noises of shock and sorrow and panic.

As they emerged into the court, thunder split the night above.

Klyton tilted back his head. He shouted in a harsh male scream, up into the sky. "Yes! You've spoken. *Yes*."

Adargon put his hand on Klyton's arm and Klyton turned, a snarling lunatic. Adargon who also had never beheld Klyton in this shape, faced him solidly. "My lord, don't let them see. They'll think hell gapes enough already."

Klyton's eyes seemed to give off a shot of fire. Adargon, even Adargon, started. But then they heard the tearing shriek.

They turned and stared, and in the courtyard, men called aloud, while the horses swerved and squealed.

The thing came blazing down, sizzling, and shattered on the paving. Red fire ran like dye and glittered out.

"A thunder-stone—a bolt from heaven—" Adargon blurted.

Klyton's eyes had cleared somewhat. He was back inside them. "Look. More of them."

The soldiers and the slaves, the Sun Prince and the King, stood with their heads tipped back, as if at some scenic instruction.

From the thunder-riven dark, the stars had sped away, or else they were dashing down to the earth. A rain of shrieking fires was falling like hail. As they hit the ground they smashed, each a vessel of seething matter that burst. On the palace roof, rattling, glittering. Through the garden trees they rushed. A blow of fire ignited, and there were black silhouettes before a curtain of red. Everywhere, the thunderbolts were cascading. The sky was birthing them. And on and on they came.

Klyton ran to his horse, mounted it, and held it wheeling, neighing, as the groom tumbled away. Seeing this, those who had held back, also mounted up, while their servants ran for cover.

The band of men raced from the palace, a stream of bronze and steel, along the shore road towards the town of Oceaxis, while the rain of fire-coals plunged all about them, lighting their path with kicks of fire, and from the sea crashed waterspouts of the form and heat of smelted swords.

The wild gardens, and the groves that led towards the. sea, were burning. I stood transfixed on my terrace, watching the deluge of the thunderbolts, and seeing the trees flare up to cups of gold. Birds swarmed from the conflagration, black, like bees, on the red cloud of the smoke. They blew between the shards of fire. Their cries and wings sounded like the cries in the palace, and my women's commotion and rushing. Slaves rushed too, below, with vessels of water, which they spilled in their terror.

The sound—the sound—beyond the screaming and the outcry of the birds—notes like the missiles of a million miniature catapults, the air unseamed—

But down there, twelve years old, I had sat while the women danced. The sky so tranquil that evening, and the lucid sea silken on the shore. And Klyton came to me the first.

The tamarinds cooked with an appetizing smell. The air smelled, too, of metals, and a yeasty fermentation. And of lightning.

I wished the women would die to stop their noise. Where was Hylis? Even the white dog had run away, and in their cage the doves huddled all together, trembling like the firelit leaves.

By the time Klyton and his men reached the town, several houses were on fire there. The streets were full of scurrying slaves, the town guard called out, drays with water-barrels pulled by half-petrified donkeys, men and women who cried and milled about, their heads muffled from the fiery storm. The thunder-stones seemed less, but as Klyton climbed above the town to the Sun Temple, whose building had been begun, it was said, by eagles, Oceaxis spread away like a map, and was a scene of punishment, and nightmare. The ruddy pall of the fires, the smolders, the constant abstracted human movement, one great house that had gone to a pillar of flame, and sent up a tower of pitchy smoke. And through it all, the livid bolts which still intermittantly fell. On the temple hill, the crying sank back to a rumble, but now and then the gongs were beaten in the town, to warn, perhaps of a new conflagration. Beyond the harbor, the sea looked bubbling, and not like water. Klyton turned his face to the temple and rode on. And the pines and cedars, the huge oaks and marroi, draped the town from view.

Lektos had come out and positioned himself at the stairs' top, on the uppermost terrace. Behind him, the temple burned yellow from the torches and the lamps, and two hundred of his five hundred men, stood in ordered ranks, their shields in front of them. In Lektos's hand was yet that naked sword.

Klyton dismounted. Adargon and ten others walked behind him up the steps. It was enough. Klyton was the Great Sun.

Lektos, though, did not give way. He waited, the shields at his back.

The smell of smoke was acrid in the groves and on the stair. But the thunderbolts seemed not to have fallen here at all, or if they had, they had done no damage.

Klyton reached the terrace, and Lektos. They faced each other, and Lektos said, "My lord, the Queen-Widow—"

"Yes." said Klyton. "Why do you think I'm here?"

Lektos faltered, but did not falter sufficiently. He did not shift. And at his back his men were like icons of soldiers, unseeing, shields locked.

Adargon said, "Stand aside, Lektos. The King is here. Can't you see?"

Lektos said, "My lord the King—the King is behind me. The priests say so. In the temple. The King—is Amdysos."

Klyton bellowed. His voice smote the trees and rang like a hammer on an anvil. "Your *King* came up from a pit—your *King* has killed my *mother*—your *King*—*Get from the way!*"

"Not—not Amdysos," Lektos warbled, backing a step, firming himself and standing still again, "the child—it rent her and ran off into the passages—they closed the doors to keep it in and hunt it—but it was the instrument of the God—"

"*Udrombis!*" Klyton bellowed. In a movement like that of some machine, his hand loosed the sword with the eagle in its pommel. In one smooth stroke, he cut the weapon from Lektos's hand. Lektos was openmouthed, foolish now. And in the silence they heard again the outcry of the town, and the whistling of another of the bolts falling somewhere near, but below the trees. Klyton said gently, "Move yourself."

Lektos planted himself more steadfastly.

"Someone shall fetch a pr—"

Klyton's sword stripped through the light: a flare, a dart of color. It had taken Lektos, who was generally armored, between throat and collarbone, where the throat-piece and helm had been dispensed with. Lektos hiccuped, face splashed with his own blood, and turned slowly around, crashing face-down before his men.

The shield wall disbanded. The soldiers leaned at angles, staring. A young handsome man, with a scarred chin, made one stride forward. He was a son of Lektos's earliest youth, by a woman of the palace. Neither Klyton nor Adargon knew his name, but Lektos had been reasonably good to him.

He said, blatantly and loudly, "You killed him, but you're not the King anymore. Amdysos is. Can't you see all the gods are raging at you, throwing fire down from heaven? They chastised the old witch—" incredibly he meant Udrombis—"for her poisonings and plots. It's you, Klyton, who must step down."

And Klyton looked at him, at the sword the boy had drawn and the baleful libertine eyes. Klyton cut sideways now, and took off the hand with the sword, and as this adversary also slumped away, sightless with surprise, the other soldiers on the terrace came trampling forward, swearing and yelling, their eyes not blind at all but bulging with horror and anger.

The world truly gave way. They fought Klyton, there on the terrace. The army of a King, clashing against a King's sword their own. And others now were pounding through the trees, not knowing who it was they must war with, but knowing it was war.

Adargon dragged Klyton back down the stair, both men hacking away the attack as they went. All but two of their ten were gone. Adargon howled for the rest of the escort, forty men, and as these cleared the area below, forced Klyton towards his horse. "Leave it, my lord—Klyton, *leave* it—they're too many and they're out of their minds—"

Klyton remounted. His face was bloodless and empty. He allowed Adargon to push him from the riot. Those of the escort that could, extricated themselves from Lektos's battalion in the sacred groves, and galloped after, killing, as they went, men in armor and on foot—who were only shouting to know what had gone on.

All the women had vanished, as if they had felt and taken exception to my fear of their fright. As the gardens by the shore faded to a blackened wasteland, little birds that had flown into the trees beneath my terrace, fluttered anxiously, piping, unable to settle. Slaves called to each other in the gloom. They had not, before, needed lamps, and now everything was dark, even though the cruel moon had risen on the Lakesea. The smoke had veiled her and colored her like a hyacinth. I thought I saw the drawing of the face of Phaidix there, a profile with one indifferent and unlooking eye.

In the room with the pool, the turtle would not come out of her shell. She had ceased to be an animal and become instead a cold slab of onyx. The doves continued to huddle together. I spoke softly to them, but they paid no heed. Did they blame me? To the beast, men seem like gods, able to do and cause so much. Therefore, are not all things in their power? And when the lamp goes out or the plate is bare, or the snow comes, that too must be their fault. I pondered, wandering my hollow rooms, if we then misjudged the gods, who were able to do and cause so much that we could not, and yet perhaps, like us, must sometimes wait helpless on the whim of other, mightier beings.

I had seen a red glow pulse above the hidden town, but that too had died away. The levinbolts had ended. At the edge of my terrace one lay that had burned only for an instant. It was merely a gritty ash now, that would be easy to sweep aside.

A hand scratched on a door. I gave admittance, and one of my women entered. I asked her where Hylis was, and the woman lowered her eyes. "I don't know, madam, but I was sent to you. They say, keep to your rooms." This was like before. Perhaps I knew, for what else had I done? "Bring me some juice, and water, please," I said, for I had drunk dry the pitcher. She bowed and went, and when she had gone, I asked myself who "they" had been, that "sent" her. In any case, she did not come back.

The palace, after the commotion, was now deathly still. I had heard horses once, and men's voices lifted, but that, too, ceased without explanation.

At last I walked to the outer doors and opened them. The guard there did not turn to look, and he was no man I knew, but then, when did I notice them?

"I wish to send word to the King," I said.

"Pardon me, madam. I can't leave my post here. One of your women . . ."

"My women have disappeared."

His eyes then slid to me. I was young and a fool, the eyes seemed to say, no other Queen would let herself be abandoned so. And he, for his bad luck, must linger here to guard this imbecile.

"Some have gone away," he remarked, enigmatic.

The lamps were failing, but another light crept in the corridor. It was the dawn beginning.

I left the guard and moved again into my chambers, to watch the harsh Sun appear, as the cruel moon had done, over the sea which was a lake.

Now I seem to picture those eyes, that face, repeated, the shuffling of their booted feet, between the torchlight and the rising of the Sun. Men urged and tugged away, uneasy at the gods, thinking of the riddle and the death in the temple, and hearing of Klyton's deeds there. The soldiers of Akhemony, ordered that night to ring the palace round, slipping off in twos or threes, then by two hundreds and three thousands. Glancing back perhaps, to note that high golden roof, the landmark of Oceaxis—*See that? The palace.*

As the Daystar followed the Sun, both of them wan and soiled from the smokes, the King's House, perched above the land, hollowed out as I had felt it to be.

An hour after Sunrise, someone came in not knocking, or else knocking so lightly I never heard.

I went into the outer room.

There stood my slave, pretty Nimi, and with her the child from the Temple of Thon, and on a leash they had the white dog, who seeing me, wagged his tail and smiled.

"Lady Calistra." said Nimi. By this title she nearly always called me, though I had risen to be High Queen. I had never chided her. Had I never felt myself quite Queen enough? "Here we are. We found your dog. Choras caught him, he was afraid. But there was some food in the kitchens."

Choras, the Thon-child, held up a silver platter they had piled, winningly, with little girl treats, sweets and small fruits, and some wine and milk, and a meat bone in a napkin for my dog.

I saw Choras had been made pretty too. Her black hair was curled, her lips rouged, and in her ears were two tiny colcai rings.

We sat in the inner room, for the terrace looked now out on to desolation. The dog gnawed at the bone without any seemliness. He had been used to having an amber dish. The girls ate their sweets, and I drank some of the wine. Nimi asked after the doves and the turtle. Then she went to see. When she returned, long silver threads of tears were on her face. The doves had escaped through the undone cage, the unwatched door, over the open terrace. They were in the living trees, ruffling and cooing, no longer nervous. The turtle, she said, had died inside her shell. She was so very old, Nimi reminded us, had Kelbalba not said so? And now, maybe she had lived more than she wanted.

But we were young, I not so much older than they, and our leaden dignity of sadness did not last. New iridescent fear rushed quickly in where loss had been.

The guard was gone from my door, so Nimi had already advised me. Soon, another guard arrived, twenty men fully armed, whose leader announced that Klyton would presently be here.

But the smoke-tinctured day yawned on, and Nimi and Choras played a board game on the floor, and I went away in my clothes to sleep on the bed. The white dog pounced up beside me, not to be my guard, but for comfort.

As I lay there dozing, Klyton was pacing out a floor, while Adargon and others watched like gazing blocks of earth.

"I was *given* this," Klyton said. "*All* this."

But Torca stood before him in the white and gold of the priest, his black beard dividing him, his black lips pressed shut, parting only to say, "My lord, it wasn't given, but loaned. Now you must give it up."

"What to? That *thing* you have in your temple."

And, "Yes, sir. To the Lord Amdysos."

And Klyton shouts now. He reiterates, *that* is not Amdysos.

But Oceaxis is in ferment, and although the men of bronze still ring the palace, still hold the road, the burnt places scream with their own voices, and thousands of men are out on the land, also men of bronze, and with them two thirds of the Sun Princes of Akreon's line. Lektos lies on a bier with his arms by him, a wronged hero, his son close by. Udrombis's mutilated cadaver is kept concealed in the Vault of Night.

When Klyton finishes his tirade, his faction—for this is what they have become—observe him with eyes cast sidelong. Eyes that seem to regret he is so young, perhaps a fool, and they have served this imbecile.

He had been like the Sun itself, but now he is a ranting child. The toy was given him. The gods gave it. He will not—*not*—render it again to the other one, the mysterious and god-reborn, whose rightful thing it is.

"Damn him," Klyton says. He has left off shouting. His color cools. His beauty is all they perceive, and there is a weird lesson in it, for Amdysos's beauty was struck from him, and he has been brought back a monster. The gods have chosen what is not the best.

"All right," Klyton says. "Call the council. I'll debate it there."

But like water from a surface of fine polish, the world and its chariot are slipping from him. Udrombis and her cleverness are dead. He seems to hear a rumbling, a whistling and turning in his head, the noise of the town as the firestones smote it.

No, of course he does not think of me. He is alone among his loyal men. His back is to a wall that has been shaken down. Clear as the writing in the book of stone, he sees it all.

5TH STROIA

SUN'S ISLE: THE LAST MARCH

I

Annotation by the Hand of Dobzah

The nightingale has come back, to the tree beside the pool under the tower. Sirai is pleased and sits listening as it trills in the blue dusk.

She reminded me that in Akhemony, they called it the kitri, the honey-bird. And of the song she made, which compares the nightingale to memory, flying as it wills, returning often to a particular tree, where sometimes it so sweetly sings. But shadows come also to the tree.

I REMEMBER HOW THE ROWERS sang on and on to the beat of a drum, louder than the heart of Akhemeny, working us through the hot, windless sea. They were Bulote men, the ship a Bulote ship, one of two he had taken at the little port of Belba. They had been turning for Oceaxis, but Klyton paid the men to put the cargo off, and board us instead. They did not know who he was, and took him for some Akhemonian noble. Their dialect is complex, and in it the word for king is like the word for lord. Only the title Great Sun has a separate meaning, and this was never used in front of them.

They did not want to go, either. But they were given gold.

A temple to Thon Appidax sat on the shore, facing out the way we would be making, to the Island. It was not like the houses of Thon elsewhere in the region. As Appidax, Thon is a youth, comely, with long black hair, a form the Death god assumed once, when he went, unusually, wooing. For the sake of that human lover, Thon Appidax may be placated, and asked to desist—or at least to wait. The dying often sought such shrines, to beg more days, or those on a dangerous journey bribed the god.

From the temple, which had four pillars dyed with cobalt, and a roof of red tile, our sailors and rowers came to the ships, laden with amulets and blessed bread for the voyage. The oracle, an old sightless woman masked only by her blindness, had assured them only one of the party would suffer immediate death. Though they were unnerved as to whom that would be, the felling of one among so many seemed worth the risk. Besides, the fatality might be in the ranks of the noble and his men, not theirs.

Adargon had said, "Klyton, my lord, no one goes there now. The Island is cursed."

"Then it will suit me, won't it. No, naturally I don't mean that. The thunderbolts were my omen, Adargon. I must go where I am shown. That brought me the crown of the Sun Lands. I won't believe the gods intended it to be snatched away."

He had spoken very much in this vein. He would pace, or sit almost still twisting something—a knife, a fruit—in his hands. And he would say to us, those close about him, *I was given the Kingship. This was never meant. There will be a way to put it right.*

As we rode from Oceaxis, he had already decided on a portion of his course. He had Daystar wives in Uaria and Oriali, little girls he had wed deliberately too young, then garlanded and gifted, kissed on the lips, and left intact with their families, until they should be fifteen or sixteen, as old as his present Sun Queen, Calistra. But with Artepta a betrothal had been arranged, a princess of eighteen years, daughter of one of the triumvirate Pehraa, their kings, who ruled always by three, and whose bloodline had run also in Udrombis. This princess had been kept for the Sun House. Artepta was a powerful and isolate land, peaceful and slow to move, but with a vast army of priest-warriors, and the capabilities for many things, which the scholarly reckoned above anything known elsewhere. Esoterica, magic, marvels of architecture and science, and weapons, too, beyond anything employed in the upper Sun Lands. One had heard the tales of what Arteptans were. Udrombis had been an awesome ambassadress, though only partly of their blood. And I do not forget Torca who had enabled me to walk, and helped drive Klyton from his Kingdom.

Klyton said to me, "I must marry this woman, and perhaps another daughter, from one or other of the three kings. Don't mind it that I seem to value these women. You see why."

I was meek and affectionate, pliant to his will, trained like the dog. And so much had gone against him. I must not, even in the slightest thing. It was not that I had come to be afraid of him, not yet. But, as once before, I seemed not to know him. He radiated a hard and fascinating light. Not much more than a thousand men, some three hundred of them Sirmians, had followed him from Oceaxis. Those held by the fire of him, hung from his Sun, now too brilliant, and now in cloud.

We had been making for Sirma, so it was thought. Then Klyton drew us up again, northeast, to Belba. He had said to Adargon, no ship would have put out from Oceaxis for the Island.

At Belba, he gave the bulk of the soldiery over to Adargon, and in the wagons put presents, selected on the night we chose our possessions for our future life. "Go and speak to them in Artepta. You have my letters to the Pehraa. Add what you like. Only the facts. You only need set them out. I am King. Artepta is always gracious, and worships justice, and so on."

With about sixty men loaded on the larger Bulote ship, a vessel of two oar-banks and double sail, Klyton put himself and his household, such as it now was, with ten guards, into the lesser galley that had fifty rowers and a single sail the color of brown Bulote mud.

Our ship had for her figurehead the goddess of the river up which they had sailed into the Lakesea. They wreathed her but bound her eyes. They did not want her to see the direction they were steering her. Which was to the Sun's Isle where a piece of the Sun had fallen, in the time before time.

They had called their council in Oceaxis. By then, a deputation had come from the Sirmian troops in Akhemony led by a kinsman—so he called himself—of Klyton's: one of the spear-wife Bachis's uncles. He declared the Sun Lands would be plunged into anarchy if the King was no longer King. But the Sirmians were thought mostly savages, and did not have the weight of savage Ipyra, who had not yet learned the plan. If Klyton sent the Karrad-king, my grandfather, any word, I do not know. Probably not. Ipyra might fly either way, to Klyton's standard or back into her rebellions.

The days dragged on for me there, shut in the tiny continent of my royal rooms. Food was brought, elaborate and artistic, and I shared these feasts with my dog and my two women, Choras, who was ten, and Nimi who was only a year or two older. One of my new guard came in to remove the dead turtle. My throat closed and ached at this, but no tears would come. He said he would have them scour out the precious carapace, and bring that back to me. Then I felt a piercing. I told him no, she must be buried with her shell intact upon her. But I saw his eyes. So I said, distractedly, I had changed my mind, we would see to it ourselves. I did not want to offend him, because danger seemed all around. Nimi and I carried the turtle to a huge chest, and put her down on silks, and covered her. Choras sprinkled spices. We locked and sealed the chest from the air, and got it away into the vacant rooms my women had occupied. I wrote on the lid in the script of Akhemony: *A faithful one lies here. Leave her untouched. Alcos emai.* Ancient queens had buried pets in this manner in the distant past, having the caskets installed later in their own tombs.

As for the doves, they never returned. Like the doves, my women. It interested me vaguely when we were on the road from Oceaxis going South at first towards Sirma, that Bachis the spear-wife, and her child, had managed to keep most of their small retinue. She might as well not have bothered, for Klyton set all but one girl and the Maiden loose on the road, as too much baggage.

I had told Klyton, in their hearing, that Nimi should now be my Chief Maiden, and Choras a Maiden too. Nimi blushed with delight. Her mercenary innocence warmed me. Choras only gazed at me raptly. To her I was almighty, having rescued her from Koian Thon. I would do no wrong, and could, ultimately, never myself come to harm. And this unmercenary faith chilled. But I scarcely noticed. They were only there, with the dog.

Through all the days and nights until that afternoon, I had not seen Klyton. He had penned me one letter. He told me he was sorry for my discomfort. It would soon end.

Then, when he came—without all the customary flurry, for no one was there to make much fuss—he had people with him. A guard, and a secretary, an old slave he had kept by him since boyhood. The slave took an itinerary of my wants, and Klyton led me aside into my—our—bedroom, where despite the ravishing food I was brought, no one had been to sweep or tidy, to see to the perfumes for the bath, or clean it.

"Calistra—"

This was when I saw again that I did not know my husband. He burned so bright. He laughed and the shining coins of his laughter struck the walls.

"I've brought you down. The God knows, no fault of mine. Trust me, it won't be for long. Isn't that what the hearty peasant says to his wife in the bad year when the orchards don't ripen? The God's Heart, Calistra. What can I say?"

Then he told me they had made the fake Amdysos High King, that he was to be crowned Great Sun. Certain of the princes, jointly, would rule for him, until his recovery was complete.

"Recovery—what, put back the crushed brain and sew it in, as they do in Artepta? This mad, crippled stick—because of a shower of thunder-stones blown in from some fire mountain of Ipyra—yes, that's what Torca—even Torca—says they were. Volcanic debris. And for this—for this—But then, Torca believes that obscenity is his true King. I know Torca. He'd never sink down to this unless he did believe it." And after that, pacing across the room, Klyton began one of his speeches, which till then I had not heard. How the gods had chosen him, making him wait, preparing and purifying him, snatching Amdysos away, the sacrifice, leaving the enthroning world to Klyton. And this—this was some aberration as if some word spoken in a fever were taken as the pronouncement of destiny. The fever would pass. They would see what they had done. Then they would cry after Klyton and he would forgive them, and gather them again into his hand.

I listened. The dog listened. Outside I heard the old slave talking sensibly to Nimi.

Did I grasp that Klyton's golden sentences were only decorated ribbon's tied about a rotten fruit, as they do it in so many markets in time of festival, to hide what must at last be smelled and seen?

That night he appeared again the beautiful young god I had married. He pushed me backwards on the stale bed, and mounted me as an animal does. But, I was all his, my sex at least knew him well. We struggled to the Paradise of the flesh, and then he slept exhausted at my side. And once two tears ran from his sleeping eyes. I saw, for that night I did not sleep at all.

Next day, the old slave, Sarnom, came alone and told me with a gentle courtesy I should select what I must have. His face was like a mourning carving. But old men and women, I thought, often looked sad, as sometimes they looked wicked.

I chose what I predicted I should require for the trek to Sirma. Here, I had been, told, we would go—to find friendly loyalty, and an army, whereby to persuade mistaken Akhemony.

What did I hold inside myself? Only a heavy dread that was not completely real. For I, too, had been led into the Sunlight, and gained what I should never have had. Surely, surely, the gods who helped me, would not leave me in this plight?

Outside, the gardens smoked still on the shore. What I had seen there so often, removed in an hour.

I offered to Gemli and to Lut. Both seemed like little made things of stone and wood. Not gods at all. But did the air hear? The moon-glow on the floor? The gods were presently engaged. Soon they would recollect us.

That night. The night when I had chosen what I should need and want, finding only later I had picked out usually nothing of any use, leaving behind me the dearest and the best. Alone on the bed, the covers thrown away, the hearing air so hot, so merciless, and the crack of moonlight streaming through the outer room and under the door.

The moonlight had blackened over in one spot.

Waking, I saw, and then that a woman stood up straight there, in her black robe, the gems lit like dark moons on her wrists, fingers, at her throat. It was Crow Claw. Now I imagine that she spent some of the ten years of her earthly wandering, prescribed by God after death, there in the palace at Oceaxis. This accounts for her ghost, the intrusions she made on us

"What do you want?" I said. And sitting up, "Have you brought some better tidings?"

The dog saw her, too. He did not seem alarmed, his tail even quivered, as he watched her, head on long paws.

"What's your name?" said the witch, as long ago, in my childhood.

"You know my name. Calistra."

"Sun Queen Calistra. No. Now you're Cemira again."

I started violently, and made the circle.

She shook her head. "Remember, the Cemira is one of the Secret Beasts of Phaidix. Both names are yours. Shun neither."

She had sung me to sleep in that long ago.

Not now.

I said. "Why are you here?"

"To bid you farewell, Great Queen. I'll see you no more." The mooolight caught the side of her crone's face, as with a living thing it would. But she looked younger tonight. Not any older than thirty years. This was curious. No one had ever seen her young, since her death. "Nothing ends with death," said Crow Claw. "Even the unborn don't end there." She pointed at me. Involuntarily I glanced down, to look where her ivory claw indicated. But nothing was there, beyond my own slender shape, the dirty pillow.

"Crow Claw," I whispered, "do you speak with the gods? Do you see them walking? Beg them for me to give back to him what he's lost."

"But," she said, "he has lost nothing at all."

I cursed her, and she was gone.

We behold and cling to the rock, but the rock is a vapor. We tumble through space, shrieking, and in the night that is All-Night, open our wings. But the promise we are born with, in the land of illusions we forget.

The dog licked my tears, disliked them, and moved away. I held myself firmly and pushed off the weeping. Tomorrow we would go to Sirma. I was a Queen, and must act as a Queen would, even in exile.

Under the mud-brown sail the rowers sang and the oars churned and the sea had a flat poisonous iridescence. We had been two days on the water, and one night between.

The Sun's Isle.

Here the thunder-stone had rushed from the Sun. A priesthood, it was said, had tended the place for centuries, and always they died, the young, the vital, died on Sun's Isle. Animals there were monster-like, mythical. Few came there now. The force of that chip of the living Sun sucked out the life of men. And we were rowed towards it. It was the hub of the universe.

I sat under an awning, looking at the Lakesea. I had never before crossed it. The atmosphere had by now a peculiar glimmering film. Last night the stars had seemed of a thousand altering colors. The fish they had caught today was unnatural. It was the size of a calf, and almost snapped the line. It had three eyes and two mouths each packed with pearly teeth, that the pearl-loving men of Bulos pulled from the jaws.

But, they did not eat the fish and threw it back. By then it was dead. Things were done too late, or not at all. Nimi had had a terrible dream. The sky was torn open and a flaming creature dropped to the deck.

The Heart Drum of Akhemony had been audible at Belba, yet on the ocean it grew muffled, unknown, more distracting in its change.

Klyton talked to the captain. He had charmed them all, even in their superstition and unwillingness. We would sight the Island by Sunfall, or with the dawn. Ancient maps described it. It had the shape of a huge lizard lying in the sea.

2

In Bulos, they drive out the Scapegoat every year at winter. They mark a ram, or other animal, or even a criminal, and tie him with little tokens written by the priests, notes of various sins and omissions. Then they thrust him away into the river marshes among the man-high reeds. Possibly the Scapegoat dies then, of cold or hunger, or eaten by wild dogs, or large water reptiles. If a man survives, he never goes back. Ten years after, if they knew him, they would kill him, for bringing home their transgressions.

Perhaps the Bulotes no longer do any of this.

But I was thinking of it in the Bulote ship.

Did I say to myself that Klyton was the Scapegoat of Akhemony? A council of old men and priests had asked of him that he go away, perhaps to an estate at Airis, or better, to Sirma, where the Sirmians had given him land before even he was crowned King. Nexor, when unwanted, had been disposed of in just this way, into Ipyra. Klyton called his men, such as would go, and left. And around his neck were hung the stooping eagle, and the flight of firebolts, the drought that was beginning, and any other unlucky thing.

The second vessel had dropped behind yesterday but now, as the Sun began to rise at our back, we saw her again. The ships hailed each other with horns. A dismal mooing.

It had not occurred to me that Klyton could have resisted his dethronement and expulsion more vigorously than he had. Even there, on the ship, it did not. I saw Akhemony had closed to him like a door. He knocked and shouted, he raved. There was no answer so he came away to find a battering-ram.

During all the short voyage, the sea had been odd, so very flat, the waves scarcely stirring. No birds were seen once we were an hour out.

The dawn Sun looked very red, but as it lifted into the sky, it metamorphosed. The sailors started to cry out and call prayers. The Sun—behind us, reflected before us on the flat and half-dead sea—was an emerald. Its path was the shade of fresh grass. This lasted for some twenty heartbeats, the Heartbeats of the Mountain. After that the greenness dissolved and the Sun was the Sun, only dull, the track on the water faint as if under a skim of oil.

In silence, when we turned again, we saw the Island, the Sun's Isle, pushing from the sea before us.

To me it seemed to have no particular shape, despite what had been said, only a dark scoop of land, with night still caught around its skirts.

Soon I could make out the sluggish waves dragging up on its rocky beaches, with hardly any frill of foam. Big stones stood out into the ocean, shapeless, or weathered into low arches. Even now there were no birds. But a scent sighed off the Island. It was rich and heady, as of perfumes and citrus fruit, and then like burning incense mixed with alcohol. And then it grew sweetly rotten, like decayed flowers.

A natural harbor had been shown on the maps. Here the sea was deep enough for the ships to stand close in.

The maps also stated that a hale man could walk round the entire scope of the Isle in a day. To reach its center where the Sunstone had fallen, took half a day. The ancient temple was planted there, and even in quite recent times, less than fifty years before, one man had dared the Isle and seen it, the Stone lying in its cradle. But the country was unsafe. They said three-headed beasts roamed the Island with snakes for tails, and womanlike things with snakes for hair, and a white lioness that had leapt down from the Daystar after the Stone.

Klyton left all but fifteen of his men on the ships. We heard later, aside from their captain, the soldiers had drawn lots, to see who must go. This was allowed.

After Sun's Isle we would sail down the great river to Bulos, and so press on, marching overland to Artepta. But Klyton wanted his omens first.

Sarnom went ashore with Klyton. The slave had declared he would go. But Partho, the Sirmian boy, who seemed at all other times in love with Klyton, had become sick and was left on the galley.

Klyton sat down with me under the awning.

"Calistra, I know you can't walk far over this terrain. But will you come ashore? I'll leave you ten guard. And the others will be near enough on the ships."

I replied, "Yes," not considering. We were adrift wherever we went. And I have said, I did not want to cross him.

"You're brave," he said. "You always have been. But if they see it in a girl, their Queen, it will give them courage. And besides, besides . . . We're far away from the Heart." He looked out to the crinkled water, the Island beach where, as we could now make out, the mass of a forest descended. "I dreamed once that I flew with wings—did I ever tell you? I should not have done. But you anchored me to the earth. It was you. I don't want moving water between us. If you will."

His tone was thin and wooden. He smiled, as if he had said something mundane.

"Whatever you want, my lord."

"Dulcet Calistra, like the dove. Look, do you see the shrine there, and the path like silver for your silver feet?"

I stared. There was a sort of building above the beach. A sort of path. Would I be able to manage it, even with my cane?

He read my mind. "No, of course. One of the men will carry you over the pebbles."

Nimi approached when he had got up. I told her she must stay on the ship. But she shook her head. She put her chin back and said, sternly, I was the Queen and must have an attendant. I realize now her bravery made any of mine into a grain of dust. I was bemused. And she had heard, in her short life, all the stories of the Isle, which I never had.

A boat rowed us over, and went back.

By now the Sun was much higher, ambered, a huge smothered spark. The Daystar could just be seen, mauve and opaque.

There were no clouds. A kind of shivering luminescence hung on everything, and seemed to slide through the stony beach, and drip down off the clustered forest.

A few moments after we had got from the boat, a bird began to sing.

Nimi exclaimed, and two of the men made warding signs.

At first the song seemed exquisite, resembling the notes of the kitri. But then it sharpened, splintered. As with the odors of the Island, it was firstly pleasing and next disgusting. It scratched the nerves with needles. Then the song ended and did not resume.

Klyton walked at once away and up the path, which had originally been paved, and was now quilled by slivers of rock that must have shot up, perhaps, in a tremor. The ground was woven with brambles and creepers.

Five pillars were at the entrance of the shrine, and were black from age, with horrible shafts in them that showed out yellowish white —protuberant bones. The creepers had gone round and round like serpents. The roof was gone, smashed in on the floor below. This floor had had mosaic, a picture of a Sun with cat-animals running about it, but no colors remained in it, and something, maybe only the years, had pulled fragments out and thrown them everywhere.

Klyton told his men to clear an area in the shrine and put down for me some rugs, and the chair which had been brought.

I had after all managed the beach, and was now on the path, but going very slow, Nimi and one guard assisting me.

As I ascended, I studied the trees of the forest. They were twisted in extraordinary shapes, some like open hands stretching out cupped, clawing fingers, and some lying sidelong against each other, then bending back to run another way. There was one like a great ball, the branches thrust out as spines do from a hedgehog. All the bark greasily shone, and unlike the mosaic had deep, throbbing colors, a syrupy green, orichalc, and magenta. While out of some of the trees strange slender trickles of moisture flowed, red like magma, or greenish like sap.

The canopy of the forest had dark leaves at least larger than a man's hand, and in places as big as a shield. These flags hung motionless, but as we climbed, we saw, threading through and through, a type of snake thing, pallid and scaled, long, rope-like, yet seeming to have a head also at the tail's end. But it was blind, it had no eyes. It paid no attention to us or the men heaving out the rubbish from the shrine. When it vanished, we climbed on.

The creepers and brambles were also curious. They had the highlight of silk, black wizened berries.

In the shrine's back, the altar had been split by the roof coming down.

Nevertheless, Klyton there offered wine, and some meal from the store on the ship. Only when the incense was lighted, it stank.

There had been a tale King Okos had had grapes brought from the Isle, to make a wine. He gifted it to an enemy, who died.

The bird began to sing again. With strands of burning liquid glass it webbed together the tree tops, then tore its web in splinters.

Klyton drew me aside. He kissed my mouth. He tasted of the char of the offering, but I did not recoil. Had I started to be afraid? Had I? Oh, yes, surely. But then, I loved him.

There was a film on his clear irises like the film on the sea. Behind the film, his eyes glittered.

"We'll be back by nightfall." And then, very low, "Pray for me, Calistra. The temple is ruined but stays holy. You can feel—the air's like granite, weighing. The most holy ground in the world."

The soldiers watched respectfully as we parted, and followed him out.

My guard sat dicing heartily, with frozen faces, on the path, three standing watch. The rest constantly looked up and around.

Out on the level, greyish sea, the Bulote galleys shimmered as if haloed or on fire. We knew, though standing in so near, they were miles off from us.

He told me, in the ship by night, on our last journey. And in Artepta told me again and again, along with his repeated speech of the favorable giving of the gods, this other tale. His dreams I listened to also, unless I could wake him. Until our situation was altered. Then she will have heard them. Or woken him. And later she used her soothing drugs.

Sometimes for battle, the prince puts on a badge or a particular high crest, to show his men at all stages where he is. Then it is the keynote, that sigil, of his fight. And for this final fight, this last march, Sun's Isle is the blazon, how to find him and know him, the keynote to the ending.

The legend of the island I had heard. Kelbalba had recounted it, and more than once, for as a young girl I liked it.

Before history had begun, the center of the Sun Lands had not been a hollow lake of sea, but filled in by land. Here lived a despotic race, advanced in sorcery, who warred on the people of Akhemony, then only a tribe which lived about the hills and plains, in villages of dirt-brick. However, their priests were wise, and had found out that the Sun god was supreme, and worshipped him. So then Akhemony's priesthood invoked the Sun.

The god had invented the act of breathing, to cleanse and fuel the bodies of humankind. Now he embued the breath of the Sun priests with sacred fire. Lying down on the earth, their feet pointing outward to all stations of the world, and in a circle that mimicked the Sun itself, they produced in unison one mighty outward breath. This, magically altered by the god, rose upward as a wind, and the form of it was mirrored ever after in the chimney of Akhemony's temple. Spearing on, it entered the uplands of the sky, and here provoked a solar gale. Which in turn, by the god's will, broke off a part of the greater Sun, and hurled it down upon Akhemony's foe. So colossal was the detonation, the land sank there and filled instead with sea, as a hoofprint fills with rain. Only one small island stayed afloat, and on it an enormous fragment of the larger Sunstone. As Akhemony grew in might, this Isle became sacrosanct. A temple was erected there to contain the Stone and dedicate the victory. But the priests who served it were withered by the power of the Stone, and died, and the Isle itself was transformed into a place of marvels and monstrosities.

Sarnom walked behind Klyton, as they went up through the colored forest. An old man, he had stayed healthy and alert. He did not seem fearful.

The soldiers and their captain came after Sarnom, their eyes everywhere. They had drawn their swords, specifically to cut away the foliage and creepers, as Klyton did with his knife.

The forest was thick. It made them dizzy with its perfumes and effluvias. They passed through only one glade, and here there was no grass but a floor like obsidian, fused and sheer. On it, they saw a black shelled creature, like a sort of crab, and great as a mule, but it did not move, it might only have been another rock.

Some while after they found frog-like things, which appeared constructed from bright silver, and jumped away. They had each two pale eyes, and a third eye at the middle of the back, lidded and blinking.

When the forest ended, which it did without any scrub, the boundary drawn straight as a rule, there were hill slopes of tawny grass, brittle as baked sugar, that snapped, and smelled of new bread. Once or twice they heard the bird sing again in the trees, or another like it. On the first slope, there were scarlet ants the size of mice, or a little bigger. The soldiers tried to stamp on them to kill them, but, having done it, as they raised their boots, the ants, too, rose unharmed, and scurried off again through the grass.

Above this slope were others, but they were empty. Then the slopes became burnt, like meat, and scattered with boulders all eaten out, and cold, they said, to touch.

Something made a sound here, reminiscent of grasshoppers, but they did not see any. Aside perhaps from the crab, and the hideous ants, so far they had seen no creature that lived.

They continued. There were plants, bulbous things, which spurted juice when sliced at. They had colors, Klyton told me, which have no names. He said, colors like the eye of a storm, like the pain of thirst. They could hardly stand to look at them.

Where the crown of the highest hill was, they beheld a skeleton, old as for ever, brown and terrible, a beast that had, as in the tales, two heads, one much smaller than the other. Through the huge blackened skull, and the tinier skull like soiled bronze, an antique sword and knife poked up, rusted and brittle as the grass below: the remembrance of some hero's battle, which he had won.

They had climbed up the hills of the Isle, and now went down into its valleys. But it took them less than half a day, because the blunted ember of Sun was not at the apex when they reached their goal. When they had cloven through a wall of dead and murky trees that once might have been oaks, they saw the temple of elder time lying over the lower hillside, before them.

It was black as a carious tooth, the temple, but steps went up to it, and columns held up a roof. There were said to be five hundred

columns, a number of the Sun, but by now many had toppled. Even so
the roof was whole, noduled by statues which seemed to have blistered,
melted, becoming shapeless. Over this place, immanence had formed
like a slab.

About the temple, grazed a flock of things. So you might see
sheep, clustered around some little Sunlit fane of the hills of Akhemony.
These were not sheep, though about their size.

The men stared, and Klyton stared, down at them. The flock
was composed of rats. But they were bald rats, pinkish, with dim
dark eyes as though their heads were full of rivers. There reached,
even here, the rodent smell of them. And what they grazed on had
had bones.

Klyton said to me, he meant then to go down alone, killing where
he had to, to gain the temple.

But abruptly the Sunlight congealed, as if before a storm. And
then a wind thrust up the hills, throwing the grasses and the plants
together, snapping them, so the air was suddenly full of the odors of
bread and mutton. The wind bent even the men over. It roared as it
passed, and going down around the black temple, it danced, spinning.
The rat flock fled from the wind.

But in three or four minutes, the wind died. And now the light
itself was of a shade no man there could describe. In this they picked
their way down, and over the carcasses of indecipherable dead items,
and pellets of rat dung like loaves, and walked up the temple steps.

There were snakes on the steps, sinuous and whip-thin, and they
sank into holes.

One of the men began to howl there. The captain hit him in the
face. "Steady. You've seen worse." This was a lie.

A friend helped him up and they went on.

The temple was a casket, and the door was down. Inside, light
entered at a hundred cracks. Most of the pillars stood, and an aisle led
to the great altar. This was of a washed-looking white marble that had
scarcely darkened. And on it, above the place for offering, the Sunstone
rose the thunderbolt, in a cage of black metal.

The soldiers stopped. They went to their knees. Perhaps they
forgot the giant rats. Only Sarnom stayed at Klyton's back.

Klyton strode forward through the temple and came to the altar,
and faced the mythical Stone that was real.

He put back his head, to look.

The Stone from the Sun was black and rough, and veined with ores. It was my height, he said, no more, the height of a girl. It had an unlikely image, for it was also shaped like a woman. So he saw it. A head and breasts, tapering to a pair of little feet which were, he said, because of the ores, silvery.

From his clothes, Klyton took the jewel he had brought. It was a ring of golden leaves, finely crafted, set with a flawless topaz. He laid it on the offering place, before the Stone.

He spoke to the Stone, but without words.

The temple sang, he said, like a huge harp, a sithrom. And it glowed like a cave of the sea, all phosphorescent. He felt some substance of the temple spread over his skin, on the orbs of his sight, and in his mouth he knew its flavor. A spirit of the wind still twirled in the aisle, in and out of the pillars. One might see dancers in the wind, or the priests who were dead, advancing with a sacrifice, a pale stallion that had five eyes . . .

Deep within his brain Klyton now experienced the rippling glimmer of the Stone, reaching in and tasting him, like a snake sipping a cup of milk.

The god spoke then, muffled and soft, inside his brain, his mind. A tiny voice. Almost nothing.

No.

The god said only this. It was impersonal.

The god had forgotten him, for Klyton, a Sun, of a line of chosen Kings, was only mortal. No more. Nothing else.

No.

The impact wrenched through Klyton. He steadied himself, as the man had been told to do outside. He whispered, too low for the waiting soldiers and slave to hear, "Very well. Take my life. But give me just one year more of glory. Give me what you vowed to me. Since you said it should be mine."

The god did not speak again. And the Sunstone was grey-black and cindery and ugly, and had silver feet.

Sarnom, seeing Klyton turn with tears lying out under his closed lids, reached up quickly and flicked the drops away, as if attending to flies.

"Thank you," Klyton said. "We'll go back now." He added, "They must eat and drink nothing here. Do they know? Did I tell them?"

* * *

My guard had stopped dicing. They stood together drinking from a wine sack, at the bottom of the path.

Nimi and I sat watching the forest.

I wondered what Bachis was doing, aboard the smaller galley, and whether she felt favored or demeaned by being left there. Though the vessel was not big, she had kept elsewhere on it and did not share my awning. She knew her place, a lesser Daystar. She fed her baby herself, cloaked by the sturdy Maiden. This led me to remember my own childhood, Phaidix's garden, Ermias, the turtle.

The day went slowly but also very swiftly. I cannot explain this. Perhaps I sometimes slept, without knowing it.

Conceivably, too, I was terrified that Klyton would be attacked within the Island, and so shut my mind numbly away in reveries. Yet I see I did not for one moment believe in his death, as I did not in my own.

Every so often, the bird splayed its glass web and destroyed it.

The guards talked of finding and killing it. Its song was so interesting, it might eat well. Or it might contain venom. They loudly laughed and at their noises, the song did not cease, as if it could not until its sequence was complete.

Then the Sun was low, and it came to me a Sunset was beginning, and the colors were at fault again.

Like the darkest carnelian the Sun sank, and the sea was henna. But as the solar disc went under the water and the land, there was a green lightning violent enough that it caused one of the men to cry out. And then the sky seemed to glow more tremendously than the Sun, and it was purple and beryl, and two shades that I, also, cannot name, though I have seen ghosts of them sometimes, in other substances.

Nimi murmured a soft prayer. She put her cool palm on my knee, as if to comfort me. She said, prosaic as a mother, "The dog will be missing us."

But the guards were pointing into the sky. "Birds! Birds, do you see?"

I stood, and went out and positioned myself on the path. Nimi and I gazed upwards. Across the supernatural Sunset, out from the Isle and back again, the flying things streamed, but they were not birds but insects, great as dishes, and they turned the sky black.

The soldiers were shouting and on the ships I noted some activity. But then the winged things settled down again into the forest, the way dregs do in a goblet.

In an utter quiet, the bird sang once more. Its song was very close. After all this, Nimi gave a tiny shriek.

There on the path, between ourselves and the soldiers, was a cricket made of green chalcedony, through which the afterglow shone, revealing its inner life, bladders and arteries pulsing with dim blood. It was, this entity, almost of Nimi's own height. And with its forelegs it strummed at its own body, and from it shrilled the web of glass, its ghastly song.

But it was beautiful. In memory I see its beauty as I did not then.

And while I was transfixed, one of the soldiers threw his shield. The shield slammed against the cricket; it toppled through the ethereal light, and the shield covered it, all but the edge of one spun-silver chitin wing.

Nimi and I turned away as the soldiers slew the giant cricket with rocks and bits of the Island they uprooted, yelling, cursing, retching. They would not touch it even with their swords, and the man who had thrown his shield, did not reclaim it.

In my belly, a deep aching.

Nimi, the mother, had buried her face in her hands. I put my own hand over her head a consoling gesture I had seen her make herself, with Choras or the dog.

As the upheaval died down, the glowing day color ebbed, and a glowing night descended. The hundred lips of the sea were lined with gilt. Daylight left behind.

And Klyton and his men walked from the forest, calling to us cheerfully, as if we were at home, and they had only been hunting on the hills.

3

Beyond this point, I find I can say little of Klyton, that is, of his thoughts, his mind.

Although with memory it seems I knew him before ever even he spoke to me, after Sun's Isle I do not know him. And this is not the alienation of the past. Ah, no. He is now a stranger I see at a distance, as if from a high wall. A stranger who lies beside me, sometimes, and sometimes works on me the enchantment of lust, and who sleeps where I can hear his mutterings, and who in sleep, now and then—though so distant—strikes me a slight glancing blow, as he battles with an invisible other. "Amdysos," he said once, "I didn't wish you dead." And then, "Of course you didn't. Leave it behind."

Klyton burned on, torchlike, often at the ship's prow, looking forward, talking with the Bulote men, who forgave him the Isle as soon as we turned from it. Despite the prophecy, none had died. With his own soldiers he flared on, like a comet. Having seen nothing, yet they assumed his private omens on the Island had been favorable. Indeed marvelous. He played his part for them I think, from shame. Or did he yet not credit his gods had forgotten him, even while their *No* was branded black into his brain.

The Lakesea changed herself as if to abet him. By the third day, birds flew over, sunny white. A score of small islets passed, with willows that the god is fond of.

Meanwhile I endured the laval ache in my womb. My courses had always been irregular. No doubt the journey, the Island, had brought it on after delay. But the cramps grew worse. I, too, burned with fever. I lay down and the motion of the galley made me sick. Then I was being carried through the shallows of the sea, to one of the little isles. I was in a tent beneath a pine, and Nimi bathed my forehead, and blood was all over my skirt.

Near evening, I saw another attendant had arrived. Bachis had sent me her Maiden, fifteen years old, a stout, strong girl from the country round Airis. I did not know, but the Maiden was a skilled midwife and had assisted Bachis in the act of birth. Now, she bent over me. An hour later, in a torrent of pain and awful blood, something was drawn out of me.

Though professional at her work, the Maiden was not canny with her tongue.

"Oh, lady, see. Is perfect. And would have been a boy."

I had not, in my absorption, having no proper symptoms, and misled by the irregularity of my menses, known I carried Klyton's child. He was the length of my last finger, under the filth, like a totem of white-fat jade, perfect, as she said. One might see the shape of all of him that was to come. He had hands, unopened eyes, lips, a phallus like a paring of the moon. And he was the bud of a flower. I stared at him, half delirious, and cared nothing at all, wanting this done with. It was in later years he haunted me, the only child I ever bore.

"They keep such aborts, in Sirma," said the Maiden knowingly, "in a box of spice, with the lid sealed tight."

Like my turtle, I thought. And slept.

I think Klyton did come in. Recollection seems to glimpse him, distracted, a man of affairs, who must pause at women's business, from politeness.

To this day I am not sure if they told him, or if they did, whether he understood. Having become true strangers, we never spoke of it.

By the time I was well enough to notice, the Lakesea had narrowed to a long river, which the Bulotes call Her Plait. They worshipped still a mother goddess, and her river tresses were strewn through Bulos, but this waterway was three rivers on one, therefore *plaited*. Their goddess has pearls, too, in her hair, of course, and on the river, as always in that country, you found pearl fishers, boys and men, diving from the decks of thin brown boats, one coming up once, that I saw, with weed on his shoulders, a pearl like an egg clenched in his grinning mouth.

We had traveled through Bulos before, when we were a King and Queen, but not along this river. Anyway, none knew us now, though I heard Bulotes in the river villages speak on two occasions, in my presence, of that summer when the Great Sun went by on the road, his Chief Queen with him. And they spoke as of something momentous, and lucky. But we were only foreigners.

One sultry night on Her Plait, waking, I thought I heard something go overboard, very heavy, cumbersome. Maybe I dreamed this. But never again did I see Klyton bring from the baggage Amdysos's shrine.

There was a minor summer festival about this time, seldom much observed in the royal house. I recalled Kelbalba had, a couple of times, laid flowers for Gemli, and Ermias sneered at them, before we were friends.

Klyton decided we should put ashore, and honor the festival and the summer goddess. We were near the end of the river. They would have to march afterwards, mostly. Klyton wanted the horses off the bigger galley to be exercised, and the men. We landed near some villages and made a camp, and when the people saw the two ships, they came to sell or barter food, and milk their cows into our buckets.

For his soldiers, he organized games, horse riding, and throwing and shooting at a mark. He gave extravagant prizes from his own goods, astonishing some of the men, cups of silver, boots of bullshide, belts fringed with bullion, scabbards staring with gems, and often with a steel sword in them.

He spoke to them at their games, praising their faithfulness and endurance. He said he would not forget. They had started the wine ration by then, which was lavish, and they cheered and banged on their shields.

As he sat overseeing the contests, he was impeccable, and magnificent. No one could quibble at such a leader. But there was a flaw now, *behind* his face, under his eyes. Could I alone see it? I think not.

I, too, must sit to applaud the games. The Sun tired me out and I knew I could not lapse, not drop asleep. It was an agony.

Quite near me, Bachis sat too, with her stout Maiden fanning her, and her child in the slave's lap. Klyton's Daystar queen had plumpened rather after the birth, now she was short but round. Having come to him with not much, she was almost always in silk, and in winter in the palace, she had been hung with furs and pelts, summer foxes and leopards, with strings of whole tails trailing after her. She had jewels, too. Knowing she liked it, he had loaded her, for she was an ideal secondary wife, prepared to learn and never to demand. At these games in pastoral Bulos, she wore glinting, silver-sewn white, and on her head, I see it as clearly as if she posed now before me, a circlet of electrum with flowers of every colored metal —electrum, gold, silver, colcai—tumbling down through her darkish hair, to her fat, satiny shoulders.

She must have been about my age, I suppose, sixteen or seventeen, and the boy almost a year. He had pale gold hair that caught the sun. I glanced at him now and then idly. For I too had almost done what Bachis had, produced another living creature.

After all the feats and prizes, Klyton gave the soldiers a feast from the bounty of the villages.

The men roamed about, or sat around the cook-fires, where whole cows, one of whom had given us milk, were now roasting. Klyton's household was in the greater tent, his two captains, and the two royal women, she and I.

The day cooled to twilight, and stars Bachis might have liked to have, spotted the enormous sky. On the river, swans had gone by, and the soldiers had shot one, being frisky. But here the swan was thought sacred to the summer goddess, so they did not dare eat it, and the river pulled it away.

I see the swan, too, in my memory. Its waste. For it had lived.

He was drunk. I believe so. His beauty was alight and his movements slow, or rushed. Then the drunkenness went down to melancholy, as it can. He had been acting out for them, on and on and over and over, his victory and hope. And somewhere in the Bulos starshine, he could not play any more the King and the Sun.

He seemed to sit in thought. He missed what was said to him. His eyes grew heavy. They turned black. I had seen this happen sometimes in desire, but never like this. There was no light in them, only a gloss slicked over.

Klyton began to gaze about at us all. He smiled once at me. It was a smile of forgetting. He had not meant to hurt me. On the captains who had stayed with him, he turned his black eyes, considering. Who were they? One jested, and others laughed; Klyton nodded. He could manage nothing else, for they spoke another tongue.

It was then Bachis's son shook his rattle—naturally silver, with silver bells—the Maiden had given it him to keep him jolly and awake.

The black eyes sunk on to the face of the laughing, primrose-headed child. The eyes lightened. All the darkness left them, and they were colorless.

He said to Bachis, "Let me have my son."

She fluffed up like a proud hen, and snapped her fingers at the slave.

They did not tell him, or they did. He and I did not speak of it, not then, nor ever. That bud of white jade buried in the powder box under a pine. Perhaps this had nothing to do with that.

Klyton took the child from Bachis. He gazed at it. The boy was solemn now, only waving his arms, slowly, and, as if to flatter, drunkenly.

Without another word, Klyton rose and carried the child outside the open tent.

Bachis's mouth came open. What was Klyton doing—taking the child to the other tent, maybe, to wreathe him in jewels?

None of the men paid much attention. They, too, had drunk well. A father with his son. He might be showing him the stars.

About half an hour after this, Klyton returned, and told us the feast was done. He was unaltered, but his arms held nothing.

Bachis, who never demanded, went up to him in a slinking, fawning way. She put one finger on his sleeve and whispered something.

Klyton frowned at her.

"Don't let it concern you."

I saw her face fall in like an old woman's, and it was the sensible Maiden who conducted her away.

The soldiers went, mumbling, uncertain, somewhat confused. In the camp, not many had noted that Klyton had not brought the child back again to the open tent. Could not a father lay his child elsewhere to sleep?

So he had. They discovered it before Sunrise. The scintillant hair was put out, dark and wet, and just so was the stone on which Klyton had broken in the child's skull.

I know they said of Klyton that, having become insane, he killed the child, timid it would rob him of status, as his brother, Amdysos, had. And also there was a story he sacrificed it to the god, for better fortune.

He said to me, "I had nothing to give him but suffering. I myself can't bear it. How could I make him heir to that?"

And I held the murderer in my arms, this evil and unspeakable thing he had become. Do not judge Calistra. She will judge herself more coldly. But she would hold him yet, I will not lie.

In the morning, most of the men had made off. Such country swallows those who wish it to.

But Bachis stood with her slave and her Maiden among the sparse heap of her baggage, those items she had accrued and been able to keep. She stood as if grown into the ground, her fallen face as white as naked bone, and her eyes staring at him. She said only she would not move, no, never. She had a look of Udrombis, indomitable, and perhaps for that he left her there, where she had rooted herself. The Maiden bulked behind her, crying. I think the villagers buried the child. I do not know what became of Bachis.

4

South, the summer seemed it could never end, yet trees had autumn in them, when we got down to Artepta.

They said in Thon's hells, where men were made to suffer for the worst earthly crimes, there were no seasons, yet there could be extreme heat or cold. A wind blew in the south that might have come from there. They call it in Artepta, *Fire-Breath*.

Adargon was waiting in a fortress house in the marshes, where all but one of the rivers end. It was a building Arteptan kings had had made long ago, partly ruinous now. The huge window spaces looked out at the miles of reeds, taller here than men, that rattled in the firewind like spears. Between were pockets of ale-dark water. Violet irises grew about them, these the height of a girl, on stems like brass. Great lizards couched in the mud, and vented a pig-like barking.

I had been able to exercise my body very little on the journey, confined to a ship, a tent, traveling overland in a litter between two mules. Then another man ran away, and he took a mule with him, and I rode the remaining animal awkwardly. I was stiff and in pain, and in the chamber I had in the fortress, at last tried to undo the knots of my body. Nimi rubbed me with scented oil. And the crocodiles barked from the rushes.

Artepta had sent Adargon emissaries with amiable words for Klyton, saying we would be welcome in her city. They had offered Adargon a ship, which had arrived, and lay now at the edge of the marsh, on the last narrow river that went to the sea. But, Adargon said, Artepta spoke of Klyton only as of a prince. Kindred, not lord. And there was another thing. Of the men left to Adargon after the desertions of his own march, scouts had tested Artepta. There were bizarre reports of a massive fleet, anchored out beyond the islands. True, the scouts had not seen it, but had met with those who had. The fleet came, perhaps, from the Benighted Isles. But that place was primitive, and the fleet, purportedly, like artisans' work for sophistication.

It might be only a tale. Artepta spoke a language unknown elsewhere in the Sun Lands. Though the scouts had mastered it somewhat, possibly they were not as lingual as they thought.

Was the fleet Artepta's own? If so, why anchored far off? And why clandestinely?

Adargon looked worn. Not like Klyton, for Klyton burned on. After what had happened, after what had been done, he was yet brilliant as the Sun. Until the shadow came, which was often. Adargon was raddled, unhappy and at a loss, but his mind was perfectly transparent. He must have heard soon enough about the murdered child. But Adargon did not deviate. He would do his best. The gods would expect that, but no more.

All told, Klyton had reached the marshes with fourteen men, the old slave and the boy, and three women: myself, and my two little girls. Adargon's contingent now numbered seventy-six men.

In this panoply we would sail to Artepta, who might prove strange or false. But, beings of action must go somewhere on a road, and there was no turning back.

Artepta knew our numbers were low, too, for the ship they had sent was single and not significantly large.

Nevertheless it was not like anything I had seen. It had two decks. All the wood was gilded, even the oars, and the mast was twined by gold with a crimson and black sail crossed by a rayed Sun that became the crescent moon of Phaidix's bow. There was a sort of pillared house amidships, and here Klyton and I were to sit, as one had seen gods did in Arteptan carving. So we dressed in our best and sat down, under the awning, with the sail unfurled above.

Nimi and Choras were at my feet, with the white dog, who now took notice only of them.

The soldiers had been positioned down on the lower deck. They were orderly and had polished up their gear.

Two slaves on the ship fanned the deck-house with leaf-shaped green fans. They were black, as the rowers were. There is a light strain, too, in Artepta, like malt or mahogany, even sometimes paler. But mainly you see slaves of this tone. And though at one time I thought I saw a noble and his company of this paler type, I was mistaken. The higher classes have skin like ebony. It came to me in Artepta, that Torca gained his blood from the higher caste. But Udrombis, whose blood had been mixed, was white.

So they rowed us downriver between the clashing reeds, the pale purple irises, where the water-lizards slid under the surface, disdaining us.

Then we saw wide fields, yellow and too ready, bending to the firewind, worked by black shapes whose scythes crackled with light.

In less than a day we came between two great statues, taller than the palace roof had been in Akhemony, sculpted of black granite that gleamed. They were so old, their form had become simplified, two giants, seated, their eyes up on the sky.

But from the stone lips of the right-hand statue boomed out the words sailors told one of: *Who passes?* And our ship flashed up its oars, saluting the statue which had spoken. Many believed, without this, it would not let us by. I did not believe it, however. With the death of hope had come the death of all wonder and awe. Magic belongs with life.

5

They gave me a house on the north shore above the Straits, looking back to the mainland. It was a mansion, with gardens and fountains. In the morning the rising Sun blonded an image of white marble to the left of the house. At Sunfall another, to the right, of porphyry, became a blood-kissed rose. I had servants there, and slaves. I had a Maiden with coal-dark skin, highborn, whose ten-times braided hair fell to her ankles like ropes of black wool.

In this place I saw the winter come, as it does in Artepta, mostly windless and never really chill. But dry, in some cold fashion, dry as age.

He was kind to me. He visited me every day.

I had become a secondary wife, a Daystar.

And *she*—*she* was Calistra.

He said. "I've put you aside from *love*. I mustn't taint you, now. Say you see it, Calistra."

But that one thing I would not comply with.

The beat of the Heart of Akhemony had faded beyond the Lakesea. Some claimed still to feel it, hear it. I heard it in my ears as I lay unsleeping. The heart decides. A murderer, I loved him. Lost to me, I would not agree that he was gone.

Usually he entered the house at noon. He would frequently sit without speaking, smiling, as if to reassure me, at the floor. After an hour, he went away.

Sometimes I was given the speech of the god's bond to him. Sometimes of the breaking of the bond on Sun's Isle. Once, only once, he said, "He took the she-pig from me. Then the Sun Race. And then my Kingship. Everything."

The sea here was louder; it came far in on the land, at particular times, day and night, or drew away. Crossing it, I had felt dizzy, half afraid, as if above some endless drop. It copied whatever shade the sky was. Over it, from the house, I saw huge Arteptan monuments along the farther shore, or risen from the waves, one like a lion with a serpent's head, crowned. And three white towns lay out there, with mansions and gardens like mine, that sloped to the water.

I existed for noon. I was extinguished after an hour. When he got up, and kissed me, I did not cling to him. I had never learned to importune, only to dissemble, a pleasing and dignified woman. Nothing improper.

Her name was Netaru.

At first, rooms were awarded me in the palace in the city of Artepta, and to Klyton an apartment near to mine. I never saw this.

We were treated like wished-for guests, given attendants, brought clothing, wonderful silks, and Arteptan linen that is thinner than gauze. At night, we dined in the palace hall. It was not like the halls of the northern Sun Lands, being open on pillars at three sides to the gardens. If the night turned colder, drapes were let down.

The Arteptans have canny acrobats, and their dancers would rival any in the world. There was always something to see. Sorcery was used too, now and then, as an entertainment, amazing things. Birds flew out of glass bottles too small to have held them, and flowers grew to twice their size, and turned another shade. One mage had trained a monkey to speak very clearly, with an accent like that of a child from a different country. By this, one saw their private sorceries, and those offered their gods, were profound.

There was a festival of Bandri, the birth goddess, and I saw the procession. There were male priests too, padded like the women with huge pregnant bellies. They say ejaculation in the male is also a birth.

If Klyton spoke at other times to the three kings, the Pehraa, of wresting back Akhemony, I never knew. Certainly he must have done. It had run off them, then, as the sea of the Straits ran off from the land.

The kings were men in middle years, Rhes the youngest of them, at thirty-four or -five—it was hard to reckon, for their calendar was not the same as ours, and their months of other lengths. The daughter of Rhes was the betrothed they had pledged Klyton, and despite dethronement, Klyton and she were apparently considered still handclasped, as they said, which made Klyton kin to them, and myself also.

In our presence, the Arteptans spoke the tongue of Akhemony. Klyton had asked to be tutored in the Arteptan tongue, at Oceaxis, but not spent much time on it. Now he asked for a tutor once again. It would have helped to fill his hours.

But I saw Rhes's daughter, Netaru, from the first night. She sat on the women's side, among the black and stately princesses and queens. The wives of the Pehraa wore, all of them, helms of gold and silver, similar to that Udrombis put on for Klyton's coronation. Netaru had only jacinths in her hair, which was not black, but the sheeny light brown of an acorn. Was this hair considered a lessening of her—and for that reason had they given her to Klyton? You could not be sure, with Arteptans. Besides, apart from her hair, she was so black her features, other than her eyes and lips, were hard to make out. And she was beautiful. The eyes one saw were long ovals, tapering at the corners and outlined with gilt, smoky white agate set with black. Her mouth was like a plum for color, and with the plum's succulent indentation.

I do not think I was jealous. It was terror I felt. It was not immodesty but sense to know, before, I had had no rival. Though if we had been in Akhemony, his destiny unbroken, I think I would not have feared. And then, too, I would have prayed to the gods. If he loved me, he would come back to me . . . but all that was done.

Klyton behaved only as he should. He wooed her decorously. He showed that she was delightful, but that, as a prince, he did not dwell only on her. And he sought me every third night, although he never stayed long. Nor did he lie down with me. He talked of the god's bond, and of Sun's Isle. Or of the weather.

News had flowed, and Artepta learned, when we did—or rather earlier—that Amdysos had been crowned with an autumn crown in Oceaxis, his Queen beside him, in one ceremony, to spare him too much labor. Princes of Akreon's line had uttered his words for him. Torca was one of the priests who officiated.

I visualize then, the Great Sun Amdysos, and his Consort Elakti, much as Udrombis had beheld them under the temple. Except the child is not on Elakti's knees. Nothing was said of *that*, though Adargon had told Klyton the abomination was still at large, so it was reckoned, in the Precinct of Night. The priests left food for it, and went armed. It was sacred, yet profane.

In Artepta, they do not perform a wedding. There it is announced, if a woman of equal status goes with a man to his house, and stays a day and night with him there, they are husband and wife. And though a man may have more than one wife, in archaic times, they say, so might a woman, and their babies inherited through the maternal line, no one being sure of the fathers.

Since Klyton's palace apartment was his "house," they had only to go there. For that reason too, the kings gave me the mansion just outside the palace, whose gardens fell down to the sea.

But I witnessed the Blessing. It was etiquette I should, being his other wife in Artepta.

There was a feast. More of their vegetable dishes and dark red beans with hot eggs served on them, and sweetmeats in the forms of all the gods, of which they had, Kelbaba once told me, a thousand.

Then Klyton and Netaru, with garlands of irises, went to her father, and he blessed them simply, the same words an Arteptan peasant uses on such occasions. And he gave her, as the peasant does, a small pot of perfumed oil, with which to make fragrant her new home. The pot was gold, of course, with a ruby stopper.

Klyton laughed and so did she. He looked happy, like a young man again. The way I had seen him so often, with me.

Before they went out, Netaru came to me, her ladies rustling after, and kissed me on the lips. A man's wives must be friends and sisters. She smelled of dusk on a lily, and her skin peppery and enticing.

Together they departed to his rooms, and stayed there the prescribed time. Actually longer. By then, I was in my house.

After a few days, Klyton entered the house for the first of his daily visits. He seemed washed free of all of it, and I was gone with the rest. But when he had spoken to me for a while about silly, domestic things, I saw the dark sink through him, as it had come always to do. No, the grief and rage, the bewilderment and shame, had not withdrawn. Only the joy of the other life, the glory, only they had been dismissed. Though with these bright things, I, too. Whatever stayed with him, Calistra was not there at all.

But then suddenly he said to me, "The tears run down your face like the fountain outside the window." So I was weeping and had not realized. I turned away, and he said, "Calistra, Calistra. I can't take you with me where I must go. Don't you see?"

Should I have cried out that I would not be parted from him, would lie at his door like a dog, and follow him to the earth's edge, and down into hell? Once there had been that time of passion, when I thought him lost to me before. But now I could not say it. He did not want me, and unwanted I could offer nothing, even my life.

Klyton said, "Don't cry for losing me. Be glad. I haven't tarnished you. No. You're like the fountain, more than your tears. Look how it overflows its alabaster basin, and pours away in a stream to the sea. It vanishes in darkness and runs underground in darkness, to return again to the fountain's source, and overflow once more. This is you, Calistra. But I'm the fire. A burning jet, and now burned out. There's nothing left. Let her have that, then," he said. "She knows. She's generous and kind from her indifference. She asks nothing of heart or mind. It's what I need. All I deserve."

When he had gone I wept on for hours, but like the fountain, always more tears evolved. Surely *he* had been my source. I must only go back to him.

I remember looking so often from the windows of that house, at the slender strip of sea, at the gardens. White owls and sea-eagles nested on my roof, as in other high buildings and statues of the city. In the gardens I frequently saw Nimi and Choras at play with the dog. They were not despairing here. And my black Maiden told them stories. They had come to admire and trust her, as the dog had come to rely on them.

Without me, Choras would have had no life but for her penance in Thon's Temple of misery. But then, without Udrombis, I also would never have come up into the day.

I could not imagine for myself any future. It was as if prophetically I knew my future would be unimaginable unlike anything I could ever foresee.

The winter moved smooth as cream. I exercised from long habit to the beaten drum of a musician girl, whose flesh was of the tone of brown bread.

She put me in mind, by her lightness, of a youngish man I had seen sometimes in the three kings' hall. But his skin was not quite like hers, though resembling her unblackness, dark more in the way of smoke. He grew the hair on his upper lip. But some Arteptan men went bearded. Additionally, he dressed in finery, and gave evidence of military power—the way he stalked about, his manner, the sword cut on his left hand. One saw the soldiers of the Arteptans, who were of above average height, and each man's breastplate crossed by the skin of a leopard he had killed.

The dark man did not seem, however, much like them. He had

two servants, pale as he, sometimes others with him, also well-dressed. And he was treated with by the kings as a high prince, given far more subtle respect, in fact, than Klyton.

That I took him for an Arteptan is not surprising; I had never seen before a man from Pesh Sandu.

At last, the orchard trees under my seaward window put on a sugar of blossom. They alone, of all the native trees, had lost their leaves. The other plants, and the palms of the garden, had only grown sulky and sombre.

Something in me, finding the blossom, catching or pretending a quality of spring was in the light, raised its face and glanced about.

I was young. I looked for something. If seasons transcend, why not other things.

That morning, I was aware of a great many ships out in the Straits, and faintly now and then some sound of horns would lift up to me. There was always trade, and business. I thought nothing of it.

At noon, Klyton did not come. That filled me with perplexity, and a fresh distress. Then a letter was brought, asking me to excuse him. Messengers had docked from the Benighted Isles, so far as he understood. Artepta would be winning to them, as she was to everyone. And he was, he said, curious.

Did something wake in Klyton too? Did he, hopeless and resigned, scent the spring and look about him, for some unthought-of chance?

A statue of an elder king, visible from my mansion, for it was the height of two houses piled on a third, let out its bell-voice to the Sunset, as it always did. And the porphyry beast in my garden flushed, then was the grey of ashes.

I recollect I puzzled over an Arteptan book that evening. I found the language difficult, and the substance of it has disappeared from my memory. Quite early, exhausted as I often was from boredom, I went to bed, without a single warning. And slept without one portentous dream. Not until my black Maiden came to wake me did I feel alarm. So the sacrifice only guesses, when its nostrils widen to the altar's previous blood.

Many years longer than Klyton, my brother, lover and husband, I knew the Battle-Prince Shajhima. His last heir, now that Prince Shajhima whom I sometimes see, was born in the Battle-Prince's sixtieth year.

At twenty-seven, he was strong and tall, and handsome in a way unusual to me, and at the time unseen. His hair was blue-black, and his eyes also blue-black. His smoldered skin had been clad in the azure of the Pesh sky, and ornaments of gold and silver, as he sat at the table of the kings of Artepta. Besides this he wore the great sword, made of the white steel that the Pesh call Immortal Moon, and which can cut through any other metal. This steel is feminine, and represents, as we know, the moon goddess of the Pesh, who they put away centuries ago, in order to seek the Ultimate God. Decades after this time, I said to Shajhima that the Pesh stood therefore behind a woman when they slew their enemies. He answered nothing, but later told me I had been correct. For the Pesh—then, women were so much less, that no blame could attach to them for obedience to a man in war.

But the steel of the Sun Lands was pherom, which also descended to us from Phaidix, a moon goddess.

He had sat quietly through winter, Shajhima, his warriors about him, only a handful in the kings' hall. In the city were more. And south beyond Artepta, the fleet of the Pesh covered the sea as gulls cover a pool.

At the marriage rite that was no rite, when the pot of oil was handed to Netaru, I recall Shajhima frowned.

But he remained dumb. For Pesh had allied with Artepta, great power lying down beside great power, claws sheathed. And any way, the triumvirate had given one sanctified oath, which mattered very much.

That night when Klyton was curious, thinking to see the wild-men from Kloa and her Isles, was the night this oath was to be honored.

It was not Islers who walked into the hall, where the three walls of draperies were drawn up and the gardens were visible, black on the black sky, fountain-starred below with singing waters, silently starred above with stars.

Klyton was sitting, as was normal, among Artepta's princes, but tonight he had been given a chair beside King Rhes. Adargon was on Klyton's other side, and there were three of his captains, nobles from Akhemony. They had been talking since morning, trying to learn more about the Islers and their coming. But had learned very little, it seems.

Netartu had gone to the women's place, and sat with her sisters, playing with a lion-cub.

The hall was built to face east, for moonrise, and Sunrise at dawn. Centuries before the Arteptans had considered Sunset ominous, and avoided, where possible, looking at it, marking its passage with raucous cries and blown trumpets. So the blind side of the hall was to the west. East, north and south, the drapes were raised, and Shajhima, the Peshan, had he been remarked, was on the north side, quite near to the Pehraa.

There was no preliminary for Klyton.

The silver horns sounded, and through the gardens, from east, north and south, came a long wide band of men. They were dressed in indigo and bronze, helmed in the Pesh helmets that cover the cheeks and are topped by spikes, which can, in battle, offer another weapon. They carried their ceremonial spears, chased with silver, and bound with white ribbon, which demonstrate they come in friendship not hostility.

Anyone could see at once now, these men, walking measuredly into the hall, were not Arteptans. And as Shajhima rose, they saluted him, raising their arms and tamping down with the spears. It was evident that he was their master.

The elder of the three kings also got up. He nodded to the phalanx, and then looking to Shajhima, he inclined his head.

Then the Peshan warriors drew back to the sides of the hall, and up the central floor was walking an old man heavily bearded, in a robe of dark silk, an embroidered cap upon his head.

The king spoke to the old man, in Arteptan, which Klyton understood by now reasonably well.

"You are very welcome, Teacher. Will you sit by me, here?"

The old man glanced aside at the royal women, and he drew his brows together, then loosened them. He gazed at the three Pehraa with hot and inky eyes. Then came up among them, and was sat down there between Rhes and the eldest king.

Rhes turned to Klyton. "This gentleman has traveled from Pesh Sandu across the Endless Sea, to teach us how to worship the True God."

Klyton had no expression, though he had watched everything unblinking. He said quietly, "Did you not know how, sir?"

"It seems, not quite," said Rhes.

Then turning back to the Peshan priest, he spoke to him in the Peshan language, which Klyton had never heard.

Adargon said, "Klyton, I think—they are Outlanders."

"From the fabled continent beyond all the seas," said Klyton. "Yes."

He had meant to go there, if it existed, and grip hold of it. It took no great effort to reason that something like this had happened in reverse.

Rhes returned to Klyton and said, with the utmost politeness, "Pesh Sandu makes a holy war. Artepta does not war at all. So we have agreed to learn about God, and to reshape ourselves somewhat, in order to display to him our reverence. The Teacher will assist us."

"And these armed men," said Klyton, "will they also assist?"

"Some. But the bulk of their army, of which there are many, many thousands, will press on through the countries of the mainland, towards Akhemony."

Klyton did not speak.

It was Adargon who said, "You mean, king, to make *war* on Akhemony?"

"To conquer Akhemony."

And Rhes smiled. The smile was not villainous, nor sorry. Events came and went around Artepta as the sea did, and like their carved statues that stood in the sea, Artepta would remain.

Adargon swore and surged up. A slave, coming with wine for the old teacher, skipped back, and the drink was spilled.

"A bad omen for your friends," said Klyton.

"They don't believe in omens quite in that way."

"Then do they believe in swords?"

As a prince, and kinsman, he was permitted to feast with the kings, armed. Now he touched the red hilt of the sword, where the eagle poised.

"Please calm yourself, prince," said Rhes, unruffled. "Nothing can be done. You need fear no insult. You are son to the Pehraa now, and your other wife is our daughter, as Netaru is. Your household, your half brothers, are held within our own safety."

"Insult, and safety," said Klyton, still in Arteptan. "You might," he added casually, "have warned me. In the anteroom, say, before we came in, and looked so foolish."

They had trusted probably he would not make a fuss. To how many had he said, as to me, he was a fire burned out?

But they had forgotten burned ground keeps heat a long while, and sometimes plants grow there, like the memories of flames.

Klyton drew the sword, but when Adargon also moved, Klyton put him mildly back. Klyton said to Adargon, "I see now I was brought

down to this, for the moment that the gods have sent me, here." And
then he pointed with the sword, barbarously, across the elegant tables,
the crystal bowls of lilies, the alabaster lamps, the glimmering of
women's gowns and skin, and all the shining of the angerless, acquies-
cent night. Pointed at the Peshan who was Shajhima. "Is that one their
commander?"

And Shajhima, who could speak Arteptan better than Klyton, said
in a carrying voice, "I am the commander of the force of Pesh Sandu.
What you are doing means you wish a combat with me. Or have I mistaken your rudeness?"

"No," said Klyton. "No mistake. I mean, very rudely, to cut your
flyblown heart out of your stinking body. Will that do?"

Shajhima shrugged. He said, "Tomorrow, then."

"Now," said Klyton.

Rhes stood up—

And Klyton snatched a wine cup from the table and hurled it into
the open floor, where the dancers, acrobats, and magicians had worked
their lovely patterns all winter.

"I'll meet you there," said Klyton. "Now, before all this wondrous
people, who have no word in their language for honor."

Shajhima said, "I'd heard Akhemonians are savages, with kings
who act like slaves."

Klyton said nothing. He had been recognized, that was all it
meant. He went down to the floor and kicked the thrown cup out of
the way. But for its rolling, there was no other sound

Shajhima bowed to the Pehraa, and made a salute to the old
teacher. "With your indulgence."

He, too, had sat armed. But for ceremony, the sword of the metal
named Immortal Moon, was curved, like Phaidix's crescent. Shajhima
drew it from the scabbard, and offered the blade to his god. Then he
went to meet Klyton.

Klyton had said, for Adargon remembered and wrote it in his own
chamber, wrote it on the white wall in his own last blood: I was brought
down to this, for the moment that the gods have sent me, here.

Klyton. What is in his mind—only the words that have left his lips?

Does he see the lamp-glow on their cool faces, on the face of
Netaru, who has not left her seat, while the jewels move slowly over her
breasts that he has kissed. Does he see the Arteptan night of fountains
and stars? Or does he see only the past?

Not Shajhima. He does not see Shajhima. Nor does that count, for the moment sent is not for the hero, but for the sacrifice.

I cannot, even from the air, gaze down into their fight. Will not, perhaps, see it. Refuse.

The swords, curved and straight, ply to and fro. Light slides and drips from the blades. It is easy to become mesmerized, missing the instant, after all.

Klyton. He had grown old, in Artepta, this young god. He had lost his skill. Does he stumble? Does he hear that noise in his head he has complained of occasionally, the sound the thunderbolts made, bursting on Oceaxis?

Perhaps a glint from some jewel interferes with vision. Or he is only weary. Or simply knows what the moment is, and consents. The King must go first for his land, to slay—or be slain. If he will not, he is no king.

And, he has been dead some while.

No, never can I say it. Cannot have written the words. Let it not be said or written, then.

Only the spinning of steel, the sudden flash of goldenness, then of scarlet. Stars going out, not eyes. Smoke moving, not life, away, away, and into the darkness for ever.

Oh, my beloved, says the song of Pesh that the women sing under my tower, when they wash garments at the lower pool. Oh, my beloved, my mouth is stopped with emotion. My heart has been stolen and hidden under a stone.

I had become a shadow with him, and to regain myself, must lose him. But losing him, only the shadow remained of me.

I was a shadow. But, early in the morning or late in the night, the black Maiden woke me, to tell me so.

TELESTROION

The words spoken, at a distance,
when the dance is ended

HE DID NOT RAPE ME. I had expected it of him. I did not then know the
customs of the Pesh and Shajhima had claimed me as a battle prize—
that also was a custom. Netaru, of course, he did not have, for he was
the ally of Artepta.

I see Nimi standing before me, saying valiantly she must go
with me. But she was afraid—since the giant insect on the Sun's Isle she
had mislaid her care, her bravery. I said I was no longer a Queen, and
needed no attendants. Now I was a slave.

Choras stayed with Nimi, both absorbed, I have no doubt with
ease, into the Arteptan court which would patronize their whiteness,
but not with cruelty. The white dog had forgotten me entirely, and quietly padded away with them. The inlaid doors close upon them all.

Guarded and ministered to by Shajhima's own people, I lived in
the house on the north shore until full spring. There were only two or
three women slaves to tend me. They were from the Benighted Isles,
and barely spoke my tongue. But I needed their assistance. Shajhima
had at once taken away my silver feet. So I could not walk, and was
returned to childhood, a cripple, helpless.

Will any ask why I did not pick up a fruit-knife, or a strong silk
girdle, and conclude all this. What can I say to you. I seemed to myself,
as he had been, already dead. What happened therefore did not matter.
Also I partly believe I thought, if I should die, the priests were wrong

and I should not find him there. At least in the world I was allowed my thoughts, my dreadful searching dreams.

Klyton, the Arteptans put into a tomb. They did not burn even their own kings. In Akhemony, he would have ended as Akreon had done, on the great altar, in fire. Here, he went into a box, with his image painted on the lid. It was like him, for I saw it. And it smelled of myrrh, as he had sometimes done in life. The priests who mummified his body wrote that it was, excepting its war scars, completely perfect in all but the brain. How could they see such a thing? But there.

Before these rites, Shajhima had pared off a nail from Klyton's middle finger, cut a lock of his hair, and dipped a square of linen in his blood, for a Muhzum. Though demented and unholy, Klyton had been a High King and died in fight.

Calistra walked at her lord's funeral, the last time she was allowed to walk on the soil of her own continent.

I see Netaru sprinkling red flowers, like the flowers that grow after the fire is out.

In mid spring, Shajhima and his troops began their march across the Sun Lands. I was taken too, among the baggage train, which included already many captive women. I saw the armies of Pesh, sparking and gleaming in the Sunlight, covering the earth like great waters. But they meant nothing. I cannot speak either of the battles, how hard they were, or simple, what strategies were employed, how many gave their lives on either side. I have to this night no notion of the manner in which the princes of Akhemony joined to fight the Pesh. I can neither conjure or draw the picture of the twisted and wrecked un-King on his golden Sun Throne, cast down, and trampled.

Torca died, but I cannot say how.

I was a shadow.

There is only one half-colored scene, that room in the palace at Oceaxis, the King's Apartment. I had been housed there, and some other women with me. I do not know why. Shajhima scorned for himself these royal rooms.

I looked without any feeling beyond the eternal pain that encompassed me like air, or blood. The white rearing horses, the mural of the god, the painted ceiling, the bed-frame, stripped. Men came by, carrying out the scrolls and books from another room.

As I stood in this bedchamber, the men who had been sent to the Heart Mountain, reached their goal. They had put wax in their ears to protect them from the Drum, and climbing up to the sacred cave, they saw the Drummer at his task, which few Akhemonians had ever done, bringing down the drumsticks on the enormous Drum that never ceased, save to pause at the death of a Sun King.

On the route to Akhemony, I had heard the Heart come back. The troops of Battle-Prince Shajhima had not liked the sound. It made them dizzy and they prayed to their god, who then was not mine, and who I should never have thought would ever come to be. As indeed I would never have thought the man who killed my love and took away my feet, would ever become my champion and the friend of my soul.

But what had *I* felt in my agony hearing the Heart? Let me be truthful. I felt no more than for another thing—nothing. I think I did not, even, strictly hear.

Yet I heard the Heart stop, and stop for ever.

Having got up close to the cave, they found a horn to blow, and did not bother with it. The Pesh warriors climbed on, up platforms of rock, through the glacial rush of a stream. Green blossoms, they said, were growing in it.

The Drummer did not see them, they said. He sat amid his own excrement, around him the pieces of food he had not yet eaten, which deaf women brought him, and which he gathered with his teeth. Above him hung the filled gourd of wine and honey he had only to tilt with his cheek to drink. His eyes were like two voids of light.

Unhindered, the Pesh moved around and behind him. Two held him and another sliced his throat. He drummed on, even as his thick gore spurted from the wound. They said he drummed a minute more than any man could, for he was immediately quite dead. Then he sank forward on the brass Drum, and it was stilled.

The precious green flowers that grew there were consumed and blackened by the blood. Or so I think someone has told me. But who, who could it have been?

In Akhemony, when the Heart stopped, a terrible mad shrieking rose. And since the Drum did not resume, the shrieking did not finish.

As birds are dashed from the sky, so men were dashed to the ground. Within the palace alone, ten or twenty persons died. Perhaps disturbed by this vibration, after about an hour, the huge gold King's lamp came crashing down from its chain, in the bedchamber. The other captive women here, Islers, Bulotes, were merely frightened by the noise and screaming, and the lamp, which had missed us.

And Calistra lay in her chair, and she only thought, *Is that all?*

However, sometimes I hear it still, the Drum of the Heart of Akhemony. In the voiceless core of night. Or after the desert wind has risen and gone away.

We were at Oceaxis a year. I forget what I did. Then Shajhima marched some thousands of men back across the world to the sea, and I was carried south again, to a ship, and brought towards this land of Pesh Sandu a captive cripple and a slave, and a shadow.

QUTM

*The verse spoken after all the dances, which
often includes an invitation to the audience
to indicate if they wish to see more.*

DOBZAH HAD BEGUN TO FOLD away her writing materials. I asked her
if she wanted to add any words herself. But she shook her head, and her
eyes are heavy. I must recollect she is no longer young. I wonder if she
will write *that* down?

Annotation by the Hand of Dobzah

See, I have written it!

Outside in a darkness like blue velvet, the nightingale sings on, as if all
the hurt and happiness of the earth mean nothing, unless her song can
render them as they are. Well, she is quite right. What poet can com-
pare with a nightingale?

And I have said enough presently to exhaust myself and my
scribe, let alone any who may read it.

My days in Pesh, how I ascended from the status of a slave, and
gained the power of a visionary and poetess, and was made great in this,
my adopted land, and how my life stole back to me, up out of the darkness, in a chariot brighter than the moon—these things I will not
otherwise speak of here, in this, which became at last a book of shade
and sorrows. That is another story.

But I will recount a tale I heard in Pesh, long ago, one final anecdote of Oceaxis.

Before the One God of Pesh, the Sun Temple was disgraced. The Pesh entered it and it was changed. Also they went down into Night's Precinct.

Five men—the Sun's number, by strange coincidence—glimpsed there a monstrous creature, part bird and part dwarf which, when they went after it, scuttled away.

The men pursued. Then, in the black, with most of the torches out, they began to see that, before the bird-dwarf there danced along two small pale things—which they took at first for littler birds. Abruptly though there was a torch alight, and then they saw what ran there were two small white child's feet—having no body attached to them. These seemed to lead the dwarf on.

The Peshans had gone down under this temple of idolators prepared for sorcery, and they did not shun it when it came.

But presently the passage they were in revealed its ending, where was a wall of stone. Here a young woman stood, beautiful, they said, with long dark hair and sable garments, and midnight jewels around her throat. And she, opening her cloak, beckoned both the little feet and the hideous dwarf into its refuge.

Accordingly the feet skipped in under the robe, at once, and the creature was folded to her side, as if by a black crow's wing.

Then the woman opened the cloak again, and nothing was there.

Daunted now, the men of Pesh had come to a halt. They said the woman smiled. Such boldness, in women, they did not care for, but she was like a queen. Then she spoke. This is what she said: "Tomorrow I shall be younger than I am tonight." And she vanished like a star at Sunrise.

Alcos emai:	So it is.
Sharash J'lum:	So it is, through God's will.

The nightingale sings
Down all the centuries.
And all things alter:
Still the nightingale sings.
But . . . it is another nightingale.